MOTHER
OF
INVENTION

ALSO BY CAELI WOLFSON WIDGER

Real Happy Family

MOTHER
OF
INVENTION

A NOVEL

CAELI WOLFSON WIDGER

Published by Little A, New York

www.apub.com

Amazon, the Amazon logo, and Little A are trademarks of Amazon.com, Inc., or its affiliates.

ISBN-13 (hardcover): 9781503950078
ISBN-10 (hardcover): 1503950077
ISBN-13 (paperback): 9781503951846
ISBN-10 (paperback): 1503951847

Cover design by Derek Thornton, Faceout Studio

Printed in the United States of America

For my mother, Cathy Schwarzkopf Wolfson,
who knew me first.

PART ONE

When provided with every practical support option and no logistical restraints, women may inhabit motherhood wholly, but without compromising their relationship to their work or themselves.

—*Tessa Callahan*, The Seahorse Solution: A New Approach to Motherhood

1.

On day one of the Seahorse Trial, Tessa Callahan awoke at 4:45 a.m., eased into consciousness by the dawnlike glow of the KindClock on the nightstand. Her husband, Peter, slept on his back beside her, wearing only plaid boxers, his rib cage rising and falling in slow measure. Outside, it was dark, the streetlamps of Atherton still haloing the sidewalks, dew just beginning to form on the wide lawns of houses as perfect as designer cakes. Tessa's own was a five-bedroom Georgian neoclassical, which she'd purchased and renovated four years ago, after Loop Industries had gone public and made her rich. She'd married Peter that year also, the year they'd both turned forty, and they'd turned the property into a suburban oasis: two gardens—succulent and vegetable—infinity pool, guesthouse/"Zen den" in the backyard.

Peter had trepidation about living so well—he'd been in a railroad apartment in the Mission District of San Francisco since finishing grad school and was a minimalist by nature—but Tessa was unconflicted. She'd worked hard, harder than most people she knew, even here in Silicon Valley, where a forty-hour workweek was considered part-time. She'd put herself through business school without racking up a cent of debt; founded two hit biotech startups, both of which had released products that improved the world; and was currently running a third—Seahorse Solutions, her most ambitious project yet. Part of Tessa's stock portfolio went to cause-based investing. She gave generously to charity, ate low on the food chain, volunteered at a nonprofit that taught young girls to write software code. She'd earned her life.

Tessa sat in bed and raked her fingers through her "new" hair, which her stylist had recently transformed from the blunt bob Tessa had worn since college into a cap of choppy layers. The stylist had also insisted on lightening Tessa's natural auburn locks to a blonder, "more approachable" shade. The change somehow made Tessa feel both younger and more authoritative. It also showed off the aloe green of her eyes and her good skin, which was still relatively porcelain, while minimizing what her stylist referred to as Tessa's "strong nose." Ever since Tessa's PR people had assigned her a RAW (relatability, accessibility, warmth) quotient of four out of ten, every one of her handlers seemed hell-bent on raising her score.

Secretly, Tessa was proud of her RAW number. It aligned with the ideas she'd promoted in her book, *Pushing Through: A Handbook for Young Women in the New World.* Don't be pleasers, she instructed her readers. Embrace your unlikability. Practice confrontation. Banish your guilt. (She'd even banished it from her book itself, referring to it only as *the g-word*.) Her imperatives resonated intensely with young women all over the country and the world; *Pushing Through* was an instant bestseller and went on to spend thirty weeks on the *New York Times* list.

Across the bed, Peter moaned softly in his sleep and shifted from his back to his side. Their golden retriever, Python, raised his head from his fleece-covered bed on the floor and stretched his nose up toward Peter. Then he tucked it back down by his tail and returned to sleep. Animals loved Peter; he and Python had a near-telepathic connection. Python had been Tessa's when she and Peter met, but now she could hardly remember the last time she'd taken the dog on a walk. He was completely devoted to Peter, in a manner so pure it made Tessa reflect on her own devotion. She knew how much she loved Peter, but did she show it enough? Did he have enough evidence to believe her?

It had been so easy in the beginning. He'd been her coach in preparation for the annual Tech Tread in San Francisco, a charitable fundraiser in the form of a swim race in the Bay. Historically, all the big Silicon Valley execs participated, and hordes of spectators turned up to watch the well-known billionaires compete against each other in the frigid water. Tessa was a weak swimmer and had never participated, but the year after Sheryl Sandberg won the race, beating a field of mostly younger men, Tessa felt compelled to sign up, to the delight of her PR team. To help her prep, they'd hired Peter Grandwein, a longtime member of the local Polar Bear Club with a great reputation for teaching open-water swimming to beginners.

Swimming in the Bay, it turned out, even sealed in a wetsuit, terrified Tessa. The water was freezing and opaque, and absurdly, she could not stop thinking about old photos of the Loch Ness monster that had thrilled her as a child. When she looked out to the Alcatraz and Farallon Islands and imagined being alone in the water, far from shore, her heart beat so fast she felt she might hyperventilate.

Peter never told her not to be afraid. He never dismissed her panic. Instead, he suggested she visualize the water holding her up. To pretend she was a part of it. To give herself over to it and trust her body. He was so supportive, so kind, so nonjudgmental, and so totally in control. Swimming lessons were one of the rare times Tessa felt vulnerable and actually enjoyed it. They were a reprieve from her life on land, where she was perpetually managing, controlling, fixing. Also, Peter was so different from the men Tessa worked with, with their laid-back demeanors and little-boy clothes. Her colleagues in Silicon Valley were approachable in appearance but actually entrenched in an airtight boys' club. They were men who said one thing and meant another, who played video games with the exuberance of teenagers. Men who'd been labeled *brogrammers* or *boy-kings*. Men like her co-CEO at Seahorse Solutions, Luke Zimmerman.

Peter was nothing like Luke or the rest of them. Where they were cagey, Peter was straightforward. What Tessa disliked about the men in tech was the disparity between the lassitude of their surfaces and the cutthroat ambition underneath. No one got that rich by accident.

After one swim lesson, she hadn't been able to get Peter out of her mind: the clean angles of his jawline, the haze of stubble across his face, how his brown eyes held hers and didn't let go as he talked about bilateral breathing, head turns, stroke angles. She nodded and did her best to imitate him, noting the broadness of his shoulders as he told her to think of herself as *part* of the water, as *in sync* with the Bay.

After four lessons, she was beginning to swim with confidence, completing the half-mile swim from the dock to the buoys and back in faster and faster times. She hit her goal of completing the route in under thirty minutes, and instead of issuing his usual high five, Peter pulled her into a hug. They stood together on the dock, Tessa shivering against him, her heart at a gallop, her mind finally, truly devoid of thoughts. All that existed was Peter's body against hers.

After her fifth and final swim lesson, the idea of never seeing him again seemed tragic.

She asked him to dinner. Two nights later, after work on a Friday, Tessa met him at his favorite taqueria in the Mission.

At dinner, she'd asked him about his passions, and he'd talked first about swimming and rock climbing, both of which he taught for a living, and then about food. How he'd gotten his master's at Berkeley in sustainable nutrition and had always dreamed of opening a store that reflected his vision of locally sourced, package-free products. A store that created zero waste, left no trace, carried not a scrap of plastic or paper.

"Zero-Sum-Yum," Tessa had said, off the top of her head.

"What's that?" Peter leaned closer to her, across the table.

"Your store. You could call it Zero-Sum-Yum."

His face broke into a grin. "That's brilliant."

"So what's stopping you?"

He'd shrugged.

Later, when they'd become a couple, Tessa didn't think twice about giving Peter the capital to open his store. She was in love with him, and she certainly had the money. She funded his business and, a year later, accepted the engagement ring (sapphire, passed down from his grandmother) that he presented during a weekend trip to Napa, his voice quavering as he dropped to one knee.

Tessa had never regretted saying yes to Peter's proposal, but she wished she'd thought twice about funding his business. ZSY had closed after just fourteen months, after operating at a steady loss. The loss didn't concern Tessa much. She knew it could take three or four years, five even, for a specialty brick-and-mortar retailer to turn a profit, and privately, she'd never really expected to see a return from ZSY. Her goal had been to provide Peter with fulfillment. A sense of purpose. Instead, he'd become more rudderless than ever.

"The store is failing," he'd told Tessa over seafood tapas and sangria on Valencia Street, after ZSY's accountant had delivered another quarter-year's worth of abysmal numbers. "*I'm* failing."

"Don't be ridiculous. This isn't about money. Not yet. It's about seeing a passion through. It's about putting your values into action. The numbers might be modest, but you've got repeat business. You've got a base of loyal customers. What we've got to do now is grow that base. Build the brand. Create name recognition. ZSY needs to become synonymous with *delicious, conscionable food*. Its mission needs to inspire consumer action."

Peter dropped a shrimp tail onto his plate and stared at it. "Tessa, stop," he said, his voice just above a whisper. "ZSY is not going to make it. I'm in the store every day. I feel it."

"Businesses don't run on *feel*."

"Fine. But I can't live with blowing through your money this way."

"*Our* money," Tessa corrected.

"Whatever. I still can't live with it."

Maybe you should try harder, she thought, but she could hear he'd made up his mind.

"Okay, so you close the store," she said, as gently as possible. "Then what? Back to teaching?"

Peter stabbed a small, sharp fork between two halves of a mussel shell and shook his head. "Most swim coaches are in their twenties. I don't want to be the old guy."

"What, then?"

His eyes searched for hers in the dim light of the restaurant. He seemed to be summoning courage.

"I want to be a full-time father."

His statement hung in the air like an unidentifiable scent.

"A father to whom?"

"Well." Peter cleared his throat. "To our child, ostensibly."

"Our child."

"What?"

Tessa reached for her sangria and drained the last of it. "We've already been over this. We're too old. The planet is overwhelmed. We're not parental types."

"But maybe we are. It's not too late to find out."

"It is," said Tessa calmly. "We're in our forties now. Way past peak fertility."

"People do it in their forties all the time."

"True," Tessa said. "Just not me. Even if we could get pregnant immediately."

"Why not?"

"Because I will fail," said Tessa.

"You won't fail. You'd be an amazing mother."

"No, I wouldn't. I'd be a scrambled, exhausted, guilty one."

"And that would be okay. That's how all mothers feel."

"But they shouldn't," Tessa said. "Our standards as a culture keep sinking to new lows. It's no longer a question of whether women can do it all. It's just assumed that we will. It's assumed that we can be great careerists and mothers and spouses and still magically keep the laundry in check. Which is not only impossible, it's mass exploitation. It's keeping women in a permanent state of fatigue and anxiety. I can't be a part of it."

"Hear me out," he said. "What if I committed to doing all the parenting? The feeding and the night-waking and the pediatrician appointments. The diapers and the spit-up and the screaming. All of that will be up to *me*. You could literally do nothing but hold the baby when you felt like it. I will commit to this one hundred percent." His voice grew husky with sincerity and emotion. The din in the restaurant seemed to be growing louder.

"Why? Why did you decide *this* was the answer?"

"Honestly? Because of you. I look at you and how much satisfaction you get from your work, and I'm jealous. I want that level of fulfillment, but I'm never going to have a career that I love the way you love yours. Look at how I ran my business into the ground. I'm just a different type of person."

"You didn't run ZSY into the ground. The natural foods market is tough."

"Still. I need something else. Something more challenging and mysterious. Something bigger. Otherwise, I'm going to be in limbo until I die."

"Peter." Tessa could see the disappointment claiming his face as she spoke his name, assuming rejection. This triggered a deflating sensation in her own body, like air leaking from a tire. "I . . . I wish I could give you this. There's nothing I want more than for you to be happy."

"But?"

"But your logic is flawed. It's endearing, but it's idealistic. A mother cannot extricate herself from the parenting process. It's impossible."

"It's possible, Tessa. You don't even have to breastfeed. I'll use milk banks and wear a prosthetic."

She almost laughed.

"Don't laugh," said Peter. "Isn't this right up your alley? Practically straight out of *Pushing Through*?

A server materialized at their table. "Dessert?" asked the young man brightly. "Pistachio flan, perhaps?"

Neither of them looked up.

"I'm promising you, Tessa. If you'll give birth, I'll do the rest. One hundred percent. We'll be a triumph of modern parenting. You can write your next book about it while I'm at the playground with the baby. Think of the title possibilities." He paused, thinking. *"The Hands-Off Mother: Maternity, Revisited."*

Tessa couldn't help smiling. "Not bad."

"Fathering the Storm," Peter went on. *"Trading Places, the Sequel."*

"Have you been thinking of these?"

"Maybe." He clasped his hands together and leaned them on the table. "But seriously, Tessa. If you would be open to reconsidering a baby—just *one*—I would take full responsibility. I would work my ass off without a single complaint."

"Do I come across as hopelessly unmaternal?"

"Of course not. I just know your priorities."

Tessa felt a dovetailing in her mind, her aversion to childbearing suddenly cleaving into the logic of Peter's argument, reshaping her original stance—*absolutely not*—into something new. This was one of the reasons she'd fallen in love with him: his ability to surprise her with his thoughts. She'd had no idea he'd been thinking about stay-at-home parenting and surrogate breastfeeding. She found this oddly touching.

Whether or not it could actually work, whether such an unconventional arrangement could abate the devouring effect children had on their mothers' lives, well. Tessa wasn't sure. But the fact that Peter had proposed such alternatives with so much earnestness, the clean line of his jaw tense with conviction as he spoke, made her love him more than ever.

He understood her. Most men only pretended to. Tessa felt it in the rote, dismissive quality of their nods, how their eyes slid away from her as she spoke about biological injustices and the unique burden reproductive capabilities posed to modern women. While many men mocked her (and they did, behind her back, or on various media platforms, or sometimes to her face), called her *bitter*, referred to her as a *Silicon cougar*, accused her of being *antifamily*, Peter loved her for who she was. For the things she cared about. Never mind that he'd given up on ZSY. Never mind that he was still adrift at the midpoint of his life. None of this mattered in the face of the way he loved her.

"Just the check, then?" said the waiter.

"Yes," said Peter and Tessa, together. When he'd left them alone again, against the choppy hum of the growing crowd in the restaurant, Tessa reached across the table and cupped her hands over Peter's.

"Look, I'm listening. I'm hearing you. But I need some time to think about it."

She watched the change settle over his face, an easing, as if a valve had been released. He did not actually smile, but she could feel it.

"All the time you need," he said.

In the end, she'd said yes. Peter had been elated and grateful, and Tessa had found her own excitement at the prospect of a baby growing—not as much as Peter's, but still. They'd begun "trying." And trying, and trying. Two years later, after the failure of IUI and IVF, after countless hormone injections and four miscarriages, not including the ectopic pregnancy, Tessa had had enough. Their looping monthly cycle of hope followed by the dashing of hope was unacceptable. Not to mention the ongoing physical discomfort. Her body was saying no, and her spirit wearing down.

A child was simply not in the cards.

"It's time to stop," she finally told Peter, surprised by the lump in her throat, when yet another white plastic stick flashed the words NOT PREGNANT at her. They'd been sitting on the duvet of their freshly made bed, late-morning sunlight playing on the wood floor. They were both forty-two years old.

Peter was silent for what seemed a long time.

"Okay," he half whispered.

"Maybe it will just happen," Tessa said. "You hear about it all the time. The couple finally lets go, and then . . ."

"I've heard," Peter said.

"So we'll stop all the interventions, but we'll stay optimistic."

"I guess," he said sadly.

She took his hand and they sat without speaking.

Then he said, "What about adoption?"

Tessa felt something turn and retreat inside her. She thought of the vast amount of paperwork adoption required, about the viewing of children's profiles—*Is she the one? Is he?*—about how the agencies would favor younger applicants over Peter and her, stretching out the timeline indefinitely. She thought of the old book *Are You My Mother?*, which she remembered finding achingly sad when she'd read it as a child.

No. Adoption would only present a new set of major hurdles. Even if it ended well, even if they were able to adopt an infant (she did not have the confidence for an older child) in less than the year it typically took, the process would claim too much of her mind and effort. She'd gone through enough in the past two years. She needed to get back to work.

She squeezed Peter's hand and looked into his eyes. "I'm so sorry," she said, her voice quavering. "But no."

"What about a surrogate?" Peter was beginning to sound desperate. "I've done a little reading on the process."

"So have I," Tessa sighed. "It's a legal nightmare. And bringing a third person into the mix is potentially messy. I've read too many cases of surrogates forming attachments and wanting to be involved with the baby." She did not add her third concern, which was the harsh public speculation that would surely arise if she paid another woman to carry her child.

~

The next morning, when she'd awoken, she had felt happier than she had in ages. Lighter, full of new possibility, the future suddenly bright and beckoning.

She had an idea. She went straight to her office and began drafting a proposal for what would become Seahorse Solutions, a blueprint for the revolution of motherhood.

~

Beside her, Peter continued to sleep. Tessa considered waking him; she had just an hour until she needed to leave for the Seahorse Solutions Center in Moss Beach, headquarters of the company she'd conceived of on that morning two years ago. Today, Seahorse would begin a clinical trial of its most radical component: a breakthrough reproductive elective called Targeted Embryonic Acceleration Technology (TEAT). Because of the sensitive nature of the Trial, Tessa and her co-CEO, Luke Zimmerman, would spend as much time as possible at the facility for the nine-week duration of the Trial. The facility had a number of residential suites, and today Tessa would move into one of them. She'd be less than an hour from Peter, and he was welcome to visit, but still. She would be fully occupied with the Trial. She would probably not lie in bed with him again until it was fully under way, and the women of Cohort One were secure in their pregnancies.

The separation was critical to her work but would not be good for her marriage, which, it had turned out, was a thing that needed constant tending, like a garden of delicate flora. She tried her best, but it was tough to find enough time to be with Peter, and when she did, it was sometimes hard to get it right. When they had "downtime" together, she too often got the palpable sense of some invisible, sound-less countdown taking place—an imposed urgency that distracted her. Then Peter would ask her if she was *really present*, which never helped.

She wanted to be more present with him. She did. But she often failed.

Last night, for example: Peter's lips eager on her neck, his fingertips tracing the curves of her sides. Why had she stopped him? Why had she been unwilling to sacrifice a measly ten minutes of sleep? Why had she felt so entitled to that sliver of time, so impelled to claim it as her own?

She reminded herself of her own mantra.

Never apologize for your honest desire.

Time is a feminist weapon.

Banish the g-word.

But she couldn't. The sight of the pile of clothes strewn across the bedroom floor—Peter's jeans, inside out; a gray silk work shirt of hers, twisted up with her black bra—triggered the familiar, unpleasant sensa-tion in her chest: regret. The heap suggested an urgency she'd wanted to inhabit last night. She'd wanted to be a wife who couldn't keep her hands off her husband at the end of a weeknight dinner date. Who wanted him so much that she couldn't bother to properly unbutton her two-hundred-dollar silk shirt.

Last night, she'd *almost* been that wife.

She reached over and grazed her hand over his head, enjoying the bristle of his short, dense hair against her palm. She felt desire stir inside her, a sensation of weakening. She maneuvered to Peter's side of the bed and curled her body into his. She already missed him, preemptively, intensely.

Where had her tenderness been last night?

Their farewell at Angelini, the tiny Italian place in Palo Alto. They'd shared their ritual meal—the mushroom toast, the squid ink pasta, the bottle of Mendocino Syrah—and managed to avoid the fraught topics, as they'd agreed in advance: Peter's unemployment, Tessa's overemployment. Most of all, the Seahorse Trial.

Tessa had proposed the moratorium on work-talk, though the Trial was all she wanted to talk about. But lately, with Peter, the topic only led to one place: his skepticism. To his same old questions: *What's wrong with natural design? What's wrong with human pregnancy as it is?*

Tessa's perennial answer: *almost everything*.

For most of last night's dinner, they'd managed to avoid the topic, to keep the conversation light, even buoyant. His mother's growing assortment of pet pigs. The progress of the young girls Tessa worked with at the coding academy. They'd laughed and netted their fingers together on the little table, their knees touching beneath it, candlelight throwing ghost-shapes on the wall beside them. Tessa actually felt *romantic*. Somehow, they'd entered one of those suspended spaces, free of context, when only the other person mattered. It hadn't happened in a long time.

But then Peter had looked up to speak with the restaurant's owner, Sylvio, who was a friend, and Tessa excused herself to the bathroom, where she checked her messages.

Kate Lavek: I'm a little bit terrified. Hurry up and get here.

Luke Zimmerman: OK to push up meeting time to 9am? My office.

Gwen Harris: Residence rooms are beautiful though I find the "dumb-waiter" unsettling. See you tomorrow.

LaTonya Sims: SUPERHEROINES. Just reminding myself.

The three women composed Cohort One, chosen from a pool of over a thousand applicants who'd applied to participate in the Trial. Tessa couldn't help herself; in the bathroom stall, she responded to each woman's text, uniquely reassuring each of them, though her hand sweated onto her phone.

To Luke, she replied only, "Y." When she returned to the table, Sylvio was gone, the butterscotch pot de crème had arrived, and Peter's mood had shifted. The change was subtle but Tessa detected it like a scent.

"Everything okay?" Peter said. "You were gone awhile."

"Definitely okay," said Tessa, too quickly.

"You seem preoccupied."

"Just tired."

Obviously, he *knew* what was preoccupying her. The Trial. Which, tonight, was off-limits.

Tessa wanted to reenter the loving, easy place where she'd been with him ten minutes ago, but found it impossible. The Cohort's messages had reconfigured her attention. Instantly, they'd made her see Peter in a slightly different light, filtered with a colder hue. The pot de crème was untouched between them and Peter's cappuccino still thick with foam, but Tessa was ready to leave. It was 11:00 p.m., almost officially April 4, day one of the Trial, and the Cohort needed her. As Peter spooned the dessert into his mouth with what seemed like deliberate slowness, Tessa's impatience bloomed. He was still talking—now about his *epic* afternoon surfing at Mavericks—but she could no longer listen. She could barely restrain herself from reminding him that he was forty-four and thus might consider spending less time on a surfboard.

The names of the women in the Cohort began to loop in her mind with a percussive insistence: Gwen, Kate, LaTonya. Gwen Kate LaTonya. *GwenKateLaTonya.*

"Earth to Tessa," said Peter.

"Roger." Tessa mustered a smile, some eye contact.

"I can see you're ready to go," he said, nodding down to the inch of Syrah left in his glass. "Let me just finish this."

This irked her. He'd already finished his cappuccino. He never returned to wine after coffee.

"Sure," she said. "Take your time."

"Do you want to talk about it?" Peter's voice softened. "If you do, it's okay." He did not need to say what *it* was.

"No, that's okay," she said. "I'm enjoying the break."

"I'm proud of you," he said. "You know that, right?" He reached for her hand across the table.

"Yes," she said.

GwenKateLaTonya.

She tried a bite of the pot de crème; it tasted burnt.

Back home, he'd begun kissing her in the foyer while Python nosed at their legs, the silk of his fur tickling Tessa's ankles. Peter paused to rub the dog's head and shoo him away, then returned to kissing her, more greedily. She tried to savor the familiar sweep of his tongue against hers. Soon, he'd led her by the hand upstairs. She'd tried to stay present. *In the moment.* She'd pulled off her clothes quickly, with his help, as if she couldn't stand to wait. But then, when they'd landed on the bed and Tessa had caught sight of her KindClock—12:09 a.m.—she'd felt official permission to stop. It was simply too late. Tomorrow would demand everything of her; she needed her sleep.

She stopped kissing him. Removed her hand from his inner thigh.

"I'm sorry," she murmured. "It's just . . . tomorrow."

"It's still tonight," he whispered, his teeth at her earlobe.

"I need all my resources."

He didn't stop grazing his lips across her throat. He didn't remove his hands from her breasts. He was not listening.

"Peter," she said, at normal volume.

Now he stopped. Rolled off her, onto his back.

"I'm sorry," she repeated.

He sighed. "No big deal. We'll have another chance in a mere nine weeks." Sarcasm—a rarity for him.

"That's not true. We'll see each other."

"Maybe," said Peter.

"Not maybe. You'll visit the Center. I can pop home."

"We'll see."

"I love you," she said, with too much emphasis.

"You too," he'd said, rolling over, and was asleep within two minutes.

How were men able to do this? Tessa had wondered as she'd lain awake beside him. What did it feel like to get those solid seven, eight, even nine hours, night after night? For him to have his biorhythms restored while she lay wide-awake, fending off the g-word and worrying about the Cohort. Were they sleeping now, on their high-grade mattresses in their guest rooms at the Center, or were they wide-awake also, staring into the darkness?

GwenKateLaTonya.

Eventually, Tessa had slept. A little.

Now it was 5:16 a.m. She wanted to be on the road in an hour, to beat traffic, but she wasn't ready to get up, not just yet. Peter had half woken, draped himself around her, and fallen back asleep. It felt good to be lying against him, his breath deep and steady. At the bottom of it, she detected a faint wheeze. He had asthma, long controlled with a daily corticosteroid, but when the season changed from winter to spring, the wheeze emerged. The sound seemed like evidence of his vulnerability, and Tessa thought of all she'd denied him. Vacations, weekday dinners. Lingering in bed in the morning. A baby. He accepted so much about her—her choices, that her career came first.

Why had she denied him last night? Would it have killed her to have gone through with it, to have given him a little more time, to have actually made love?

Tessa moved her arms across Peter's back, massaging him awake. She looped her arms over his torso to reach his stomach, planed her hands over his taut, defined body, pulled him over to face her.

He blinked in the glow of the KindClock.

"In a better mood this morning?" He smiled. His teeth strong, white, even. He'd already forgiven her, in his sleep. Upon hearing Peter's voice, Python awoke and hopped onto the bed in a single motion. Peter scratched him behind the ears and then pointed to the door.

"Downstairs, dude," he said, and Python trotted off to wait by the front door for their morning walk.

"Yes, a much better mood," she answered. "I'm sorry for last night."

"You can make it up to me," he said, pulling her onto him and slipping off her tank top in a single motion.

"Okay," she said. She tightened her legs around him and lowered her face to his. She could still be in the shower by 5:50, on the road by 6:15. She raked her fingers lightly up and down the sides of his body and he shuddered. Tessa felt her guilt lighten and lift, evaporate like raindrops under hot sun.

2.

2021

Early on the morning of April 4, in San Francisco, Luke Zimmerman eased out of bed, pulled on jeans and an army-green hoodie, brushed his teeth, and ran goop through his curly hair. Then he jogged down the gleaming walnut staircase of his restored Victorian, enjoying the slick feel of the polished banister under his palm.

In the kitchen, he grabbed the coffee waiting at the base of the preprogrammed Italian espresso machine, added a splash of Brain Octane oil, and stepped outside into the wispy air of dawn. He spoke a command into his phone and on cue, the garage door opened and his self-driving Elan—not yet available to the public, MSRP $585,000, solar-powered—glided into the driveway. On the half-hour ride from the city to the Seahorse Center, south on the 280, then straight west on Highway 1, Luke sipped his coffee and listened to a podcast of a Buddhist nun detailing the difference between transition and change.

"All life is flux," said the nun, her voice like heavy cream. "We must inhabit the discomfort of perpetual motion."

"Fuck that," Luke said, and then regretted it, as if she could hear him through the car stereo. "Sorry," he added.

But he'd been *inhabiting discomfort* for a long time, and he was sick of it. "Failure" was a darling concept in Silicon Valley. Everyone loved to talk about how much they'd failed and how invaluable the experience had been. How essential to their character. How inextricable from their later success. They wrote books and gave speeches about it—*after* they were sitting on the other side of their first billion, or had been credited with an invention that altered the course of humanity. After they were officially, objectively *successful*. Then came the "humble" reflections and condescending platitudes. *Fail harder. The gift of failure.* His best friend, Mustafa "Moose" Lodha, had done it via a TED Talk after Yumlets, his twice-a-day capsules that provided one hundred percent of a person's daily nutritional requirements, designed to eradicate world hunger and malnutrition, were approved by the FDA.

Before Yumlets, I was sharing a two-bedroom with six guys in the Tenderloin, Moose said to a packed theater, *and eating dried ramen for breakfast. I'd been fired from two tech jobs and cashed out the seven hundred bucks I had in a 401(k). (Laughter.)*

Now Moose was credited with virtually ending food shortages in Zambia and Comoros. He also owned a Cessna, an assortment of rare vintage cars, and eight hundred acres of a Hawaiian island.

Luke's own father, Reed Zimmerman, had also loved to claim failure. Never mind that he'd founded the world's most popular social media network, LikeMe, which was also one of the most successful companies of all time, part of the "Power Quad" of tech behemoths: Apple. Google. Microsoft. LikeMe.

I was a college dropout with no girlfriend and a net worth of three maxed-out Visa cards, Reed was fond of saying in interviews. *I couldn't get a job, because then how would I stay up writing code all night? (Laughter.)*

By the time Reed was delivering self-deprecating commencement speeches at Stanford and Harvard (his *dropout-mater*, as he called it, ha ha), he was a household name with an estimated net worth of $40 billion. Over a billion people around the globe used LikeMe on a daily basis. The company had its own *New York Times* beat. Reed was unequivocally one of the most successful people of his time.

But then, abruptly, shockingly, Reed Zimmerman *failed*. Or rather, his myocardium suddenly failed to pump adequate blood to his body, and he collapsed jogging up a steep trail on Mount Tam. He had been preparing for an Ironman the following year. He was fifty-five years old, divorced, with one child: Luke, then age eighteen.

Luke had hardly known his father. He'd been raised by his mother and a series of nannies, while Reed had been off empire-building. Luke's father had barely recognized his existence. Still, his death had jarred Luke; he'd always imagined his father on some far-off horizon, pointed toward shore. One day, Luke assumed, they'd get to know each other.

That day would never come.

Instead, what *had* come to Luke was a massive inheritance, along with the mandate from his father to *do something radical and extraordinary*. He'd written this in a letter to Luke, many years before his death, printed on a single white page in Courier font. Luke kept the letter stashed in each of the series of cars he'd driven since Reed's death. Now, a decade later, it was tucked into the glove box of his Elan. Luke's memory of opening the letter stayed with him, in vivid detail. How, for a fleeting, idiotic moment, as he'd unfolded the paper, he'd imagined it might contain something heartfelt from his father. Some love that had been left unexpressed by Reed's workaholism and the engineer's aversion to sappiness. Some confession of a deeply held, unspoken feeling Reed had for Luke. *Even if I'm not great at showing it, I'm proud to have you as a son . . .*

But no. The letter read more like a half-jokey, half-motivational email Reed might have written to his LikeMe employees.

Luke, [Not *Son*. Not even *Dear* Luke.]
You're reading this, so apparently I've been downsized to a half dozen pounds of ash. But just because I'm inert doesn't mean I'm not still expecting big things from you. I've left you a couple of bucks as a sort of

insurance policy that you'll not only do something big, but something radical and extraordinary . . .

Blah blah blah.

Move fast and break things.

RZ

He'd signed his initials not by hand but via a digital signature. He couldn't bother to fish out a pen, Luke thought.

Luke remembered how his hands had trembled as he'd refolded the letter and shoved it back in the envelope, giving himself a paper cut in the process. He felt he'd been socked in the gut. But he'd also never felt more motivated in his life. First by the money—the "bucks" Reed referred to amounted to $65 billion in cash and stock—and then by the rage.

Luke's body tingled with new ambition.

He would not let himself be crushed by something as clichéd as an under-loving father. He would not wallow in Reed's lack of approval. He would not spend another second wishing his father had been proud of him.

Instead, Luke would *move fast and break things*. Indeed.

~

That was ten years ago. Luke was twenty-nine now. By twenty-nine, Reed had already made *Luminary* magazine's annual list of the world's 100 "great influencers." He was already *radical and extraordinary*.

Luke was not. At the moment, he was best known for being the son of Reed Zimmerman. Lower-grade digital media had assigned him a host of humiliating nicknames: *The Billionaire Skateboarder*. (True, Luke liked to skateboard. What California-raised male didn't?) *The Little LikeMe Prince*. The media had also loved reporting that Luke had invested large chunks of his father's money in a series of failed Silicon

Valley startups. The flying car company. The virtual reality travel company. Perhaps most embarrassingly, the insect milk company.

But how things could change in just a handful of years. Luke leaned back in the driver's seat, keeping only his fingertips on the wheel as the Elan's autopilot software held the car's speed at a perfect fifty-three miles per hour on Highway 1, navigating its curves like a seasoned, confident chauffeur. Out the window, the rising sun burned through the fog lining the hills, bringing them into focus, and Luke felt his own mind sharpen and clear, his spirit rise alongside the brand-new day.

Soon, they would no longer laugh. Not the reporters or the tech bloggers or the social media influencers. Not his superstar peers like Moose Lodha or the millions of LikeMe users who still worshipped Reed and thought Luke was a joke.

Insect milk and the rest of his failures may have deserved their laughs. Now that Luke was on the other side of those mistakes, he could admit this. The mockery no longer bothered him. Not since he'd embarked on his newest venture, Targeted Embryonic Acceleration Technology, TEAT for short. When the world learned that Luke had designed a way to safely reduce the duration of human pregnancy from nine months to nine weeks, no one would be laughing. Of this he was completely certain.

Luke exited Highway 1 and switched the Elan into manual mode as the road grew narrow and winding. The fog reappeared and blotted the sun. Out his window, horses grazed behind a fence.

He slowed as he approached the entrance to the Seahorse Center, a wrought iron security gate flanked by a thick hedge. The Center's landscape was strategically designed to obscure visibility from the road, its hedge outfitted with a wireless security system.

"Everything that happens," said the nun, "happens today."

"Yes," said Luke, lowering the car window and offering his palm to the square black sensor affixed to the guard booth. "Yes, it does."

The palm-recognition software flashed its green light of approval.

"Good morning, Luke Zimmerman," said the digital voice of Zeus, androgynous with a slight British accent. Zeus was the Center's custom AI tool, a far-superior Siri, named through an employee vote.

The two halves of the iron gate began to retract, and Luke eased the Elan through. Directly ahead, the twin domes of the Seahorse Center— known by staffers as East Lobe (clinical) and West Lobe (corporate)— rose like bronze mountains. Luke parked the Elan and sat for a moment, watching the peach blush of morning sunlight on the surface of the buildings. It was just after 8:00 a.m. One hour until his meeting with Tessa. Four hours until the three women of Cohort One were scheduled to report to East Lobe for orientation.

Today was the day. The Trial. The end of his period of "failure."

3.

Tessa arrived at the Seahorse Center an hour before she was due to meet with Luke. She wanted to check in with the Cohort first. She parked in the staff lot, hoisted her wheeled suitcase from the trunk, and followed a footpath to the building's entrance, feeling soothed, as always, by the Center's lovely grounds: acres of lush grass studded with sprawling live oaks and curly-topped pepper trees. Topiary and bright flower beds. Outside the building's entrance was a fountain in a round pool, surrounded by western coneflowers, their deep purple heads protruding like gothic strawberries from toothy green leaves. Tessa paused to skim her fingers through the cool water of the fountain. She shivered against the morning fog. Here, along the peninsula's coast, it commonly became all-day fog, hemming in the Center three hundred days a year, enhancing its sense of privacy.

Ahead of Tessa, the twin domes of the Center gleamed through the mist. The burnished exterior was derived from a combination of copper cladding and smoked glass. At the center of the conjoined buildings was the image of a fetus protruding from the metallic surface, a sculpture rising out of the smooth planes of the building like an artful tumor. Tessa loved the building; sometimes, out of nowhere, a stray glance at it would shoot tears to her eyes. And how many times had she gazed at it? Thousands.

Today, the tears rose. Tessa swallowed them down and summoned a firm smile for the uniformed security guards standing on either side of the Center's main entrance, guns snug at their sides. They were both former Army soldiers. Both had served years in Afghanistan. Both were muscular, tall, stone-faced. Luke had spared no expense when it came to guaranteeing the safety of the Center, its workers and visitors. Reprogenetics was a hot-button field.

"Morning, Dino," Tessa said brightly. "Morning, Michael."

"Morning, Ms. Callahan," said Dino. Michael gave his customary grunt-nod, and the Center's doors, military-grade reinforced glass, opened to admit her.

∼

Inside the Center, Tessa felt, as always, the sense of arriving home. It was the interior's unobstructed space, ironically, that made her feel secure. Reassured her that the Center could accommodate the activity inside it, no matter how big or radical. Above her, the central cavity opened like a wide throat, eight stories up, creating a sense of soaring inner space. The labs and offices were constructed around the inner periphery and connected crosswise by a network of clear tubular hallways. People could be seen moving from one side of the floor to the other. The footbridges were so transparent that they appeared to be walking on air. Elevators peeled up and down the interior walls like zippers. Tessa stepped into one at the base of East Lobe and took it to eight, the Residence Floor, where she and the Cohort would live during the Trial. Kate, Gwen, and LaTonya had arrived yesterday. They were required to stay through the delivery of their babies, plus an additional postpartum week, before heading to Bonding Camp for a month of intensive connection-forging with their newborns. Tessa could hardly wait to see them.

The elevator opened right into the common living area of the Residence Floor, where Kate Lavek was curled under a blanket on one of two sleek white couches facing one another, reading *The Economist*. She wore fashionable violet-framed glasses and her shiny blond hair was pulled into a perfect French braid. Tessa had seen Kate construct that braid in under a minute, while doing a host of other things: leading a teleconference, drinking iced coffee through a straw, evaluating a spreadsheet. She was a gifted multitasker.

"Tessa!" Kate tossed the magazine onto the coffee table. "Thank God." Kate hopped off the couch and gave Tessa a fierce hug, her petite body hard with muscle beneath her stylishly fitted Seahorse Solutions Center tracksuit, in midnight black; Luke had provided an array of branded "couture comfort-wear" for the Cohort to wear during the Trial.

"How're you feeling, dear one?" said Tessa, hugging Kate back, then settling onto the other couch.

"Perfect," said Kate. "Physically, at least."

"And otherwise?"

"Oh, you know. Right on the edge. Still wondering if I'm batshit for doing this. Still getting texts from my mom telling me I *am*. Along with the usual insults from Damon. Was I really ever married to that person?"

"You're not anymore," said Tessa. "That's what matters."

"One or the other, I could handle. My mother *or* Damon. But having both of them in the We-Hate-Kate Club—"

"Neither of them hate you," Tessa cut in. "They're both just extremely limited people. We know that. It's best not to engage with them."

Kate sighed. "I'm *trying*." She sat back down on the couch and drew her knees to her chest. "But my mother's so infuriating. She refuses to acknowledge that for practically my whole childhood, she openly complained about her AOF. That she whined all the time about her miserable pregnancies, all the miscarriages, how badly she wanted more children. How much I *deserved* siblings, blah-fucking-blah."

From her mother, Kate had inherited a condition called acute ovarian fatigue—AOF—which made her odds of conceiving a child after age thirty very low. Perhaps worse was the fact that Kate's likelihood of miscarrying if she *did* manage to conceive was very high, as was her chance of experiencing hyperemesis gravidarum, extreme "morning sickness." Kate's own mother had long suffered through all of these circumstances.

Kate had revealed all this to Tessa a decade ago, through uncharacteristic tears, when she'd been Tessa's top employee at Loop Industries, one of a half dozen companies on the peninsula that had entered the race for life extension therapies and technologies. Kate's job was to solicit donations from ultrawealthy individuals to support the firm's anti-aging research. The work was complicated and nuanced, and steeped in rejection. It also required a deep understanding of Loop's work, and the ability to then explain it persuasively to skeptical, inaccessible, and often eccentric billionaires. Kate had routinely pulled fifteen- and sixteen-hour days, doing whatever it took to book meetings with prospects, then hopping on planes, armed with statistics, slides, and samples, ready to pitch Loop with confidence to extremely powerful individuals, nearly all of whom were male. And she'd killed it, raising nearly a half-billion dollars in her first year. She and Tessa gradually progressed from colleagues to friendly coworkers to close friends. Now, nearly a decade after they'd met, Tessa liked to think of Kate as a niece. When the Seahorse Trial came to fruition, Tessa called Kate immediately. She was a perfect candidate: mentally and physically fit, with a clear medical justification for accelerated pregnancy, and temperamentally suited with her sales-hunter mentality.

Kate was tough. Except, Tessa knew, when it came to her mother. Then Kate became a little girl again, craving approval.

"She dumped all her fertility issues on me, for years," Kate was saying now. Tessa had heard this fact countless times over many conversations with Kate, but still nodded sympathetically. "And now that I'm taking actual steps to avoid them myself, she thinks I'm morally deficient."

"You know that's outrageous," said Tessa. "She's just fearful. And she didn't have a career, remember."

"How could I *forget*," said Kate.

"So she might not fully understand how hard it would be to do your job if you felt sick for nine months." After working for Tessa at Loop, Kate had gone on to an intense career in high-ticket software sales, regularly closing the six-figure deals that had earned her a spot as the top performer at RogueTech, and a renovated Eichler house in Mill Valley. Nine months off her game could mean a loss of millions in commission to Kate.

"Right?" said Kate, sounding gratified. "You know how *on* I need to be in my pitches. Am I really a terrible person for wanting to avoid nine months of morning sickness?"

"Of *course* you're a terrible person." LaTonya Sims drifted up behind Kate, wearing a fuzzy yellow robe, her perfect crimson nails in formation around a cup of coffee. With her free hand, she gave Kate's shoulder an affectionate squeeze. "Kidding, Kayters."

LaTonya, a fashion model from the Bronx, and Kate had formed a rapid bond when they met after being selected for the Trial a year ago and had since developed a sisterly dynamic, with an easy physicality that made Tessa envious. They were forever slinging arms around each other, leaning a head on the other's shoulder. Tessa had always felt uneasy with this type of affection—*why?* she wondered, as LaTonya took a seat on the couch next to Kate and leaned against her.

"Morning, Tessa," said LaTonya. "Thank *God* you're here."

"Sorry to barge in so early," said Tessa. She was always startled by LaTonya's beauty, especially first thing in the morning, when LaTonya had clearly just rolled out of bed. Her eyes were still half-mast and her face bare of makeup, but she looked every bit the supermodel she was: six feet tall and impossibly narrow. Dramatic cheekbones, full lips. Lustrous dark skin. She was determined to have a baby with minimal interruption to her career. Her multimillion-dollar contract with the French label Tropez did not permit the lengthy interruption of natural pregnancy. Nine months would be a deal-breaker. Nine weeks, however, was not a huge deal. She'd already booked a personal trainer known as the Miracle Worker in the modeling industry, a man famous for guaranteeing women a "complete body recoup" just three weeks after giving birth. As for other postpartum logistics, Seahorse would provide each member of Cohort One with a customized prosthetic breast, wearable by anyone and infused with the mother's scent, designed to "lactate" formula tailored to mimic her biochemistry. Each Cohort member would also receive a tiny two-way VR device that, when worn by mother and baby, would allow them to "be" together, regardless of physical location.

Bottom line: LaTonya could resume shooting for Tropez a mere four months from now, max, lithe as ever, minus the guilt that would ordinarily arise from working twelve-hour days with a newborn at home. "Barge in?" said LaTonya to Tessa. "Give me a break. We're lost without you."

"Oh, you're completely fine without me," said Tessa. "But I'm happy to see you, too."

"I was just filling Tessa in on my mother's latest take on my life choices," said Kate. "Which is still that they're super shitty."

"Your mother's a mindless bitch," said LaTonya easily. "We all know that, Kayters."

"Thanks for the reminder," said Kate.

"Well, *I'm* extremely proud of you, Kate," said Tessa.

"Spare me the mom compliments," said Kate.

"The mom-pliments," said LaTonya, propping her long, slender legs on the coffee table.

"I'm not your mom, Kate," said Tessa. "And I'm neither mindless nor bitchy, at least by my own estimate. So I think my opinion counts." She liked saying the things to Kate that Kate's mother never did. And they were all true. Tessa was wildly proud of Kate—her mentee, her ingénue, her former colleague, and now dear friend—for defying the opposition of both her mother and her ex-husband and enrolling in the Trial. "And my opinion is that you're extremely brave. I don't say that to many people."

Kate tried to look irritated and failed. Tessa could see her holding back a smile.

"I'm with Tessa," said LaTonya. "You're a badass, Kayters. My parents were basically cheerleading for me to do Seahorse, and I'm still scared shitless."

"Yeah," said Kate. "Shit. Less."

"Seriously, you two?" asked Tessa, feigning surprise. "At this point?" She'd anticipated this—the Cohort's last-minute jitters, doubts, the urge to back out. Completely normal. It was Tessa's job to soothe them back to their full commitment. Doubts caused the risk of flight and more.

"Really," said Kate.

"Well, let's talk about it," said Tessa. "What are you afraid of? What's really at the bottom of your fear, after all these months? Don't think, just speak from the gut."

"You mean, aside from a higher chance of miscarriage and birth defects, not to mention societal condemnation and death?" said Kate. She smiled as she said it, but Tessa could hear she was only half joking.

"Also, our bellies splitting open," said LaTonya, with a nervous laugh.

"Very funny," said Kate, not laughing.

"Of course you're afraid of those things," Tessa said kindly. "But remind yourself that we've taken every possible precaution. That you have the best clinical staff in the world dedicated to you twenty-four seven."

"Milford's such a stick-in-the-mud," said LaTonya.

"His bedside manner's not the warmest," agreed Tessa. "But he's a superstar. He has a Lasker. The most coveted prize in clinical medicine. He ran the Mayo Clinic for seven years. He's considered one of the top embryologists in the world."

"I like Gupta," said Kate. "She's still going to be there when Milford does our transfers, right?"

LaTonya feigned a shudder. "She'd better be. Otherwise I'm not letting Milford up in there." She gestured between her legs.

"Of course she'll be there," Tessa went on. "And speaking of credentials, Dr. Gupta was part of the team that invented the artificial womb. She's won a National Medal of Science. Dr. Akabe was a part of the group in Japan that converted skin cells into eggs and sperm."

"We know all this, Tess," said Kate.

"I know you do. But I'm just reminding you of the caliber of your staff. They're brilliant doctors. They've thought of all possible aberrations in the Trial. Put a contingency plan in place for every single one. They've designed Seahorse to protect you, at any cost. I would never—ever—have brought you here otherwise."

"But what if—" started Kate.

"No, Kate," said Tessa. Firm, gentle. "Optimism. It's the only logical position. TEAT was already in year four of intensive clinical tests when Seahorse acquired it. I've personally seen it applied successfully to dozens of different species, including chimps. Ninety-eight percent overlap with human DNA."

"Two percent non-overlap," said Kate.

"Kate. Remember that you held the baby TEAT chimps in your own hands. In fact—" Tessa pulled her phone from a pocket and held up a recent picture of Esther, one of the original TEAT baby chimps, now full-grown. In the photo, she was munching an apple.

"Awww," said Kate, smiling.

"I was just up in Eureka, at the Animal Preserve, on visiting rounds last week," said Tessa. "The whole community is thriving, mothers and children. You're welcome to have a look at the documentation."

After a pause, LaTonya said, "I don't need to see it. I've got the faith."

"Me, too," said Kate.

"Someone has to be first," said Tessa. "Think of Margaret Sanger and Lesley Brown. *They're* the reason birth control and IVF became everyday options. You're following in their footsteps."

"Courage is the mother of progress," said LaTonya, raising her coffee cup.

"Radical precedes ordinary," said Kate, without missing a beat. "Vision is nothing without activism."

Tessa smiled. All were *Pushing Through* quotes she'd often cited to the Cohort.

"Yes, yes, and yes," she said. "Now we're getting somewhere."

Down the hall, a door opened and closed.

"Gwen's awake," said Kate.

Momentarily, Gwen Harris appeared in the common area, already dressed in khakis and Birkenstocks, holding an insulated travel mug, long brown hair wet from the shower. When it dried, Tessa knew, gray threads would appear, suggesting Gwen's age, which was forty-seven.

"Morning, all," said Gwen, eyes gliding past Tessa. "Already chanting the *PT* mantras, are we?"

Gwen was the least agreeable Cohort member. She was the least moved by the deeper ideas of Seahorse, far less of a fan of *Pushing Through* than Kate and LaTonya, who both owned first editions. Like the two younger women, Gwen wanted a child as quickly as possible, but unlike them, her career did not factor into her decision. She'd already retired from a twenty-year career teaching high school math in Texas, though she'd never "had" to work; she was an heir to her family's oil wealth. From Gwen's application, Tessa knew that her longtime partner, Linda, had died of a swift-moving ovarian cancer five years ago, shortly after they'd begun the search for a sperm donor. The plan had been for Gwen to donate the eggs and Linda to carry the child, a plan cruelly undone by Linda's illness. Gwen had written in her personal statement that since Linda's death, she'd begun to crave a biological child with *brutal intensity*. That was the phrase Gwen had used in her application, in a paragraph so honest and raw it had given Tessa a lump in her throat.

But her personal statement wasn't the reason she'd fought so hard to admit Gwen to the Trial. And it *had* been a fight: Luke and the docs disliked the fact that Gwen was approaching fifty. They were concerned with the risks her age would bring to the Trial. But her age was precisely the reason Tessa wanted her: when Seahorse became a mainstream elective option, older mothers would likely be widespread early adopters. Women whose biological clocks ticked louder by the day, who were less physically resilient than their younger counterparts. Who was Seahorse—especially TEAT—for, Tessa had argued with her team, if not women like Gwen: over forty, single, reasonably healthy, struck in midlife with the desire for a child?

Tessa had fought hard to bring Gwen here and was proud to have won. She just wished she liked Gwen more. Tessa often had to remind herself she'd titled an entire chapter of *Pushing Through* "Against Likability." Gwen's curmudgeonliness, her lack of interest in making other people comfortable, was a quality that, in theory, Tessa wanted to admire.

"Morning, Gwen," said Tessa brightly. "How are you?"

"Tragic," said Gwen. "I'm about to drink my last cup of coffee for nine weeks." She nodded at her travel mug. "I'm in a state of preemptive mourning."

"Don't remind me," said LaTonya. "I'm trying not to think about it."

"Six ounces of coffee is permitted," said Tessa. "Or ten of green tea."

"My heart says yes," said Gwen, sardonic. "But my head says no."

Kate nodded. "I didn't come this far to screw things up over a little caffeine."

"Me neither," said LaTonya, sighing. "Maybe my teeth will get whiter."

"That's not possible," said Tessa. "You could do a toothpaste commercial right now."

"Thanks, honey," said LaTonya, flashing her snow-white smile at Tessa. Tessa smiled back. She enjoyed the feeling of inclusion in the Seahorse Cohort, that LaTonya called her *honey*. Most of her social interaction in the past decade had been with colleagues and direct reports; she was often friendly with them, but she kept a layer of reserve, a clear professional boundary. With the Cohort, it was different. In order to keep them focused and calm—fully committed—she'd had to refrain from acting as their manager. She'd had to become their friend.

Positive manipulation, Luke called it.

But Tessa didn't feel manipulative. Not even toward Gwen. She felt propelled by a genuine camaraderie, an unfamiliar tenderness. She couldn't remember the last time another woman called her *honey*. Tessa emphasized the importance of female friendships—*grow them like investment accounts,* she'd advised in *Pushing Through*—but the truth was, she didn't have that many herself. Not since her days at Weldon, two decades ago. There she'd made dear friends—her roommates, her lacrosse teammates—but those women were scattered across the country and the world now, immersed in careers, raising families. Tessa kept in touch with them, but she'd lost the dailiness of their friendship long ago. She missed it. The Cohort, in some ways, had brought it back.

Gwen set her coffee down on the table, too hard, and leaned back on the couch. "Fucking progesterone," she said with a groan. "I feel like a dog that just swallowed a ham. Bloated and lethargic. And it's eight thirty in the morning."

"The hormones are rough," said Tessa. To prepare for their transfers, the Cohort had been on a regimen of hormone injections. "But hang in there, Gwen. You only have a few hours to go."

"You sure we can't take the supplement *now*?"

"You probably could," said Tessa. Part of the Seahorse Solution was NauseAway, a supplement that eradicated "morning sickness" and maintained energy levels throughout pregnancy. "But it hasn't been tested exhaustively at the pre-procedure state yet. We know after an embryo transfer is successful, the supplement is completely safe. Your transfers are happening in"—Tessa glanced at the clock on the wall—"four and a half hours. Then you can take the supplement."

Gwen rested her head against the white leather of the couch and covered her eyes with one arm. "Just wake me when I'm pregnant, okay?"

"I'm starving," said Kate. "I think it's the hormones. I've never cared so much about breakfast."

"I never cared about breakfast until yesterday," said LaTonya, "when I had an almond croissant in the dining room here. It's like God in a pastry form."

"Oh, good," said Tessa. "They're made by a friend of my husband's."

"When does Dreamy Pete get to visit?" said Kate.

Tessa shrugged. "We haven't planned anything yet. No visitors at all until you three are settled in." She kept her tone casual, almost dismissive, though it made her feel guilty, as if Peter could hear her. In truth, she missed him already. But none of the Cohort had a husband or significant other; this was a requirement of their participation. Their harvested eggs were already prefertilized with the sperm of anonymous, well-screened donors. They'd also been enhanced with cells derived from the skin samples of natural AG mothers, to jump-start fetal growth. The Cohort's pregnancies were manipulated, coaxed, and designed in a lab. It was incredible, but it was not romantic.

Eventually, of course, Tessa and Luke envisioned the Seahorse Solution as a decision a couple made together, as an enlightened team. But for now, allowing another person's opinions and emotions into the mix was too risky. To linger on any details of Tessa's own marriage, even those as minor as Peter's visiting schedule, would remind the Cohort of what they did not have: partners. It risked making them feel more alone.

"Doesn't it bother him?" Gwen said, as if reading Tessa's mind. "That you've ditched him for us?"

"No," said Tessa. "He understands the importance of our work here. He believes in it as much as we do." She wished this were true.

"Peter's basically perfect," said Kate. "He's like a Ken doll, hiker edition."

"Can he be my donor?" said LaTonya. "Is it too late?"

"Very funny," said Gwen, sounding unamused.

"Let's keep our eye on the ball," said Tessa. "The Trial is about the three of you. It's about the future of motherhood."

"Damn straight," said LaTonya. She stood and stretched, her body a graceful stalk. "I'm going to throw on clothes. And then I *need* to go get a croissant."

"I think I'll go back to bed," said Gwen.

"Come with us to breakfast," said Tessa. Gwen seemed grouchier than usual, which was not a good mindset for the TEAT transfer, just hours away. It was best not to leave her alone to ruminate. Success rates correlated, to some degree, with mood and stress. Tessa added, "We want you with us."

"We do," said Kate.

"This isn't summer camp," said Gwen. "There's a fully stocked kitchen right here. I don't need to relocate to eat breakfast. The whole dining room seems redundant, doesn't it?"

"You're right," said Tessa, forcing agreeability. "We built the dining room on another floor for variety. So you'd be able to cook some meals and not cook others. So you could change up your meal settings."

"I think we're changing things up enough as it is." Gwen pushed up from the couch. "Breakfast locale seems rather petty, next to gene editing."

"This is true," said Tessa, forcing cheerfulness. "You do what you like, Gwen. We'll bring you a croissant."

Tessa walked with LaTonya and Kate down one floor to the dining room.

"What do you think's up with Gwen?" said LaTonya, as they settled around the table. With two crimson nails, she picked a sugared almond slice off her croissant and nibbled it. "She seems kind of hostile today."

"Today?" said Kate. "As opposed to most days?"

"She isn't hostile," said Tessa. "She's just guarded. And probably scared. We should have compassion. Try to support her, no matter what. We're a Cohort of one. A single unit." She enjoyed using *we*, even though she was not technically a member. "In a matter of hours, each of you is going to begin changing the world."

"Amen," said LaTonya, raising her glass of orange juice.

"To Cohort One," said Kate, lifting her water, and Tessa her mug of tea. The three of them clinked a toast, the sound solid and reassuring. Tessa thought of Peter, how they'd tapped their wineglasses together in the dim light of the restaurant just one night ago. Already it seemed like long ago, their lovely home in Atherton light-years away. Right now, Peter must be on his morning run. She pictured the seep of sweat darkening his T-shirt, Python hustling at his heels, leash-free, the muscles of Peter's legs tensing and flexing as he strode over the sidewalk. His absence suddenly felt physical, as if a part of her body had vanished.

4.

TEAT began with Luke's job at Configuration Labs, a Palo Alto–based biotech company doing pioneering work in genetics. He'd gone to work there after his serial failures in insect milk, flying cars, and VR travel. Perhaps a day job in the hard sciences would clear his head, he told himself. Grant some perspective, spark a real idea. He would not jump into something on a gut instinct or the thrill of its coolness. This time, he would research and self-educate until he'd found something just right—the thing that was destined to become *radical and extraordinary*. He knew only that it would be in the biotech sector. Back at Harvard, he'd been on track to double major in biology and computer science, and the convergence of the two had always fascinated him—but he didn't yet have *the* idea. He'd tried to keep up on what was happening in the field, subscribing to long-standing journals like *Nature* and *Cell*, plus edgier publications like *Experimental Biology* and *Reprogenetics*, and even to radical ones like *Technological Self Transformation* and *Consumer Eugenics*. He got his hands on any paper that had come out of Carnat, the radical French biotech lab, and taped a modified quote from transhumanist Zoltan Istvan onto his refrigerator:

I will use science and technology to radically change and improve the human species. For real-world experience and possible inspiration, Luke got a part-time job (volunteer, unpaid) at Configuration Labs, where one of Reed's old friends was CEO. One of Luke's duties there was to organize and digitize Config's archives, a room filled with medical journals and scientific papers. It was in the archives that he'd first learned of accelerated gestation. AG, as everyone in Luke's circles called it.

Config staffers had been among the many scientists, ranging from evolutionary biologists to molecular geneticists, who'd tried to crack the cause of the AG phenomenon. They'd obtained tissue samples of the babies and mothers but, despite rigorous analysis, failed to determine why several dozen American women in the late 1990s and early 2000s had experienced their pregnancies on fast-forward, birthing full-grown, healthy babies just nine weeks after they'd conceived. Deliveries—mostly C-sections, but some vaginal—were normal. The infants were of typical size and weight, between five and nine pounds. Completely normal, but for a small cleft at the top of their heads—the response of the fontanel to the uterine pressure. The effect resembled the dip of a lowercase *m* and was strictly cosmetic, devoid of neurological impact. A thatch of hair could conceal it.

Their mothers recovered as if from standard pregnancies—even faster, in some cases. The media was rabid at first, relentlessly covering the AG births in the daily news cycle. Coverage spanned the full political spectrum. One extreme right-wing outlet called it an "elaborate left-wing hoax cooked up by pro-choice fanatics"; counterparts on the left worried that AG might lead to "radical setbacks in reproductive rights." Popular culprits for the cause, Luke learned, ranged from tainted water to industrial food contamination to estrogen disruptors leached from plastic. Other speculations included bad Chinese vitamins, a chemical weapons attempt by Al-Qaeda, divine intervention, and pharmaceutical interactions.

A few women—Luke noted the names of each who was willing to reveal it—made appearances on the talk show circuit, others did *People* magazine covers or interviews for a *New York Times* feature. Social media was in its nascent phase when AG first occurred, but Luke was able to identify heavy trending of the topic on the few platforms—LikeMe, Friendster, MySpace—as well as furious debate in AOL chat rooms and Blogger.

Long after midnight, Luke sipped energy drinks in the silent, empty archives of Config Labs and pored over every old piece of media he could find on AG. Coverage was heavy for roughly eight months after the last birth, he learned, and then began to taper off steadily. The reason for the waning, Luke surmised, was that fresh information on the cause of AG failed to emerge, and the mothers and babies who'd experienced the extraordinary nine-week gestations went on to begin utterly ordinary lives together, the media-unworthy daily routines of diaper changing and feeding and sleep training. Apart from their clefts, the infants were indistinguishable from other infants: loud and demanding and cute, and of little interest to most people beyond immediate family. Certainly not to the drama-craving news cycle. By studying the media trends, Luke could see the public's interest in AG wane steadily. Other stories took over: new wars and the latest acts of terrorism, political circuses, school shootings, natural disasters, and ugly celebrity divorces.

Acceleration did not repeat. No one knew why. Eventually, the NIH declared the phenomenon a *spontaneous aberration of indeterminate cause*. The number of reported cases—forty-eight—was small enough for acceleration to be deemed another of nature's enigmas, like the rapid aging of children with progeria, or one fetus growing inside the other. Twenty years later, it seemed nearly everyone had forgotten. Forty-eight documented cases of accelerated gestation gone to the ether.

Luke couldn't imagine forgetting. Acceleration was grotesque and triumphant, an unsolved mystery, unduplicated.

He attempted to contact the few AG mothers who had identified them-selves publicly: Danielle Auslander of Racine, Wisconsin, and Jane Ford of New York City, both of whom had openly appeared in print, on television, and online. He tracked down the name of another, Irene Brenner, from Austin, Texas, through poorly secured electronic hospital records that indicated a live birth from an AG pregnancy in the spring of 2000. Luke's investigation of each led him nowhere. Danielle, of the *People* cover, appeared to now live in Australia, with four children in their teens and twenties, none of whom Luke could identify from Danielle's social media pages as the accelerated one. They all looked perfectly normal in photos at the beach and graduation ceremonies, curly-haired and grinning at the camera. He sent her messages through LikeMe and Twitter but got no response.

Jane Ford was too generic a name; his search in the New York metro area yielded dozens of results.

Irene Brenner had died in a car accident in her twenties. Luke found only a few brief obituaries that mentioned some biographical details: she had been an excellent student and athlete who'd gone to Yale and rowed crew. She was killed on impact when a drunk driver blew through an intersection. Survived by her parents. No siblings. No mention of Irene's baby. Luke wondered if the child hadn't survived, or if Irene had given her up for adoption. Despite the cold leads, accelera-tion continued to fascinate Luke. He felt he'd discovered a lost key to some forgotten door. Who knew where it led? He wasn't sure what he might *do* with the faded story of accelerated gestation, but his gut told him there was an important discovery within it. No one had been able to find it yet. Perhaps they hadn't looked hard enough.

Luke resolved to look harder.

In the end, it was Reed, of all people, who'd provided the answer. The most valuable thing he'd left to Luke, it turned out, was not the billions in cash and stock but unrestricted access to LikeMe. Reed had died while multiple machines were up and running in his Tiburon mansion; Luke was shocked to discover his father's relative sloppiness with his personal devices. Then again, Luke was very good at hacking, something he'd taken up as a sort of hobby at Harvard. It took him just a few weeks to crack Reed's exclusive access to the deep inner algorithms of LikeMe, which had granted him passage to every user profile, every group, every chat, every status update, message, photo, video, rant. That Reed had granted himself rights of entry was wildly illegal, easily worthy of several lifetimes in prison. Luke was not surprised to learn what a liar his father had been, publicly championing the sacredness of online privacy while granting himself full access to every scrap of data ever posted to the site.

Luke was disgusted and thrilled at the same time. What his father had done was egregious, and yet the ability to lurk anywhere on LikeMe, undetected, made Luke feel as if he'd gained the one superpower he'd longed for as a kid: invisibility.

He tried to use his all-access pass sparingly. Despite the excitement of being *able* to spy on anyone in the world, there weren't many people Luke actually wanted to secretly observe in their digital habitat. Plus, it was unethical.

But then he discovered the CleftKids, and his conviction wavered. The CleftKids were a chat group on LikeMe classified as "ultraprivate," which meant only users who'd been invited by the organizer *and* passed a triple-layer ID verification could join. The group was open to only one minuscule segment of the population: children of accelerated gestation.

It took Luke under two minutes to fully access the group, which had just a handful of members, all teenagers, ages ranging from thirteen to sixteen. As he scrutinized their conversations day after day, his future clicked into place. Connections appeared between the scattered milestones of Luke's life—his internship at Config, his failed business ideas, his father's death, his inheritance of LikeMe—like a pattern of stars cohering into the shape of bears or huntsmen. As he lurked, undetectable, in the CleftKids' virtual room, an idea began to form in his mind, a composite of all he'd learned over the summer. At its center was accelerated gestation, surrounded by everything else he'd learned on those long, silent nights in the lab.

5.

Tessa stepped into Luke's spacious office in West Lobe, from which he enjoyed sweeping views of the Seahorse Campus, eight floors below, and the blue spark of the Pacific just beyond. It was almost identical to Tessa's office, just down the hall, but minus any personal touches. Luke's desk, custom made in Italy, was made from thin planes of opaque glass. Its height could be adjusted with the touch of a button; Luke often stood while he worked, though he also (somewhat reluctantly) enjoyed the ergonomic desk chair gifted to him by the CEO of Aeron as a condolence gift after Reed died. Luke's desk was as bare as an ice rink but for two large, nickel-thin monitors arranged side by side; his phone; and a green fidget spinner. Adjacent to Luke's desk was a whiteboard wall covered in dry-erase marker scrawl. Tessa had written half the notes. The only other furniture in the room was a clear Lucite chair for visitors and, beside the far wall of windows, a napping pod—a white orb dangling from a fixture like an upright fishing pole. The floor was polished concrete and the blue-gray walls bare of decor. Luke claimed "environmental asceticism," as he called it, kept his mind clearer and more productive.

"Callahan," he said, poking his head around one of the monitors. He pushed his curly hair away from his forehead with a pinky finger, a gesture he performed with tic-like frequency. He should have gotten a haircut for once, she thought, for the sake of the Cohort. They would probably prefer the cofounder of their Trial to look like a grownup. Luke could still pass for twenty-two. "Where've you been? I thought we were meeting half an hour ago."

"I needed more time with the Cohort," said Tessa, sitting down in the Lucite chair and crossing her arms and legs. The chair was hard and its arms were slightly too high; it was impossible to get comfortable. "We had breakfast and then I walked them over to Clinical for their morning evals."

"Right." Luke nodded. "Milford should be sending the results over any second and officially green-light the procedures for noon. How's the Cohort?" Luke tapped his finger to his temple, indicating mind frame, which was Tessa's job to assess. "Let's start with LaTonya."

"Excellent. Eager, high spirits. She's an unwavering optimist."

"Good. Lavek?"

"Kate's somewhat anxious, but nothing out of the ordinary."

"How anxious?"

"Mildly. Remember that having your genes reconfigured and your womb manipulated might cause just a little bit of stress, even in a perfectly stable person. Kate's high-strung by nature, a typical high achiever. But she's also completely grounded."

"What about her divorce?"

"What about it?"

"Is she still communicating with the jerky ex?"

"Minimally. It won't be an issue."

"Are you sure?"

"Of course I'm sure. Emotional and situational readiness of the Cohort has been my *job* for the past year. I would have flagged Kate weeks ago if I had concerns about her ex-husband's influence."

"Hey." Luke held up a hand. "No need to get defensive, dude. You know I trust your judgment." He smiled; it was a joke between them, calling her *dude*. He'd called her that by accident during one of their first conversations, many years ago, and now he reverted to it when he sensed she might be annoyed with him, an attempt to quickly win her back over. They worked best when in sync. Sometimes the *dude* worked. Other times, like now, she ignored it.

"Moving on to Gwen," said Tessa. Luke grimaced.

"Don't make that face," she said.

"Sorry." He picked up his fidget and spun it between his thumb and forefinger.

"Look, Gwen's the least affable of the three. She continues to display some contrariness. She's naturally solitary. But I maintain that she's ready."

"Why?"

"Because she's tough. She's got grit. The same qualities that make her unpleasant to be around will keep her grounded during her pregnancy. Pragmatism. A lack of sentimentality. These are strengths."

"But are they good *maternal* qualities?" asked Luke.

Tessa knew where he was headed; she'd expected this. Luke had been skeptical of Gwen since he'd seen her initial psych eval, ten months ago. It had been high enough to qualify for the Trial, but just barely. Tessa had insisted on accepting her anyway, a decision Luke claimed to find risky, though Tessa suspected he was simply turned off by Gwen's age.

"We've been over and over this, Luke. Gwen represents a critical demographic. Older mothers stand to become Seahorse's biggest adopters. Women in their forties are done living to please other people. They're over being accommodating and agreeable. Gwen is just acting her age."

Luke shook his head. "I'm still struggling with her."

"It's too late now. You've had ten months to deal with this."

"Is it? Too late?"

"Too late to cancel her procedure? Are you kidding me?"

Luke pushed sideways in his Aeron and then deftly maneuvered the chair with his feet across the polished concrete floor to the front of his desk, until his long legs almost touched Tessa's. He placed his fidget on his denim-clad knee and leaned in toward her, as if delivering a secret. She could smell him—a mixture of musky male skin, a few days unshowered but inoffensive, and a vague whiff of fruit from the acai energy drinks he constantly consumed.

"Hear me out for a second," Luke said quietly. "What if Gwen absconds? Freaks out? Causes us problems? If she disrupts the Trial, we're both going to regret it."

"She won't do any of those things. Gwen's bristly. Not unhinged."

"She's given me nothing. Just a lot of scowling and unnecessary questions, every time I talk to the Cohort."

"Like what?"

"She likes to get personal. Yesterday, she asked me what I'm doing here. Just like that: *I'm curious, Mr. Zimmerman, as to exactly what makes you want to be a part of the Seahorse project.*"

"And what did you tell her?"

Luke looked irritated. "I told her the truth. That I've been in the biotech space for my entire career and that inventing TEAT has been a longtime passion. And then she goes, *But why? I'm just trying to understand how a young guy like you decides to make reproductive technology his passion.*"

"It's a reasonable question," said Tessa.

"She seemed more accusatory than curious."

"Try to see it from Gwen's perspective. What if a woman much younger than you was a key player in determining the future of your body? Of your child? Wouldn't you want to ask her some questions?"

He seemed to ignore her. "Should we delay her procedure and do one more psych eval?"

"The Cohort's procedures are in *two hours*, Luke. Delaying Gwen would only make her upset and suspicious." Tessa tried to stay calm, though she felt like shoving Luke's chair away.

Luke said nothing, looking down at the fidget resting on his knee and flicking it into action. Tessa stared at the blurry green whirl, then reached out and clamped her hand over it.

"Hey," he protested.

She kept her hand on his leg. Sometimes, physicality was required to get through to him, as with a toddler. "Luke. Stop this. The procedures are at noon. Gwen's included. No more psych evals."

He met her eyes and she saw him soften. This was their dynamic; they pushed and pulled each other, until one of them suddenly understood. He dropped his hand over hers and they sat silently for a moment, until a notification pinged from one of Luke's monitors.

"Results of the morning evals," said Luke, and they stood up together, the fidget falling to the floor and skittering across the slippery surface. They ignored it and moved back to Luke's desk, leaning in toward the screens to review the Cohort's morning charts. The news was good: vitals, viscosity, and hormone levels were optimal in each of the women. Gwen's numbers were the best, Tessa noted with satisfaction. There was no reason to postpone procedures, no need for last-minute reevaluation or second opinions. The Cohort was ready for the Trial.

Luke straightened from the monitor and turned to Tessa. "Showtime," he said, his face relaxing into a genuine smile for the first time since she'd entered his office.

Tessa, returning his smile, felt the tension in the air dissipate, their usual camaraderie settle in. "Shall we head over to Clinical? It's time. They enter prep in half an hour. I want to escort them."

"Everything that happens, happens today," said Luke, offering his elbow to Tessa. She looped her arm through his and they exited his office together, bound for the tubular hallway that crossed from West Lobe to East. As they approached it, the warm, cultured voice of Zeus wished them a *fruitful day*, and the glass doors to the footbridge slid apart.

6.

From studying the CleftKids' posts on their LikeMe page, Luke learned they were like an alumni club: bound by a shared past but occupied by the present, only occasionally referring to the thing—accelerated gestation—that had brought them together. When it did come up, Luke snapped to full attention, his heart rate rose, he studied and restudied their posts. One member in particular, he noticed, broached the subject most often: Vivian Bourne, a sophomore at Oceanside High in Newport Beach, California. Of the CleftKids who frequented the group, Vivian, a.k.a. VivversOC, was Luke's favorite. Even through the sloppy, abbreviation- and emoji-riddled chat of the group, Luke could tell she was the smartest of the batch. The most confident. He ran a quick data scrape on her and found that she was an honors student, played lacrosse, liked to surf, and was hoping to attend Weldon College, the prestigious all-women's school outside Boston.

VivversOC had written Luke's favorite CleftKids post:

I'll show u mine if u show me yrs #cleftpride.

Below was a picture of the top of her head, parted and lit strategically to reveal the irregularity at the crown. Luke had to squint to make it out, but there it was: a three-inch dent running lengthwise, perfectly centered as if marking the head into two equal lobes. Shortly, ten other postings with scalp photos went up.

VivversOC: That feels kinda good, right? No one but my parents + docs have evr seen mine. Like a little secret u don't want.

LindsEE! (Lindsey Wyatt, 16, Melbourne, FL): What about ur boyfriend?

VivversOC: Don't have bf

Xavey (Xavier Hartley, 17, Lowell, MA): Now u do, babe. [lip emoji]

VivversOC: In your dreams dude.

LindsEE!: when my bf noticed I told him it was a scar from surgery I had as a kid

Stoph1 (Christopher Dunn, 16, Chicago): what like brain surgery?

LindsEE!: he didn't even ask lol

VivversOC: omg, how incurious. What abt when u get a haircut? Don't u think they notice?

Xavey: I buzz my own hair yo.

Stoph1: I goto supercuts and skip the shampoo lol

LindsEE!: hair peeps notice 4 sure. Its just too awk to mention

VivversOC: that's what I think.

Luke printed out Vivian Bourne's photo and hung it over his desk.

With Reed's money, he formed a new company, his "biotech incubator," ZimLabz. He situated it in Daly City, away from the startup-swarmed suburbia of the peninsula. He kept his former workspace in the Mission, though, a converted garage he'd been using for years, for when he needed privacy.

ZimLabz mission statement: to transcend imperfections across the human experience, via intersections of technology and the natural sciences.

Intersection no. 1: Targeted Embryonic Acceleration Technology. TEAT.

Now Luke just needed the talent to make it happen. He hired a headhunter to start building his team. Despite Luke's own spotty entrepreneurial record, Reed's network had been so vast and deep, and his reputation so dazzling, that almost no one turned down a meeting with his son. Luke got a green light to visit the Mayo Clinic.

With the help of his headhunter, Luke poached best-of-the-best talent. First, he brought on his reprogeneticist—Roger Milford, of the Mayo Clinic, recent winner of a prestigious Lasker Prize. Then Kenzo Akabe, the stem cell biologist who'd first created embryos from human skin cells in Japan, came on as a consultant. Rita Gupta from UCSF, the obstetrician from the team responsible for the first successful artificial womb. She had been a particularly tough hire, strongly opposed to the idea of the nine-week pregnancy when he'd first met with her.

"It's an unsound concept," she'd told him. "Women need nine months to prepare for the profound changes a baby brings."

"But how can they really prepare," Luke asked, "when the child is still in utero? How long does it take to set up a nursery?"

Gupta had laughed with disbelief. "I don't mean *logistically*, Mr. Zimmerman. I mean psycho-emotionally. Even hormonally. A lot of necessary internal changes happen during pregnancy, and they happen gradually. For a reason."

"I respect that," Luke had said. "But perhaps you'd be open to talking with my new clinical chief, Roger Milford?"

"What?" Gupta seemed suddenly sharper, more tuned-in. "Roger Milford is working for you?"

"Starts a week from Monday," Luke had said.

Soon, Gupta joined his staff too.

In addition, Luke had needed research assistants and lab techs, finance people and legal wizards. Handlers and veterinarians for the animal trials.

In order to recruit, he'd needed to discuss the origin of his source material, the tissue samples he'd taken from Config Labs and preserved pristinely in deep freeze. Voluntary donations, he'd explained, riffing on actual historical events, contributed by AG mothers and children. He'd even located a document forger in Russia who provided him with an array of beautiful consent forms "completed" by every legal adult who'd donated her and her child's tissue to Luke's project, thereby authorizing him to "utilize the material for any purpose directly supporting human advancement."

It took years to get the team in place, to lure each new person away from a fabulous job, negotiate extravagant compensation packages, assist with relocation, complete stacks of nondisclosure and noncompete agreements. Luke's lawyers worked around the clock. His list of enemies lengthened as ZimLabz recruited top talent away from legendary institutions. The director of the Lincoln Laboratory at MIT referred to Luke as *a shameless poacher of human capital, seemingly bent on exploiting his father's legacy*, and Google's moonshot factory filed a lawsuit against him, claiming "tortious interference," which Luke's lawyers assured him would go nowhere. He was not worried. Every step he'd taken to build ZimLabz was absolutely necessary. Ruffling a few feathers along the way was inevitable.

When it was done, Luke paid his headhunter an astronomical commission and sent him on his way. There was still one more person to recruit to the team, but Luke wanted to handle it himself.

7.

Peter had gone trekking in Nepal alone. He'd strongly wanted Tessa to accompany him on the Himalayan adventure, but she was working fifteen-hour days preparing to launch Seahorse, and still had one foot in Loop Industries. She couldn't afford to be away until after the opening bell clanged on Wall Street and the company began trading. Declining Peter's invitation to Nepal had triggered a healthy dose of the g-word in Tessa, but the timing could not have been worse for her to be on the opposite side of the globe. Probably with altitude sickness.

Two nights after Peter left on his trip, Tessa had gone to a networking event in San Francisco, a shmoozefest thrown in celebration of a new company vowing to disrupt the beauty industry with AI-infused, ultralifelike robotic fashion models. Such events in the tech scene were often preciously quirky, and this one had been no exception. Held in a soaring barnlike space in the Mission, it featured small-batch bourbon and unidentifiable pickled things on trays, served by gorgeous "women"—actually bots covered in "skin" made from whipped latex and silicon—who moved through the crowd on "smart" roller skates.

Tessa normally skipped such ridiculous showcases, which made her feel excessively mature and unwhimsical, but several other major execs from buzzy Valley companies like Loop were rumored to be attending, so she decided to make an exception. Plus, she was feeling good. The IPO would solidify her place as a serious player in biotech—not an easy spot for a woman to capture—and spike her net worth on paper by a staggering eight-figure sum.

She'd gone to the robot model party with Kate Lavek, who promptly disappeared into the attractive, youngish crowd clad in the sort of low-key, skater-chic outfits that suggested high-balance bank accounts. Kate seemed to know everyone under thirty-five in the Bay Area. Tessa settled alone near the bar, where she was sipping her requisite bourbon and scanning the room, plotting her first introduction, when a tall, floppy-haired young man approached her.

"Tessa Callahan," he said. "Queen of the Loopers," using the term the media had assigned to Tessa's employees.

"Should I know you?" Tessa said.

"You sound suspicious."

"I am," she said lightly. The bourbon and her impending IPO had giddied her mood.

"Mutual suspicion is a gateway to mutual trust."

"I think you just made that up."

"Nope. Napoleon. I'm Luke Zimmerman, by the way."

"Zimmerman? As in—"

"Yes. Reed was my dad."

"Your father is missed," said Tessa. Reed had been a casual acquaintance of hers and she'd been as shocked as the rest of Silicon Valley to learn of his sudden death.

"Speak for yourself," said Luke.

A server whizzed by on her skates, glossy humanlike hair (horse, actually, Tessa had read) fanning behind her. She stopped on a dime to lower her tray of fresh drinks to a group of tech bros in graphic tees and Vans—Tessa knew the look well—and then pushed off in a three-sixty twirl, somehow managing not to crash into anyone.

"Smart ghost in that machine," Luke said, nodding to the bot.

"I'm impressed," said Tessa. "Grudgingly."

"Same," Luke said to Tessa. "Hipster nonsense like this is why I want to move out of this city."

"That's why I just did," said Tessa.

"Seriously?" He turned his focus on her like a tuner; she suddenly felt as if she were the only visible person in the room. "Where?"

"Atherton. I'm not ironic enough for San Francisco."

"To the post-ironic world," he said, clinking his water glass to her bourbon.

"To adulthood," she said, clinking back. "Except you barely look like an adult."

"You should see inside me," he said. "I'm approximately seventy-two."

"I'll take your word for it," she said, and felt something like a flush come over her. There was a disarming earnestness in the way he'd said *you should see inside me*, as if it were an actual invitation. But also a hint of aggression. She liked it.

"I'm working on something I thought might interest you," said Luke.

"Go on."

"You'll have to sign an NDA first."

"I can read and drink." She extended her hand.

"I don't have one on me. But my office is pretty close to here."

She texted Kate: *Already hit my quota for bourbon and bots. See you tomorrow.*

Then Tessa and Luke stepped out into the foggy San Francisco evening.

Luke's "office," south of Market, was little more than a garage with blackout shades over the few small windows, the space inside aglow with computer monitors and lamps emitting underwater shades of blue and green. A painted whale covered one of the walls. The only seating, aside from desk chairs, came from a few large hay bales scattered around the room. The other walls were mounted with large whiteboards, scrawled with numbers and notes and code. Tessa couldn't make sense of any of it, apart from TEAT written in large block letters at the top.

"What's TEAT?" she asked.

"It's why I brought you here," he said. "But I'll get to that later." He extended a palm and made a sweeping gesture around the room. "This is just my think-space. My company has a large lab in Daly City." He gestured to the hay. "Have a seat."

"Your company?" Tessa eased onto one of the bales. The straw poked through the thin wool-blend of her black trousers.

Luke didn't answer. He'd crossed the room to a small open kitchen along the far wall and was assessing the contents of the refrigerator. Then he shut it with a clang and joined her at the hay with a glass bottle of arterial-colored liquid in one hand and a sheaf of papers in the other.

"Beet juice?" He extended the bottle to her.

"I'm good, but thanks."

"Well, here's your NDA then. I'll tell you all about my company after you've signed. Take your time."

He sat down on a hay bale facing her and sipped the beet juice while Tessa read and signed the document. After she handed it back to him, he folded it into his pocket and fell silent, knees on his elbows, as if considering an important decision.

"Okay. My company is called ZimLabz. We're committed to the most cutting-edge biotech research on the planet."

"I've heard that before," said Tessa.

"Wait. Listen. We're working on a particular project. Highly confidential." He tapped his temple. "No one but my staff has heard what I'm about to tell you."

"I'm all ears."

Luke began to talk. His voice had a languorous California drawl, surfer inflected, but his pitch was eloquent. As it gathered momentum, he sat up straight and his long fingers flew through the colored light, throwing shadows on the walls.

Tessa listened.

The more he spoke, the more awake she began to feel. His sentences felt extracted from somewhere deep inside herself.

Women are tethered by their own biology . . . Human reproduction is the ultimate weapon of the patriarchy . . . Technology is a feminist weapon . . .

His idea was outrageous. A nine-week pregnancy, modeled after the accelerated gestation phenomenon of the late nineties and early aughts. AG was the inspiration, but TEAT would be a new and improved version of that unexplained anomaly, adjusted and controlled by the world's greatest experts in genetics and biotechnology.

"Think of AG as the organic fruit, and TEAT as the GMO fruit," Luke said. "But the best kind of GMO."

"Sounds like a PR nightmare."

Luke nodded. "Point taken. It's a bad analogy. But you get my point."

"I do."

TEAT would be offered as an elective add-on to IVF, he explained. Possibly, in the future, it would be available alongside natural conception as well, perhaps in a format as simple as a pill.

Tessa sat on the edge of her hay bale, captivated. The idea was wild and impossible and mind-blowing. She was half-incredulous, half-smitten by it. She had a million questions. But her gut told her TEAT could be perfectly symbiotic with the work she was doing at Seahorse.

"Look, I'm intrigued," she said, when he finally paused. "This is . . . radical stuff. But why are you telling *me* all this proprietary information?"

"Isn't it obvious? I need the world's best minds in biotech on board with this. And I have them, at least on the clinical and research front. But I still need someone on the business side. Someone who's overseen the build-out of transgressive products from scratch and made them crazy successful."

Tessa suppressed a smile. "I may know someone like that."

"I've heard about what you're doing at Seahorse Solutions. The proxy nursing device, the virtual separation-reducer. Plus all those genius accessories that make pregnancy less burdensome. I think it's genius."

"Thank you."

"In short, Tessa, I want *you*. At ZimLabz."

Tessa laughed. "I've already got my own company, remember?"

"Then let's merge. Think of the possibilities if our product lines merged. Between TEAT and Seahorse, pregnancy, birth, and early postpartum would become extremely low impact for women. Think of the benefits for their careers, their stress levels. Their *time*."

"I *am* thinking about those things," she said quickly. "Basically all the time."

"So? Then how does a merger strike you?"

"I'd want to keep my brand," she said reflexively. "Seahorse is here to stay."

"So keep your brand. ZimLabz will fold into Seahorse."

"I'm flattered. But I'd need to think about it—a lot. And get a lot of questions answered."

"Ask me anything." Luke set his empty juice bottle on the floor and leaned back on his hay bale, as if settling in for a long conversation. "Right now."

"For starters, I'd need to vet your technology. What's the basis for it?"

"Gene editing, essentially. CRISPR technology. The newest application of classic Mendelian inheritance."

Tessa nodded. "All the rage. But editing from what source material, exactly?"

Luke paused for a beat. Tessa thought she detected a slight change in his breathing, as if he were suddenly nervous. Understandable; they'd just met an hour ago, and he was essentially divulging his greatest trade secrets to her.

"Skin samples of natural AG mothers and babies," he answered, swiping his hair off his forehead with his index and pinky fingers. "Mothers and babies. Donated by anonymous volunteers. TEAT technology involves base code drawn from a combination of dozens of those samples, which my team then analyzed and altered and replicated. We're already at the animal trial phase. The goal is a human trial two years from now."

"How does your team alter the base code?"

Luke shrugged. "I can't pretend to understand the details. I haven't won any Nobel Prizes, like some of my new colleagues. But in layman's terms, they quality-control the source material by snipping away the risky stuff."

"Eugenics," said Tessa.

"In a way," said Luke. "But the positive, market-based kind. The same kind that's helping cure diabetes and cancer."

"And what's *your* stake in all this, Luke? You're Reed Zimmerman's son. I'm guessing you have a fair amount of . . . resources at your disposal. You probably could be doing anything you want. Traveling to space. Living on a private island. Why this?"

Luke flicked his eyes toward the ceiling and back to Tessa. "My father helped invent social media. Which I think is basically evil. In the end, LikeMe and all its garbage spawn just make people feel bad. It created a massive, ubiquitous system of artificial desire and reward. It made personal experience an object to be displayed and judged. It's done nothing but wedge humans apart from one another."

"I agree," said Tessa.

"And, mark my words, it *will* die. LikeMe usership peaked in 2017 and is incrementally declining. Twitter's in serious trouble. Even Snapchat has a million fewer users than it did two years ago."

"I know. But what does this have to do with TEAT?"

He began tapping one foot on the concrete floor.

"Well, when my dad died, he managed to turn even death into a popularity contest. Do you *remember*?" Luke's voice grew fervid. "The VR service with people all over the world weeping? Holding up signs that said shit like *The World Will Never Be the Same*?"

"I remember," said Tessa.

"It made me want to do something that was the exact opposite of what my father did. Something tangible and physical and *real*. Some kind of breakthrough that trends and taste and pop culture and fucking *likes* couldn't touch."

"And so you just decided to reconfigure women's reproductive systems?"

"No. It was more like the decision found *me*. I stumbled upon some information about AG, and suddenly the lights went on. I can't explain it. But it felt like an epiphany." His eyes searched for Tessa's in the dim, aqueous light of the garage. "Like suddenly I had the key to unlocking a new kind of freedom for women." He exhaled loudly, as if he'd worn himself out.

Tessa took a moment to absorb what he'd just told her. To let his passion and his anger settle. Clearly, he was full of both.

Then she asked, "Might you have anything other than beet juice to drink?"

Luke grinned. "I've got room-temperature La Croix. And a bunch of bourbon. Same artisanal shit they were serving at the roller-bot party."

"I'll take some of that," said Tessa, rising from her hay bale. The straw had left crisscross patterns on her palms where she'd leaned them against it.

Then they talked and talked, the evening melting into night, the gap between their knees on opposite hay bales growing narrower. But. Tessa felt she'd encountered some alternate version of herself. In his presence, she felt open and unfettered, as if she could say anything. It was absurd; he was a baby. Yet their rapport had a chemical pull. At some point, she'd literally let her hair down, pulling it from the professional low ponytail she'd worn to the meeting so it fell around her face.

Perhaps—*perhaps*—they would end up working together.

She had a lot of thinking to do first.

When she finally left his garage, it was 4:00 a.m., the streets of the city gauzed with fog and weak streetlights, but Tessa was wide-awake, teeming with brightness. She waited until she got home to Atherton to call Peter in Kathmandu, who assumed she'd just woken up for the day, and she let him believe it.

8.

Tessa stood beside Kate in a procedure room of East Lobe, dressed in blue scrubs and a surgical mask, holding Kate's hand. Kate lay on the exam table, her body bisected just above her belly by a white sheet that extended from a rod over the table. On a mount at her eye level was a monitor on which she and Tessa would be able to watch the transfer. The room was cold and Kate was shivering lightly, despite the fleece blanket covering her from the waist up. A Chopin sonata drifted through the spotless, bright room done in white soapstone and stainless steel.

"What's taking them so long?" asked Kate. Her blond hair was pulled back and tucked under a hairnet and her face was free of makeup, making her look younger and more vulnerable than usual.

"They're not taking so long," said Tessa. "It just seems that way."

Dr. Milford and Dr. Gupta were scheduled to arrive in Kate's room shortly, after they completed LaTonya's and Gwen's transfers. Kate had requested to go last. Targeted Embryonic Acceleration Technology required neither surgery nor anesthesia, nothing more than a speculum and catheter, but still, Kate was nervous. Tessa could feel it in the dampness of the young woman's slim fingers, in the fierceness with which she clutched Tessa's hand.

Kate palmed the monitor beside her with her free hand. "Am I sure I want to watch this?"

"Yes," said Tessa. "It will demystify the experience. I'll be watching it right alongside you."

Kate smiled. "Fear is proportionate to its vagueness, right?" It was a line from *Pushing Through*.

"Exactly," said Tessa.

"I'm not afraid of the transfer," said Kate. "I'm just afraid it won't work. I wish they'd implant more than one embryo. The odds seem so low. Statistically, only one in—"

"Kate, no stats. Every detail of this trial is by design. We're conserving embryo supply on purpose. Not because we expect TEAT to not work, but to guarantee that it *will*. Even if we have to go through a second round of transplants. Which I'm confident we won't."

"I hope you're right. I'm not sure I can do this more than once."

"Gupta, Rita, MD. Authorized to proceed." Zeus's voice through the speaker interrupted Chopin. "Milford, Roger, MD. Authorized to proceed." The exam door clicked open and the doctors stepped through.

"Knock, knock!" said Gupta, the obstetrician a fortyish Indian woman with lustrous hair and skin, her voice a melodic soprano. "Kate, Tessa, good afternoon."

Milford, the reprogeneticist, grunted a greeting. He was in his sixties, white-haired, slightly stooped, with an underhydrated look. Seahorse's two lead physicians formed a perfect yin and yang of medical horsepower, a triumph of Luke's networking efforts.

"Are we ready?" Gupta smiled at Kate.

"How'd it go with the others?" asked Kate. "How are Gwen and LaTonya?"

"No complications," said Gupta. "They're both perfect."

"Lie back, please," said Milford. He tapped the monitor beside Kate to life and its screen glowed dark green. "You can watch here." He moved behind the white sheet and Gupta joined him.

"Knees wider, please," said Milford. "You'll feel some coldness."

Kate latched her eyes to Tessa's.

"Now relax," said Milford.

"Oh my God," said Kate, looking at the images on the screen, which resembled several round pieces of coral, pocked with holes.

"Everything's fine," came Gupta's voice. "Please try to stay still."

"Kate, you'll feel a dull prodding sensation," said Milford. "It may be slightly uncomfortable."

Suddenly, Kate drew in her breath, a sharp suck. "Oh!"

"Got it," said Milford. "Sorry about that."

Kate's eyes glossed with tears. "That hurt," she whispered.

The screen went dark.

Gupta snapped her gloves off and tossed them into the gleaming trash bin. "You did beautifully, my dear. Now you'll just lie here with your legs elevated for a few minutes. Then the nurses will come to transport you back to the residence. You'll want to rest for several hours."

"When will we know if it worked?" said Kate.

For the first time, Milford smiled. "In forty-eight hours we'll administer pregnancy tests."

"Usually we'd wait two weeks," said Gupta. "But these cells are fast."

Tessa thought Kate's face looked bare and childlike. "Is it okay that I've done this?" She sounded unlike herself, close to panicked. "Tessa, is it okay?"

"Dear one." Tessa took both of Kate's hands in her own. "It is absolutely okay."

9.

After the Cohort's transfer procedures, Tessa spent an hour debriefing with Luke and the clinical team. They were all restraining their optimism over how well the transfers appeared to have gone. They offered one another tempered congratulations. Only Luke dared use language like *about to stun the world* and *just a matter of time until you're all household names*. But he always spoke that way; the team was used to it. Tessa hardly even cringed anymore.

At 4:00 p.m., they broke for the day. Tessa took a walk on the grounds of the Center. Later she would spend time in her office, catching up, and then eat dinner with the Cohort, but now she just needed to be alone. To decompress. Outside, the fog had burned off and the sky was lucid, vibrant blue. As she walked along the footpath lining the bluffs, she called Peter.

"Smooth sailing," she told him. "No victory laps yet, but we're on our way."

"Aren't they scared?" said Peter. "Kate and the other two? That another human has probably already started growing inside them, on fast-forward. Isn't it just a little bit terrifying?"

"Of course," said Tessa. "Fear is a natural part of the process. But what matters is that they've learned to keep it in check. And it's not *fast-forward.* It's a carefully engineered, calibrated acceleration process based on a preexisting genetic template."

"In layman's terms, fast-forward."

"Okay, okay. That just makes it sound . . . manic. When it's carefully controlled. Anyway, how are you?"

"Fine. Python and I did a great run on Pulgas Ridge. But I'm curious to see the action at Seahorse. How long until Python and I can visit?"

Tessa bristled. She'd been gone less than a day. "I'm not sure. After my trip to Boston. I'm back on the twenty-third."

"Oh, right. Your Weldon speech. So we'll come on the twenty-fourth."

"Let's wait to lock it in."

"Okay." Peter sounded disappointed.

"I'm sorry," she said. "It's just going to be . . . really intense around here. Until the Cohort settles into their pregnancies."

"I understand," said Peter, though he didn't sound like he did.

"I'll make it up to you."

"Do you . . ." He spoke slowly. "Does being around all this pregnancy activity make you sad at all?"

"Honestly"—she paused, deliberating how truthful to be—"Honestly, no. Not yet, anyway. Maybe when I meet the babies I'll feel differently. But it was so hard for us. I'm relieved not to be going through it any longer. I'm just focused on supporting the Cohort in their experience."

"Oh." Peter sounded let down. "Well. I was just wondering."

"Does it bother you that I'm not upset?"

"Should we get into this now?"

"We don't have to. I just asked a question."

Peter was silent, then said, "*Bother* isn't the word. It's more like *perplexed.* Sometimes I just can't understand you."

"What don't you understand?"

"How you can compartmentalize like this. We wanted to get pregnant. We tried every natural and unnatural option out there and we couldn't. And now you're this . . . sort of *coach* for a group of women with these ultraengineered pregnancies. It's just hard for me to understand how you can be in this position and not feel . . . conflicted."

Tessa felt her palms dampen around her phone. When she spoke, her voice sounded tight. "I *am* conflicted, Peter. I just can't let it interfere with my work."

"But you're not working right now. You're talking to me."

"Would it be better if my voice were shaking? If I were expressing more angst?"

Peter sighed. "No, Tessa, that's not what I mean. I just want to make sure you're really okay."

"*Okay-ness* isn't a real thing. You can decide to make something okay or not. Men do this seamlessly all the time and no one questions them. Do you think a male CEO has ever been asked if he's *really okay?*"

"Hopefully by his spouse, yes. I'm your husband, Tessa. Not some colleague. I'm trying to communicate honestly with you."

Tessa felt herself release and soften. "I know you are. I'm sorry. I have no choice but to stay focused. I can't afford to let any personal issues interfere with Seahorse right now. It's a slippery slope."

"I know. It's just that sometimes it seems there are two Tessas, *my* Tessa and work Tessa, and I miss mine." His voice dropped and strained. She felt a pang of the g-word, mixed with irritation and tenderness, picturing him standing in their bright kitchen in his running shorts, phone between his head and shoulder as he chopped vegetables on the cutting board, Python curled on the floor. She missed him. She also sometimes wished he were different. That he didn't need quite so much from her.

"I love you," she said. "I'll see you soon, okay? As soon as I'm back from Boston and get my bearings."

"Okay," he said. "Bye."

He didn't say he loved her, too.

Tessa cut over to the footpath that traced the edge of the bluff and sat on a green bench, facing the ocean. It was a rare clear afternoon, the clouds a light smear in the sky, the breeze a soft rustle. At the base of the cliffs, the Pacific bucked and churned. Behind her, the domes of the Center gleamed in the sun.

She wished Peter hadn't brought up the baby issue. It was in the past, a healed wound. Their life was rich and full. She wished he'd just congratulated her. Said he was proud and left it at that.

A few hours later, he sent a text:

Eric & Dalton hiking the PCT. Invited me to join for part of it. Probably a couple weeks. Might be good timing, since you're busy. Could bring Python along. Thoughts?

The message startled Tessa. Eric and Dalton were old buddies from Peter's Polar Bear Club days; he hadn't mentioned them in years. Hiking the Pacific Crest Trail had been something he'd dreamed of when he was younger, Tessa knew, but he'd stopped seriously hiking after ZSY went under, claiming it gave him too much time to think.

That he would now suddenly want to embark on such an adventure with distant acquaintances struck Tessa as strange.

Could he be trying to punish her?

That wasn't Peter's way.

Still, she was vaguely hurt by his request.

But how could she possibly say no?

10.

B ack in his office, after the debriefings on the procedures, Luke settled into his desk chair and tapped his phone to lower the taupe shades over the broad windows facing the ocean, obscuring his panoramic view. Often, he found the natural world distracting. People spent far too much time in pursuit of beautiful settings. In Luke's circles of entrepreneurs and innovators, it was practically a sport. The splendor of the California coast was not enough for them. Nor were traditional places of grandeur, like Europe or Hawaii. No, Luke's peers insisted on Antarctica, on Easter Island and the Amazon. Then flaunted their conquests in real time on social media, grinning smugly at the camera.

Luke had been almost nowhere. This was on purpose. He'd had a VR room built in his house and owned all the most state-of-the-art accompanying equipment, and it was enough. In that room, he'd taken a safari to Kenya and stood atop the summit of K2, without risking his life or taking interminable plane flights or getting a single insect bite. More importantly, he hadn't eaten up weeks and weeks of his valuable time. Travel, in Luke's opinion, was an inefficient endeavor, on its way to eventual obsolescence. It pleased him to be ahead of the curve on this, even if it meant incredulity from his friends and mockery from the media.

He propped his feet on his desk and twirled his fidget, fixing his eyes on the round bearing at its center, trying to focus on breathing deeply. Meditation, like travel, also seemed a waste of time, but a knot of anxiety had settled in his chest after the Cohort's procedures were completed a few hours ago. It had yet to dissipate, despite the jog he'd taken around the periphery of the campus, and the two cans he'd swigged of ClearCalm, a drink containing the root of a South American plant that purported to "soothe the central nervous system while simultaneously promoting mental acuity."

Currently, Luke felt neither calm nor clear. A few hours ago, at the postprocedure debrief, when the doctors declared the Cohort's transfer procedures successful—inasmuch as success could be determined so early—he'd experienced a wave of elation. The whole staff had exchanged jovial hugs, even Roger Milford, who reminded Luke of some upright crustacean. Luke hugged Tessa last, and as they embraced, she'd whispered in his ear, *Two days until it all begins, Zim,* and held on to him for a few extra beats.

Of course, she'd only meant that the day after tomorrow, the doctors would know whether the women of Cohort One were pregnant. Her comment was merely one of excitement, of camaraderie, an iteration of obvious fact, but to Luke, it also carried vague menace. Yes, the day after tomorrow was the beginning of everything. But it could, theoretically, be the beginning of the end. He needed the Trial to run smoothly. His stakes were high, higher than anyone else's. He'd known this from day one, from the first moment he'd learned of accelerated gestation, years ago, back at Configuration Labs.

He had total confidence in the Seahorse team and the work they'd done to bring TEAT to the world, to improve every iteration, working from mice to rabbits, then from rabbits to rhesus macaques and chimpanzees, and finally to the Cohort. He believed in Milford and Gupta, in Kenzo Akabe. He believed in Tessa.

It was not the risk of the Trial, exactly, that was making him edgy. It was the surrounding circumstances. He reminded himself of the most basic principle of science, taught in grade school: correlation does not imply causation. That he'd noticed, several weeks ago, the presence of some anonymous visitor to the CleftKids group—a ghost troll whose account and IP address he could not trace, nor could his go-to hacker friend in India—meant nothing. That Tessa was soon leaving on a short trip to Boston to speak at her alma mater, Weldon College, where Vivian Bourne was currently a senior, slated to graduate in just eight weeks—also meaningless.

But yet, combined with the momentousness of the Trial, Luke could not help feeling unsettled by these events. Even though Tessa had informed him months ago of her obligation to speak at Weldon, as part of a series the college ran called Influencers. Even though LikeMe "ghosts" were not uncommon—hackers were getting more intrepid by the day—and it was only a matter of time before the company's cybersecurity division would nail whoever was lurking among the CleftKids. Still, both developments left Luke unsettled. He could not afford mistakes, especially not now, when his reputation and the entire course of his future was at stake.

Once the Cohort settled into their pregnancies, he'd feel calmer. Once TEAT was fully under way, and he could view the babies and know with certainty that he'd made all the right decisions. Once Gwen Harris, the questionable member of the Cohort, had improved her attitude. Which was inevitable, Luke thought, from a hormonal perspective. Once the oxytocin began swirling in her brain, she would surely lose her sourness, which had felt vaguely threatening to Luke from the moment he'd met her.

He closed his palm over the fidget and jutted his head to the right, then the left, hoping to elicit some cracks that might relieve the tension at the base of his neck, but nothing happened. His office with its blotted windows felt suddenly stifling. Perhaps he'd have to resort to a view of nature after all. He tapped his phone to open the window shades, and they peeled up to reveal the sky and sea before him, so bright he could hardly look.

11.

Before the baby, when Irene Brenner was just a regular college student, she'd loved the white winters of Connecticut, the exuberant springs. How the air on campus teemed with possibility, with any number of amazing things ahead, endless permutations of greatness. Nothing like the languid Texas Hill Country where she'd grown up, in a big house in the suburbs outside Austin, where it was green and warm most of the year. Yale was a revelation. The seasons, the sense of exclusivity. She was happy there, happier than she'd ever been. She went out for crew on a whim, because it seemed a quintessential college experience, and fell in love with the sport. It ignited an ambition in her she hadn't known existed, a competitiveness, a superiority. Rowers got up earlier than anyone else and trained harder. The rigor was part of the reward. There was no individual glory; the nine teammates were part of a single organism, bereft without one another, worthless.

Irene rowed coxswain. Perched at the tip of the boat, she faced her team, guiding them, a conductor of eight. She loved the distinction of her position, the pressure, the challenge. She wasn't a typical cox—at five foot six, she was taller than most so she had to keep her weight down to stay competitive with the shrimps who coxed other boats. Maximum weight requirement was 110, and staying as far below that number as possible was crucial to winning. This required constant self-denial that both maddened and inspired her. She conditioned herself to pass up the sundae bar in the dining hall, the late-night orders of chicken parm delivered in a red-handled insulated bag from a pizza place in town. In doing so, she relinquished a tradition of college life: indulging with friends. But the repercussions of indulgence were never worth it to Irene. The consequences always brought far more regret than the original pleasure. She'd done what it took to stay light, stay fit, stay strong. She studied, lifted weights, did cardio, rowed. She took her supplements (multivitamin, folic acid, fish oil) and drank plenty of water. She went to her annual physicals, to her gynecologist. She was not a virgin, though her boyfriends had been few, rare enough that she'd never taken regular birth control. Marriage and family seemed far away. They didn't interest her at all. Rowing crew interested her, pushing her body past its natural limit, winning. She loved her friends. She would have liked a boyfriend, but what she had fulfilled her enough.

At her annual gynecological exam, during her junior year, she'd turned down her doctor's push for her to take birth control. "It just makes sense," the doctor had said. "Even if you don't have a partner now. Better safe than surprised."

Irene declined. Artificially manipulating her body as insurance against some stupid hookup seemed lazy. Unnecessary. If Irene were ever in that situation—which, in those days, felt unlikely—she'd just use a condom. Easy enough.

"Thanks, but no," she'd said to the gynecologist. "I'm probably the least likely person on campus to get pregnant."

Famous last words.

"No problem," the doctor said. "But while we're talking about these sorts of choices, I wanted to mention a fantastic new option for women that's just been approved by the FDA. It's a mild hormone stimulant, designed to optimize your fertility for longer. It works cumulatively, over time, so if you begin taking it now, your fertility will remain robust for longer than it might otherwise."

Now Irene was confused. "And why would I need that?"

The doctor looked mildly irritated, as if Irene were missing the obvious. "A woman's natural fertility window—nineteen to twenty-six—is out of sync with modern career paths. Education and work are so consuming that we're not able to find time to have children until well into our thirties, sometimes forties. Which can be a very tough time to get pregnant. Egg count is low, stress is high."

"What about freezing our eggs?" Irene asked. "I just read an article about it for my women's studies class. Why not just do that?"

The doctor laughed. "'Just do that'? Oh, if only it were that easy. Egg freezing is cumbersome and expensive. It involves hormone injections and multiple doctor visits. It's physically demanding and unpleasant. That's why I'm so pleased about this new option. Just a daily pill. No side effects or interactions with other drugs. Just a simple way to keep your future options open without compromise."

"I don't know," said Irene.

"There are other benefits. It promotes a general sense of vitality and well-being. If used in conjunction with a healthy lifestyle, which I know you have, it can make low body fat and physical fitness easier to maintain."

Now Irene scanned the office wall for the doctor's credentials. Yale medical school, with a PhD in biology to boot. She turned over the words in her mind: *low body fat and physical fitness*. A nurse had weighed Irene before her exam: 112. Two pounds over the coxswain's maximum. The Essex Regatta—one of the biggest crew races of the year—was coming up in two weeks. So was her macroeconomics midterm. This semester was very tough. She could use all the help she could get.

Irene left the gynecologist's office with a prescription for Juva, a daily pill to be taken "to support vitality and long-term reproductive function."

Two weeks later, Irene's crew beat Harvard and Princeton at the Essex Regatta, and she'd gotten a ninety-seven on her econ midterm. Ahead of her were a few precious days free from studying and training.

So she let her roommate, Violet, drag her to a party.

It was the sort of night with an identifiable tipping point. Irene went from dancing to OutKast with her roommate in a group of girls, all of them tipsy on spiked punch, to doing shots of some amber, fiery liquid, to making out in the corner of the room with a guy she'd just met. A handsome senior with curly brown hair and glasses, named either Ryan or Bryan. The music was intensely loud—she'd had to yell into Violet's ear to let her know not to wait for her. That Irene would find her later. And then she'd let Ryan/Bryan guide her across a quad to another dorm and up to his room, a single on the top floor where the moonlight beamed in through the trees. He'd put on the Shins, the album everyone played all the time that year, and laid Irene on his bed, where he'd lifted her shirt and kissed her stomach, one hand on each of her breasts, and continued undressing her, asking, "Is this okay?" several times, to which Irene murmured, "Yes, yes," because, at the time, it was. Sex was neither sacred nor fearsome. She'd had a great night, a rare few hours of cutting loose, and sleeping with a handsome senior didn't seem like a bad way to end it.

Except that she hadn't realized quite how drunk she'd gotten. She'd done an additional shot—in the company of Ryan/Bryan—just before leaving the party, and its impact didn't fully hit her until she was in his bed, naked, underneath him. It was at the most inopportune moment when a tide of nausea rose within her, and she had to summon every ounce of her focus toward *not* throwing up. The moment Ryan/Bryan was up on his knees, fumbling with a condom, muttering, "shit, shit, shit," when he tore into its plastic sleeve too zealously and ripped the latex along with it, then leaning to her ear and whispering, "I don't have another, is it still okay?" Irene was too queasy to emit anything more than an indecipherable groan, which Ryan/Bryan interpreted as an affirmative, heaving into her as the room began to wheel, and he took her "Oh Gods" as declarations of pleasure.

Until he came and went limp, still inside her, he kept murmuring, "Was that okay? Are you okay?"

He wasn't a bad person. Whether his name began with an *R* or a *B*, Irene never ascertained. Other guys surely wouldn't have reacted so kindly when Irene turned her head to the side and vomited all over the mattress.

He'd wanted to help her, in fact. He threw a towel over the mess and brought her a can of cold club soda from a mini fridge. Her mouth cottony, head beginning to throb, Irene swigged the water, gagged on the bubbles, handed the can back to him.

"I have to go," she'd said, bending to the floor for her underwear, her jeans, her tight knit top. She was far too wobbly to attempt her high-heeled boots.

"Don't go," he said. "I feel bad. I didn't know you were so drunk. Why don't you sleep here?" He was sitting on his bed with a pillow in his lap, covering himself. Irene's vomit pooled underneath the towel beside him.

"I have to leave," she said, swaying a little and stepping toward the door, boots dangling from her clammy hand.

She walked in nothing but thin trouser socks, carrying her boots, all the way across campus to her dorm. It was April but the night was still cold, and the soles of her feet were numb and black with dirt by the time she opened her door in Durfee Hall. Violet didn't even stir as Irene entered.

Three months later, when Irene left New Haven with the baby, a girl, strapped into the back of the Toyota Highlander handed down from her father, she was glad she'd never learned the father's name. If he'd had a more distinct identity in her mind, she might have felt more compelled to find him. To tell him.

But why would he have wanted his life disrupted by such a bizarre event as becoming an unintentional father in the span of nine weeks?

Who wanted direct association with a freak occurrence? Irene had done Ryan/Bryan a great favor, she thought, as she steered her dad's old SUV south on I-95 in the first of the thirty hours between New Haven and Austin, her hands trembling on the wheel. She hadn't yet told her parents. Hadn't yet told anyone. She'd withdrawn from Yale right after she'd gone to Planned Parenthood to verify the positive result of her home pregnancy test. She'd also planned to schedule an abortion. Just a few weeks had passed since the Ryan/Bryan night and her missed period, so she knew she wasn't very far along.

Except that the nurse at Planned Parenthood (she was too embarrassed to return to her usual gynecologist, under the circumstances, since she'd refused birth control during her last visit) informed Irene that she was fourteen weeks pregnant. Irene stared at the ultrasound screen, unable to speak as the nurse pointed out all the standard features of a fourteen-week-old fetus.

"It's not possible," Irene had said finally. "It's just not."

"It's common to feel that way," the nurse said sympathetically. "But you're not alone here, and we can talk through your options. Termination is still available if . . ."

But Irene, who had always been vehemently pro-choice, couldn't bring herself to do it. Not now, when she could see toes and fingers and a nub of a nose.

That afternoon, she submitted a form to the college dean, requesting an immediate leave of absence for personal reasons.

A week later, she stared at the latest ultrasound in horror and awe. At the thing ballooning inside her, limbs and fingers already visible, the sex organs fully formed just five weeks after the night of the party. A girl. Developing normally but on fast-forward. It was more than Planned Parenthood was equipped to handle. She checked into Brigham and Women's Hospital.

Then, just over two months after Irene had rowed in the Essex Regatta, a nurse wheeled her into an operating room, flanked by an anesthesiologist and an obstetrician specializing in high-risk deliveries. The C-section was over in forty minutes, free of complications. The nurse and doctors couldn't conceal their amazement. A healthy baby girl, normal but for the shape of her head. The tiny creature felt wrong in Irene's arms, writhing and squirming, sucking greedily at her plastic bottle, guzzling the foul-smelling formula, because Irene couldn't bring herself to try to breastfeed. Mostly, though, she'd held herself together, despite her scrambled mind and frozen heart. She'd gone through the motions. Had refused painkillers for her throbbing incision. Learned to feed, to bathe, to change. She was capable. But the situation felt like pure dream. A punishment for a crime she hadn't committed, a long hallucination. Yet the baby continued to exist. Continued to wail and feed and sleep. And the sorrow settled over Irene, webbed and clingy, impossible to see through. Blocking the light, blotting her comprehension. Blunting her ability to feel what she knew she *should* feel for the tiny, needful thing.

Her baby.

But it was impossible to see the girl as her own. It had all happened too quickly, too strangely.

She couldn't stay here.

It was near the twelfth hour of her drive from New Haven to Austin that she'd cracked. The child yowled in the back seat, inconsolable despite many bottles and the vibrating pad Irene had purchased at Target and shoved under her car seat, guaranteed to soothe.

But the baby would not be soothed. She bleated on into the night, Irene weeping at the wheel, searching the radio desperately for something that might bring them an iota of the comfort they deserved.

She hadn't wanted this. Not in her wildest imaginings. She was twenty years old. Children were nowhere near her radar, nothing but a vague notion, like a mortgage or gray hair. *Probably, someday.*

After so many other things had happened.

Her daughter was two weeks old now. Six pounds, one ounce, declared healthy by the OB who had delivered her, by the NICU neonatologist, by the pediatric geneticist. Her doctors released her from the hospital reluctantly, along with free blankets and flats of formula and a protective helmet for the baby. She was to keep the baby's protective helmet on at all times, except when she removed it once a day to apply a salve. The helmet was designed to protect the skull and her ultradelicate fontanel and to gently reshape it over time. It looked like an old-fashioned swim cap and covered up the tufty dark hair the girl had been born with, making her pinched face even more pronounced. As if she'd been squeezed at the cheeks with two viselike hands and frozen that way.

It was hard for Irene to look at her.

She promised her doctors she'd return with the baby for follow-up appointments every two weeks; the aberrant nature of her pregnancy demanded close postpartum monitoring of them both. The doctors seemed desperate to see her again. She assured them she'd be back and allowed a front desk person to tap a half dozen future appointments into a computer, which Irene pretended to note in her planner. She had no intention of ever setting foot in Brigham and Women's Hospital again.

She drove south from Boston, on I-95, through Virginia and the Carolinas, then west toward Tennessee. Toward Texas. To her parents. They believed she was simply coming home for summer break. They knew nothing of her leave of absence.

Nothing of the baby.

Now: July, 4:30 a.m. Irene wasn't sure which day of the week it was. She'd lost track. Driven through the night. The baby had slept for a stretch after Irene had given her a bottle, but she was awake now, before the sun, screaming her head off.

Irene couldn't take the pain. Hers or the baby's. She didn't know what to do with it. With herself or the girl. All she knew was that she *could not do it.*

She cracked the windows, hoping that the sound of the air in the car might placate the baby until she could bring herself to pull over. Feed her, change her.

And for a moment, the swirling helped. The child's cries subsided, receding back into her throat with gasping, staggered sounds. The cool morning filled the car. The wind's whipping sound drowned out the classical music Irene had found on the radio. Inside the white-noise moment of silence, a glimmer of peace.

She saw a sign for a rest stop, pulled over, scooped powder into the bottle, felt the usual pang of guilt for not breastfeeding, added water, shook. Climbed gingerly into the back seat, wincing at the throb the motion sent to her C-section incision, and sat beside the car seat. Fed her four ounces of formula, until her eyelids drooped again. She decided not to change her but to apply the protective salve to her scalp instead. One mechanical chore was the most she could handle.

She squinted her eyes and crossed them, to blur her vision while she removed the helmet and spread the ointment around the baby's cleft, just as the NICU nurses had demonstrated (improvising, they admitted, based on the protocol used for preemies). She was then supposed to wait ten minutes before putting the helmet back on, so that the baby's scalp could absorb the medicine.

In the brief time it took Irene to remove the helmet and apply the salve, the girl had fallen back asleep.

Irene left the helmet off and climbed back into the driver's seat. Ten minutes could feel like an eternity. She started the engine, turned on the radio, and swung back onto the interstate.

A few miles later, Irene saw the brown road sign: **GREAT SMOKY MOUNTAINS NATIONAL PARK ENTRANCE, 4 MI.**

She'd never been to the Smokies. But she imagined the park as a welcoming place. The mountains old and mellow, deep green. It was summer now. Warm and fragrant, high tourist season just beginning. A safe and wholesome place, where people came to hike, swim in rivers, spot wildlife, introduce their children to the wonders of nature.

Nature. Was it responsible for what had happened to her? Or was it something larger, less tangible, a force with some inscrutable plan for the earth and its people, the sort of nonsense Irene had never believed in?

Or was *she* responsible, somehow?

Irene followed the signs to the park entrance. Past a welcome station, a brown hut, no guard. Drove into the park, the two-lane road winding. The baby was still sleeping. A woodsy smell entered the car, its sunroof still open, a mixture of sap and soil and flora. Up ahead, a sign for the Cades Cove Inn. **GORGEOUS ROOMS, STUPENDOUS VIEWS, KIND FOLKS.**

The caption gave her a flicker of comfort. It seemed like an omen. *Kind Folks.*

She pulled into the parking lot of the Cades Cove Inn. Full of cars but quiet. Too early for people. She found a patch of grass near the side of the rustic building, clear from the path of cars and far enough from the main entrance to give her a little time before anyone made a discovery.

She pulled on her sunglasses, although it was still mostly dark, the sun just beginning to rise, the light gently pinking. Put the Highlander in park without turning off the ignition. Climbed out of the driver's seat and opened the passenger door. Removed the car seat along with its base, an easy latch release.

The baby did not stir. Irene placed the car seat in the trimmed grass, kissed the girl's cheek, and returned to her car to get the note.

It was where she'd tucked it days ago. A sheet of plain white paper, folded once. She scanned the ground for a suitable rock. Found one—smooth, palm-sized—in the soil from which irises and passion-flowers grew in a patch flanking the log cabin–style siding of the inn.

Back to the baby, rock in one hand, paper in the other. Knelt down beside the car seat and gazed at her daughter, nestled in footie pajamas printed with yellow and pink butterflies. She slept with three fingers in her mouth, cheeks pulsing as she sucked on them, tiny palm pressed to her chin.

Irene unfolded the paper and smoothed it on the ground beside the car seat. Then she placed the rock over one corner to keep it from blowing away.

In large black lettering, penned with a Sharpie: *Please love me, because my mother cannot.*

She returned to the Highlander. Closed the passenger door. Climbed back into the driver's seat. Fastened her seat belt and drove away. She glanced over her shoulder once to see the car seat in the grass, just beyond the throw of a streetlight, as she swung from the parking lot back to the main road, closing the sunroof overhead, shutting out the tree smells, the blooming dawn. She silenced the radio.

"Goodbye," she said. She hadn't given her a name.

She'd exited the park and made it a handful of miles down the highway before she remembered the helmet. She glanced behind her to see it lying on the empty back seat. Like an abandoned shell that had once housed something alive.

Seeing the little cap on the black vinyl seat knifed something deep in Irene's center, and she felt a pang of horror.

At the steering wheel, she released a howl, a ragged, foreign sound from the center of her chest, her being, a sound she didn't recognize as her own. Her face was suddenly on fire, her body clutched with frantic electricity.

The baby needed her helmet.

The baby needed *her*.

She floored the accelerator, veered off the highway at the next exit, and horseshoed the car back toward the eastbound ramp of the interstate.

Back to the park. Dawn just beginning to break in earnest. The whip-poor-wills trilling, a shrimp-colored sky. The last layer of darkness lifting but still obscuring Irene's view from behind the windshield.

But she reached the parking lot of the Cades Cove Inn too late. Near the spot where she'd left the baby was a white BMW. The driver's side door was open, and a man was standing in the space between the door and the body of the car. He was beckoning toward the side of the building, waving his palms in front of him, as if summoning someone back from where Irene had placed the car seat.

Then he left the car, door still gaping, and walked over to the side of the inn, to the baby. Walked fast.

From Irene's vantage at the entrance of the parking lot, the white BMW blocked her view of the spot alongside the building where she'd left the baby. Heart slamming, Irene pulled the Highlander behind the BMW. Out the window, a dozen yards from where Irene sat in the car, were the couple. The man from the BMW and a woman with the car seat hooked on her elbow. The woman was looking up at the man, speaking intently to him, while the man shook his head from side to side, with force.

The woman was swinging the car seat back and forth, gently, deliberately, as she spoke to the man. Trying to soothe the baby, Irene saw, or perhaps keep her asleep.

In what felt like a single, attenuated motion, Irene lifted the helmet from her lap, exited the Highlander, and ran to the BMW's open door.

She dropped the helmet into the driver's seat and, like a relay racer on her final leg, tore back to the Highlander. She didn't look back at the couple or her little girl. Glanced only at the license plate of the BMW—California, 4EVRFIT—before driving away. This time, for good.

～

When the officer from Child Services located Irene, she was lying in bed in her old room at her parents' house in Austin. She hadn't gotten up in three days. Her parents were beside themselves. But Irene wouldn't talk. She just burrowed in her old twin bed and slept, the weariness dropped over her like a black cloak. The officer was a pretty black woman in her thirties with a badge that read **VERONICA HART**. Irene spoke to Veronica Hart privately, in her childhood bedroom behind a closed door. This infuriated her parents, though it was Irene's right, Ms. Hart explained: she was a legal adult. Irene answered questions. Ms. Hart told her that, under Tennessee's child abandonment laws, Irene would face a considerable fine, and possible termination of future parenting rights.

"Is she okay?" Irene asked, sitting up in her bed, back against the headboard, pillow clasped over her stomach.

"The baby?" Ms. Hart sat in the chair of Irene's old desk, where she'd written her application essay to Yale. That seemed like a different, pretend life. The officer smiled gently at Irene. "Yes, she's perfectly okay. She's in state custody in Tennessee. A couple on a road trip found her and brought her to a safe haven. It took us a few days to track you down. We thought you were up in Connecticut."

"I c-c—I can't," said Irene, feeling her throat close like a fist.

"Can't what, honey?"

The room blurred around her. "I can't take care of her," she whispered.

Ms. Hart rose from the desk and sat on Irene's bed. She took Irene's hand in her own and squeezed it. Irene would remember precisely the feel of Ms. Hart's slender fingers, the clean French manicure on her nails. The gesture felt like an overwhelming act of kindness.

"You've got options, sweetie," said Ms. Hart, softly. "I can tell you're going through a rough time. But it's going to be okay."

Irene collapsed against the officer's starched blue shirt and began to weep.

12.

Three for three. They're all absolutely perfect," said Rita Gupta, beaming as she waved a silver pointer toward the video capture of three ultrasounds projected side by side on the monitors behind her. At 8:00 a.m., Tessa and Luke and a half dozen of the Seahorse clinical staff were gathered for their morning status meeting in a conference room of East Lobe. They sat in Lucite chairs around a surfboard-shaped conference table as Gupta, in a crisp white lab coat and slingback heels, presented her daily analysis of the Cohort's pregnancies.

Tessa stared at the screens, transfixed by the distinctly human shapes of the images wobbling on them. Inside each form was the dark, fast-pulsing bead of a heart. It was day fifteen of the Trial, but she'd still not grown accustomed to the experience of seeing the babies growing inside Kate, LaTonya, and Gwen. Each morning, viewing the fresh ultrasounds caused her breath to quicken and left her almost dizzy with awe. Her friends were really, truly pregnant. TEAT had worked. Their babies were growing beautifully, just as normal fetuses should, only four and a half times faster. They were already the size of kumquats.

"Here we have an ear," Gupta said, clicking the wand with her thumb so that a red dot appeared on the middle ultrasound—Gwen's.

Tessa squinted to make out the dark squiggle. It *was* earlike. "And up here"—Gupta raised her wand and the dot jumped—"is an eye."

Across the table, Luke asked, "How did Ms. Harris respond to her view today?"

Tessa cut in, "Is it really necessary to ask this every morning?"

"I was asking Rita," said Luke.

"Psycho-emotional reactions across all members of the Cohort are very positive," said Gupta. "We see no indications of prenatal distress in the mothers. They're engaged and excited."

"When can we distribute the INR-Views to the Cohort?" asked Tessa. Part of the Seahorse Solution was issuing each mother her own patent-pending portable ultrasound device, so that she might check in with her baby whenever she wished. It was an elegant machine, the size of a small hand weight with a flat sensor that, when skimmed over the flesh of the abdomen, transmitted a 3-D image of the womb to any connected device.

"They haven't arrived from the manufacturer yet," said Roger Milford from the head of the table, his hands clamped around a coffee cup. "And regardless, we're waiting until 7.5 weeks to administer them. Until the pregnancies have entered their lowest stage of risk."

"What?" said Tessa. "Kwak told me they'd be here last week." Her friend John Kwak had invented the INRs and agreed to provide Seahorse with four prototypes. "And 7.5 weeks is practically the end of the pregnancies. I'm calling Kwak right away. We need them sooner."

"We've already spoken to him," said Luke, somewhat coldly. "Kwak moves at his own pace. Plus, the Cohort already *has* daily ultrasounds. That's far more than most pregnant women. The INRs aren't necessary."

"Necessity isn't the point," said Tessa. "Their dailies are administered by our doctors." She gestured toward Gupta. "The idea of the personal INR-View is to put the mothers in control of when they check in with their babies. It's designed to enhance a mother's sense of control."

"We're all aware of that objective," said Luke. "But it's less critical than preventing any unnecessary worries that frequent viewings might trigger in the Cohort." He swiveled his neck toward Milford. "Right, Roger?"

Dr. Milford cleared his throat. "Correct. I recommend waiting until the fetuses are further along."

"We do need to maintain balance between maternal sense of control and trust," added Gupta.

Tessa felt heat rising to her cheeks.

"They deserve to see. They've already proven a high lev—"

Luke cut her off. "Doesn't your flight to Boston leave in a few hours, Tessa? Can we table this discussion until you're back from your trip and refocused on the Trial?"

Tessa felt he'd given her a light slap. *Until you're back and refocused.* His disapproval over her leaving Seahorse to speak at Weldon was palpable. Even though she'd be gone for a measly five days, and even though she was working on some Seahorse-related meetings with a progressive biotech firm in Boston, Luke acted as if the trip indicated a skew in her priorities. It was ridiculous. He was acting like a toddler with separation anxiety.

"That's right, Luke," she answered calmly. "I am indeed headed to Boston to give a talk at my alma mater." She panned her eyes around the room at the doctors. "It's part of Weldon's Influencers lecture series. Gabby Trace was there last quarter." She spoke the name of Britain's prime minister slowly. "And I think it was Imogen Bijur before that." She watched Roger Milford's face soften with approval at the mention of the famous astrophysicist. "So I believe my participation is quite positive for the Seahorse brand. The title of my talk is 'The New Frontiers of Choice.'"

Around the table, heads nodded in approval. Except for Luke's.

"Brilliant," said Gupta.

Tessa went on. "I'm happy to table the INR discussion until I return. In the meantime, I'm going to nudge Kwak again, and Luke, I want you to follow up with him while I'm gone."

Luke crossed his arms. "Fine."

"Any more questions?" said Gupta brightly.

"Fantastic job, all," said Tessa, standing. "Sorry to cut out, but I do need to get to the airport." She panned her palm in farewell around the table, and rested her eyes on Luke. He held her gaze, as if meeting a challenge, his expression half-insouciant, half-needy, and Tessa felt a familiar stirring in her chest. Luke was forever difficult, but she needed him. They needed each other. Seahorse was incomplete without the both of them.

For a moment, the room was completely silent.

"Ciao," said Tessa finally, and she turned to leave the room, feeling Luke's eyes at her back as she went.

13.

Five years after she'd released the baby for adoption, when Irene was living in Austin and working as a glorified secretary for a nondescript financial services company, having never returned to Yale, she saw the ad in the *Houston Chronicle*:

> Config Labs, prominent Bay Area startup conducting a study on the phenomenon of "accelerated gestation," seeks female volunteers who have experienced full-term pregnancies in a fraction of the typical 40 weeks. Submit a relevant skin cell sample from you and/or your baby and receive an instant stipend. See www. AGvolunteers.com to learn more.

The language was dry and clinical, but it made Irene weep. Until she'd read it, she hadn't realized just how profoundly lonely her experience had left her. She'd gradually become aware of other accounts of fast pregnancies as a handful of women came forward with their stories, but until she'd seen that ad in the *Chronicle*, on a bright winter morning in Texas, she'd still felt alone. That she was a freak. A wild anomaly, genetically miswired. And also, a terrible person who'd abandoned her baby in a national park.

But she was not. The ad proved that enough other women had experienced her sort of pregnancy that a research group knew of it. It even had a name—accelerated gestation—a phrase Irene had not heard before.

She suddenly felt desperate to learn something—anything—about so-called "AG." Anything that might make her feel less isolated. Less guilt-racked. On an impulse, she went to the website, from which she requested a sample kit. It arrived in the mail, instructing her to press the enclosed tape on the skin of her arm, yank it off, and then place it back in the mail, using the packaging and postage provided.

She sent off the sample, but never heard anything back or got the "instant stipend." A few weeks later, the AG Volunteers website disappeared, a 401 error page in its place. She found an 800 number for Config Labs, but when she tried calling it, a recorded voice with a British accent informed her it was no longer in service.

~

2021

Tessa's flight from San Jose to Boston was overbooked, and she sat in first class for a half hour past the scheduled takeoff while irritable passengers negotiated seats and flight attendants called for volunteers to give theirs up. She caught up on a few messages; reviewed a proposal from a potential manufacturer for the Mammarina, the prosthetic breast Seahorse was developing; sent a text to Peter—*sitting on overheated tarmac, love you*—and then tried to read on her tablet. But she could not concentrate; the plane air was too warm and the legs of passengers standing beside her, in an unmoving line toward the back of the plane, were just inches from her face.

"Lap of luxury in here, isn't it?" said the man in the window seat beside her. He looked midthirties and had an intense, vigilant air that Tessa had noticed when they'd boarded. He'd kept his sunglasses on even after he'd settled in his seat, silver aviators that he now removed and snapped into a case. Without them, his appearance softened.

"Flying is pure function nowadays," said Tessa. "I keep my expectations low."

"Smart woman," he said. "I'm Wayne."

"Tessa."

"Nice to meet you, Tessa. What takes you to Boston?" Wayne was almost handsome, with reddish-brown hair, slightly receded, and a boyish face, though she saw crinkles at his eyes and a weariness behind them.

"A quick business trip," said Tessa. "You?"

"Combination of things," he said. She noticed faded scars above both jawlines—perhaps from old acne?—and that his skin was over-tanned, slightly weathered, as if he worked in the sun.

"What type of things?" Normally she did not open the door to chatting on planes; she worked when she flew.

"Work-related. All equally dull. I refuse to bore you. Are you in Silicon Valley?"

"I am. In biotech."

"Interesting. I'm looking forward to being made obsolete by a robot."

Tessa laughed. "It'll be awhile. A couple of years at least."

"Silicon Valley's a weird place, isn't it? All that brainpower and ambition, but hidden underneath a kind of . . ." Wayne paused, searching for the words. "Laid-back skin."

"Well said. Do you live in the area?"

"Negative. California's not for me. Can't speak the language."

"I understand," said Tessa.

"I'm in grad school, out at MIT."

"Impressive," said Tessa. The phrase *out at MIT* sounded strange, as if he might be playing a joke on her. He also looked old for graduate school, but she reminded herself not to be ageist, that people might decide to get advanced degrees at any time.

"Nah. I think I filled some diversity quota. I'm old. I'm from Montana. Not a classic MIT combo."

"Montana's gorgeous," said Tessa. "I skied up near Whitefish once."

"I'm from the plains. The ugly part. Anyhow. I'm sure you've got plans for passing these next six hours. I'll leave you alone. I just make it a point to be neighborly on flights. Try to counter the misery of the experience just a tick." He pulled an in-flight magazine out of his seat pocket and opened it, as if demonstrating his willingness to leave her alone.

"I appreciate that," said Tessa, though she felt surprisingly willing to talk to him. There was something compelling about him, a lack of inhibition that bordered on brashness. It was refreshing; typically, no one bothered to look up from their screens on a plane. She couldn't remember the last time a man, other than Peter or Luke, struck up a conversation with her for purely social reasons. Over the cabin loud-speaker, a voice instructed them to prepare for takeoff. The cabin filled with the noise of the plane's gathering speed. Tessa pulled a blackout eye mask from her purse and put it on. She was always mildly anxious during takeoff and landing, a weakness that perplexed her, and found the darkness soothing.

As the plane leveled off, she left the mask on, weariness overtaking her. She'd been up extra early to spend time with the Cohort and ensure they were comfortable with her brief absence from the Center. They were all in good spirits, especially since they'd been authorized by the docs to start the NauseAway supplement, which drastically reduced their morning sickness. Gwen still complained of discomfort, but less, and Tessa had come to understand that it was her need for self-assertion that led Gwen to behave disagreeably. That it was partially an act. Being a contrarian was simply part of her identity, and she was obviously determined to not let pregnancy take it away. Underneath it was a flinty stability. Luke had trouble understanding this, no matter how many ways Tessa attempted to explain it. He refused to see her as anything other than a bitch, as a disruption to the cooperative mood of the Seahorse Trial. Tessa, on the other hand, had come to admire Gwen.

Still wearing her eye mask, she found herself wondering how her seatmate, Wayne the grad student, was passing his time on the flight. She pushed the mask up just a little to afford a view of Wayne's hands, skating over the screen of a tablet. His fingers were ruddy but well formed, with clean, square nails. On his left hand he wore a bulky ring; she could make out an animal on it, a horse or a cow. Very Montana-ish.

On Wayne's screen, Tessa saw a photo of a young woman with dark, curly hair past her shoulders. She watched as Wayne enlarged the image, then quickly reduced it again. He zoomed in and out a few times, too fast for Tessa to register the details of the woman's face, by which Wayne was apparently transfixed.

His girlfriend, Tessa thought. Sweet, that Wayne was so arrested by her photo. Perhaps she was the reason he'd been in California, and they'd just parted ways. Perhaps he was missing her so intensely that he could do nothing but stare at her image.

Tessa tried to remember when she was preoccupied with Peter this way. She recalled their earliest days together, when Peter was living in a crammed Victorian in the Mission District of San Francisco. How once she'd needed to get up the creaking stairs and into his arms so urgently that she'd parked her car on the sidewalk, knowing she'd return to a three-hundred-dollar ticket.

She removed her mask and blinked into alertness; she did not want to think of Peter, not now. It led her straight to the g-word. She pulled out her tablet and opened her notes for the Weldon speech. Beside her, Wayne had also gotten to work, apparently. The curly-haired woman on his screen had been replaced by words and images of indeterminate content, a clutter of charts and graphs; Tessa slid her eyes over them but couldn't make out details.

Tessa didn't have much to review for her talk at Weldon. At this point, talking about Seahorse came as naturally as breathing. She'd presented the topic to dozens of groups. She loved public speaking, especially on a topic about which she felt passionately, and was at home in front of a crowd, rarely experiencing anxiety.

The Weldon speech, though, was different. For starters, it would be her first time speaking about Seahorse as a reality instead of mere concept. That it was being tested at this very moment lent a new gravitas to her talk. Also, since she was an alumna of the college, she felt an extra sense of responsibility toward the students who would form the audience. Many of them would be seniors who'd soon face critical decisions about work and family. Tessa could not risk steering them in the wrong direction. She needed to present Seahorse as a powerful and liberating option, without polemicizing or pushing. She needed to emphasize the concept of *choice*, while also generating excitement for the Solution's potential role in their futures.

From her screen, the familiar diagram glowed. Even now, long after she and Luke had first sketched out the new logo on a whiteboard, the visual of the Solution still gave Tessa a twinge of pride. It fortified her, every time.

Tessa sensed Wayne glancing at her screen; had he also felt her stealing a glance at his, even from behind her eye mask? She closed the diagram, opened her speech, and read through it, making a few notes. Although Wayne was now watching a movie, something futuristic and battle-filled, teeming with flashy special effects, Tessa was too conscious of his presence to focus on editing her talk. He had a magnetic appeal she didn't quite understand; he was physically unremarkable and had not said anything to her of particular interest. Perhaps it was just charisma, she thought, that elusive biochemical force field.

A blond flight attendant materialized, and Tessa surprised herself by ordering a Bloody Mary. She did not typically drink on flights, or much at all, but her nerves were twitchy. A consequence, she supposed, of being away from the Cohort, the various disapprovals emanating from Peter and Luke, her impending speech at Weldon, and now, the distracting presence of her appealing seatmate. When he asked the flight attendant for a seltzer, Tessa regretted her own order. Booze was sloppy, especially midafternoon on a weekday.

Oh well.

When their drinks arrived, Wayne lifted his plastic cup in her direction, a suggestion of a toast, and then returned to his movie, where creatures with humanlike bodies and insect heads were huddled in some sort of control room, conferring urgently. Tessa forced her eyes away from the screen and sipped her drink, enjoying its spicy, sodium burn. She thought of Peter, on his way to the Pacific Crest Trail, Python's head out the window, the furred silk of his ear flattening back in the wind. Of Kate, ambling the grounds of the Center, hand resting lightly on her belly. By the time Tessa returned from Boston, Dr. Gupta had told her, the Cohort's bellies would have "popped." She felt irrationally uneasy leaving the women at the Center without her.

Halfway through her drink, she began to feel drowsy and light-headed. She had eaten little since breakfast. There were still hours to go until she'd land in Boston and have dinner with an old friend, one of the few women who ran a hedge fund on Wall Street.

Tessa never napped. Napping was anathema to her work ethic, to her pace, practically to her worldview. But after handing her empty drink to the passing flight attendant, she tipped her head back onto the headrest and promptly fell asleep.

She woke as the plane touched down in Boston, and her head throbbed with a vodka headache.

"We made it," said Wayne, zipping his tablet and a textbook—*New Frontiers of Data Science*—into a black backpack. "Congratulations."

"I can't believe I slept," said Tessa, smoothing her hair. Her mouth was dry and she felt disoriented. She combed her purse for Advil but found nothing. She shouldn't have ordered the damn Bloody Mary.

"Need something?" said Wayne.

"Do you happen to have ibuprofen?"

"Affirmative," he said, pulling a plastic Advil cylinder from a compartment of his backpack. He dropped two brownish pills into her hand and stood to deplane. "My parting gift. Nice meeting you."

"Thank you. Vodka at high altitudes is a bad prescription for me."

"Try whiskey next time," said Wayne, winking at her and pulling a miniature plastic bottle of water from his jacket pocket and handing it to her. "Have this. And take care, Tessa Callahan." He touched her arm, lightly, just above the elbow, and joined the stream of passengers filing out of the plane, before Tessa had even gathered her things.

He'd *winked* at her. Ridiculous. And yet, the wink, followed by his hand on her arm, had boosted her mood. Even triggered a small, fluttery sensation in her chest. She'd found that being over forty, combined with her status as a business exec, had virtually eliminated instances of passing flirtations with men. It was refreshing when it actually happened, like a visceral reminder of girlhood, of a former desirable self. Of course, Peter still looked at her with desire on a regular basis. That should be enough. Most of the time, it was.

Outside the Boston airport, evening had fallen and a light spring rain spattered the clog of cars and buses circling the terminal. She replayed the moment of Wayne's departure in her mind, embarrassed to be thinking of it but allowing herself to anyway.

Take care, Tessa Callahan.

She didn't remember telling him her last name. Had she? Perhaps he'd recognized her but hadn't admitted it. Played it cool. That must be it; *that's* why he'd looked at her with such interest. *Pushing Through* had brought her widespread media coverage, plus a tour on the talk show circuit. It was not unusual for strangers to know her face.

Her driver arrived in a black sedan, and Tessa climbed into the back seat.

Outside, rain streamed down the tinted windows as evening closed over the city.

~

Tessa arrived early to her dinner at a soft-lit, minimalist sushi restaurant. She sipped Pellegrino at the bar, thumbing her phone, catching up on messages. All was well with the Cohort, Luke had written. They were starting to itch—a good sign, a symptom of active fetal growth, easily relieved with a topical cream they'd developed at Seahorse when the animals had begun to scratch themselves. There was a text from Peter on the PCT with a photo of Python and him, beside a river, steep ochre cliffs in the background. Message: *Your boys miss you.* Tessa appraised the photo with relief; Peter would be happy there, in the wilds of Oregon, at least for now. There he would need her less, resent her less. His dog and his friends and beautiful views of Crater Lake would distract him from his disappointment in her: her lack of attentiveness, her lack of presence. Their lack of a baby.

All the *lacks* she'd created.

Tessa turned her mind to the forty-eight hours of work ahead of her. Tomorrow, she'd spend the day at One-Fifty, a biotech company in Brookline focused on life-extension products. It claimed it was close to bringing a product to market that would reliably extend the human life span by sixty to seventy-five years, and had agreed to give Tessa an early look. The following morning, she'd give her Seahorse talk at Weldon, followed by a reception at the dean's house.

Normally, the prospect of such days filled Tessa with eager anticipation. She swirled the ice in her glass with a straw and tried to locate her usual excitement, but found she could not. She just wanted to check off her obligations in Boston and return to the Seahorse Center, where Cohort One needed her, as soon as possible.

ISA – OFFICIAL EVIDENCE

👻

VivversOC: Do you guys keep links to AG—like articles and stuff we've sent to eachother?

LindsEE!: u mean like bookmarks?

VivversOC: or whatever, just keep track somehow

LindsEE!: Im not that organized lol

Stoph1: why? its automatically saved in ur browser history

VivversOC: I know dude but when I try to go back thru my history all the links are dead

Stoph1: probly an issue with your settings.

VivversOC: that's what I thought but it's not.

Stoph1: u gotta remove your "clear history" window.

VivversOC: dude I know how to work my settings i'm not 60 yrs old

Stoph1: sorry miss sensitive

VivversOC: can u guys just check? If you don't have the URLs i will send links

Stoph1: ok boss

Xavey: viv I checked my links don't work

LindsEE!: Mine either weird right?!!?

Stoph1: nah it's just linkrot

VivversOC: ???

Stoph1: linkrot = urls to webpages that no longer exist. Usually for content that's really old

VivversOC: so it just expires and like falls off the internet?

Stoph1: nope, somebody pulls them down

14.

Irene Brenner sat in the rocking chair on her porch, watching the sky shift from its monochromatic dome, flat and still as pool water, into the chaos of sunset. The look and feel of her "town" were deceiving: colonial brick, white columns, humidity pumped into the air by some unseen machines. If you strolled through its center and looked straight ahead, you might think you were in New England. If you drifted out into the "neighborhoods" here—Irene's blue Craftsman bungalow was situated on an unnamed street lined with eucalyptus trees and more bungalows identical to hers—you might think you'd been transported to some spot in northern California, perhaps Berkeley or Oakland. Some of the bungalows on Irene's street were painted in other colors of the resident's choosing, an option granted after sixty consecutive days of good behavior.

As if paint color mattered.

Irene's house had been blue when she'd moved in.

The architecture of the landscape was incoherent, but there was no disguising the singular desert sky overhead. No way to mute its bright, hard stars. As a young woman, the summer before her senior year of high school, Irene had driven from Austin to Los Angeles to look at UCLA, and the desert states had been her favorite passageways: their starkness, their scorching days and freezing nights, the wild panoply of stars. She established a vague intention to end up in New Mexico or Arizona, but higher education was second-rate in those states——and Irene wanted better for herself. Yale was her first choice and when she was accepted, she didn't think twice about going. She could live in the desert later.

And here it was—later—and she was doing it. Living in the desert. In *a* desert. In *some* desert. She'd been here for years and still did not know its name. The staff referred to it only as the Colony. She could not point to it on a map. Long ago, she'd stopped asking them where she was. The answer had always been the same: *information will become available after you've agreed to cooperate.*

Irene had never agreed. She'd considered it, at certain times, like when she stared out the window above the lone twin bed of her bungalow at night and calculated how old her daughter would be. Where she might be living, and with whom? There had been the California license plate of the people who found her, so Irene settled on images of her girl sitting under a palm tree beside the ocean, reading poems, sun on her face. Irene tried to imagine what her face looked like, whether her eyes had stayed blue (they often changed after infancy, didn't they?), whether she'd inherited the slight bump in the bridge of her nose, the one Irene had always longed to have corrected.

As if a young face needed correction of any kind.

She tried to imagine the shape of her daughter's body. She wondered if she loved sports, as Irene had, and books, and the sound of language. If she, too, hated dancing and found most boys nearly impossible to talk to, except for the ones she longed for, with whom it was completely impossible. She wondered if her daughter was also too hard on herself, endlessly seeking out her own flaws.

If only Irene had known how perfect she'd once been. She wished she could somehow tell her daughter this, wherever she was: *you are perfect.*

Although Irene had last seen the girl as an infant, her car seat receding in Irene's rearview mirror, she pictured older versions of her daughter and somehow missed *that* person. She pictured a mane of dark hair, soft blue eyes, a strong jawline, and bold eyebrows. She saw her wearing braces and Velcro sneakers, kicking a ball on a playground. For a time, in Austin, when she was working as an admin and eating tuna straight from the can at night, she was obsessed with these imaginings. Who was tucking her into bed at night, making her breakfast, driving her to school? She thought of the white BMW that had pulled into the Cades Cove Inn, of the two people who had emerged from it.

Was the girl with *them*?

At Irene's lowest point, a year after the birth, she'd paid several hundred dollars online to trace the license plate of the BMW. *California, 4EVRFIT.*

Were they the ones who adopted her?

The car had been owned by Lawrence D. Bourne, of Newport Beach, California. A real estate developer. He was married to Elise S. Bourne, née Brocken, a fitness professional. The report was several years old. It made no mention of children.

Irene stopped reading the report, her tuna stuck in her throat; she was no longer hungry, her body electric with despair. She would not research the girl further. She would live and grow in Irene's mind only. Real knowledge was too painful.

At work, she'd started to hear of people writing "blogs"—then a brand-new format—and the idea appealed to her. She'd always liked journaling but found it lonely and aimless. The prospect of a few readers—even invisible strangers—was oddly comforting.

She signed up for a Blogger account and began posting about her experience. For weeks, she had no followers. This emboldened her; she began to write more openly about Yale, about the night of the party, about the pregnancy. About how it unfolded, in those terrifying nine weeks. About giving up the baby, and how it had cracked her heart in two.

The more she wrote on her blog, the more her sadness gave way to anger.

> I birthed a child a little more than two months after becoming pregnant. It disrupted my entire life and derailed the course of my future. I AM NOT MAKING THIS UP. I know that this has happened to other women. Why aren't scientists obsessed figuring out WHY?? IS ANYONE LISTENING? Why is it not in the national conversation??

One morning she woke up, and she had followers. Three, to be exact.

I'm listening, one of them, Danielle-A, wrote. This happened to me, too.

Later, after Irene had gotten deep into blogging about AG, Henry Duarte showed up at the front door of the little house she'd rented in Leander, claiming to be a gardener looking for new work. He had a pickup truck with *Duarte Landscaping* on the side, a business card, a lawn mower in the bed of his truck. He'd been so young, with his ramrod posture and apple-hard muscles and lineless face.

She had fallen for him before she'd even hired him to work on her yard once a week. It was textbook head-over-heels, biochemical attraction. Infatuation that kept her wired at night as she tried to fall asleep, and barged into her mind first thing upon waking. Henry eclipsed her brain; he made her stupid, craven, in a permanent state of yearning. She cringed at the cliché of it: she was a lonely secretary (Yale educated!) and he was her *gardener*.

Six months later, he'd brought her here, to this blank space in the desert.

Why didn't she hate him? For a time, she had. For a time, her hatred for him had burned white-hot. But she also understood. He was just a man, doing his job. Carrying out his assignments to investigate any private citizen this employer deemed a potential "threat" to the U.S. government. He'd been just a boy when they recruited him, so naive and vulnerable, so desperate to escape his barren, violent life on the high plains of Montana.

He'd told her all about his life.

In a way, she loved him. The romantic fixation had long subsided, replaced by something deeper. She'd forgiven him. She couldn't help herself.

For a time, Irene had considered cooperating. Considered walking into the stucco administrative building near the Great Wall, which ran the perimeter of the whole area, and making an appointment to meet with Borlav or Winger, or any of the other thick-necked oafs on the Inner Panel, the group in charge of the Colony. She imagined sitting across a table from one of them and saying finally, *Okay. Yes. I'll cooperate. Just tell me what I need to do.*

But what sort of life would she have if she did?

It would be like life on a stage, scripted and directed by the Inner Panel. Her choices would be dictated by them. Her mouth would belong to them. They would be watching and listening, verifying she uttered not a word pertaining to her own history. They would repackage the story of her pregnancy and disappearance with elaborate, specific details—her "revision." An entire division of the Colony staff was devoted to inventing this content. Irene would be forced to rehearse her revision until she knew it so well that she almost believed it herself. Until she could deliver it seamlessly to the people who had once loved her, who had been bewildered and devastated when she disappeared.

Yes, if she mastered her revision, she would be free to leave the Colony. But what sort of freedom would it be? She'd still have to live by their rules. They would still be monitoring, listening, watching.

Worst of all, if she returned to the outside world, she would not be allowed to contact her daughter.

So what was the point?

She let her window to cooperate expire. After a time, the Inner Panel deemed her resident status "permanent."

She'd gone permanent, a rare choice. At any given time, there might be as many as five hundred Imports in the Colony—there for any number of reasons, the vast majority unrelated to AG—but most of them eventually revised and departed. Whatever they'd done to earn a classification of "threatening" to the government, they were usually happy to undo it in order to earn back their freedom. Only Irene and a few other stubborn souls remained, month after month, year after year.

She didn't regret her decision to be permanent. It seemed the best of her bad options, at least for now. At least until Henry Duarte returned to the Colony—and he always did—and she could speak to him about her other plan. He'd promised, when he'd brought her here, all those years ago, that he would help her. Somehow she believed him. Somehow she still considered him her friend—her only friend, really, unless you counted Johanna the nurse—even though Henry had deceived her before. But that had been his job, back when he cared about his job.

He cared less now. Irene could tell. But he still cared about *her*, a great deal. It was an unspoken truth, an energy she felt between them like an electric current, not exactly sexual but not devoid of sex, either.

It was that feeling that made her believe Henry would help her get what she wanted.

Irene continued to sit on the porch and rock as the oncoming night bruised over the setting sun. She'd observed this sky for so many nights that she could now recognize the altered configurations of stars each evening, the shifting phases of the moon. She thought frequently of an Elizabeth Bishop poem she'd studied at Yale: *He thinks the moon is a small hole at the top of the sky / proving the sky quite useless for protection.*

Yes, it was quite useless.

She reached for her juice on the small table beside her chair, and the simple extension of her body was difficult. The stiffness of age was a particular cruelty. She didn't mind the wrinkles so much, or the inches lost in height, or the color of her hair—in fact, she'd come to love its downy white—but not being able to move as she once had was terrible. Once she had lived so fully in her body, taken such pleasure in its abilities, in how it would respond when she pushed it. Of course, she'd also been harshly critical of it, but she hadn't known any better.

Now she knew better.

She went to her bedroom, changed into her nightgown, brushed her teeth at the sink. Johanna always offered to help with these tasks, but Irene refused. They took her a long time to complete, yes, but what was the rush? There was an intimacy in revealing her body to herself, a renewed fascination every time. The loose and creased flesh, the hump at the top of her shoulders, her downward breasts that lay almost flat against her chest. Her body had always been so generous, so cooperative, that she felt she deserved to witness what she'd done to it. This sagging, dying husk.

No one wanted to acknowledge the nudity of the elderly. Anyone would shield their eyes from the sight of her.

Except that Irene was not elderly.

She was just unlucky.

Of the forty-eight documented cases of accelerated gestation, only three of the mothers—one in sixteen, insofar as Henry knew (and Henry, as a senior agent at the Agency, which ran the Colony, knew a great deal)—had ended up this way. As for the children, well, it was hard to know. They had not been rigorously tracked, despite the Agency's mandate that all obstetricians report the delivery of an AG baby.

Perhaps her daughter was okay. As healthy and normal as she'd seemed at two weeks.

Perhaps she was not.

She'd probably never know. She'd trained her mind to veer away from the topic each time it began an approach.

But according to Henry, most of the other mothers—Irene's peers—still looked their age.

Which, in Irene's case, was forty-two.

ISA – OFFICIAL EVIDENCE

VivversOC: anyone there?

Xavey: YRU awake?

VivversOC: YRU?

Xavey: its not thaaat late in Denver. Ur in Boston now right? At that girlz school?

VivversOC: women's college, yeah can't sleep. do u ever wonder why AG isn't more of a thing?

Xavey: a thing??

VivversOC: like why it's not more famous, more research etc?

Xavey: there was already a lot, it didn't go anywhere

VivversOC: can I ask you a personal question?

Xavey: fire away

VivversOC: how did ur mom die?

Xavey: car axydent. I wasn't even 1y/o

Xavey: hello???

VivversOC: shit I'm sorry I sort of froze, I'm sorry to bring up yr mom

Xavey: np.

VivversOC: so yr dad raised u?

Xavey: no, my aunt and uncle. my dad was in the car too

PART TWO

Do not implore the women to change. Implore the system.

—*Tessa Callahan,* Pushing Through: A Handbook for
Young Women in the New World

15.

After sitting in the stubborn remnants of rush hour traffic between Logan Airport and Cambridge for nearly an hour, rain sluicing his windshield, Wayne Bridger finally arrived at his apartment on Chauncey Street, a few blocks from the Charles River. His apartment was sparse and tidy, a railroad flat with hardly anything on the walls, a blue couch in the living room, an IKEA coffee table, his desk against a wall in the bedroom. His employer, the Internal Stability Agency, encouraged its field agents to "personalize" their apartments according to the tastes of their aliases. They even offered to send an "aesthetic specialist" to assist, if interior decorating wasn't your thing, but Wayne had never bothered. The ISA hovered over his life enough as it was; he didn't need their grunts hanging bad art on his walls, too.

He opened a can of tuna and a diet ginger ale and sat at his desk, leaving the bedroom dark but for the glow of his laptop, the drizzle outside streaking his dark window. He clicked to his latest report, yet another spreadsheet dense with stats and notes on Viv. For the first time in his career, the reports made him feel slightly sick, how they reduced a person to a clutter of numbers and shorthand. How many had he submitted over his nineteen-plus years with the ISA?

Thousands? He sipped his ginger ale and did the math: in his two decades with the Agency, he'd imported dozens of PITs—panic instigation threats. Viv would be the last, his final assignment before he could retire.

Some of his Imports had been rough, but not until now had his job begun to feel unbearable.

He'd hung a Post-it on the right corner of his computer with *8/15* written on it in thick black ink. He kept it to remind himself, in moments when his doubt immobilized him—like now—what his goal was. Retirement. On August 15, he would hit his twenty-year mark of service with the ISA, and assuming he'd fulfilled the terms of contract, he would be a free man. No more importations. No more quarterly treks to the Colony, to be scrutinized by the goons of the Inner Panel. No more trailing, no more stories to keep straight, no more calculated "friendly" conversations with "strangers," like the one he'd just had on the plane with Tessa Callahan. No more reports. No more shitty, anonymous apartments. No more lies.

He had to stay focused. To keep a clear head, his eyes fastened like bolts to his goal: Retirement. Freedom.

On some level, it had always been a struggle. Deep down, he knew his job wasn't entirely honorable. But he'd been so young when the ISA had approached him, a teenage kid on the high plains of Montana, desperate to get out of the double-wide trailer with its threadbare carpet and fridge containing nothing but Natty Light and ketchup, his father permanently splayed in front of the TV. The situation had made him ripe for recruitment—Wayne's own, and the larger situation in the country: a fresh assassination attempt on the president, Dewey Falk, a Washington outsider, a "rogue" who teemed with rage and bravado, newly reelected by a razor-thin margin. The attempt was handily thwarted and Falk got away without so much as a bullet graze, but the country was shaken to its core. Falk, on the other hand, seemed galvanized by the attempt on his life. Almost gleeful, as it had granted him the all-access pass he'd craved. When the dust from the would-be assassination—allegedly the work of a lone wolf—settled, the president announced the formation of the Internal Stability Agency. Its mission: *to anticipate, prevent, and correct situations that trigger undue, harmful, or potentially threatening anxiety among American citizens.* The president insisted that his goal was to "quiet the storm of vitriol poisoning the American air."

Wayne hadn't known the meaning of *vitriol* when he'd heard President Falk say it on TV, but he'd sure as hell known *poison.* His entire life had felt poisoned: with poverty and bad weather, a school full of pocketknives and OxyContin, parents who drank and fought, drank and fought, their anger shuddering the aluminum walls of the trailer.

Has America become no different from the deplorable Muslim states we've tried so righteously to defeat? the president had asked from his protected podium, which encased him in a pod of bulletproof plexiglass during all public addresses, a new standard after the incident. Wayne had watched the speech from the living room of the double-wide, where he sat on a brown couch scarred with cigarette burns. Beside him, his father snored in a Natty Light–induced coma, the hard hill of his gut rising and falling.

Wayne listened as the president insisted that the United States had reached such an *apex of rampant misinformation,* had become *so angry, so accusatory, so divided,* that the formation of the ISA was a *no-brainer. We are living in a toxic fog of anxiety,* said the president. *This is not the America you deserve.* He thrust a balled fist toward the clear wall of his impenetrable enclosure. *You. Deserve. To. Feel. Safe.*

At the time, Falk's words had rung true and brave to Wayne. At the time, they were a comfort.

Ha. What a child he'd been, a boy so rudderless he'd found comfort in the promise of surveillance.

Wayne's plan had been to join the Marines right out of high school and get the hell out of Harlem, Montana. He'd just turned eighteen and was set to head to Basic in San Diego when a recruiter emailed him out of the blue, claiming Wayne had been identified, via a national database, as a potential job candidate for an "exclusive" new opportunity with the Internal Stability Agency. The Marines were aware of his eligibility and would be happy to save his spot in Basic, should he choose not to pursue this other prospect. Would Wayne be willing to meet for a preliminary interview, that very week, in Billings? The invitation was essentially coming from President Falk himself, the recruiter added. .

Wayne had been willing.

Eight months later, he'd emerged from training as a member of the ISA's first team of field agents, with a new chunk of money in his new bank account—more than he'd ever had in his life—and his first alias: Henry Duarte. He'd hated that name—*Duarte Fart-ay*, his colleagues ribbed—but the Inner Panel had pinned it on him, and he had no say in the matter. He learned to turn his head, to look up, to snap to attention at the sound of it. Eventually he thought of himself as Henry Duarte.

Just as now, nineteen-plus years later, he thought of himself as Wayne Bridger. All the names he'd had before were inert. Dead to him.

As a field agent, his task was always the same: to access individuals identified as panic instigation threats—people engaged in the *widespread dissemination of harmful misinformation*—and relocate them to a *contained but comfortable* facility. There, at the Colony, they'd be given the opportunity to "revise" their lies and rejoin public life with proper self-restraint. If all went smoothly, they could be in and out in under two weeks.

Wayne and his team did all they could to avoid coercion of their PITs. The Colony was not jail. It was a thoughtfully constructed community, complete with landscaping and recreational options, for those requiring extended stays. The PITs were not criminals; no probable cause had been established. Only, as the president phrased it, *probable propensity to cause harm.* Once imported, the PITs had a chance to redeem themselves. The Colony, Wayne had been taught during his initiation, was a place of second chances.

And if they refused their second chance . . . well.

It was Wayne's job to ensure that they didn't. Usually, he succeeded. A few times, he hadn't.

In his first years at the agency, the PITs had posed obvious threats. Importing his first ones had felt like acts of heroism to Wayne: removing danger from the streets, giving it the opportunity for redemption. It felt like noble work, snagging those would-be troublemakers from the public arena, like defusing bombs for a living. He'd nailed a group of Black Web programmers who were building an entire alt-internet of lies, angry feminists on the brink of violence, and a few serious would-be terrorists from basements in Ohio and Texas.

As time passed, some of Wayne's assignments felt less noble. Were his PITs less threatening, or had Wayne simply begun to grow up, to see the world in gradations of color instead of black-and-white? The PIT who'd leaked "fabricated data" on endocrine disruption, threatening the multibillion-dollar plastics industry at its core, had insisted that her research was valid and refused to back down from her position—that unborn males were facing a widespread risk of hermaphroditism—even after ten months at the Colony. She would not budge. She was still at the Colony today, along with other PITs who refused to revise their alarmist agendas: the pollution guy from Riverside, for example, who'd tried to convince thousands of cancer patients that their condition was a direct result of merely breathing the air of the Inland Empire. Or the women in Brownsville, Texas, along the Mexican border, who insisted their water supply was tainted with lead.

Criteria for importation had loosened since Wayne had joined the ISA, that was for sure. When he'd been assigned to Vivian Bourne—part of the ISA's effort to assemble civilians affected by accelerated gestation—he'd almost laughed. What threat did a bunch of college kids, mostly at tony, soft liberal arts schools, pose to the general public? To the administration? What did it matter that tech geeks out in California were newly fascinated with accelerated gestation, a phenomenon that had faded out twenty years ago?

The situation, it turned out, was complicated.

But it was not Wayne's job to get mired in the details. His job was to slip in and out of his PITs' lives like water. He was merely an order-taker, an executor of protocol. The justifications were the responsibility of the Inner Panel, the top brass hemmed inside their desert fortress in New Mexico. Strategy happened from inside the Colony. Action—Wayne's job—happened in the field.

Action, they'd taught him in training, must never involve attachment. Whether a PIT got attached to him, well, that was beyond his control.

Mutuality had never been a problem. Until now.

Never had mistaking the locations of his contacts for home been an issue for Wayne. He'd been trained to live in the moment, blind to context, his focus pure as new snow. The spirit of a good ISA agent was necessarily vagrant. Homeless. From nowhere. It was part of how they convinced their PITs to come willingly to the Colony. It was part of why he'd almost never resorted to force.

Almost never.

Outside Wayne's bedroom window, the rain had begun to fall harder, tapping the glass like jittery fingers. He clicked on Viv's file and opened her latest report. He'd begun it on the plane, after he'd closely reviewed his latest photos of her face, and the x-rays of her upper left leg, but he'd been unable to properly focus, on account of

Tessa Callahan in the seat beside him. His proximity to Callahan was deliberate, of course. The ISA had wanted some read on the activity of Seahorse Solutions, her biotech company that was currently meddling in accelerated gestation. So they'd sent Wayne on a quick intel trip to the Bay Area, where he'd found Tessa practically impossible to access, cordoned behind an airtight security system at what appeared to be a high-end research compound. When he'd learned she was traveling to Boston, via a conversation he'd accessed between Tessa and her husband, he'd booked his own return flight according to hers, in hope of a break, and voila, she'd granted him a gift. While he'd pretended to work, she'd spent a full five minutes gazing at colorful visual diagrams detailing the nature of the work happening at Seahorse Solutions—precisely the information the Inner Panel had pressed him to deliver.

He'd memorized as much as he could, employing mnemonic devices he'd learned in early ISA training, and documented it on his own tablet when Tessa dozed after drinking a Bloody Mary.

Tessa's presence on the plane had made it hard for him to concentrate on finishing Viv's report. He kept imagining her jolting awake and somehow, in a single glance, absorbing all the data on his screen.

Which was impossible, of course. Even if Tessa had gotten a long look, she would not have been able to make sense of his work. His edginess was unfounded. Clearly, he'd become irrational in matters involving Viv. Clearly, he was edgy about his pending retirement. *Sensitive, emotional . . .* Lately, he'd been displaying all the qualities antithetical to the success of a good field-op.

Wayne drained his ginger ale and set the can down hard inside the tuna container, calling himself to attention.

An ache knotted his chest. He swallowed hard and clicked open the two images that would form the basis of his report: the first, a closeup of Viv's face, unsmiling, neutral, per ISA guidelines. The second, an x-ray of her upper leg, where her femur was anchored to her hip bone with a titanium pin, the result of her accident on the lacrosse field last fall.

Slowly and lightly, as if the keyboard were too hot, Wayne began to type.

Thirty minutes later, he finished. He paused before sending it to the Inner Panel. Once they reviewed it, it was usually just a matter of days until they'd summon him to the Colony for a final meeting before the importation. To discuss his "action plan." Wayne loathed those trips: the white-hot desert sun, the claustrophobic gravitas of the Blue Room, the subterranean office where he and the IP buffoons would discuss the final logistics of importations.

He did not want to think about going to the Colony. Not now. There was no point in ruminating on the inevitable. It was as futile as dreading nightfall. It would happen, regardless of how much you worried or didn't.

For now, he would try not to worry.

Five minutes later, he clicked "Send," snapped his laptop shut, and lay down on his bed, fully clothed. He sank into the pillow and rested his forearm over his eyes, listening to the rain. He wanted to call Viv so badly, to hear her voice, but he'd lied about his return date by twenty-four hours, to give him some cushion if he needed it. He'd also lied about his destination. Necessary lies that he'd been trained to tell and had told to so many PITs for so many years that they usually felt true. But with Viv, it was different. Even the smallest untruth felt like a transgression, unsavory and clumsy and wrong.

But the lie, like so many before it, was already done. He'd just have to live with it and wait. He'd see her soon enough.

He was just beginning to drift into sleep when his phone buzzed with a text.

I, um, miss you.

Reading Viv's message jolted him like a hit of some narcotic. He was suddenly both more lucid and more distracted, his desire to see her like live voltage through his body.

He typed back. *I'm pretty sure I miss you more. See you Saturday?*

Cornball, she responded immediately, with a heart emoji. *And yes. Sat.*

Corny but true, Wayne wrote back, because it was.

He willed himself back to work.

ISA – OFFICIAL EVIDENCE

VivversOC: what do yr docs say about your AG?

LindsEE!: pretty much nothing why?

Stoph1: my health ins is too shitty for me to goto the doctor unless im literally dying

Xavey: mine says its just cosmetic and I can ignore it unless it starts bothering me somehow like "itching or throbbing"

LindsEE!: just threw up in my mouth thanks

VivversOC: my doc says the same, don't you think it's weird they aren't more curious?

LindsEE!: weird why?

Stoph1: paranoid much?

VivversOC: like we are total medical anomalies and our docs aren't even interested?

LindsEE!: why would they care, don't they just want to be done and go golfing?

Xavey: idk, I agree w/ Viv I think it's kinda weird.

VivversOC: thanx, Xave. At least someone listens to me.

LindsEE!: VIV!!! don't be so sensitive! ♥

16.

"When I fell asleep last night, it wasn't there," said Kate, her face filling the screen of Tessa's phone, "and when I woke up this morning, it was."

On the morning of her Weldon Influencers speech, Tessa was sitting at The Buzz, a café in the Henrietta Steiner Center for Student Life, the heart of the six-hundred-acre campus. At 9:00 a.m. on a Sunday, the café was completely empty but for the tattooed barista who'd made Tessa's latte, now wearing earbuds and glued to her phone behind the coffee bar, oblivious to Tessa's video chat with Kate. Dawn had hardly broken in California, but Kate had been up since 5:00 a.m., she told Tessa, woken by the sensation that her body had something it could not wait to tell her.

The news: overnight, Kate's bump had arrived.

"It's not just a paunch, which would be entirely plausible," Kate was saying. "Since I'm essentially living on pastries. But no. It's a firm, bona fide bump."

"Show me," said Tessa.

Kate hopped off her bed, pushed up her shirt, and angled her phone toward her midsection. Tessa drew the phone closer to her eyes, her throat tightening as she focused on the image: just seventeen days pregnant and sure enough, Kate's belly rose in a pretty sine curve.

"Wow" was all Tessa could manage.

Kate raised the phone back to her face. "Right? It's so utterly crazy, and yet I'm calm. It just feels right, like something that's supposed to be happening."

"What about the itching? And the nausea?"

Kate shrugged. "Since we started taking NauseAway, I don't feel queasy at all. And just like you said, the exhaustion went away. The salve totally helped the itching. I feel pretty incredible. Luke brought in a prenatal yogi for us yesterday morning, and LaTonya and I had such an amazing session with her."

"No Gwen?"

"No Gwen. Yoga's not her thing. No surprise there."

"She is who she is. We need to support her."

"LaTonya's great, though. Such a strong person. I'm so grateful to have her here."

"*You're* such a strong person."

"You always say that."

"Because it's true," said Tessa.

Seeing Kate gave her an intense urge to be back at Seahorse. But she was scheduled to deliver "The New Frontiers of Choice" in just an hour and a half, and she wanted some time to stroll the campus before reporting to the steps of Phipps Tower, where she would speak to hundreds of undergraduates beneath a canopy of red oak trees with a carillon of bells overhead.

"I should go," she said, reluctantly.

"We miss you," said Kate. "Especially me. Hurry back." She blew a kiss to the screen.

"Three days," said Tessa, returning the gesture.

Outside, Tessa breathed in the cool air, rinsed clean from yesterday's rain, and marveled again at the loveliness of the lush campus.

Just thirteen miles from Boston, Weldon was its own private world of Gothic buildings, grand old trees, sweeping lawns, and a private lake. Tessa followed a footpath from the Steiner Center toward the trail that led around Lake Nabaw. Newly bloomed dogwoods quivered in the breeze.

As she walked along the lake, her urge to be back at the Seahorse Center dissipated. Weldon had always had a grounding effect on her: the beauty of the campus combined with the presence of two thousand women living together—thinking, working, moving the world forward. The place was an inspiration. She thought of her days as a Weldon student, recalling the sense of continual awakening, of beginning to understand that the world offered a drastically different experience for women than it did for men. She remembered the late nights in her cramped dorm room in Pomeroy Hall, drinking cheap boxed wine with her friends, discussing how they might, someday, make the world a better, gentler, more equitable place for everyone. Back then, Tessa's friends all had "radical" ideas, most of which would never emerge from the walls of the dorm. The majority of Tessa's classmates graduated and went on to succeed in ways that were admirable but also conventional: they became lawyers and journalists, bankers and doctors, corporate big shots. Policy makers and professors. Some went into tech, though usually to the high-profile establishment companies, the Googles and LikeMes of the world. They settled down with partners from other elite colleges and then had children, usually two. They worked and achieved, worked and achieved, but few of them were interesting to Tessa. This was not to say they weren't changing the world; in small ways, many of them were. But they'd played it safe.

Tessa had never been interested in playing it safe. Perhaps that was why she hadn't stayed in close touch with her friends from Weldon. Perhaps it was why, improbably, she currently felt a stronger kinship with the women of Cohort One than she did with any of her fellow alumnae. LaTonya, Kate, and Gwen did not merely talk about taking risks; they *took* them.

Tessa sat down on a log beside the lake and turned her face to the sun, closing her eyes. She thought of Peter, who was certainly much different from the Harvard and MIT grads her classmates had married. More solid, more genuine. *In* the world, instead of hovering smugly above it. A pang of missing him gripped her and she opened her eyes, blinking in the bright sun. Farther up the lakeshore, she spotted a line of goslings trailing their mother goose, like an illustration from a children's book. They reminded her, somehow, of the Cohort, and she smiled to herself. Her phone pinged and she saw a new message from Peter, as if he'd sensed her missing him. It was a photo of him hanging on to the face of a sheer rock wall, grinning at the camera. Tessa brushed her lips to the screen, wishing he could be there with her right now, beside Lake Nabaw. That he could stand on the green lawn in front of Phipps Tower and listen to Tessa explain the new frontiers of choice. Perhaps if he could be there, in the midst of so many passionate young women, he could come to understand her better.

But Peter was in Oregon, and Tessa's speech was slated to begin in half an hour. She stood up from the log, brushed off her black trousers, and stepped back onto the footpath.

17.

"You know what cracks me up?" Vivian asked Wayne. "Imagining you as a baby."

"You can tell I was an unusually ugly baby? I thought I'd grown out of it."

"No!" she said, kicking him under the table. They were eating an early breakfast of pancakes at the Piehole, a diner on Mass Ave., before Viv's bus back to Weldon. She wanted to be back in plenty of time to get a good seat for Tessa Callahan's speech. She'd invited Wayne to come along. He'd declined, blaming work.

"What I meant was," Viv went on, keeping one of her legs pressed against his, "that it's hard to imagine calling a *baby* Wayne. It's strictly a grown man's name. Was it a family name or something?"

He was always ready for this. "I'm named after an old cowboy. I grew up in Montana, remember?"

As a boy, his favorite book had been *The Illustrated Cowboy Encyclopedia*, originally published in 1949. He'd found it gathering dust on a back shelf of the Havre Elementary Library, checked it out, and never returned it. Wayne Bridger was the toughest cowboy in the book, a loner known to strangle snakes with his bare hands and sleep in snow caves he'd built himself.

The ISA allowed employees to choose their own name for an assignment, or they'd generate one for each person. Over his two decades of working for them, Wayne had always let his employer choose. What did it matter? Choosing your own required filling out a tedious form for the pricks of the Inner Panel, who ran the ISA, and Wayne preferred to have as little contact with them as possible.

But for the last assignment of his career, he'd felt compelled to submit the old cowboy's name. The Inner Panel approved. *Wayne* had been in the top four hundred male names given to male infants in 1995, his designated birth year for this assignment, making it plausible but not obvious. Then they'd assigned him to Vivian Summer Bourne, a senior at Weldon College and child of accelerated gestation who'd begun presenting negative physical symptoms four months ago. Thinning skin, hair depigmentation, rapid decrease of bone density.

The usual signs.

But God, she was so beautiful. Sitting across from her now, he didn't even register any of the new wrinkles near her eyes or the slight slackening of her neckline.

Hard to believe he'd only known her for four months.

"Of *course* I remember that you grew up in Montana," said Viv. "Women love biographical details. It's an intimacy-builder for us. For men, not as much."

"Oh?" Wayne lifted his eyebrows, feigning fascination. He loved teasing Viv about her all-women's college.

"I'm *serious*." Viv lightly kicked him under the table, then kept her leg pressed to his. "You guys are more broad-brush in your sexuality. Details turn women on. You should come with me to the Tessa Callahan thing. It'll be hot."

He reached for her knee under the table and massaged it. Remembered it was her left leg and went softer. It was the one with the titanium pin inside.

"Remind me who she is again?" he said. He didn't even have to pretend he didn't know, or will himself to forget he'd sat next to Tessa on the plane two days ago. The lie was effortless, required no thought; he'd gotten *that* good at his job.

"Are you kidding me, Bridger?" Vivian said, dipping a piece of pancake in a small ceramic bowl of syrup. "Do I really have to tell you who Tessa Callahan is?" Wayne found this detail inexplicably endearing, how she primly dunked each bite so that the stack on her plate didn't get soggy. Then again, he found most things about her endearing. He was in trouble.

"She's an, uh . . ." He pretended to consider. "Feminist porn star?"

"You wish," said Viv, whacking his shin with her toe again. "Seriously. She's only one of the most important feminist thinkers of my *generation*."

"Oh, right. Can you just remind me what her thoughts are?"

"She's a sort of Silicon Valley guru. Runs biotech companies. She's figuring out a way for pregnancy to be easier."

"Isn't it already pretty easy? Don't you just wait around for nine months, getting massages and letting people give you their seats?"

She sighed theatrically, trying not to smile. "You're hopeless," she said, and kicked him again.

A server set the bill down between them. Wayne swiped it off the table while Viv was still rummaging in her purse.

"Hey," she protested, "I was going to get this one."

"Nope. The man always pays, little lady," he said, exaggerating a Western drawl.

"Watch your language, cowboy. Talking like that will get you skewered at Weldon."

"Speaking of which," he said. "Why don't you skip going to Weldon this morning? Come back home with me and take a nap instead."

"Tempting, but no. We can rain check the nap, but Tessa Callahan reschedules for no one. She's possibly the busiest woman in America."

"Well, she can come take a nap with us, too. Sounds like she needs the rest."

"Very funny, Bridger."

He held her elbow as they crossed the restaurant, noticing her gait, which was still slightly uneven from her injury. She'd told him she was doing physical therapy twice a week and never complained of any pain. Still, the more time they spent together, the harder it was to witness her limp. He was plenty familiar with broken bones. That broken leg of hers had to be throbbing sometimes. He wished she'd tell him when it hurt.

Out on the sidewalk, both of them jacketed against the cool spring morning, Wayne pulled her into his arms and kissed her, closing his eyes to blot out everything but the feel of her, both taut and soft beneath her sweater, and her scent, a touch floral from the lavender oil she used, underpinned with a distant tang of dried sweat, a reminder of the night they'd just spent together.

"I have to go," she whispered.

"One more sec," he said, not letting go of her. "Tessa Callahan can wait."

He ran his hands down her sides, between her jacket and sweater, savoring the curve of her.

"We're in public, you know," she said, and giggled, but she didn't remove his hands.

This was the time in Wayne's day he relished the most. The mornings even more than the nights (amazing as they'd recently been), because kissing her goodbye on the street, with any passerby to notice, was an act of public honesty. With his eyes shut and his awareness contained entirely in the realm of Vivian, everything felt simple and true, exactly what it appeared to be: a young couple, newly in love on a perfect spring morning. He could almost forget all the nights he'd lain awake in bed, Viv's breath deep and steady against him, trying to calculate how much time she had left, wondering where she would be when it happened. Not *if* he would lose her—because he certainly would—but precisely how.

But for now it was morning, and she was warm and alive in his arms, and he could almost forget the future.

18.

Seahorse does not imply that the female biology is imperfect," said Tessa from the podium, looking at the crowd of Weldon undergraduates before her, young women of all shades and shapes and sizes, from all corners of the world, dressed in everything from ripped jeans to tailored dresses to hijabs and saris. "Because it is perfect, indeed. The flaws that Seahorse strives to address are the drastic imperfections of our unreasonable culture. A culture that, increasingly, expects women to 'do it all.' Yes, our voices are louder than ever. We are leading corporations, communities, governments. We are leading research in the sciences, making incredible contributions to the arts. We are side by side with men in our military, some of us on the front lines of battle. We are, in short, *killing it.*"

From the crowd, whoops and cheers.

"But let's not fool ourselves. No matter how hard we work, no matter how much we achieve, one immutable fact remains: *we are expected to bear children*. And most of us do. By virtue of our biology, no matter how evolved and involved our partners, no matter how devoted our caregivers, no matter how supportive our organizations, *no one but us* will get pregnant and give birth. No species on the planet has managed to circumvent this responsibility. The closest is the seahorse—namesake of my company—a species in which the male acts as a sort of surrogate during gestation, physically carrying and releasing eggs. It is not true male pregnancy—the females still produce the eggs, simply depositing them into the male's pouch to carry until the babies emerge—but it is a good start. It was with the seahorse in mind that I founded Seahorse Solutions. With Seahorse, I sought to create options for women that would not force them to decide between *children* or *no children*, but give them an opportunity to experience motherhood in the least debilitating manner possible. In time, the Seahorse Solution will enable women to limit the demands of pregnancy and early motherhood. Because, let's face it, those are the years that debilitate us the most. They are the years of discomfort, of exhaustion, of physical transformation that changes the way we are treated in this culture. This is not to say motherhood isn't 'worth it.' It is not to say that in those years when our bodies swell and split, when our nipples crack and breasts leak, when sleep and self-centered pleasures feel like distant dreams, we are not moving toward a deeper level of experience. Although I do not have children myself, I have heard over and over that these sacrifices are 'worth it.' I have no doubt they are. But I do doubt the fairness of these sacrifices, in a world when we are expected to get right back to work, to have domestic talents—let's face it, this is *still* expected, even if not consciously"—whoops from the crowd—"we are expected to draw resources from a single pool: *our own strength*. Because no matter how much support we have, two hard facts remain."

Tessa paused, for dramatic effect, and to center herself before delivering the crux of her speech:

"One: *women are responsible for pregnancy.* And two: *babies need their mothers, more than anyone else.*"

Again, whoops from the crowd, though less vigorous now. She could sense a tentativeness from some; this was to be expected.

"During early motherhood, women like you will likely have the support of your partners. You will likely have caregivers and involved families. You have heard, probably ad nauseam for most of your life, that *it takes a village*. But here, even in the privilege of the first world—perhaps *especially* here—let me make one fact crystal clear: *there is no village*.

"It's you, my friends. From the moment of conception until, at the very soonest, your child enters kindergarten, *the mother matters most*. I've been presented with endless anecdotes arguing otherwise. Case after case of fathers as primary caregivers, of a child who cries for her nanny at night. There are certainly plenty of men in same-sex relationships who do a beautiful job raising vibrant, happy children. These stories matter. However, they are also exceptions to the rule.

"The mandates of motherhood are simply too much, my young colleagues. Too much need is placed upon us. We give and we give and we give until we are uncertain where we end and others begin."

The crowd fell silent. Tessa waited a few beats. Then she added, "Trust me, this is not a problem for men."

A smattering of applause.

"These are radical times for American women. I know it's a dramatic word, *radical*, but I cannot think of a more appropriate one. In recent years, our country has been led by a series of men who, to put it bluntly, wish to demote us."

The crowd came back to life.

"Although they do not state it explicitly, we have reverted to rule by an elite, oppressive regime of men who seem to have just woken from a hundred-year nap. We must do everything in our power to resist their intentions, which, though perhaps not stated explicitly, seep into our collective consciousness like toxins into groundwater. No one would *say* that the recent administrations have implicitly instructed women to get back to looking prettier, to cheerleading more loudly for their men. But I believe that to be the case. At the same time, we're already in the fixed position of carrying fifty percent of the economy. We can't very well step back now. In fact, we must *lean in*"—Tessa paused and lifted her hands high, hooking her fingers into air quotes, invoking the famous phrase—"further than ever. We must lean so hard that we *push through*."

The audience resumed cheering.

"The same old solutions—split the housework fifty-fifty, hire more help, live closer to family, commit to your yoga and biweekly pedicures, *take care of yourself*. Wake up earlier. Be present. Download a meditation app. Unplug after 9:00 p.m. Have a girls' night. Have a date night. Have family dinner. It's the same old tired suggestions, over and over."

"Ay-fucking-men!" someone yelled.

"Women of Weldon, these suggestions are often no more than well-meant bromides. There are only so many hours in the day. There are only so many years in your life. Reprioritizing and reassigning duties are a good start, but they *are not enough*. We need bolder solutions. More concrete and less burdensome on the individual woman to execute. Sure, you can have it all. As long as you find an enlightened partner committed to domestic equality, live within a few miles of a large, supportive family with plenty of time on hand to help out with your kids, and earn an income large enough to provide a sub-income for your children's caregivers."

The crowd was thrumming at a louder volume now, full of claps and whistles and whoops.

"For decades now, we've turned to elective medical technology to enhance our lives. It is a foundation of modern life: pills and patches to control ovulation, to control unsavory moods, to slim down, to help us sleep. Surgeries to tighten skin and lift breasts. Procedures to improve our fertility, to help us get pregnant when our bodies resist, to make birth less excruciating. As it stands, these offerings are piecemeal. You must continuously decide which is right for you and when. Seahorse seeks to diminish, if only a little, the endless litany of decisions that await you when you step off the campus of Weldon College after graduation. It is a unified, elegant option to alleviate the anticipation and profound aftereffects of early motherhood.

"Seahorse Solutions is my contribution to a new type of support for women approaching motherhood. Before I explain it, let me issue several caveats: One, it will not be right for many women, nor is it intended to be. Two, it is inherently controversial, and will remain as such for the foreseeable future. Three, it will not necessarily be an option for your generation. Back in the Bay Area, where I live, we are working hard to test and validate a very early iteration of the technologies at work. As I speak, a very small group of brave, pioneering women are personally testing the Solution. Once their success is proven, *and it will be proven*, there will be years of testing and retesting, of convincing layer upon layer of bureaucracy that women deserve Seahorse, should they decide it is right for them."

Tessa panned her eyes over the crowd, the sea of young, lovely faces in every hue and shape, the hair of every length, sunglasses and cardigans, visors and cargo pants. Their young, unlined skin, their faces earnest and open. So vulnerable, so capable. Headed straight into the impossible. *This* was why she'd chosen her work: not for fame or legacy or wealth. She did it for *them*, these women in front of her, full of potential, wide-open to possibilities.

She talked briefly through Mammarina and FormuLove and the Intimizer, saving TEAT for last, when the crowd was as warm and receptive as possible.

"And finally," she said, "for those who truly comprehend the value not just of every year, of every month, of every week, but of every *hour* of their lives, Seahorse will, someday, include the option to significantly reduce the duration of pregnancy."

She felt a new kind of attentiveness settle over the crowd. A new curiosity, bordering on fear. This was common. She never delved too deeply into the details during her speech; she left that for the Q&A. Best to ease the audience into the idea, to let them guide the revelations.

"By condensing gestation," she continued, "we diminish not only the logistical impact of pregnancy, but the psychological interference as well. There will be less time to anticipate the identity shift that comes with motherhood, less time to unconsciously lean away from all that came before."

Tessa forged into the final lines of her speech.

"Wherever you go after Weldon, let me urge you to do this: Give yourselves a break. Give yourselves the gift of *less*. Give yourselves the gift of time. Perhaps for you, perhaps for your daughters, this gift can include the Seahorse Solution. Today, I ask nothing more than that you open your minds to the idea. For the sake of your daughters, and your daughters' daughters."

The crowd was fervent, the applause at full throttle, some waving blue flags with white *W*s on them. One redheaded woman even held a sign that read TESSA FOR PRESIDENT.

Tessa nodded and waved and gave a thumbs-up. This was always the best moment of all, the one she wished would go on and on, when she and her audience became one.

~

Holly J. Mackaday, dean of Weldon College, placed a light hand on Tessa's arm as they crossed Phipps Green to the car waiting outside the Steiner Center. The Q&A following Tessa's speech had just wrapped, and the dean was hosting a lunch reception at her lavish home a half mile off campus.

"Well, that was certainly the liveliest Influencers talk in recent memory," said Holly. She was fiftyish and trim in a fitted charcoal suit and black suede heels.

"Lively in a good way?" asked Tessa.

"Oh, absolutely," said the dean. "I was watching faces around the crowd as you spoke. Some of them were positively enraptured. Others were obviously uncomfortable. Or *challenged*, rather. This is what we want from our Influencers."

"It was an honor to be part of the series."

The dean issued Tessa an impish look. "Oh, come on, Tessa. We've been trying to get you on campus for years. You're even busier than most of our alums, which is saying a lot."

"Seahorse demands everything from me," said Tessa.

"Just like a child," said Holly.

Tessa laughed politely. "Yes." Had she detected a note of sarcasm in the dean's tone?

They reached the edge of the green and stepped onto the sidewalk, heading toward a silver SUV with a Weldon logo on its passenger door idling by the curb of the Steiner Center. The dean's heels clicked against the cement. Students had begun to clear out of the area, headed back to their dorms or the library or to throw Frisbees by the lake, resuming their normal Sunday routines. A few stragglers passed by Tessa and the dean, some pausing to thank Tessa on their way. She responded graciously, still riding the adrenaline rush of her speech, but she'd also had enough. The past ninety minutes had been intense, and she'd given the students all of her energy. The late-morning sun had grown warm overhead, and Tessa was drained. Also, she found Holly Mackaday stilted and hard to read—she probably opposed Seahorse—which made spending time with her arduous. Tessa would have loved to skip the reception, which would be full of repetitive conversations for which she would have to summon maximum energy and charm, but not attending was out of the question.

"Excuse me, Ms. Callahan?" They were just a few dozen feet from the SUV when a young woman fell into step beside Tessa, out of breath, as if she'd sprinted to catch her.

"Yes?" The woman, clearly a student, had curly dark hair and light blue eyes, a striking combination.

"Hi, Dean Mackaday. Sorry to interrupt. I was hoping to talk to Tessa for a quick moment? I just listened to your talk, but I didn't get called on during the Q&A."

"I'm sorry, we're just on our way to a reception," the dean answered for Tessa. "But you can post further questions on the Influencers LikeMe page, and Tessa will respond personally."

"It won't take long," said the woman. "I'd really like to speak to Tessa in person."

"Absolutely," said Tessa. "Holly, you can go ahead if you like. I can get myself to your house."

The dean issued Tessa a cold look. "If you're sure. Lunch is being served in twenty minutes."

"I'll be there," said Tessa, and the dean clipped off.

"Thanks," said the curly-haired woman. "I hope I'm not getting you in trouble."

Tessa laughed. "Hardly."

"I'm Vivian Bourne. A senior here."

"Shall we walk and talk, Vivian? Or would you prefer to sit somewhere?"

"I mostly go by Viv. Do you have time to sit somewhere? I heard what Dean Mackaday said about lunch being served."

"I have time." Lunch could be served without her, Tessa decided. The dean could deal with it. Vivian had an intense look about her, as if words were burning inside her.

"Really? If we could go sit at The Buzz for a few minutes, I'd really appreciate it."

"The Buzz it is," said Tessa. As they walked together into the Steiner Center, Tessa noticed Vivian limping slightly.

"Lacrosse accident," said Viv quickly, pointing toward her left leg. "Still in physical therapy."

"I played lacrosse here, too," said Tessa. "Second home."

"I know," said Vivian. "Except you were really good. I was just so-so."

"That's a generous assessment. What happened?"

"Collision with a teammate. A bad landing. Broke my femur."

"Your femur? That's cruel. I'm so sorry. You must have landed in the most perfectly awful position."

"Bizarre, right?" said Vivian, almost sharply. "To break a femur?" She must be sensitive about her limp, Tessa thought. She regretted allowing her gaze to linger on it long enough for Vivian to notice.

"Unlucky. Not bizarre. Lacrosse can be violent. I always resented its civilized reputation."

"I guess," said Viv, offering nothing further about her accident.

They entered the Steiner Center and made their way toward The Buzz at the back of the building. The tattooed barista had been replaced by a pale-skinned blond in a denim apron, but the café was as empty as it had been that morning.

"So," said Tessa, when they were settled at a corner table, each with a steaming mug of green tea. "You had some questions about my talk?"

Viv scanned the room, as if looking for someone. Then she placed one hand on each side of her mug and leaned toward Tessa.

"Some comments, actually."

"Even better," said Tessa. "Fire away."

"Actually." Viv took a breath. "It would be easier just to show you. Can I show you something?"

Tessa paused. "Of course."

Viv pushed her mug to the other side of the table. She stood from her chair and tipped her head downward, as if curling herself into a ball, or preparing to perform a somersault. As her dark hair spilled forward, she separated it down the middle of her scalp with her hands, pulling it down tightly into two sections.

"Look," she said to Tessa.

"Look at what?"

"The top of my head."

Tessa stood and looked at the pale white line of the girl's scalp.

"I'm looking."

"Look harder," said Viv, her voice muffled by the curtains of her hair. "Or better yet, touch the top of my head, right at the crown."

Tessa glanced at the barista. She was hunched over her laptop, tapping away, oblivious to them.

"Go ahead," said Viv, impatient.

Reluctantly, Tessa moved an index finger to the top of Viv's head and lightly touched the designated spot.

"Come closer," said Viv. "Look right at the spot you're touching. Press down on it. It's okay, really. I need you to do it."

Tessa moved from across the table to beside Viv. She lowered her face closer to the young woman's head.

And then she saw it: a narrow divot in the center of her scalp, about three inches long and a quarter inch wide.

A cleft.

"I see it," said Tessa, and removed her hand.

Viv straightened and her hair tumbled over her shoulders. She sat back down in her chair and Tessa followed suit, feeling something like a caffeine buzz run through her body, though she hadn't yet touched her tea.

"So yeah," said Viv, reaching for her mug. "I was an accelerated baby. The real deal."

A message chimed on Tessa's phone.

Holly Mackaday: *ETA?*

She ignored it.

"Okay," said Tessa, trying to sound casual. "So my speech this morning probably struck you . . . differently than the rest of the audience." She met Viv's blue eyes. "I'd love to hear your reaction. And I really appreciate your sharing your personal story with me."

"It's not really a *story*," said Viv sharply. "It's a major event in history. That, like a lot of major shit, people were interested in for"—she snapped her fingers—"about ten minutes."

"I'm interested," said Tessa. "I actually care about it a great deal."

"Because we gave you the idea for your project, right? We're the spark that lit the Seahorse empire, right? I wouldn't call that *caring*. I'd call that a self-serving connection."

"That's a fair point. It's more accurate to say that your situation was a source of great inspiration for me."

"Why? What inspired you about a bunch of babies who grew at warp speed? Are you drawn to freaks?"

"You're hardly freaks. I've studied all the data that's available. It indicates that accelerated babies became normal adults. I can't say what your private experience has been, though I'd like to know."

"Why?" Viv's tone was addled.

"I'm curious. Learning about your origin had a powerful effect on me."

"And how did you? Learn about it?"

Tessa spoke carefully. "The early aughts aren't that clear in my memory. The web was young. But I'm sure I read about it online somewhere. The *Times* or the *Wall Street Journal* or *CNN*. It could have been any number of sources."

"No, it couldn't have."

"Excuse me?" Tessa took a sip of her tea. It was cold.

"Run a two-minute web search and see for yourself. There's practically *nothing* on the entire internet about us. A couple of puff pieces and a happy-ending *New York Times* story. That's it."

"Archiving wasn't standardized back then. The cloud barely existed."

"So? There's endless original reporting on 9/11 still up. Plus a zillion other news stories, major and minor. Remember the Y2K panic? The downfall of Winona Ryder? Elizabeth Smart getting kidnapped? This is all stuff I've learned about straight from twenty-year-old content I googled in about five seconds. But when it comes to AG"—Viv made a slicing motion at her neck—"practically zilch."

Another message pinged on Tessa's phone.

Holly Mackaday: *Tessa? Hello?*

"Excuse me," said Tessa to Viv, and quickly typed, *Indefinitely delayed on urgent matter, deepest apologies.*

Then she turned her phone off.

"I've already searched," she said. "I've read everything on AG that's publicly available. Plus a number of scientific papers."

"And don't you think the amount is scant?"

"I think perhaps there were too many other things going on," said Tessa. "As you mentioned, it was around the same time as 9/11. But I'll take another look."

"You should," said Viv. She flicked her thumbnails together and stared at the tiled tabletop, as if contemplating saying more.

Tessa lowered her voice and spoke slowly—her *management voice,* Peter called it. But it worked—people usually opened up.

"If you're open to talking about it, I'd be curious to hear more about growing up as a child of AG," she said. "I'd love to buy you lunch. Turns out my reception is delayed, so I've got time."

Viv looked up, looking mildly exasperated. For the first time, Tessa noticed the tiredness of the young woman's face, the dry, lightly creased skin around her eyes, as if she hadn't been getting enough sleep. Viv was so pretty at first glance—the contrast of her dark hair and light eyes— that it was easy not to notice that she actually looked rather worn down.

"That's the thing," said Viv. "There *is* no more."

"No more what?"

"No more to tell you. My childhood was perfectly normal."

"What about your parents?"

Viv shrugged. "My father's a lawyer. My mother runs a gym. It's called Elisercise, because her name's Elise, get it?" She gave a short, disdainful laugh. "She talks about her AG pregnancy like it was one of her workout challenges." She hooked her fingers into air quotes. *"Very high intensity, but I trusted my body and ended up being grateful for the experience."*

"She really says that?"

"Yep," said Viv. "And about a hundred other variations of it. My dad isn't any better. He claims to hardly remember it. *I was definitely pretty scared* is as deep as he'll go."

"Do you have siblings?"

"Nope. So it's not like my birth is blending together with a bunch of others."

"It must be hard to get such superficial descriptions," said Tessa, "of an event that's usually a monumental experience."

"Like the birth of your only *kid?*" Viv bobbed her head in agreement. "Totally. It drives me crazy. My parents are somewhat idiotic. I mean, they love me, but . . ." She trailed off, then seemed to catch herself. "But that's not why I dragged you to a coffee shop. Not for some therapy session about my parents. I just wanted to talk to you before Seahorse explodes and your acceleration technology becomes this big buzzy thing I'm reading about everywhere. I just wanted to remind you that AG already existed, before you and your *team* invented it."

"I . . . I'm glad you brought that up," said Tessa. Viv's tone had taken on a subtly hostile edge. For the first time since they'd sat down, Tessa felt uneasy. Viv had struck her as outspoken and direct, but now Tessa could hear anger beneath the girl's confidence. Tessa spoke carefully. "Acknowledging our original inspiration is a critical part of the Seahorse Solution's value proposition." She watched skepticism darken Viv's face when she heard the corporate lingo. "What I mean is," said Tessa, flustered, "I will make sure the natural AG children are remembered. And honored."

"Um. Thank you," said Viv. "But I'm not all that interested in being honored. Neither are my AG friends. All we want to know is *why* this happened to us."

"It's been investigated over and over," said Tessa. "I'm sure you know that."

"Then help us investigate again. That's why I asked to talk to you, Tessa. Because your project has the potential to throw AG back into the national spotlight. To make people interested again. A *spontaneous aberration of indeterminate cause* might be good enough for most people, but when you've got a weird dent in your head"—Viv tapped her cleft—"that you try to hide from everyone, especially your boyfriend, plus a birth story that's downright bizarre, it's not good enough. I need to know why I'm like this."

"You're right," said Tessa. "We should do better."

Viv stood up from the table. Tessa could see her lips quivering.

"Then make it better," Viv said and walked out of the café, gingerly on her left leg, heavy on her right, obviously in some discomfort from her injury. Tessa watched her recede, imagining her fall on the lacrosse field: the stun of the crash, the swift free fall through the air, her dark curls flaring, then the sickening crunch of the landing, her left leg bent at an impossible angle. As Viv disappeared from view, Tessa had the sudden, intense urge to run after her, to protect her from some looming threat out in the world, though she could not name what it was. Perhaps, she thought, this was what a mother's instinct felt like.

19.

O utside the Albuquerque airport, Wayne spotted the black car idling at the curb and angled for it. As he approached, the driver popped the trunk. Wayne set his duffel inside it, keeping his hard rectangular case of work supplies on his person at all times, per ISA code. He slid into the back seat of the Lincoln, the Freon chill of its AC enveloping him instantly, and nodded hello at the driver, a kid with a fresh buzz cut in aviators and camouflage.

"Morning, Mr. Theroux," said the driver. "Any stops before we head south?"

"Negative," said Wayne. They exited the airport and swung onto the I-25, the landscape all hues of brown and dull green, the Sandia Mountains bulging like turtle shells in the distance. An all-body weariness seeped through him; he'd barely slept the night before. The drive to the Colony would take two hours, and he certainly wouldn't have any downtime once he arrived. The tight-asses of the Inner Panel liked to book him solid for a full three days. In addition to an assessment of the preso he'd written of Viv, Wayne would have to attend endless meetings, trainings, and strategy sessions, a biannual requirement of all ISA agents, no matter how senior. No matter how close to retirement.

At least he would get to pay a quick visit to Irene. Seeing her was the only thing he ever looked forward to at the Colony.

Two hours later, he woke from his nap in the car in time to see the familiar sign: **ENTERING U.S. MILITARY GROUNDS. NO UNAUTHORIZED ACCESS.** The Internal Stability Agency's headquarters. Wayne sighed and pulled his badge from a pocket of his camo pants, then looped the lanyard around his neck. The rest of the world was trusting retinal and handprint scans for IDs, yet the ISA still clung to physical badges after consultants deemed the newer technologies too vulnerable.

The driver slowed at the guard booth and Wayne rolled down his window. He recognized the guard on duty as Mike Jensen, the pale-complected, orange-haired rookie from Nebraska.

"Theroux," Jensen said as he held his scanner to Wayne's badge. "Nice to have you back."

"Don't get used to it," Wayne said. The scanner flashed green and the guardrail rose.

The driver steered the Lincoln onto the curved road that lined the crescent of low-slung buildings where the Inner Panel and their minions worked. A ring of squat stucco buildings rose from the desert floor, all roughly the same color. The structures blended right into the landscape of scrubby trees, rocks, bleached dirt studded with noxious weeds, and lizards.

At one end of the semicircle, a building differed from the others: no windows. Quarantine, "the Quarry," as staffers called it, was where all Contacts went first for examination and confiscation of their phones and other electronic devices. They would stay at the Quarry for a week or so, for general observation and communication designed to help them understand and accept their situation. Eventually—it might take a week or a month, or longer—they would either be deemed "compliant" and released, or "noncompliant" and moved to the residences until they reconsidered accepting a revision.

The Quarry would be the first place Viv would go, when he brought her, that blank beige building. Wayne looked away from it.

"Where to, Mr. Theroux?" asked his driver.

"The Blue Room," said Wayne, checking his phone. His presentation was slated to begin in less than fifteen minutes.

"Straight to a meeting with the IP, eh?" said the driver, pulling up to the entrance of Building 3.

"None of your goddamn business," said Wayne.

"Sorry, sir."

The kid hopped out, extracted Wayne's overnight bag from the trunk, and handed it to Wayne with a salute.

"Pleasure, sir. See you on the drive back."

Wayne grabbed the bag without answering. Overhead, the sun was dead center in the sky, a burning hole.

Wayne took the elevator down to a subbasement where the Blue Room was. Inside, it was the same as always. Same dim lighting, same faux-wood conference table at the center with cushioned swivel chairs clustered around it, same strange sky-colored walls that gave the room its name. The bright paint was meant to add some levity to the grim space, Wayne supposed, but he'd always found its effect destabilizing; it made him feel like he'd walked into a break room at a mental institution. Three of the blue walls were blank and the fourth displayed two massive monitors, mounted side by side. One ran a constant stream of data from the Colony, while the second was dark, waiting for a presenter to exhibit his latest findings upon it.

Wayne was the first to arrive. He unlocked his computer case and set the machine up at the head of the table, synced it with the wall screen, and pulled up the preso, though he'd already sent it to the IP. They would want it up and waiting for them.

He clicked to the opening slide: a photo of Viv, taken for lacrosse when she'd made the team her first year at Weldon, with text below it.

PIT #1999-42: Bourne, Vivian Summer

Age: 21

Categorization: Accelerated Gestation (child)

Current residence: Newport Beach, CA (family) and Weldon, MA (college)

Legal guardians: Elise Summer Bourne and Lawrence Dylan Bourne

Activity of Concern: Widespread online distribution of alarmist content pertaining to accelerated gestation; creation of undue panic among other AG individuals; fixation on physical developments

Threat Assessment: Moderately Severe

Viv's hair had been shorter when the photo was taken, her face slightly rounder and fuller, her expression open and hopeful, more childlike. In the four years that had passed since the photo had been taken, Wayne saw, she'd transformed from a teenager into a woman.

Threat assessment: *Moderately Severe.*

He'd wanted so badly to downgrade Viv to merely *Moderate*, thereby postponing the next steps by perhaps a couple of months, but he hadn't been able to justify it. Viv's LikeMe posts were becoming more vehement, while at the same time, her symptoms had become more abundant: the persistent limp in her leg (the fall she took in lacrosse would not have caused such damage in a typical healthy twenty-one-year-old), the shallow wrinkles around her mouth and eyes, a few patches of whitish hair in her dark mane, indicating her melanin levels were decreasing.

It was subtle, but Viv was noticing, of course, and she was writing about it. Not just on LikeMe, but now in an essay that *Artery*, the most popular long-form site on the web, with two million daily visitors, was set to publish in a few weeks.

Once the *Artery* piece came out, Wayne knew, there would be no re-canning the worms. All the painstaking efforts the ISA had taken to eradicate speculation about accelerated gestation would be undone, and the conversation would metastasize all over again, like a returned cancer. Just when they'd almost put the Juva debacle to bed once and for all. They could not allow Viv to undo all their work now. Especially since Tessa Callahan and her crew of luminaries in California were ready to assume ownership of the whole thing, to package accelerated gestation as something they'd invented. As an *elective option* for women. They were calling it *Seahorse*—how clever!—and were running a human trial of their synthetic version of AG right now. Soon they'd be celebrating it publicly, demanding media attention, pushing their new "solution" onto consumers, and in the process, letting the U.S. government off the hook. Callahan and her rich-kid sidekick, Luke Zimmerman, were inadvertently ensuring that the public would now associate accelerated gestation with her swanky biotech startup. As a result, the original AG phenomenon would become even further disconnected from a certain major fuckup on the part of a U.S. federal agency, followed by a mandate by President Falk to erase the fuckup. The Seahorse buzz would divert whatever vestiges were left of the old AG skepticism—and there wasn't much, thanks to the ISA—straight to Silicon Valley. Away from Washington. Anyone who wanted to dig into the original cases would now likely break ground in the wrong place.

Thus, the Feds were delighted with Seahorse and let Callahan and Zimmerman run with their Trial. The government disliked meddling in Silicon Valley, anyway; the area was too critical to the national economy.

Wayne, on the other hand, was disturbed by the concept: deliberately turning pregnancy into a highly controlled, manipulated scenario, like traveling into space. Especially meddling with gestation speed. Why the hell would a woman as smart as Tessa Callahan endorse it? What was wrong with a regular nine-month pregnancy?

He hoped they were smart enough to make it work, the Californians with their crazy technology and Mensa IQs and outsize egos. They probably were. After all, the original AG, on paper, had not been a statistical disaster, and that one did not have a bunch of "geniuses" behind it. Most of the thousands of women who took Juva never suffered the side effects, and most of their children were showing no symptoms now.

Only a few dozen, like Irene, were unlucky.

Like Viv.

Wayne's body hummed at the thought of her, and his mind blanked with the singular desire to hear her voice, to feel his skin against hers.

A pit of nausea opened in his stomach as the reality returned of what he was about to do: recommend Viv's importation to the Inner Panel. As sick as it made him, as much as he wanted to grab her hand and run far, far away, flight was not an option. They'd only get caught. Viv had already caused too much noise about AG online, and though the ISA was pulling her posts as fast as she put them up, the administration was frowning on them. Or frowning on Wayne specifically, according to Borlav.

If he failed now, before Seahorse alleviated the situation and the administration declared it under control, Wayne could kiss his retirement goodbye.

He rolled his neck, then dropped to the cold floor of the Blue Room and did push-ups, desperate for distraction. He tried to count them in his head, but her name replaced the numbers. *Viv, Viv, Viv.*

~

A sharp rap came at the door of the Blue Room, and it simultaneously opened. A full hour had passed since Wayne had finished his presentation and the IPs disappeared. Now, Borlav, Winger, and Hurst reentered. They didn't thank him for waiting or for his patience, or ask if he'd like some water. Borlav simply began to speak in his mob-boss baritone.

"Theroux. Thanks for your presentation on PIT #1999-42. Excellent work. We're tasking you with fast-track importation. Thirty days, max."

He presented Wayne with various screens to sign, committing to the import terms. Standard procedure. Wayne had signed dozens of times, for other PITs, but this was the first time he felt a fissure open in his chest as he initialed the screen with his fingers. The thought of bringing Viv here was sickening. And yet, so was not retiring. He could not do this for much longer: enter a person's life as a friend, and leave it as a captor. He'd rather be dead. In fact, next to the prospect of more presentations in the Blue Room, death sounded like comfort.

He finished signing, and then, without saying goodbye to the IPs, he left the subterranean den of the Blue Room and caught the elevator up to the surface of the earth. The sun was blinding, despite his dark glasses.

He didn't even consider catching the shuttle to visit Irene in her neighborhood behind the Great Wall. He had more than enough pent-up energy to walk the three miles from Base to the Colony. Of all the Imports he'd worked with over the course of his career, Irene Brenner, formerly PIT #1979-33, was the only one, until Viv, that he'd cared for at all.

By the time Wayne completed the third mile, his throat was so dry he could hardly swallow. He'd bolted from the Blue Room so quickly he'd forgotten to bring water for the walk. The route between Base and the Colony was intentionally roadless, and the all-terrain vehicles that traversed it routinely took different routes, so as not to wear traces of passage into the landscape.

If you didn't know the way between the two settlements, you'd be unlikely to find the Colony. To the untrained eye, the "path" was merely inhospitable desert studded with ragweed and rock, disappearing from view after a few miles, when it met a rise in elevation.

But if you knew what you were doing, as Wayne did, you'd walk for forty minutes or so, gauging your route with the compass on your phone, or, if you had done it enough times, by the particular view of the Sandia Mountains in the distance, certain trees and rocks along the way. Every landscape, eventually, could be memorized.

He approached the Great Wall, which bordered the Colony. Constructed of steel-cored adobe, it rose up from the desert floor like a giant earthen crown. To pass through it, you had to learn where the invisible seams were, like the secret door to a speakeasy. You had to know where to find the keypads, several of which were buried under the desert floor. Your markers were nothing more than a certain plant or a group of rocks, indicated with a tiny X in white paint. And finally, you had to recall the cumbersome code for entry, a jumble of numbers and letters and symbols that changed regularly, and which you had to enter with your hand shoved eight inches into the ground.

Wayne could basically do all this in his sleep. Ten yards from the Great Wall, he squatted next to a spiny knot of rabbitbrush, felt for the metal nub on the ground, found it, and peeled the desert floor away from itself. He beamed his phone's flashlight into the hole to check for snakes. There was nothing inside the socket of earth but a small square console that lit up as the sunlight hit it. The screen produced a weak greenish glow. Wayne dipped his hand into the hole to trace the entry code across the reinforced glass with his index finger.

The device beeped and its screen flashed **AUTHORIZED**.

He closed the flap of ground, scattered the rocks he'd moved over the surface of the hatch, and broke into a jog toward the Great Wall. The system gave you only ninety seconds to find the entrance before it timed out. Wayne followed the periphery of the wall, his throat on fire, counting nearly imperceptible notches in the adobe until he reached eighteen. He placed his palm on the notch and waited. The wall retracting, offering a gap just wide enough for him to step through into a pitch-dark tunnel. He moved straight forward, feeling the walls with his hands, until he came into contact with another solid wall in front of him. The inner border of the Great Wall. He felt for another notch in the adobe and palmed it; the wall parted. He was in.

Wayne stepped out of the tunnel and the wall promptly sealed behind him. There was a litany of jokes among ISA staffers about getting crushed in the Great Wall, most involving dicks, always unfunny. Wayne had heard them all.

Inside, he stood with his back against the wall, catching his breath, adjusting to the abrupt change in surroundings. No matter how many times he visited the Colony, it always took a minute to adapt, to accept it was a real place and not a hallucination. To step inside it was to lose all awareness of being in the middle of the high desert. The Colony spanned one hundred acres and offered deep green knolls (the grass was fake but convincing), large shade trees, and flowers that did not grow in New Mexico—yellow chrysanthemums, white begonias, and roses. An elaborate climate-control system spritzed moisture into the air on auto-timer, creating gentle humidity.

Wayne's phone beeped a reminder that it was initiating his allotted visiting time, sixty minutes. On the screen, the timer began to count down.

59:59
59:58
59:57

He had under an hour to see the friend he hadn't seen for far too long. A person who'd once been the central companion in his life. All those mornings in Irene's sunny kitchen, hundreds of hours, reduced now to sixty minutes, the maximum visiting time the ISA permitted permanent residents of the Colony.

He began to walk fast toward the neighborhood where all forty-one permanent residents lived, plus another hundred staffers, in individual residences spread over the northern section of the property. The Craftsman-style bungalows, each with a green lawn, were built along a single loop of paved road lined with flowers and trees. He rounded a bend in the path and spotted Irene's house just ahead, the standard two rocking chairs on her porch.

He knocked lightly on Irene's door and waited. She was not expecting him. She would likely assume he was one of the Colony's medical staff who visited her daily to poke and prod. Last he'd visited her, Irene had slowed down noticeably, having acquired the tentative gait of the elderly. He waited for what seemed a long time, reminding himself that crossing the nine hundred square feet of the bungalow might take her longer than it used to.

But the woman who answered the door wore fresh pink scrubs and a cherry-red manicure: Johanna, who'd been a nurse at the Colony for as long as Wayne could remember. She stepped onto the porch and appraised him, squinting in the sun.

"Sight for sore eyes," she said, in the Jamaican lilt he'd found so comforting back in his rookie days, when he'd looked for comfort everywhere. "I wasn't expecting you, baby boy." *Baby boy.* Her hug was fiercer than ever. She smelled of the same hair oil she'd used for almost twenty years, a warm herbal smell, like grass and sunshine.

"Take it easy, Jo," he said, as she crushed against him. "I'm too fragile for your guns. How much are you benching these days?" Johanna was famous for her devotion to the Colony's gym, the muscles of her arms risen to sleek brown hillocks from years of weight training.

"One-eighty-five," said Johanna, releasing him for her usual head-to-toe appraisal. "Are you eating enough, mister?"

"I couldn't tell you," Wayne said.

"You're not." Johanna frowned. "You should let me cook for you while you're here. How long do we get you?"

"Just the weekend," said Wayne. "I'm just here for my biannual. Flash a few slides at the IP, hit a few meetings, then back to the field."

"One weekend? That's an outrage. You need more time. You look like you could use a straight week of sleep. Don't mean to offend."

"I plan to spend most of my retirement sleeping. I'm almost there, you know."

Her face dimmed. "You're leaving us?"

"This is my last assignment before I hit quota. So I can retire early."

"Oh, sweets, I'm so proud of you. I didn't realize. You know how time is around here. There's no keeping track. Congratulations." She pressed both hands against the sides of his face, like a mother to her young boy. Had his own mother ever cupped his face that way? He could not recall the feel of her hands.

"Don't congratulate me yet," said Wayne. "No jinxing."

"You're the best field-op this place has ever seen. I don't understand why those fatties in the IP don't take better care of you."

"Shouldn't *you* be retiring soon? How old are you now, Jo? I mean, you look like a spring chicken, of course."

She slid her eyes away from his. "Sixty-five last year."

"So you could go. Why don't you go?"

"Come on, baby. You know better. I've been here twenty years."

The Inner Panel had a way of breeding near-fanatical loyalty among their residential staff. Resignations or requests for transfer among onsite Colony employees were virtually unheard of.

"You should retire, Jo," he said. "Really."

"I'll do what I do, sweetie," she said. "Can we sit awhile? Irene's sleeping. Would you like iced tea?"

"Can't," said Wayne. "I have a training back at Base at two thirty. You'll have to wake her."

"Johanna," came Irene's voice from inside the house, wan with sleep. "I'm awake."

"Well, well, well," said Johanna. "Look who sensed your presence. Like those stories you hear about dogs waiting five years for their owners to come back."

"I'm the dog," said Wayne.

Johanna turned toward the half-open door and called to Irene. "Coming, honeybunny. I have a surprise for you. Give me just one second." She turned back to Wayne. "Let me clean her up and I'll bring her out. She's on Depends these days."

"Oh," said Wayne, his stomach dropping. Such developments always jarred him.

"It's nothing." Johanna waved her cherry nails. "More convenient for everyone, actually. Don't overthink it."

"Okay," said Wayne.

"I'll clean her up and then give you two some alone time."

"Thanks, Jo."

"Johanna?" Irene's voice wafted from the house again.

"Coming, sweet pea," Johanna called. "Listen, mister, don't be a stranger. You'd better come visit me before you retire. And I mean for more than five minutes."

"Will do, Jo."

"I'm here for you, doll," she said, tipping onto her toes to whisper in his ear, "If there's anything I can do for you, ever . . ."

"Thank you."

"I mean it. Everyone needs someone to take care of them. Even macho men like you."

"You could bench-press me, Jo. Who's the macho one?"

She kissed him on the cheek and disappeared inside.

He sat on one of the chairs in the shade of the porch and rocked, gazing out into the flawless afternoon that suggested no particular season or geography. It provided no guiding evocations whatsoever. It was May in New Mexico, but it might have been summer in New England.

Wayne turned to see the front door of the bungalow swinging open and Irene stepping onto the porch.

"Irene." Wayne went to her and pulled her into his arms. She felt smaller and more fragile than he remembered. She rested her cheek against his chest and he felt her body relax into his.

"It's good to see you," he said. He tried not to betray any of the surprise he was feeling. Last he'd seen Irene, she'd appeared a robust seventy, wrinkled but straight spined, her laugh still throaty and assertive. Now she appeared closer to ninety, her face a fissured desert surface, its skin both delicate and ravaged. A new hunch rose from between her shoulders. Kyphosis, Wayne thought darkly.

"Sorry Johanna is such a flirt," said Irene. "She's always had a crush on you. Never mind that she's old enough to be your mother."

"Oh, Jo is great," Wayne said, releasing her and moving the rockers closer together. He offered his hand. "Here, sit."

"All I *do* is sit or lie down. Let me stand a minute."

"Okay," he said.

"You're looking well," he ventured.

She laughed, brittle. "Oh, don't bullshit me, darling. What took so long? I've been counting the days since you left. One-eighty-six."

"I wanted to come sooner," he said, sitting down beside her. "Whether you missed me or not."

"Has there been trouble?"

"No," he said. "It's just busy. I'm retiring soon. It's not a simple process."

"Retiring. So you won't visit anymore?"

"Hard to say." He hurried on. "How are your friends? Do you still spend time with Mia and Carly?" He'd made sure to review the streams of the permanent residents he knew Irene considered quasi friends.

"Transformed into old bats. They've started a cribbage group. It's popular." She waved a knobby hand in the air. "*Cribbage*. The classic predeath game. I just can't do it. I've always been a terrible strategist, anyway."

"I think bridge is the classic," said Wayne.

"Bridge, cribbage, whatever. The point is, I'm surrounded by geezers, Henry."

"Henry isn't my name," he corrected her, gently, wincing inside. "Remember?" He disliked hearing his old aliases. He wondered if her slip was a sign of memory loss.

"Of course I remember. But it's who you are to me."

When he'd first approached Irene, back at her house in Texas, he'd been using *Henry Duarte*. Then, he'd inhabited that name completely, but since he'd moved on, the name sounded like dead words. Now—*for now*—he was Wayne Bridger. The knowledge that he'd soon shed that one, too, like snakeskin, rarely entered his consciousness. He didn't allow it.

"I can't stay long."

"You just got here." Her voice trembled.

"I'm sorry."

"When are you coming back?"

He thought of his thirty-day deadline.

"Soon. Maybe a month."

She covered her face with her hands. He rose from his rocker and stood behind her chair to rub her shoulders. Minutes passed. She quaked softly beneath his palms.

When she finally uncovered her face and twisted around to look at him, her expression had changed. She looked focused and composed, as if watching a symphony. Her rheumy eyes were dry. Calm.

"Henry," she whispered. "I made up my mind."

"About what?"

"I want the other option. The one you said you'd help me with."

He felt himself shift into slow motion. A hot dread seeped through his chest, down into his gut.

"What?"

"You heard me. I need it."

"Why?"

"I don't want this life anymore."

"But—it's been years since you've mentioned it."

"That's the problem. Too many years. I want it. You say you'll be back in a month?"

"Yes."

"That's soon enough. Bring it when you come. But don't make me wait much longer. I can't bear it."

"Irene. Why now? After all this time? You're—" He fumbled.

"What? Old as the hills? In the home stretch?"

"No. You're settled. You're in a life here."

"This isn't a life, Henry. You promised me a way out if I ever wanted it."

He searched for the words. None were available.

"Just promise me," said Irene.

"I promise."

Now that he'd said it, there was no way out.

He lowered himself onto the wood slats of the porch and sat cross-legged beside her rocker. One of her hands dangled off the chair and he held it and gazed out into the blank afternoon. Soon her breathing coarsened with sleep. Her head hung down toward her lap. Wayne stood and smoothed the loose hanks of hair away from her face. He brushed his lips to her cheek to say goodbye.

"See you soon," he whispered.

~

The plane taxied down the runway in Albuquerque. Lifted, banked, angled up into the sky. When it leveled off Wayne opened the window to the night outside. Finally, he was on the red-eye back to Boston. The route back to Viv didn't feel as good as he'd hoped. He'd anticipated feeling freer at this moment, with the chores of his ISA presentation and Colony visit behind him. A day with Viv ahead. But he found himself dreading the reunion. Dreading the work he'd have to do in order to make his importation deadline.

He ordered a whiskey from the flight attendant. She produced a micro-bottle of Jameson and a plastic cup.

"Two, please, actually," said Wayne, and she hesitated before handing over another.

Wayne unscrewed the bottle and skipped the cup. He rarely drank, but when he did, only whiskey did the job. The man seated beside him, a doughy guy in his fifties, ordered a beer and poured it into his plastic cup. Wayne watched him tip the green bottle at an angle to create an inch of foamy head, admire his pour, and take a sip.

Wayne looked away. He hated beer. It reminded him of his father, popping the tabs of his cans so hard foam spewed into the air.

He gazed out the oval window of the plane at the stars. In the distance, he saw the lights of another plane. Wasn't that supposed to be good luck?

Or was it bad?

He watched the other plane drifting parallel, no more than a few bright blips in the night sky. He thought of the lives inside it, all the flesh and blood and memory, suspended thirty thousand feet in the air. Lives that mattered deeply to a handful of individuals, but in the grander scheme, not at all. The world was a massive, thrumming force of life. It repopulated and marched on. Its memory was pliable and forgiving.

Wayne uncapped the second Jameson. The whiskey was doing its work. Loosening the locks on the disciplined compartments of his mind.

He tapped his tablet to look at a picture of Viv. There she was: midlaugh, eyes lit up, hair all over the place.

He loved her. He hadn't gotten to love that many things in his life.

When he closed his eyes, there on the back of his lids was Puke. His dog, another thing he'd loved.

When Wayne was eight, Puke slept with him at night, in the trailer on the Hi-Line. *Ugly as puke,* his father had said of the rottweiler-heeler mutt who'd wandered up to their trailer one day, dragging a stake and a chain, all ribs and mange. They'd driven him back down to the end of the road and dumped him there, but the dog kept showing up, tongue hanging from his mouth like a ribbon. Wayne had never gotten permission to keep him; he simply did, stealing ground chuck and jerky to feed him, rigging a ramp up to his bedroom window so that Puke could enter and exit the trailer without his father noticing. A benefit of living with a drunk like his father was that you could keep something like a pet dog a secret for a pretty long time. In the end, it was his sister, Bethany, who squealed. They'd been in a stupid fight, something about who'd eaten the last Little Debbie. His father swayed into the room and asked what the fuck was going on. Beth planted her hands on her hips and asked him if he knew her brother had a dog living in his room. That, in fact, the dog was in the house *at that very moment.* His father's eyes had blazed with booze and when he'd said *Horseshit. Prove it,* Beth had suddenly panicked, a light switch flipping in a ten-year-old mind conditioned from years of vigilance, and she changed tack. *Never mind, never mind, I was just kidding, it was just a dumb joke.* But it was too late.

Their father lumbered to the bedroom to find Puke asleep under the bed, where Wayne had taught him to lie. He and Bethany were already crying, gripping each other like toddlers, their own conflict instantly dissolved. Together they wished desperately to retract it, to erase the past few minutes, but it was impossible.

Their father was too drunk to shoot clean the first time, and Wayne remembered Beth's body jerking in his embrace with each of the three gunshots that ripped from the bedroom. In a minute, their father reentered the kitchen looking blasé, cracked another beer, and said *Took care of it.*

Wayne charged at him, screaming, swinging his fists with animal fury, and got a few solid cracks to his father's jaw before his father pinned him in the headlock. Despite being a fat slug, his father was still stronger than him. Strong enough to hold Wayne still with one arm while he made an inch-long cut along one of Wayne's cheeks, and then a matching one along the other.

He'd told Irene all of this. He'd had no one else to tell.

~

Wayne awoke to the mild jostle of the plane wheels meeting the runway.

"Good morning, folks." The pilot's cheerful voice cut through the cabin. "Welcome to Boston."

Outside, dawn had just broken, turning the sky pink and red.

ISA – OFFICIAL EVIDENCE

👾

VivversOC: ready for another installment of CrayCray Vivian?

Stoph1: bring it on!

LindsEE!: s'up Vivvers?

VivversOC: I'm fully prepared 4U to give me shit. Just saying up front.

LindsEE!: I won't!!!

Xavey: stoph's the only meathead here. Me & Linds r cool

Stoph1: fuckoff, Xave. Let the woman speak.

LindsEE!: I'm noticing some strange things about myself.

Stoph1: ur just now noticing?

Xavey: like I said. MEAT. HEAD.

LindsEE!: shut up boys. Like what Viv?

VivversOC: I'm gonna send a pic, it's easier than explaining. Just don't be weird about it you guys, promise? I just want to know what u think and honestly if you've noticed anything similar

LindsEE!: cross my heart hope to die

Stoph1: the suspense is killing me.

VivversOC: one sec

[IMAGE DELIVERED]

20.

Tessa's flight landed in San Jose just after midnight. She'd planned to sleep at home in Atherton but found herself navigating the fog-blurred curves of the route to the Seahorse Center instead. She went to her room in East Lobe, where she showered and dozed lightly in bed until eight. Then she crossed the building to Luke's office in West Lobe. On her way, she paused to look down at the open workspaces eight stories below. Her gaze rested on the "Thought Floor," a designated brainstorming area, where dozens of her staffers were gathered around whiteboards or hovered over screens, swigging coffee while they bandied ideas and planned their attack on the new day before them.

Tessa smiled. Thank God she was back.

Luke met her in a hug just inside his office door.

"Finally, she returns," he said, his long arms looped around her. "Welcome back. It felt like forever."

Tessa broke from his embrace and crossed the room to her usual spot in the Lucite chair. "You should consider getting more comfortable seating in here."

"Consider it considered."

"Very funny. How were the Cohort's charts this morning?"

"Straight to business, as always," Luke said. He seemed looser, more at ease than when she'd last seen him in the conference room, before she'd left for Boston, when they'd disagreed about the INR-Views. "The charts are beautiful. All three of them, on par with optimal fetal growth for fourteen-week pregnancies. Gupta and Milford are happy. Which means we can all be happy. We'll know the sex of the babies by next week, but between us, the docs can already see that LaTonya is having a boy." He propped his black Converse up on his desk, crossed his ankles, and leaned his head into his hands. "How was your trip?"

"Successful."

"Were young Weldon minds blown?"

"There was a lot of excitement for Seahorse. Reception was very positive."

"Crowds love you, Callahan."

"Something happened after my talk that I thought you'd find interesting."

"Oh?"

"A young woman caught up with me as I was on my way to a reception at the dean's. She had an intensity about her, so I suggested we sit down for coffee."

"A hater?" said Luke. "Campus Crusade for Christ or something?"

"No. A natural AG baby."

Luke uncrossed his feet and lowered them to the floor. "You're kidding."

"I'm not. A senior named Vivian Bourne. Viv."

A strange expression crossed Luke's face. "Go on."

"It was interesting to talk to her. My speech definitely triggered some issues she has with AG being overlooked."

"Issues?"

"She's dissatisfied by the lack of explanation. That the whole original phenomenon just sort of faded into the ether."

"It was more than twenty years ago."

"So? That doesn't mean she's stopped wondering. She's in the formative years of her adult identity—it's natural that she'd be ruminating on this. Why she was born the way she was. How AG plays into the person she's becoming. Et cetera."

"Sounds like you did some therapy with her."

"Not really. I just listened. I have compassion for her. But I also think she could be a useful resource for us."

"How so?" A tightness seemed to have descended over Luke, replacing his easy mood.

"I think it could be useful for the Cohort to meet her. They'd have a natural connection, since Viv directly inspired Seahorse. She's a predecessor to their babies, in a way. The Cohort has a lot of free time on their hands right now, so I thought we could fly Viv out and set up a casual conversation. It could be really meaningful for all of them to connect."

"No," said Luke.

"Excuse me?"

"Sorry, Callahan, it's not a good idea. It's way too early to invite outside visitors here for a look. The Trial is going well, but it's still a very delicate situation. Security has to be our top priority."

"Well, of course," said Tessa, annoyed with being shot down. "The Cohort would have to unanimously agree to meeting her first. I thought I could just present it as an option. If they say no, we won't do it."

"I'm saying no."

"You don't have veto power." Tessa was incredulous; it was unlike Luke to disagree with her like this. Their INR-View disagreement was one thing—he had the backing of the doctors there, so Tessa was willing to concede—but this was a nonclinical issue, just between the two of them. He never simply said no to an idea of hers.

"It's a bad idea. You're not thinking clearly. It must be the late flight."

Now Tessa was mad. "That's patronizing, Luke. I'm thinking perfectly clearly. I've been thinking about it for days, in fact. Perhaps *you* should take a day to think it over, instead of dismissing it with a knee-jerk reaction."

"I'm not jerking any knees. It would just be an obvious mistake to bring an agitated college student to the Trial. Irresponsible, actually."

"Her agitation is logical. This would help relieve it. Don't be afraid of female emotion, Luke. This is the reason you have issues with Gwen."

Luke held up a palm, as if to fend Tessa off. She had the urge to slap it down. "It would be an irresponsible mistake. We can revisit the idea later. But for right now, I'm done discussing it."

"I'm not done. I think we should at least present the id—"

He cut her off. "Irresponsible. Mistake."

"I'm shocked at how you're behaving, Luke. What's going on? You never dismiss me like this. Just tell me what you're really thinking."

He met Tessa's eyes, but there was a hardness in his gaze. He was not really seeing her.

"Mistakes have consequences," he said, speaking slowly. "You've made them. I've made them. Let's know better. Okay?"

It sounded vaguely threatening. Tessa sat silently, holding Luke's eyes, waiting for him to soften.

He did not soften. She stood from the terrible chair and walked out of the room.

21.

Tessa was almost shaking as she crossed the footbridge from Luke's office in West Lobe to the Cohort's residence in East. She stopped for a minute in the center of the clear tube, staring into the soaring space below, watching the movement of employees and steadying her breath.

Tessa was accustomed to handling him: his fragile ego, his mood swings, his resentment of famous peers. She tolerated him because, as unalike as they were, more than a decade apart and at different stages of life, she felt a primal kinship with him. What most people saw as Luke's grandiosity, Tessa knew was a genuine desire to change the world with technology. To take risks in order to accomplish that change; risks that most people would not dream of taking.

She'd felt this way from the first time they'd met, back on the hay bales in his converted garage-office in San Francisco. After they'd discussed the potential ZimLabz-Seahorse merger, Luke eased from his hay bale down onto the IKEA carpet, saying he just needed to stretch out for a minute. It felt completely natural for Tessa to lie down next to him and arrange herself inside the long loop of his arms. His body felt like a single tensile muscle against her softer frame. Pure youth. He was still in jeans but had removed his hoodie to reveal a white T-shirt that could have been cleaner.

It was there, on the floor, that Luke had asked her the question. She'd been expecting him to kiss her, but instead he'd murmured into her ear, "So what's your deal, Tessa?"

"What?"

"Your deal with Seahorse? I get that you want to make women's lives easier. But where does your own life factor in? If that's not getting too personal."

"This already feels rather personal," Tessa had said. Her head, after all, had been resting on his chest.

"So tell me."

And she'd told him.

That she'd been pregnant once, accidentally, in her twenties, during her second year of business school at Stanford. She was a different person then. The sort of young woman who'd been terribly impressed by the man who'd come to Stanford to deliver a speech on collateral pools, a Swiss structured-finance guru, decorated with AGEUS and Manheim prizes, degrees from Oxford and Cambridge, then a post at the London School of Economics. He had finger-length gray sideburns, plus a wife and two children back in Switzerland. After the lecture, there had been a party. The structured-finance guru held court, radiating an arrogance that Tessa found repulsive and thrilling. She'd spent the first half of the party captivated by his diatribe on the World Bank, and the second half arguing with him while he kept summoning a server to refill their glasses of Bordeaux. At 1:00 a.m., Tessa let the professor take her hand. She could recall almost nothing of the night except for the grip of his fingers, the chirp-chirp of the luxury car into which he'd ushered her after several drunken attempts to unlock it, and later, trying to breathe against the crisp hotel sheets as he pushed her facedown into the mattress, grunting over her, pushing himself into her.

In the morning, when she'd woken with a slamming headache and her underpants in a ball on the floor, she could hardly remember anything from the night before. She rushed to the bathroom and vomited. How could she have let this happen? How could she have made such a clichéd, sloppy, stupid mistake?

She vowed not to think of the Swiss professor. She cleaned herself up, took a hot shower, and went to class.

But then, a few weeks later, her period did not show up.

The weeks before she miscarried were the most miserable of her life. She was nauseated around the clock, vomiting until she dry heaved, barely able to drag herself out of bed. Her grades had suffered dangerously.

She'd never told anyone about it. Until she told Luke.

"I suppose the experience factored into my motivation for Seahorse," she had said, trying to control the tremor in her voice. "In a generalized way."

Luke had nodded. "You took control back from him. In a big way. You took it back and handed it over to women at large."

"Yes." Tessa had felt herself begin to smile.

"That, Callahan, is fucking awesome."

That he'd called her by her last name felt intimate. Affectionate.

"Now it all makes sense," he'd said, stroking her head. "I'm glad you told me the whole truth."

She moved her face closer to his, but he turned his head, slightly but meaningfully, in the other direction. This discombobulated her. She returned her head to his chest, her face burning with embarrassment.

What had just happened?

Luke drifted off to sleep, his arm still slung across her. When his breath deepened, Tessa extracted herself, stood up, and fumbled for her shoes and coat in the dimness of the room, dizzy with a collision of feeling, none of which she could precisely identify. She was confused and horrified and exhilarated, all at once. The g-word would come later. At the time, she'd felt a sort of dangerous high.

Luke woke up just as she opened the door to leave, blinking at her from the floor.

"Drive safely," he said. "And call me tomorrow. We're going to work together."

"We're not," she said.

But of course, they did. Neither ever mentioned the night on the floor. It was as if she'd never confessed the story of the Swiss professor, as if they'd never lain together on the floor in each other's arms, carpet fibers digging into their skin.

Sometimes, though, Tessa felt Luke conjure it. She sometimes felt he was using it, subtly but clearly, against her. Using it to remind her that he had special knowledge of her that no one else possessed—not even Peter.

Remembering that night with Luke made her cringe. Sometimes, if she let herself linger on it, she wanted to scream. At him. At herself. It shouldn't have happened.

She wished she'd told Peter about her miscarriage. But the timing hadn't seemed right and now it felt too late.

It didn't matter, she told herself, stepping off the footbridge and into an elevator of East Lobe. Peter did not need to know every misstep of her youth. The story of the Swiss professor would only upset him. It had happened twenty years ago. She was a completely different person now, a much better one.

As for Luke, she was not sure.

22.

Later, after she'd visited the Cohort, marveled over the twin hills of Kate's and LaTonya's pregnant bellies, and detected the hint of a smile on Gwen's lips as she rested her hand on her own swollen stomach, Tessa returned to her own room. She sat in the chair beside the window looking out at the bluffs and the churning Pacific beyond, barely visible through the shroud of fog that had blown in. Seeing the Cohort had heartened her after the unpleasant discussion with Luke. Nothing mattered more than the success of their pregnancies, and that all three of them were progressing so well thrilled Tessa. Their tiny babies, now the size of lemons, were healthy, but as importantly, so were their mothers—both their bodies *and* minds. Yes, the Seahorse clinical staff was responsible for the elegance of the technology behind the Trial, but Tessa was responsible for the strength of their spirits.

Which, she thought to herself, was more than Luke could say.

She continued to sit at the window, watching the fog thicken over the water. Then she reached for her phone and called Peter. Straight to voice mail, as expected. The last time she'd spoken to him, from Boston, he'd told her he was headed to some spectacular climb that required a backcountry hike, and that he might be out of range for several days.

But she just wanted to hear the sound of his recorded voice.

Peter Grandwein's robot here. Please leave a message for my master.

"I know you're deep in the wild," she said to his voice mail, feeling a lump begin to form in her throat. "But I just wanted to tell you I'm especially missing you right now. And that when we're back together, I'm going to be . . ." She lost her direction and faltered. "Just . . . better. Okay? I love you."

Next, she tapped out a message.

To: vivian.bourne@weldon.edu
Subj: Following up

Dear Vivian,

It was a pleasure speaking with you on campus last Sunday. I wanted to follow up with an invitation to contact me personally anytime, and also to visit the offices of Seahorse Solutions. I think you would enjoy a firsthand look at the work we're doing here. Let me know if you have any interest, and Seahorse would be more than happy to provide a plane ticket. I'm including my number below; feel free to use it.

Best wishes,
Tessa Callahan

Outside, the branches of the Monterey pines whipped seaward with a sudden breeze. Tessa wondered if it might actually rain. The sky perennially threatened it, but rarely delivered. Real rain would be nice for a change, she thought, as she tapped "Send."

PART THREE

While a degree of vulnerability is crucial to building trust and rapport with your direct reports, coworkers, or supervisors, be aware that too much vulnerability can allow your colleagues to feel power over you, thereby creating a precarious imbalance in your professional ecosystem.

—*Tessa Callahan,* Pushing Through: A Handbook for Young Women in the New World

23.

O n a scale of one to ten," said LaTonya, "how miserable is everyone's itching?" She pulled a glazed doughnut in half and bit into it.

Tessa sat with the Cohort, a bowl of steel-cut oatmeal with blueberries in front of her, while the other women ate eggs and pastry and bacon. The Cohort was just past the midpoint of their pregnancies: 4.7 weeks in, the equivalent of twenty-one weeks in a conventional pregnancy. The babies were growing at a steady clip, causing an intensified itching in their mothers that cream could no longer control.

"Seven point five," said Kate stoically. Tessa noticed that although she never complained, Kate had begun to look a bit miserable at the midpoint of her pregnancy, her fair skin blotchy and sprinkled with acne at her cheeks, like a teenager's. Her trim body and angular bone structure had changed rapidly as her belly grew, her strong chin softened and doubled seemingly overnight. The NauseAway had been effective in the early stages of pregnancy, less so as it advanced.

They'd need to improve upon this in the next iteration, Tessa thought. The women should feel good every day.

She turned to Kate. "Sorry about the itching."

"It's fine," said Kate.

"You look wonderful, though," Tessa added. "So healthy."

"And by *healthy* you must mean *fat as a house*," said Kate, sighing.

"Don't be ridiculous," said Tessa.

"My itch score's a twelve," said Gwen. "I never stop itching."

"Invalid rating," said LaTonya. "Maximum's ten. I'm with Kate in the 7.5 zone."

Gwen leaned toward the center of the table, the ends of her two braids brushing its surface, and pushed her plate. In contrast to Kate, Tessa thought, pregnancy suited Gwen: wrinkles seemed to have disappeared from her skin, and her gray hair had acquired more shine.

"Has anyone felt movement?" Gwen asked. "Any kicks?"

"Yes!" said Kate. "It just started the day before yesterday. A sort of rippling sensation."

"Like a wingbeat?" said Gwen.

"Yes." Kate nodded. "Exactly."

"I've got flutters," said LaTonya. "So faint that I thought it might just be gas. Because I've got plenty of that. But now I think it might actually be kicking."

"Guess what?" said Gwen, a note of rueful triumph in her voice. "I actually don't feel anything. Not a ripple, not a flutter, not a wingbeat, *nothing*. That's why I asked you two about it. Because now is when the kicking's supposed to begin, isn't it? Right around twenty-two weeks. But nothing's happening here." She hovered her palm over her belly.

"Of course something is happening," said Tessa. "*Many* things are happening inside you, right this second. Your baby is actively developing as we sit here."

"I don't know," said Gwen, somewhat cryptically.

"Sure you know," said Tessa. "You see the ultrasounds every morning. I see them, too. You're having a perfect pregnancy."

"I just started feeling the kicks two days ago," said LaTonya. "Don't sweat it, Gwenners. Every woman starts to feel movement at different times."

"I think I should be feeling something." Gwen's voice rose an octave. "I'm feeling nothing. *Nothing*."

"Conventionally pregnant women often don't feel anything until twenty-five weeks or even later," said Tessa patiently. "Your baby is just developing at a slightly different rate than the others, Gwen. It's completely normal."

"It doesn't *feel* normal," said Gwen. "You can spout all the reassurance you want, but it's not going to make me feel better."

Tessa was taken aback by Gwen's sudden harshness. She changed tack. "Worrying is completely understandable. You've all been so brave through this process. It's inevitable that anxieties will flare occasionally. Just keep talking about them, and they'll pass."

"I didn't realize you were my therapist," said Gwen.

"Hey," said Kate defensively. "Tessa's just trying to help."

"It's okay, Gwen," said Tessa. "I'm not pregnant. I can see how my reassurance feels flimsy. But don't trust me. Trust your body. Trust the immense trove of brainpower that created TEAT."

"I'm trying," said Gwen. She'd stopped eating but still clenched her fork in her right hand.

"We understand," said Kate, putting her hands on Gwen's arm. "It's okay to freak out a little."

Gwen fell silent, staring at her fork. "I guess it's not just the kicking," she mumbled.

"What is it, then?" said Tessa softly.

"Lately, when Gupta does my ultrasound, I have this weird gut feeling—" She faltered.

"Go on, honey," said LaTonya.

"It's going to sound crazy."

"Try us," said Tessa. "There will be no judgment from this table."

"This weird gut feeling that . . . something's not right with my baby."

"Did you ask Gupta?" said Kate. "She's standing right there next to you, holding the wand, isn't she?"

"Of course," said Gwen. "She says everything's fine. It's just a feeling I have. Logically I know it makes no sense, but it just keeps getting stronger with every morning exam."

Poor Gwen, thought Tessa. "Your body is in the throes of enormous hormonal changes right now. It affects every part of you, including your brain. Your emotions. I'm not dismissing this worry you're having, but I do want to remind you that your biochemistry affects your thoughts."

"Isn't that another way of saying I'm just another histrionic pregnant woman, not to be trusted?"

Tessa could see there was no way to win.

"Tessa would never say that," Kate cut in. "Come on, Gwen. You've read *Pushing Through*."

Tessa was touched by Kate's loyalty.

"Perhaps this is a matter of control, Gwen," she said.

"Control?"

"Yes. Being in the Seahorse Trial has required a total relinquishing of control on the part of you three." Tessa panned her hand around the table. "You've turned your pregnancies over to Seahorse. You sleep here. You eat here. You check in with our doctors three times a day. It's up to them to report what's happening inside you."

"True," said Gwen.

"And now that Kate and LaTonya are directly experiencing symptoms of their pregnancies, in the movement of their babies, and you're not, perhaps it feels like they've gained some direct access to their experience that you don't yet have."

"Yes," said Gwen, nodding slowly. "I guess that's part of it, yes."

Tessa could feel Gwen's anger lifting. She made a decision on the spot.

"I'm going to distribute your INR-Views. I think being able to administer your own ultrasounds, in private, without a doctor hovering and collecting data, is going to make each of you feel more connected to your babies." She turned to Gwen. "And I think it will make you feel more secure in your baby's progress, until you start feeling those kicks. Which you *will*, any day now."

"I thought protocol was that we weren't getting the INRs until the equivalent of third trimester," said Kate. "Not until seven and a half weeks. That's what Milford and Gupta keep telling us."

"Well," said Tessa. "I just changed protocol."

"You're a badass," said LaTonya. "I love it."

Tessa heard Gwen let out a breath and watched her release the fork she'd been clenching. Tessa smiled to herself.

"In fact," she went on, "I'll have them to you by tomorrow. We'll do a quick training session around . . ." She pulled out her phone to check her calendar. "Four p.m. Sound good?"

Around the table, the women of Cohort One nodded at Tessa. Even Gwen, who was suddenly smiling.

~

"Callahan, Tessa. Authorized to proceed."

Zeus unlocked the door to Medical Supply Room D, down in the basement of East Lobe, and Tessa stepped inside. The room was chilly and smelled faintly of rubbing alcohol. D was where some of the most expensive devices at the Center were kept, a windowless rectangle with sheet tile floors and rows of brushed metal cabinets lining the walls. Fluorescent lighting automatically ticked on, making Tessa feel exposed and edgy. She reminded herself she had no reason to be nervous. The INR-Views were here at the Center only because *she* had singlehandedly won the bid with its inventor, John Kwak. The device had still been in prototype phase when she approached him. Kwak was reluctant to release it for clinical use in the Trial. The wands were the size of a toothbrush and exceptionally powerful, allowing a user to see inside a body with startling 3-D clarity. Kwak believed the INRs would eventually disrupt the entire field of radiology. He did not want to unveil them until he felt they were perfect. Tessa had convinced him that affiliation with the Seahorse Trial could be the greatest PR he'd ever encounter. By the end of several long meetings, Tessa had won him over. Kwak agreed to supply the Trial with four INR-View prototypes. They'd finally arrived at the Center just yesterday, an alert from the mail room had informed Tessa, and were being stored in drawer #16 of a metal cabinet in Supply Room D.

But when Tessa unlocked drawer #16, the wands were not inside it. Instead, she found only a slip of white paper. Printed on it was INR-View™ patented prototypes 201–204 recalled for impaired functionality by manufacturer, Kwak Innovations, contact John Kwak MD, PhD.

Tessa was stunned. Kwak was *her* contact. Why would he have issued a recall request to anyone else at Seahorse?

She went straight to Luke's office, where she found him sitting at his desk, feet propped atop it, listening intently to something through wireless headphones. He did not notice her standing in front of him until she waved her hand in front of his face. Luke started and pulled off his headphones. Tessa didn't bother with a greeting.

"Why didn't you tell me the INR-Views were recalled?"

He shrugged.

"Kwak never wanted them shipped out in the first place, but his assistant jumped the gun. Kwak wanted to update you personally, but he couldn't get in touch. You were busy with the Boston stuff. Then you were busy with the Cohort. So he reached out to me."

"I'm almost always reachable, Luke."

"Well, in that moment, when Kwak was especially worked up, you weren't. He was intent on getting them back in his hands a-sap to replace the sensors. Evidently the ones on the prototypes he sent us are crap compared to the ones his team just released."

"I'm calling him," said Tessa. "He promised we'd have them. The Cohort is slated to begin using them in eight days."

Luke shrugged. "Go ahead."

When she got Kwak on the phone, his tone was clipped, and he corroborated everything Luke said. But he wouldn't commit to a date for replacing the INRs.

When they're ready, he said. *When they're accurate and reliable enough for your Cohort to use. These things are like my babies. I can't send them out into the world until I can stand behind them. Surely, Tessa, you understand the need for the highest standards here.*

Reluctantly, she understood.

~

"Hang on, hang on, let me get to a better spot."

In Tessa's ear, Peter's voice flicked in and out of static. They'd finally connected on the phone, but his reception on the trail was spotty.

"How about now?" he said.

"Better," said Tessa. "Finally. *Hi.*"

"My long-lost wife."

"You're the one who's lost. That must be some serious wilderness you're hiking through. I miss your voice."

"This trip is incredible, Tess." He sounded breathless. "I can't even begin to describe it. Each day we discover something more breathtaking than the last. These vast meadows full of Technicolor flowers. Herds of mountain goats. And of course the views . . . I met up with some experienced climbers, so we've been getting to some really high elevation. There's snow on the peaks. Yesterday we got this view of Crater Lake that was just . . ." He trailed off.

"Sounds amazing. I hope you're taking lots of pictures. How are Eric and Dalton?"

"Actually, they were struggling. With the altitude and the physical challenges. So they exited out of Summit Lake a few days ago. I'm going to keep heading north and fly home out of Portland eventually."

"Eventually?"

"I'm having the time of my life, Tessa. It's really . . . intense. Transformative. And since you're still tied up with the Trial I don't see the rush to get back."

"Of course. Take your time. So you're hiking alone now?"

There was a pause. "No. I met those climbers I mentioned, so we're hiking together. A bunch of Oregonians who do this together every few years. The PCT is a weirdly communal experience, considering you're in the middle of this vast wilderness."

"I'm glad you're having such a fantastic experience." She couldn't help feeling left out, though she knew she had no right to. "I'm having a rather intense experience myself."

"Oh? How's the Trial?"

The question came too casually; he could have been asking her about a meal.

"Successful. Not without its challenges, but a net positive so far." She'd planned to tell him everything—about her frustrations with Luke and the INR-View and Gwen Harris's difficult personality, but something held her back.

"I'm sure it'll be a huge hit," said Peter. "You'll probably be exponentially more famous by the time I get back."

"That's not a part of it," said Tessa, irritated. "But I do think we're on the way to making some breakthroughs that are going to have a major impact."

"Of course you are," said Peter. "I'm so proud. Oh, sorry, hang on."

Tessa heard a windy sound in the phone and muffled voices in the background.

"Sorry, honey, I have to get going. We have limited daylight until we have to make camp."

"Text me with your return date," said Tessa, her throat suddenly tightening. She didn't want to hang up yet. "You'll come straight up to the Center when you're back, right?"

"Of course," said Peter.

"I love you," said Tessa.

"Love you, too," said Peter. Static rasped the connection, and then he was gone.

~

At dinner with the Cohort that evening, Tessa had planned to lighten the mood. Gwen's concern over her baby's lack of movement had created an air of mild anxiety among the group, and Tessa wanted to change it. Part of her job was to keep the group optimistic and in good spirits. She'd planned to ask each of the women to share a story about her childhood; they'd spoken little of the distant past.

But when the four of them had settled around the table with poached salmon over asparagus risotto, Tessa found she wasn't in the mood to facilitate conversation. Her phone call with Peter had left her out of sorts. She took a bite of fish; it was delicious, like all the meals served during the Trial.

"How's Peter, Tessa?" said Kate, out of nowhere. "You haven't mentioned him lately." As if she'd read Tessa's mind.

"It's interesting you ask," said Tessa. "I just spoke to him this afternoon. He's having a very intense experience hiking the Pacific Crest Trail."

"Don't you get tired of people saying things are *intense*?" said Gwen. "It's right up there with *amazing*."

Tessa couldn't help laughing. "You're right. But I think he's sincere. He finds a lot of . . . meaning in nature. He's always loved to hike and ride his bike in the mountains."

"Do you?" asked LaTonya. "Find meaning in nature? Because no offense, but nature sort of bores the shit out of me. I mean, I love a pretty beach as much as the next person, but I'm more indoorsy."

"Honestly"—Tessa took a sip of sparkling water—"no. I'm not especially drawn to the natural world."

"What are you drawn to?" asked Gwen. "Where does Tessa Callahan find her sources of meaning?"

"Well," said Tessa. "In people, I suppose. And in ideas."

"What about something more concrete?" said Gwen.

"You're tough, Gwen," said Kate.

"In *this*." Tessa gestured around the room. "In the concrete manifestations of ideas."

"Pretty lofty," said Gwen. "I was thinking more of like a hobby."

"I wish," said Tessa. "I haven't found time for hobbies."

"Me neither," said Kate. "I read and watch TV and that's it. God, I'm so boring. But there never seems to be time."

"Have you noticed men always do, though?" LaTonya said. "No matter how busy they are, they always find time for their extracurriculars. Their video games, their sports, their collections."

Kate nodded. "Zimmerman hunts, doesn't he? And teaches himself Mandarin."

"Luke? Yes," said Tessa. "I mean, he only hunts nuisance populations that he can eat nose to tail. Deer and rabbit, I think. I don't know how far the Mandarin went, but he does kite surf quite a bit."

"Whatever the fuck that is," said LaTonya.

"Or maybe it's Ultimate Frisbee now," said Tessa. "Plus some competitive chess."

"But no girlfriend," said LaTonya.

"Or boyfriend," said Gwen.

"Neither," said Tessa. "His behavior is conventionally gendered. Externally facing. Action-oriented. Lower emphasis on relationships."

"I feel sorry for men," said Gwen. "And coming from a lesbian who doesn't particularly like them, that's saying a lot."

"Why sorry?" said Kate. "My ex-husband and his buddies are the luckiest people on earth. They do whatever the hell they want, pretty much all the time, with zero guilt. That includes hobbies and plenty of sex."

"Bitter much?" said LaTonya.

"Maybe," said Kate. "But I definitely don't feel sorry for him."

"They're just always searching," Gwen went on. "I actually think that conventional gender model you mentioned is pretty accurate for most men. It's not their fault. It's all because they can't get pregnant."

"What do you mean?" asked Tessa.

"Well, pregnancy and motherhood are universally acknowledged as accomplishments. As big milestones in a woman's life."

"Not in half of Africa," said LaTonya.

"Fine. Let's talk about the United States. No matter how empowered women are, no matter how badass their careers are, no matter how much money they make, those things are second-tier achievements."

"What?" Tessa said, startled. "Second tier?"

"Yes," said Gwen. "Motherhood is the first tier. I don't care if it sounds outrageous. You know it's true. A woman without a career is considered weird, sure, but secretly, most people think a woman without children is weirder."

"That's insane," said Kate. "That's not true at all."

"Actually, voluntary childlessness has held a steady percentage in the United States—around six percent—for the last twenty years," said Tessa. "But that's not to say I agree with you, Gwen."

"Let me put it another way," said Gwen, sounding more enthused than Tessa could remember hearing her. "The achievement"—she air-quoted the word—"of motherhood is available to most women. Some are infertile, sure, but most aren't. And once you've had a baby, you are a legitimate woman in this society."

"Bullshit," said LaTonya. "You need money. You need to join a certain class. Ideally you should be white. Straight. Et cetera. You're sounding sort of crazy, Gwen, and I—"

"I completely agree with you," said Gwen. "But those factors are separate from my point. All I'm saying is, most women are biologically, inherently equipped to succeed at growing another human being inside themselves, and then releasing it out into the world. Almost no one, except people who are mean or lying to themselves, doesn't think that's a cool, respectable thing to be able to do."

"Whereas men don't have that preprogrammed power," said Tessa.

"Exactly," said Gwen. "They have to start from scratch. They have to prove their worth by starting wars and making money and creating companies and . . ."

"Hiking extreme mountain trails," said LaTonya, patting Tessa on the arm, and everyone laughed.

"All I'm saying is," said Gwen, "women are born with a superpower. Men aren't as lucky."

"To our superpower," said LaTonya lightly, raising her water glass. Gwen and Kate lifted theirs and clinked. Tessa did not. She felt anger creeping through her like an allergic reaction.

"Fatherhood is profound," said Tessa. "You can't dismiss it."

"You know a lot of successful men, Tessa. How many successful men have you heard say, *Fatherhood is my greatest accomplishment?*"

"None," said Tessa.

"Fatherhood is an accessory status," said Gwen. "A minor upgrade. For women, motherhood is a breakthrough. It signifies having *arrived*."

"Speak for yourself," said Kate. "I've always been much closer to my father than my mother."

"There are always exceptions," said Gwen.

"I think your point has been taken, Gwen," said Tessa. "It's an interesting, highly simplified point of view."

"No need to patronize," said Gwen. "Just because I didn't write a book on gender and culture doesn't mean I don't have opinions."

"What's your deal tonight, Gwenners?" said LaTonya, always the diffuser of tension. "You're kind of on your soapbox, lady."

"I despise the word *lady*," said Gwen, but she smiled.

"Right up there with *intense* and *amazing*," said LaTonya, and Kate laughed.

Tessa did not.

"I saw there's key lime pie for dessert," said Kate, standing. "Anyone want to go take a look with me?"

LaTonya and Gwen stood, too.

"I'll pass," said Tessa. "I'm going to take a walk." She was still tingling with agitation.

"Look, Tessa, I'm sorry if I offended you," said Gwen. "I was just rambling. It's just something I've been thinking about. It's probably the hormones." She hovered her hands over her protruding belly. "I got worked up."

"No apology necessary," said Tessa.

Outside, the night was moonless and foggy, the outdoor lights along the footpaths blotted to a dim, smeared glow. Tessa followed the trail to the bluffs, shivering as she walked; she'd left the dining room of East Lobe without bothering to stop in her room for a jacket. But the conversation at dinner had left her full of negative electricity. Defensiveness. It had taken all her restraint not to yell, *Look at this place. Look at your bellies. Look at your lives. It's all because of me.*

How dare Gwen imply that the Cohort had a *superpower* that Tessa did not have? That her achievements were *second tier*?

Reaching the bluffs, she picked up a piece of driftwood and hurled it as hard as she could over the cliff and into the dark sea.

24.

Wayne counted to ten between reps and then began another set of bicep curls. He would pull this off, he thought. Over the hour since he'd arrived at the gym, a basement-level Dolphin Fitness on Marlborough Street, he'd located a new confidence about his situation. This was what he liked about working out: the sense of potency it gave him. The burn of the lactic acid in his muscles cleared away his doubts. The endorphins proffered optimism. Neither would last much beyond his postworkout shower, but he'd take what he could get. It would take every inner resource he possessed, every ounce of resolve, for him to complete Viv's importation.

It had been ten days since his presentation review at the Colony. The Inner Panel was getting impatient. Borlav was calling him daily, demanding an ETA. Wayne kept insisting the time was not yet right to move her. But he could not put it off much longer.

He finished biceps and moved to triceps extensions. The gym, which he'd chosen specifically for its windowless setting and no-frills offerings—plenty of free weights, minimal elliptical machines—was mostly empty on Saturday afternoon. A couple of beefy steroidal dudes, grunting through their reps, a whippet-thin older woman on one of the creaky treadmills. The air was perfumed with stale socks and bleachy cleaning product. The rest of the world was outside, enjoying the late-spring sunshine. Wayne kept his earbuds in and the volume of his music high.

He'd chosen a playlist of old-school punk and speed metal, enough cacophony to stomp any infiltrating skeptical thoughts. Normally he stuck to rootsier music, the classic country and rock that Viv teased him about, but plangent guitar and driving refrains were too indulgent for his current frame of mind. He could not let himself think too much about the task in front of him. He simply had to do it: to deliver Viv to the Colony with as little trauma as possible. To summon all the field-op qualities he'd spent the past nineteen-plus years honing—focus, commitment, imperturbability, distance—and deliver Viv to the Colony with minimal trauma. From there, he would have to step aside and let the Revision Team do its work. Hopefully, she would have the sense to comply. Hopefully, she would not be as stubborn as Irene.

Imagining all of it made him feel ill all over. Made him want to weep.

He turned his music up louder. Black Sabbath and Motorhead, with some Sex Pistols and punkier stuff mixed in, made him feel, momentarily, that he was transmitting a collective, triumphant *fuck you* to his employer. That he had a team behind him. Ozzy and Johnny Rotten and Lemmy and him. Together, they were weakening Wayne's shackles. As if those old recorded voices had specific loyalty to Wayne. As if, when they spewed lines like *Don't try to reach me / 'Cause I'd tear up your mind / I've seen the future / And I've left it behind*, they were screaming at Borlav and Winger and the whole goddamn Agency.

In the old days, Wayne had felt an oncoming thrill as an importation approached, the way he'd heard the FBI looked forward to stings. After so much covert effort, action was a relief, even if his feelings about it were complicated. He'd always been able to summon a separation from his PITs when it was time to actually bring them to the Colony. Irene had been hardest, but he'd gotten through it.

It was always the first moments in which a PIT realized he'd been deceived that were hardest. The utter disbelief that he—Henry Duarte, or Wayne Bridger, or whoever he'd claimed to be—had lied to them. That he was taking them to an unknown place, against their will. Their comprehension of this was sickening; he could *feel* it settle over them. Long ago, this moment had thrilled Wayne. As he watched his PIT try to process the information, he had experienced an infusion of power.

Now he was ashamed he'd ever felt that way.

I'm taking you somewhere you need to be, he'd tell his PITs. *A safe, secluded place. You can resist, or you can cooperate, but the outcome will be the same.*

Irene had cooperated, but the look in her eyes had nearly killed him. *I'm taking you somewhere you need to be. A safe, secluded place. You can resist, or you can cooperate, but the outcome will be the same.* Her face had changed when he delivered the line *You are now in custody of the United States government,* suggesting a deep internal shock, the way he imagined a baby might react if he looked up from the arms of his mother to see the person holding him was not his mother at all.

What? Irene had said. *What? What? What?* Like a record with a stuck needle, the same single syllable, over and over.

He couldn't imagine doing this to Viv. He could not pass through that moment and land on the other side of it, in some cold, detached place. But he had no choice. The alternative was sacrificing the second half of his life to the ISA and whatever penalties they inflicted on him.

It would not be pretty.

After Irene, he'd felt so fucked up about importations that he'd gone to one of the ISA therapists, though he didn't believe in therapy. The woman had pinned-up blond hair and a blue couch in her office, where he sat and babbled, hating himself as he talked about the despair he'd felt when importing Irene, how it lingered for months on end, relentless.

Let yourself be in that place, the therapist had said. *That place of despair. What you are experiencing is compassion for your PIT. I've worked with serial killers and assassins, Mr. Theroux, and if I can get them to conjure that place of pain over and over, then I know we are on the road to progress.*

Her words had snapped Wayne right out of his moment of "compassion."

I'm not a serial killer, you cunt, he'd said to the therapist. Her mouth formed a perfect O. He'd gotten up from the couch and walked out of the room.

~

Wayne moved to the leg press, racked a few more fifty-pound plates on each side, settled onto the bench. Then he lifted his legs up against the platform in a squat position and pushed it forward. His quads said no. He pulled in air through his nostrils and pushed harder. Slowly the platform ascended. One rep. Two. His quads caught fire. Breathe. That was what everyone prescribed for everything: *breathe.* As if it were a choice. He got through five reps and then lay panting on the bench. Shit. Having a girlfriend had left him out of shape. He'd barely noticed, from day to day. That was how it worked, with physical decline. You pretended it wasn't happening, until one day you were forced to confront it.

Viv's progressions, as of now, were moderate. Some changes in skin tone, some gray in her hair, which he noticed she'd camouflaged with dye. He wasn't sure if she was troubled by the gray. She hadn't mentioned it to him, which hurt—did she think he'd care? Break up with her? As if it mattered remotely. As if it would affect the way he felt about her.

But he knew she was aware of her changes. He read her posts to the private LikeMe group she ran, the CleftKids. Along with Borlav and Winger and a half dozen others on the Inner Panel of the ISA. The posts were what had doomed her. They made the Inner Panel nervous. She wasn't buying the "indeterminate" cause of AG, and eventually, they surmised from her posts, she would cause trouble.

When he thought of them separate from their grim consequences, Viv's posts made Wayne proud. She was smarter than all of them. Eventually, he bet, she would get to the bottom of this herself. He grabbed a blue foam mat from a stack in the corner and lay on top of it for crunches. When he hit two hundred, his abdominal muscles were searing and Johnny Rotten was screaming in his ears, *Eat your heart out on a plastic tray / You don't do what you want, then you'll fade away / You won't find me working nine to five / It's too much fun being alive.*

He flipped over for push-ups, adding a barbell for the ascent. It hurt like hell. He finished five sets and sat on the ground, catching his breath. He'd done enough, but felt reluctant to leave the underground solitude of the gym for the bright afternoon above, where he'd be forced to deal with his obligations.

He started a final set of weighted push-ups. He wanted it to hurt until he couldn't stand it. He braced and took a deep breath, then lowered to the ground.

He could do this. One last importation, and then this misery would be over, and he'd be free.

Except it would be replaced with a new sort of misery: life without Viv.

Twenty-one, twenty-two, twenty-three. Fuck. The push-ups hurt. The burn was deep and good.

Maybe there was another way.

25.

Tessa and Kate sat in Adirondack chairs in the shade of an avocado tree in the Seahorse garden. Kate had propped her feet on a wooden ottoman—her ankles had swollen so much that her lower legs looked like clubs. The women of Cohort One were required to spend at least thirty minutes daily in the private garden, cordoned off from the rest of the campus by thick hedges, for vitamin D. Tessa liked to keep Kate company while she met her quota.

"I think I'm down to either Eleanor or Harriet," said Kate to Tessa. "Partially as in Roosevelt and Beecher Stowe. Partially because I just like old-fashioned names."

"I vote Harriet," said Tessa.

Kate lifted her maternity shirt, baring her orbed belly, now the size of a desk globe at seven weeks, the equivalent of about thirty-two conventional weeks. "She should start bucking around in there any second now. It always happens about ten minutes after I eat. Here, come closer."

Tessa maneuvered her chair to face Kate and stared at her belly.

"Put your hand right here." Kate patted a spot on her right side below her rib cage. Tessa placed her palm over it. Kate's skin was taut and warm.

"Close your eyes," said Kate. "I know it sounds froofy, but she's more comfortable showing off when she's not being stared at. I think that's just her personality. Understated. Not a performer."

"So you already know her," said Tessa.

"Absolutely," said Kate.

Tessa closed her eyes and jealousy bloomed instantly in her chest. Recently, as she grew closer to the Cohort, touched them often, learned the details of their pregnant bodies—even Gwen's, whose stomach had grown enormous, the largest of the three—a sorrow-tinged envy had started to grow inside Tessa. It came and went, sometimes undetectable, but other times, like now, as she waited for Kate's baby to kick, it throbbed like a fresh bruise.

She missed Peter. He would return from his hike, finally, next week, but it seemed too far away. She imagined what he would look like now, after six weeks in the wilderness. Probably full bearded, grime mooning his fingernails, all of his plaid shirts spattered with mud. She thought of Python, perhaps tougher and more wolflike now.

She couldn't wait to see him, to touch him, to be back in their bed together.

Then she felt it: a knobby twitch beneath her hand. The feeling of bone rising up to meet her hand, then retreating again, like a darting fish. Instinctively, Tessa's eyes flew open and appraised Kate's belly, but the baby had already quieted.

Kate grinned at her.

"You felt that, didn't you?" She dropped her shirt back over her belly.

Tessa tried to answer, but found there was a lump blocking her throat.

"Hey," said Kate, noticing. She took Tessa's hand in her own. Tears began behind Tessa's eyes and she tried to swallow them away.

"Why don't you just do it?" Kate said softly. "Why don't you and Peter just have a baby?"

Tessa stared at a bed of chrysanthemums, her hand still in Kate's, struggling to get a hold of herself. "I never really wanted one," she said. The Swiss professor's face, his aquiline nose and long sideburns, suddenly flashed to her mind, and she felt she might be sick. She inhaled deeply, pushing the image from her mind. His face retreated, but her nausea lingered.

"Why not?" asked Kate. "For practical reasons, or philosophical, or . . ." She trailed off.

"Neither. It was more gut-level. Not all women have the pull. It's an exception to the rule, but I was one of them."

"I believe you," said Kate.

"But then I met Peter, and he wanted to be a father. Badly. I became open to the idea. Not consumed by it, just open. But we couldn't get pregnant. We exhausted every option."

Kate was quiet. Then she said, "That seems especially cruel."

"Cruel?" Tessa straightened in her chair, having regained control of herself.

"Well, to be unable to get pregnant, when you're dedicating your career to reproductive technology."

Tessa shrugged. "I've never really viewed it that way. My private life is separate from my work."

Kate searched Tessa's eyes. "Is it really?"

From the grass beneath her chair, Tessa's phone chimed. She leaned over and picked it up, grateful for the interruption, hoping the message was from Peter. She hadn't heard from him in days.

But the text was from Vivian Bourne. Tessa was surprised; she'd emailed Viv weeks ago and heard nothing back.

Tessa, sorry for the delayed response. I've been tied up with finals, ugh. Hope texting you here is OK, I don't use email much. Thanks for your offer to visit Seahorse. I'd love to take you up on it. I graduate next month and plan to head to my parents' in SoCal for the summer. Maybe I could come to Seahorse at the beginning of June, before graduation? Let me know what logistics are like on your end and again, thanks for the generous offer.

"Everything okay?" said Kate.

"Just fine," said Tessa. "Remember how I talked to you and LaTonya and Gwen a few weeks ago about the college student who might be visiting?"

"The AG woman?"

"Yes."

"Of course. Whatever happened with that? We were all so curious to meet her."

"Good news." Tessa waved her phone in the air. "She's coming to visit next month."

ISA – OFFICIAL EVIDENCE

LindsEE!: so I went to an estatician (sp???)

VivversOC: esthetician.

LindsEE!: she said sun damage and recs collagen and retinol creams. And also sunscreen duh. I spent like $200!!!!

VivversOC: did u tell her ur age?

LindsEE!: yep. She seemed surprised, I could tell she was trying to be polite. She goes "oh you seem really mature" nice try lol

ISA – OFFICIAL EVIDENCE

Stoph1: Viv you there?

VivversOC: yep hey.

Stoph1: so I did your assignment I tried "interviewing" my mom and guess what???

VivversOC: ?

Stoph1: surprise surprise, just like ur mom and Linds' she says she just can't remember. That it was just so long ago and all that matters is that she got me out of it

VivversOC: did you record the convo?

Stoph1: yep

VivversOC: send it to me ⚘

Stoph1: ok. u know what's weird tho?

VivversOC: what?

Stoph1: my mom never 4gets ANYTHING

ISA – OFFICIAL EVIDENCE

VivversOC: have a serious q for the 3 of u.

Stoph1: hit us

VivversOC: I've been doing some writing abt AG. Like personal essay type stuff for my creative writing workshop.

Stoph1: surprise surprise, it's yr fave topic

LindsEE!: shut up stoph

VivversOC: and my prof suggested I should try to pub what I wrote. So I sent it out to a few places and it got accepted.

Xavey: hey congrats! Who's publishing?

VivversOC: Thanks. Well . . . it's ARTERY

Stoph1: no f'n way!

LindsEE!: WOW!!! Like a bazillion peeps read that every day. Myself included. CONGRATS!!!!

VivversOC: I know, I'm excited. The thing is, they want it to be a big feature with photos. It's gonna be part of their "UNSILENCED" series. No pressure but I'm just wondering if u guys would be willing to participate

LindsEE!: like have our pics & names in it?

VivversOC: yep. Closeups of your skunk patches and skin creases and all. I know you guys think I'm paranoid but if there is something up with us related to AG that is being overlooked by society I think we should speak up, don't u think? Like why do we all have the same weird physical pat

VivversOC: hello, why is no one answering me?

26.

E vening, Roger." Luke ushered Dr. Milford into his office.
"Good evening, Dr. Zimmerman." His nightly jab at Luke. It
bothered the older doctor, Luke knew, that Luke—who did not even
have a bachelor's degree—simply referred to him by his first name and
not *Dr. Milford*. But Luke did not care for titles, especially in casual
settings. They created false hierarchies. If Milford disagreed, so be it.

Roger Milford took his usual seat beside Luke at his desk and produced the white tablet on which he kept the charts of Cohort One. He
cleared his throat. Everything about Milford, it seemed, was dry.

"The Cohort hits day fifty-two tomorrow. The equivalent of thirty-
three weeks conventional. Nervous system developments are now happening very rapidly. We'll begin twice-daily exams starting tomorrow.
Do you want to be briefed on each of those, or is a nightly overview of
both appointments sufficient?"

"Twice daily," said Luke. "I'll leave room on my calendar." He felt
the doctor bristle beside him. He knew Milford would have preferred
to simply brief him daily on the Cohort's progress, rather than actually sharing the charts, but Luke didn't want to see anything less than
his doctors did. If it were up to Luke, he'd have attended the actual

obstetric exams, but Rita Gupta had argued that it would make the Cohort too uncomfortable.

"Okay," said Milford, with zero enthusiasm. "Understood."

Sometimes the doctor seemed to forget just how much Luke was paying him.

"Let's sync up," said Luke, nodding toward Milford's tablet. Luke liked to view the Cohort's charts on one of his large desktop monitors. "Lavek first."

The image that filled the center of his screen was revolting and awesome: Kate's baby, swimming inside her, limbs tangled, shadows of bone visible beneath the face, digits fully formed. Her fetus floated in a golden nimbus of light, one tiny hand pressed to a cheek. Luke felt the familiar expanse in his chest, an overwhelming sense of accomplishment.

Milford droned through the numbers, unmoved.

"Head-to-toe length: 16.1 inches. Weight: four pounds, five ounces. Heart rate, activity level, breathing motion, muscle tone, amniotic fluid—all normal."

Luke leaned closer to the ultrasound image on his monitor to closely examine the fetus's head. He touched his finger to the screen, tracing its shape, which was smooth and round at the top. It was the same shape as millions of other babies in millions of other wombs at this very moment and, according to Milford's team, would remain round at birth. Unlike the natural AG babies, the children of the TEAT Trial, per Luke's decree, would not have cranial abnormalities. Luke did not want the new generation to suffer such a stigma. The Seahorse team had already proven, in the animal trials, that they could accelerate other species without creating a cleft in the skull. The birth of Cohort One's babies would verify they could do it in humans, too.

"Okay," said Luke, leaning back from the screen. "Sims next."

LaTonya's baby was smaller than Kate's, but also normal, and sucking his thumb.

"Excellent," said Luke. "Moving on."

"Ms. Harris," said Milford, bringing up Gwen's chart. Luke watched the image leap onto the screen, then fought not to look away.

"It's a battle for limited resources in there, huh?" he said to Milford. "Little warriors from the get-go."

"Quite the opposite," said Milford. "They're striving for symbiosis. They share a circulatory system. Each needs the right level of blood flow."

"And? Are they getting it?"

"It appears so, yes. We're monitoring carefully for signs of imbalance."

"And otherwise? Do they look viable?"

"Plausibly. But this is a high-risk pregnancy, especially given the mother's age. Complications could still arise. We should inform Ms. Harris of the situation."

"Not yet," said Luke. "You just said complications are still possible."

"Complications will remain possible up until she successfully delivers," said Milford. "We need to tell her."

"Give me survival odds."

"Better than fifty percent."

"A week ago you said thirty. So we're moving in the right direction. Let's get to seventy-five before we move to full disclosure."

"Need I bring up the ethical considerations?" Milford said in a tight voice. He stabbed an index finger to his tablet and the monitor on Luke's desk went dark.

"You need not," said Luke. "Because, as clearly stated in the consent and release documents signed by each member of Cohort One, including Gwendolyn Harris, our primary objective is to preserve the global health of mother and child. *Global* encompasses physical and psychological."

"I'm aware of the definition."

"So we wait and see for another few days."

"I don't follow your logic. The longer we wait, the longer the mother's perceived window of deception."

"*Omission.* Window of omission."

"Call it what you will." The doctor stood from his seat. "Either way, I'm not comfortable with it."

"You don't need to be," said Luke easily. "Comfort is not a priority. Bringing these babies into the world as safely as possible is my priority. It needs to be yours, too."

"You have an interesting definition of safety, *Dr.* Zimmerman."

"Get some sleep, Roger," said Luke. "I'll see you tomorrow."

Milford exited without saying good night. Luke dimmed the lights in his office as soon as the door clicked shut behind the doctor, leaving only a single soft glow over his desk, and opened a ClearCalm. He put on his headphones, selected Fauré's *Requiem* on his phone, and turned up the volume. He settled in front of his monitors as the river of voices and string instruments began in his ears and logged on to the CleftKids LikeMe page.

No new posts from Viv or the others, but the ghost had been there just twenty minutes before.

Plus five other times that day.

Goddammit.

He closed LikeMe and put his monitor to sleep, settling back in his chair to absorb the music. People often lazily assumed *Requiem* was simply another piece about death, but Fauré himself had said it was about aspiring to the sublime, about leaving the ordinary world behind for something grander. Luke related to this theme. It was the reason he'd invented TEAT. Sometimes when he listened to *Requiem*, he felt that Fauré had written the piece for him.

Thirty minutes later the piece was reaching its crescendo, the choir swelling and soaring—*Libera me, Domine*—and the music layered and broke and layered again, until its last measure. He pulled off his headphones and tossed them onto the desk. The room refocused around him, eerily silent.

ISA – OFFICIAL EVIDENCE

VivversOC: Hey everybody, I have an announcement

LindsEE!: VIV! Where'e u been???

VivversOC: Studying my ass off for finals. Haven't you guys?

Xavey: Affirmative.

Stoph1: Spare us the chitchat, I'm on the edge of my seat here. What's you're announcement dude?

VivversOC: So u know how I met Tessa Callahan last month?

LindsEE!: Yes so cool

VivversOC: Well she invited me out to visit her company in CA!

Xavey: WHOA

VivversOC: I know! They're paying for it and everything. Tessa says since I'm AG and their tech is based on it, she thinks me and her team would "benefit from some informal facetime."

LindsEE!: R U going?

VivversOC: Yes. But before I do, I wanted to check with all of u guys to see if it's OK if I share your stories with her. Like everything you've told me about your AG. I think she might be able to help us.

Stoph1: Help how???

VivversOC: Get to the bottom of why it happened.

Xavey: Fine by me. Tell her whatever.

LindsEE!: Same here.

Stoph1: 🕯 Run with it, detective

27.

Wayne bolted awake at 2:00 a.m., not from a dream but more disconcertingly, from a heavy charcoal slumber. His heart rate was high, as if he'd just run a sprint. Beside him, Viv was sound asleep, her breathing so slow it was barely perceptible. Part of his work at the ISA involved surveillance—focusing on the physical world, verified intelligence, hard data—but the other part, the more advanced one, required him to translate his intuition. To extrapolate action and facts from his gut feelings. In the past, he would have fought an abrupt awakening in the middle of the night, doing anything it took to get back to sleep: counting to ten thousand, a shot of whiskey, a sleeping pill. Now he understood that he did not tear awake from a dreamless sleep for no reason. That he needed to stay awake and wait for the reason to present itself. He believed in the transfer of energy, not in a dippy new age way but in a Newtonian way—a disturbance somewhere necessarily yielded a counterdisturbance elsewhere.

Waking up, as he just had, was a counterdisturbance.

He checked his various devices: nothing.

He studied Viv in the darkness, her curls like dark Spanish moss all over the pillow. She was an exceptionally heavy sleeper, he'd learned from these nights awake beside her. He could see a whole childhood in the way a person slept; Viv preferred to be on her back with two pillows, unguarded, without vigilance. Offering herself to the night. Elise and Larry Bourne—although shallow, as Viv often complained—had taken good care of her, protecting her not only from harm but the prospect of it. Wayne had studied Viv's childhood in depth, scouring her and her parents' digital histories: the long mornings at the beach, the tennis and soccer and surfing, the vacations to Yosemite and Big Sur and Joshua Tree.

And yet, he knew Viv felt disappointed by her parents, in that way that well-cared-for children could afford to be. It was not enough that they'd loved her to the best of their ability and provided her a life of comfort and stimulation. Like many kids of her generation, Viv craved understanding from her parents. Connectivity. A sense that they "got" her. She could not yet appreciate the fact that they'd shaped her perception of the world in such a way that allowed her to reach her early twenties and still sleep on her back. Wayne always slept on his side and often woke curled into a tight ball, like a late-stage infant in the womb. Self-protection.

And yet, he did not resent Viv and the gentle cushion of her history. Someone else, he might have resented. In his younger days, he could easily hate anyone with a history of softness.

He had never hated Viv, not for a second. Perhaps he'd granted her leniency from the beginning, from before they'd even met, from when he'd reviewed her file and learned what had happened to her before she'd been born, how much Elise and Larry had risked for her. They might be dolts—they were afraid to tell Viv they'd adopted her, for fear of her reaction, instead letting her believe Elise had birthed her after nine weeks—but they were generally loving parents. That big house in Newport Beach with the wrought iron and topiary in the backyard suggested only bad taste to Viv, but to Wayne it was evidence of how hard her parents had tried, within the confines of their own limitations, to keep her safe.

He'd never been able to hate them either.

Viv's breath changed slightly, for a moment, becoming audible, and he watched her mouth move, her lips parting and closing several times in succession, as if she were preparing to swallow something. He parted the dark shade over his bed to let the gray of the night infiltrate the room, illuminating her. Outside was the glow of streetlights but no stars or moon; a bluish haze blotted the sky and the Charles River beyond the trees. He'd let the bruised light of earliest morning in to photograph her over the past months, her deepest sleep being ideal for the full-body shots required by the Inner Panel. But he didn't need to photograph her anymore.

He just needed to move her.

But he kept freezing.

Not that he didn't register what was happening to her. The meaning of it loomed over him every minute, a low, toxic fog. He closed his eyes and drifted his right hand to the top of Viv's pillow, hovering it over her head. He thought again of Irene and the long mornings he'd spent in her blue-and-white kitchen in Austin, the sun blooming through the windows. The coffee and zucchini bread between them on the table, the smoky baritone of Leonard Cohen on the speakers. How close to her he'd felt then, like she was his only true friend in the world. Irene loved Leonard, especially in the morning: *he's like going to church, without all the bullshit,* she'd told Wayne when he was Henry.

Wayne lowered his hand to the top of Viv's head and pressed his fingertips down lightly. It never felt entirely permissible, touching her cleft, but he couldn't help himself. Still, four months into this assignment, he had the irrational, impossible hope that somehow the cleft would disappear. That it would have all been a magnificent error, these past months, and he and Viv could move on in the world, like regular people, together.

But it was there, beneath the springy coils of her hair: the dent in her scalp. He rested his middle fingertips against it and closed his eyes.

He was almost asleep when he felt the vibration from his phone, a shudder near his head. He picked it up and looked. A text from Borlav: *Call now.*

Wayne sat straight up, instantly awake. You were not told to call Borlav in the middle of the night for a minor reason. Quietly he stepped to his dresser and pulled on gym pants and a sweatshirt, laced up his running sneakers. Before he left, he pulled the comforter up to Viv's chin. Smoothed her hair off her face and kissed her cheek.

Outside, moonlight bled through the sycamore trees lining the sidewalk and played on the surface of the river beyond. The night air was cool on his face. He tapped a spot on his device and lifted it to his ear.

Borlav picked up before Wayne heard a ring. "Theroux. Hope I didn't wake you."

"It's two in the morning here, Borlav. You woke me. Let's hear it."

"Our IP meeting just wrapped. It went very late, needless to say. Bottom line is, you need to import Vivian Bourne a-sap."

"That's what you're waking me up for? To give me a directive I already have? I'm working on it, Gary. I'll have her there soon."

"Soon isn't fast enough. Her LikeMe posts have become too problematic. She's sucked her other little buddies into her conspiracy theories."

"'Conspiracy theories'?" Wayne couldn't suppress a bitter laugh. "You mean that time Dewey Falk and a bunch of other bribe-taking motherfuckers blew off proper testing of a dirty drug and let a bunch of women and children take the hit?"

"Don't be a drama queen. Dewey was in a tough spot during a tough time. Juva was an accident."

"An *accident*, Gary? Fast-tracking the approval of an undertested, ultraprofitable drug? So that Dewey could push more dirty agendas through? So he could keep making rich people richer and everyone else more scared and confused? So he could guarantee all his buddies in Washington that Big Pharma had their backs? Let's not forget that BetterLife is the most profitable pharmaceutical company in *history*. Or that it was the single biggest donor to both of Falk's campaigns."

"Settle down, Michael Moore."

"Fuck you, Borlav. Juva was golden from the get-go. BetterLife predicted it would be the best-selling drug of all time. Genius, wasn't it? A little pill that could extend a woman's peak fertility into her forties and fifties? What's not to like? President Falk sure as shit liked it."

"Are you done yet?"

"So it was such a bummer when Juva had those pesky little side effects, wasn't it? Just little inconveniences, really, like, oh, making women have their babies way too fast. Or start aging way too early. Or sometimes a combination of the two. And if they're extra lucky, their kids might get hit with symptoms also. They should've named it *Juva Roulette*."

"Catchy," said Borlav. "You may have missed your calling in advertising."

"Why do *we* have to clean up this mess, Gary? Why didn't the FDA discontinue Juva sooner? Why did it wait all those months before pulling the plug? This could have all been avoided. I could be doing something decent with my life."

Borlav ignored him. "Now Bourne's pulling Tessa Callahan into the mix."

"Tessa Callahan?" Now Wayne was confused. "What the hell are you talking about?"

"Evidently Bourne had a little bonding session with Callahan last month, when they were both on the Weldon campus. Now Callahan's invited Bourne out to visit her weird-science palace in California, and Bourne's going, with a plan to tell Callahan everything she's dug up on AG. It's all on LikeMe, if you care to look."

"I'll take your word for it."

"It's too risky. Callahan and her whole operation are supposed to *divert* attention from people like Vivian Bourne. Callahan's a big name. If she wants people to listen to Bourne, all she has to do is open her mouth. We're not willing to let that happen. And by that I mean *you're* not going to let that happen."

Wayne felt like he'd been punched in the gut. He sat down in the grass by the river and put his head between his knees, still holding his phone to his ear, listening to Borlav breathe on the other end.

"Four days, Theroux," said Borlav. "That's when Bourne is set to fly to California. You'd better deliver her to the Colony before that. So help you God if she steps on that flight to San Jose."

"Four days is too soon."

"Love must be scrambling your brain, Theroux."

"Excuse me?"

"Love. Or maybe it's just lust. We all know you're banging Vivian Bourne. Winger and Hurst and me. It's obvious. We could practically smell it on you when you gave your preso on her."

Wayne gnashed his teeth. "That's none of your business."

"My retirement is my business. The success of the ISA is my business. And your behavior, which includes inappropriate relations with your PIT, is threatening that success. You think I want to be doing this anymore, Theroux? I want out just as much as you do. But I took a vow to complete this goddamn mission, a vow to protect everyone involved. So did you. We got into this together and we'll get out of it together. But it won't work unless you get your focus back. So cut procrastinating, get Vivian Bourne to the Colony, and maybe you'll stand a chance of a brand-new life."

"You know I'm right, Gary. You're a fixer. I'm a fixer. Together we've helped an American president and a major federal agency avoid public shaming and probable disbandment. Aren't you proud?"

"You're out of your fucking mind. Get Bourne out here right now. Do whatever it takes. You have four days, Theroux, or your retirement turns into a pumpkin. You can kiss it goodbye."

"Go to hell, Gary."

"Message me an acceptance of this order within five minutes. Copy Winger and Hurst. Clock's starting now."

Borlav hung up.

Wayne lowered his phone to his side and squeezed it as if he might break it. During the conversation he'd been impervious to the cold night air, but now he was freezing. He tilted his head and looked up at a hazy smudge of stars in the sky. City stars. At the Colony, they were clear and abundant, constellations traceable with a finger, the Milky Way a gauzy net.

Pulse beating fast in his neck, he raised his phone and hovered his thumb over the keyboard. Typed "Accept." Sent the single word to Borlav, copying Winger and Hurst.

Then he hurled the device into the river.

28.

The morning was cool and fresh, dew beading the grass as Wayne steered a silver Ford Focus, rented that morning, through the lanes of the Weldon campus to its Route 16 exit, then to pick up the Mass Pike, which would connect them to I-93, a straight shot north to New Hampshire.

He'd told Viv he wanted to take her away for the weekend. An early graduation present, before her parents came to town for the June 11 ceremony. Anywhere she wanted, he said. This was a part of his process, letting them choose a destination. It kept them calm for as long as possible, created the illusion of their control. Of normalcy.

She'd wanted to hike to Arethusa Falls, in the White Mountains of New Hampshire. Fine. He'd assessed the location and found a viable airstrip along the way.

So New Hampshire it was. He'd chosen a bed-and-breakfast in a town near the trailhead. Sent her the link, to which she'd responded with the smiley face emoji with hearts for eyes.

But of course, he never actually booked the room. How he wished he could have. How he wished they were actually going to New Hampshire to hike through the pure mountain air and swim in a waterfall.

Wayne steered through the campus with one hand on the wheel and the other on Viv's knee. Staring out into the brilliant spring morning, watching her classmates amble around campus, giddy, he could almost pretend they were a normal couple, headed out on a spontaneous weekend trip. Viv scrolled through the music app on the car's console and selected something with jangly guitar and a nasally guy on vocals.

"Sensitive white boys," Wayne said. "My favorite."

"The Nocturnalists are the *best* sensitive white boys," said Viv. "Give them ten minutes and I bet you'll agree."

"You need a little punk rock in your bloodstream, babe," said Wayne. "And maybe some old-school country."

"My bloodstream will tolerate no such thing."

"I love that about you." Wayne slowed to a toll booth, lowered his window to pay it.

Beyond the toll was the interstate, and Wayne accelerated. As the Focus picked up speed and Viv played songs she loved, she watched one of Wayne's hands begin to drum the steering wheel ever so slightly, indicating that he was maybe a little bit into the Nocturnalists. Viv cracked the car window to let the fresh morning air swirl through the car. Traffic on I-93 was light and she watched billboards and green exit signs whiz by.

Wayne closed the car window.

"Hey," said Viv. "Wasn't the air nice?"

"It was. But too loud."

An exit appeared and Wayne signaled and veered onto the ramp.

"You hungry?" he said. "I'm kind of hungry. And we need gas."

Viv glanced at the gas gauge. "It's practically half full, Captain Cautious. And I just watched you eat a ginormous breakfast an hour ago. Can't you wait for lunch?"

"Sorry, can't wait," said Wayne. "Something about being on the road makes me hungry." He reached over and squeezed her knee.

He turned off the ramp onto a commercial road with a few gas stations and motels. He drove right by them.

"Hello, gas?" said Viv.

"There's this diner about two miles down I want to take you to."

As he expected, a large doughnut-shaped sign with MITZIE'S DONUTS & SANDWICHES written around it appeared. Their surroundings had turned green and pastoral: Laconia, New Hampshire. CITY OF THE LAKES, read the welcome sign. POPULATION 18,061.

Wayne parked in the lot and stepped out of the car.

"Hang on," said Viv, rummaging in her purse for her phone. "I want to take a picture of that sign."

He watched her check the pockets of her jacket, then compartments of the car door, and then the glove box. No device. It wasn't in her overnight bag on the floor of the back seat, either.

"Hey," she said, stepping away from the car. "I can't find my phone. Have you seen it?"

"Nope," he said. "But you had it at breakfast. It must be in there somewhere." He gestured to the silver car. "We'll find it after we eat."

Inside, they sat down in a red vinyl booth. A waitress with a green apron took their order: eggs and a doughnut for Wayne, a baconless Cobb salad for Viv.

"This place is great," said Viv. "How'd you find it?"

"I can't reveal my sources."

"Ha ha."

They fell silent for a minute. He reminded himself to act normal, to keep talking.

"Want to play a game?" Wayne asked.

"What, like an icebreaker?"

"Just something my family used to play on road trips when I was a kid."

"Okay."

"Okay. It's called Something You Might Not Know."

"Never heard of it."

"The rules are simple. You guess a secret you *think* I have. Out loud. That's it."

"Weird." She took a bite of her salad. "How do you win?"

"It's not a clear-cut thing. It's all in the reaction of the other person. The winning comes in the form of personal satisfaction. You want to go first?"

"Um, okay. You secretly cry at the end of cheesy movies," she said.

"Are you kidding? Of course I do. Like a baby." He took a bite of fried egg. "Okay, my turn. When you were a kid, you planned to run away."

Viv started. "How'd you know that?"

"Lucky guess."

"You're right. Bags packed, allowance saved, route plotted."

"Why'd you want to go? Was your mom really that bad?"

"I wish I could say she did something awful. That she was cruel or indifferent. I suppose, in little ways, she was cruel. Always pushing the athletics and weight control. But that was the extent of it. My dad was harmless enough also. His biggest offense was his passivity."

"So why the runaway fantasies?"

"It was this sense that they didn't understand me," said Viv. "The way all teenagers feel, right? My turn now." She paused, thinking. "You used to be religious."

This startled him. He'd never told her. "Bingo. Harlem, Montana, Church of Christ Youth Group, grades ten through twelve."

"Seriously?"

"Seriously. The youth group leader was this guy named Greg. Greg Harsell. I'll never forget him. He exuded this total peace and calm, like he'd found the golden key to existence. It was all so straightforward. Singular answers: Christ, the Bible."

"Let me guess. He ended up a heroin addict."

Wayne forced a laugh. "Probably."

The waitress cleared their plates and brought the check. Wayne paid it and stood up.

"Shall we?"

Back in their rental car, Viv remembered her missing phone and searched for it again.

"Dammit. I must have left it at Weldon."

"So you'll just go without it this weekend. Isn't that kind of romantic?"

Viv thought for a moment. "Yes. Okay. I guess it sort of is."

She clicked her seat belt into place. The day was bright and warm around them. Wayne reversed out of the parking spot and turned right out of the diner's lot.

"Isn't the highway to the left?" Viv asked.

"One more minor detour," said Wayne. "Unless you're in a hurry?"

"I'm not."

"My turn. In the game."

"Go ahead," she said, reluctantly.

"You are special," said Wayne.

"Wait, what? I thought we were playing your weirdass game."

"We are," he said. "That's my guess."

"That I'm special?" Her voice had turned suspicious.

"I'm saying that something you *think* I don't know about you, Vivian, is that you're special."

"What do you mean?"

"Not just special in the way *all* ordinary people are special. Objectively special."

"This game is making my head hurt, Wayne. I want to quit."

"Let me be more specific," he said, keeping the stiffer tone. "You're a child of accelerated gestation."

"What?"

"There's no reason you should have told me," he said. "But I want you to know that I know."

He paused.

"Hey, Viv?"

She did not answer.

"You don't have to answer me," he said.

"Where are we going? Not the White Mountains, right?"

"Not the White Mountains. But it's safe. When you get there, I want you to do exactly what you're told. Even if you don't agree with it. Even if every cell in your body tells you to resist. To run. You need to stay. It's only temporary."

"No! I don't want to go there! What about the White Mountains?"

"You'll meet a person named Johanna. She'll help you. You can trust her. And *only* her. You got that?"

"How can you possibly ask me to trust anything you're saying right now?"

"I have to."

"Well, I don't trust you. I want out of this car. Seriously. Slow down."

He did not decelerate. Outside, trees and sky smeared by. He turned up the stereo to high volume. The Nocturnalists filled the car.

"Turn that down," she said, fumbling for the volume.

"Vivian," he said, "I love you. And so help me God, I am going to get you out of this."

"Get me out of *what?*" Now she sounded terrified.

"I promise," he said.

Wayne reached into the pocket of his cargo shorts and, in a single fluid motion, pulled out the thick orange pen and moved it to Viv's throat. He felt the needle puncture her tender flesh. He knew what it felt like. In ISA training, agents had been allowed to practice on each other: you felt a sharp jab, followed by a hot sting, and then everything slurred and wheeled, as if you'd boarded a broken, lurching merry-go-round at some carnival in a nightmare. Then blackness.

29.

Three a.m. It was the safest time, Tessa decided, to cross from her residence in East Lobe to Luke's office in West Lobe. She'd chosen the time because it posed the lowest risk for running into anyone, though that was not guaranteed. At Seahorse, people worked on the "clocks of personal productivity," and it was not unusual to see employees at Corporate on their machines at midnight or six in the morning; there were always the early birds and the night owls.

Luke would not be in his office. After their afternoon staff meeting, he'd mentioned he was spending the night at home in San Francisco, in the context of a joke about needing a "proper shower," though his office had a full bathroom. Tessa wondered if he had a date. She'd never known Luke to have a real girlfriend—where would he find the time?—but perhaps he occasionally used RightNow or one of the other dating apps. She didn't want to think about it.

Tessa took the elevator down to the closest connector floor to cross the building through the clear tubular footbridge. She wore black leggings and an old UC Santa Cruz sweatshirt of Peter's. The smell of him gave her courage. Below her was the soaring space of the Center, like the interior of a planet. She kept her gaze straight ahead.

She reached Luke's office door and raised her palm to the sensor. Zeus authorized her and the lock clicked open. She turned on minimal lighting, just enough glow from the track lighting overhead to allow her to see her way around the spacious office. She'd use her phone's flashlight, if necessary, to find what she was looking for.

Luke's workspace was as sparse and pristine as ever, like the inside of some corporate igloo. Tessa surveyed the two darkened monitors on the streamlined desk, blanching at the sight of the Lucite chair on the other side of it. Across the room, Luke had left the floor-to-ceiling picture windows unshaded, though there was no trace of the spectacular view at this hour, just the ash-colored smudge of fog off the ocean, wrapping the building like a closed hand. In front of the window, Luke's napping pod appeared twinned by its reflection in the mirror, double white orbs.

Tessa stepped out of her canvas sneakers, to prevent the rubber tap of the soles on the polished concrete floor, and crossed the room to the window. Face almost touching the glass, she peered outside but could see only the faint, smeared glow of the iron path lights that dotted the grounds eight stories below.

Despite the vacant silence, Tessa felt a sense of Luke in the room, a sort of residual energy. She knew he was offsite—she'd checked his parking spot after dinner to verify the Elan was gone—but she still had the uneasy feeling that he'd been there just minutes before. Perhaps that was why he really kept the space so featureless, she thought: not so much to free his mind, as he claimed, but to prevent visitors from focusing on anything but *him* and what he had to say. Peter, who'd met Luke only a half dozen times, called him *narcissist lite*, which made Tessa laugh. *Contradiction in terms,* she'd said.

Whatever the case, Tessa needed to move fast. To find what she came for and get back to the residence wing.

But where to look? She turned from the window and scanned the room. Without bookshelves or filing cabinets, there were not many options. She'd come here on pure instinct, in search of the INR-Views that had disappeared from the supply room, allegedly on recall. The "replacements" had yet to show up. Tessa's gut told her they'd never left. John Kwak was not returning her calls.

And so here she was, in Luke's bare office without Luke, at 3:00 a.m.

Perhaps her gut was wrong. It was not an instinct she often trusted without question. She was not impulsive. But trespassing here had been an impulse.

She recrossed the floor to the bathroom. Marble surfaces, a single medicine cabinet in which she found nothing but tea tree oil and some "Incan" facial moisturizing lotion. For a moment, she studied her face in the mirror above the floating sink. She looked tired; her eyes were creased at the corners, her skin pale. Her highlights could use sprucing; the caramelly threads seemed conspicuous against her natural dark red.

Viv would be arriving at Seahorse on Wednesday for a short visit. The Cohort, as Tessa had predicted, was eager to meet her. Tessa had not yet broken the news of Viv's trip to Luke. She was not technically required, after all, to clear her visitors with him first.

Viv's arrival was part of the reason Tessa was searching for the INR-Views. She envisioned sitting with the Cohort as they used one to show Viv their babies. The experience would empower the pregnant women and validate Viv, perhaps make her feel less marginalized by her own history.

Also, Tessa wanted to redeem her failed promise to issue the INRs to the Cohort weeks ago. Gwen had been especially disappointed when Tessa informed her that the wands had not yet arrived. But soon she'd begun to feel her baby move, quite vigorously, and her anxiety over her ultrasounds receded.

Still, Tessa wanted to stick to her word. Plus, technically, the INRs *belonged* to her. She'd been the one to add them to the suite of Seahorse tools. The one to acquire them from John Kwak. That Luke had taken control of them was outrageous.

She switched off the bathroom light and stepped back into the office. Through the dimness, her eyes settled on the napping pod. Peter's description of Luke returned to her: *narcissist lite*.

And then she could see it: Luke hovering the wand over his own body, transfixed by the view inside himself. Gazing at his bones and organs and soft tissue. Smiling. Rapt.

She hurried across the room to the pod and unzipped it. She tapped on her phone's flashlight and shone the beam inside, where a firm white cushion was fitted into the base of the resting platform.

Moving on instinct, she worked her fingers into the space between them until she could pry up the cushion.

Underneath it was an INR-View, cool and smooth as a small missile as her fingers closed around it.

30.

From behind a two-way mirror in the Quarry, Wayne adjusted his headset and watched Johanna, wearing pink nursing scrubs, tend to Viv in a room on the other side of the glass. She was attached to an IV, lying on a white-sheeted bed opposite a large monitor affixed to the wall. He desperately did not want to watch or listen, but the IP required both. His guilt thrummed in sync with his headache. He'd been awake for thirty-six hours, since early the previous morning. On the flight from New Hampshire to New Mexico, in the ISA plane, he'd watched Viv in her chemical slumber, her chest rising and falling beneath her "Weldon Lacrosse—We'll Stick It to You!" T-shirt and felt progressively worse. He forced himself to complete the items on his Importation Task List: Ensuring Viv was in a proper and safe reclined position, seat belt fastened. Checking and logging her vitals. Timelining and documenting each stage of the day's events. Wiping her phone clean and sending all the data to the ISA's tech staff, so they could communicate with Viv's friends and family, posing as Viv herself, to keep them all from worrying. Tech was remarkably good at these deceptions, down to specific nuances of a PIT's tone and emoji use.

The thought of some floppy-haired IT guy in a plaid shirt, who was all of twenty-six, pretending to be Viv on a keyboard, congratulating himself for nailing another impersonation, made Wayne rageful. He imagined punching a window of the plane, over and over, until he'd smashed the bones in his hands. It might feel good.

As he scrubbed the data from Viv's phone, he noticed a recent text thread with Tessa Callahan. They were discussing a plan for Viv to visit Tessa at her biotech fortress south of San Francisco. Before Wayne sealed Viv's device into an evidence bag, he entered Tessa's number into his new phone, which had replaced the one he'd thrown into the river. Couldn't hurt to have it.

His to-do list completed, Wayne was free to sleep for the remainder of the four-hour flight. His body begged for it, but his mind had veto power. Each time his eyelids cinder-blocked, Viv's face flashed behind them and he jerked awake. So he sat in the seat next to hers and watched her sleep. Every so often, he applied Vaseline to her dry lips, savoring the plush feel of them under his finger, hating himself, until the plane finally descended on an airstrip just outside Tremble City.

Now, sequestered on the other side of Wayne's two-way mirror in the Quarry, Viv was just beginning to wake. Wayne imagined her confusion as she tried to make sense of where she was, to clear her fogged brain and swallow away the sandpaper-dryness of her mouth. He wondered how long it would take for her confusion to give way to fear, and then her fear to anger. How long would it take her to begin to loathe him?

"Ah, she's awake."

Johanna's lilting voice came through Wayne's headset. He sat up straighter and leaned toward the glass.

"Good afternoon, love," she said to Viv. "I'm Johanna. Don't try to speak yet. I know your throat's dry as dust. We keep you hydrated"—she gestured to the IV—"but it doesn't stop that recycled plane air from drying out your throat."

"Plane air?" Viv croaked, and the sound of her voice cut into him.

Johanna popped the top of a soda can and poured the contents into a plastic cup. "Here, have some fizzy water." She tipped the cup to Viv's lips and Wayne watched her drink with animal greed.

"Where am I?" said Viv.

"In a safe place. My job is to take care of you. You'll get a full explanation soon. In the meantime, it's best if you keep resting."

"Where's Wayne?"

She spoke the question slowly, with effort, and it was all he could do not to bang on the glass and say, *Right here.*

"Oh, you poor dear," said Johanna. "Your mind's a bit fuzzy, yes?"

"Yes," said Viv.

"It'll wear off, don't worry. It's just left over from the shot. You'll be back to yourself in no time. Don't be afraid. Everyone here is kind. They want this to be as least troublesome as possible for you."

"'This'?"

"Not my domain, dear. The team will be here soon enough to orient you."

"Team? Where's Wayne?"

"He's resting, love. It's hard work to bring you here."

Wayne took a deep breath to steady himself. It wasn't easy. "Get him for me," said Viv, more sharply.

"You'll see him soon enough, love." Johanna opened a box of crackers and offered it to Viv. "Are you hungry yet? Best to start with something bland."

Viv slapped at the box. "I don't want any fucking crackers. I want to see Wayne." She attempted to sit up and realized her restraints.

"Why can't I move?"

"Wish I could fix that for you," said Johanna, unflustered. "But you're restrained for safety purposes. It's temporary, just until you've met with the team."

"Untie me!"

"Here," said Johanna, picking up a remote from the IV cart. "Let me sit you up. This bed's magic."

"Help!" said Viv, as the bed adjusted smoothly into a seating position.

I will, Wayne answered silently.

"And let me know if you need to use the restroom again. You went before, but you weren't really awake. The bed adjusts for that, too."

Viv said nothing.

Johanna pulled her phone from a pocket of her scrubs, glanced at it, and smiled.

"Good news," she said. "The team says I can start the video without them. That'll help."

She thumbed her phone, and the screen on the wall jumped to life, displaying an animated American flag, rippling slowly. Over the flag, white text appeared and a female narrator began to read the words in a vaguely British accent.

> Welcome to the Internal Stability Agency. You are in temporary custody of the United States government. The reason for your presence is a matter of national security. Through an accumulation of evidence acquired from one or more public forums, we have determined that you are consistently engaged in activities that threaten the stability and collective well-being of American civic life. Thus, we have brought you into temporary custody to discuss the cessation of such risk-perpetuating behaviors. You have committed no crimes and will face no legal penalty as long as you enter compliance with our risk-abatement protocol. We regret that our methods require transport to our facility with minimal warning to the individual . . .

There was a hard rap to the door and Johanna snapped off the video. Viv swiveled her head, her eyes passing by Wayne's. He watched Borlav and Winger enter the room with matching strides, both in white button-down shirts and black pants.

"Ms. Bourne. I'm Gary Borlav."

"Douglas Winger," said Winger. He pulled two chairs from a table in the corner and both men sat at Viv's bedside, hulking close to her.

Motherfuckers, thought Wayne. He pressed his palms to his knees to keep his hands from shaking.

"We want to thank you for being here," said Borlav. "We realize it's a jarring experience, but soon it can all be behind you. We've taken care of all external logistics. You can be back at Weldon in time for graduation."

"Graduation?" Wayne heard panic rising in her voice. "That's still ten days off. I can't just disappear. My parents, for starters, will freak out. And I'm supposed to be on a plane to California on Wednesday. Do you know who Tessa Callahan is? She's an extremely powerful woman. There's no way she'll just—"

Borlav interrupted. "No one's going to worry, Ms. Bourne. We've covered all your bases. No one will worry. You yourself should not worry. You're here strictly for conversation. As long as you cooperate, you'll get back to your regular life with minimal disruption. In the meantime, we can guarantee your comfort and company. Our facility is climate-controlled for maximum kindness to your system. You'll have a private living space, a full-time personal aide"—he gestured to Johanna—"fresh air, and high-quality nutrition."

"It can feel like a vacation, really," added Winger.

"I want to leave right this minute," said Viv. Wayne could see her arms straining against her ties. "I demand it."

"That's not possible," said Borlav. "Our facility is a highly secured environment. Attempts to depart before we've reached an agreement would be fruitless."

"Where is Wayne? Where's my *boyfriend*?"

Wayne cringed; there was a caustic, bitter note in the way she spoke the word.

"We're getting to that," said Winger. "Wayne is your field-op."

"My what?"

"An employee of the ISA, assigned to you for the past several months. It's been his job to evaluate the validity of our concerns and to assess your activity firsthand. We don't bring anyone here who hasn't been thoroughly observed by a field-op and declared a viable risk. Unfortunately, Mr. Bridger ascertained that for you, a conversation with us was in order."

Viv was quiet for a moment. Wayne felt his heart rate pick up.

"I see," she said coldly.

"Mr. Bridger is a veteran of this work. His reports indicated a strong need for your cooperation with us. That's why you're here. We're going to let you rest a bit more, have a shower and a meal, get your bearings, and then we'll sit down and have a proper conversation. We'll tell you exactly what we need from you, and you can have some time to think it over."

"I don't need time," said Viv. "Whatever it is, I'm not cooperating."

"It will behoove you to wait until you have more information," said Borlav.

"I was just kidnapped." Viv spoke slowly. "By my alleged boyfriend. I'm now in captivity. That's plenty of information."

Alleged boyfriend. Wayne felt sicker.

Winger gave a short laugh, his furry eyebrows jumping.

"Ms. Bourne," he said, "kidnapping is a very serious crime. A federal offense, in fact. However, I regret to inform you that we *are* the Feds."

He stood up and Borlav followed suit.

"Get some rest, Ms. Bourne," said Borlav, and the two men lumbered out of the room.

Wayne saw Viv biting her bottom lip. She was fighting tears. He felt them rise in his own throat.

"Oh, honey," said Johanna to Viv. "It's not that bad, I promise. Those two come off as a couple of bullies, but that's just their act."

"I need Wayne," said Viv, her voice barely above a whisper.

You have me, he said back soundlessly, through the dark glass.

31.

Luke stood at the window of his office in West Lobe, staring out at the ocean. In the distance, the noonday sunlight sparkled on the water, and he watched clusters of his employees on the campus below, miniaturized from eight stories up, eating their lunches on benches or strolling on the paths.

He had made a good life for these people, he thought. Or at least, he'd upgraded what were already above-average lives. Provided them with meaningful work, beautiful surroundings, generous compensation. He wondered if they were grateful. Probably not. The caliber of people he and Tessa hired came with a baseline of entitlement, accustomed to being sought after, believing they had something unique to offer the world. Rarely did they acknowledge the convergence of luck and circumstance that had landed them in this special place. They were the best of the best—Milford and Gupta and the rest—but they lacked humility. After the Trial wrapped, he thought, he'd announce a Gratitude Day on campus, a sort of personal mini-thanksgiving for his staff, to see who would acknowledge being grateful for Seahorse. He was curious to find out who really cared.

Lately, he'd been concerned about Tessa's loyalty. Her attachment to the Cohort worried him. He'd rarely witnessed Tessa in the social context of other women; he had only known her as their manager. In that role, he could depend on her to keep careful professional distance, never allowing her "feelings" to get in the way of clear-eyed decision-making. But now, in her more nebulous role as the Cohort's advocate during the Trial, a role in which hierarchies were unclear, Luke felt Tessa's inner compass had shifted. Away from the practical needs of their organization toward the emotional needs—which were considerable—of the three women. Plus, there'd been the business with Vivian Bourne, wanting to bring her to the Center for some sort of vague Cohort-bonding purposes. Then her instant resentment of Luke when he'd pointed out the absurdity of the plan. When he'd tried to be the voice of reason.

It was as if, in just a handful of weeks, a mistrust of Luke had bloomed in Tessa. Mistrust with no basis that he could discern, beyond the fact that he was male, and thus stood in stark contrast to the pregnant women with whom she now shared regular meals.

He didn't like the new Tessa. Hopefully, after the Trial had wrapped and the Cohort went off to bond with their babies, she'd return to herself. In the meantime, he had no choice but to adjust responsibly. Meaning that it was not safe to share the details of Gwen's pregnancy with Tessa. He'd had to make an executive decision to eliminate use of the INR-Views from the Trial. Historically, he would have confided in Tessa and asked her to weigh in. Historically, they did not keep secrets from each other. They made decisions together, with a single eye on the greater good. Now, though, she'd probably demand they tell Gwen everything, immediately. It was too risky. As Cohort One approached their collective due date, June 8, he felt more pressure than ever for the Trial to succeed. Felt his father looming over him, whispering *radical and extraordinary. Radical and extraordinary.*

Luke struggled with withholding information from Tessa. She was the only person in the world to whom he truly felt close. He often wished he were attracted to her. If he had been, they would have been an insurmountable pair. He'd tried to convince himself to see her as a sexual being. He'd even sampled contact once, the first night they'd met. It did nothing for him. Embarrassingly, he found himself attracted only to the most clichéd ideas of women—models on catwalks, actresses in sexy superhero costumes, other demeaning iterations.

What was wrong with him? Why couldn't he have just fallen in love with Tessa?

Surely she would have left Peter for him. She'd given Luke all the signals. What would he need from her, in order to want her that way? It wasn't a matter of her physicality; she was perfectly attractive. It was more the sharpness of her mind. The same vibrancy that turned his brain on turned his body off.

But weren't they supposed to be one and the same? The brain being the body's largest sex organ and all that.

He sighed and spun his fidget on the desk. Then he tapped a monitor to life and surveyed the Cohort's latest ultrasounds and stats.

Kate and LaTonya: perfect.

Gwen: well.

The voice of Zeus cut the air. "Callahan, Tessa. Authorized to proceed."

Startled, Luke shut off his monitor just as Tessa stepped into his office. She wore a cream-colored dress he hadn't seen before, sleeveless, with a narrow red belt. Her appearance was as composed as ever, but her eyes were lit up and angled at him.

"What's up, Callahan?

She shut the door behind her.

"You know *what's up*, Luke." Her voice was tight.

"Have a seat." He gestured toward his guest chair, hoping to sound casual, though his pulse had instantly kicked up.

"I'll stand."

"You look . . . agitated."

"I *am* agitated. I'm going to be direct, and I hope you'll reciprocate."

"Consider it done," said Luke, wondering.

"I know I disregarded your opinion when I invited Vivian Bourne to Seahorse. I'm not particularly proud of that. But it was well within my rights to bring her here. I cleared it with Legal. She's a personal contact of mine. A friend. You're not allowed to decide which of my friends visit me here, at *my company*. Canceling her trip was way outside your jurisdiction. And doing it behind my back made it an even bigger overstep."

"What?" Luke felt utterly discombobulated, as if water had been slung in his face. He'd braced for a confrontation, but not this one.

"We need to stop playing these games, Luke. We need to get back to transparency with each other. Starting right now."

"You're going to have to be more specific."

"Cut the shit."

"Callahan! I have no idea what you're talking about. I didn't interfere with Vivian Bourne's trip. I had no idea it was a *thing*. I thought we'd put that topic to bed."

Tessa paused, hands planted on her hips. "You didn't reach out to her and tell her that the Seahorse legal team determined her visit needed to be postponed?"

"No! Who told you that?"

Tessa waved her phone in the air. "*Viv* told me. In a text. That she thought it was in the . . ."—she hooked her fingers into quotes—"*best interest of everyone involved* if she postponed her trip. This is a complete one-eighty—she was clamoring to visit while the Cohort is still pregnant."

"So?" Luke shrugged. He felt his pulse decelerate. He was not in trouble for anything he'd actually done. "She changed her mind."

"No," said Tessa. "I can tell this isn't coming from her."

"Do I have to spell out the possibilities? Maybe a friend talked her out of it. Maybe it was her parents. Maybe she just got freaked out."

"I'm just not buying it. Did Finance ask you to sign off on her travel arrangements? Is that how you found out?"

"Stop."

"She was *wildly* excited, Luke. Who else at Seahorse would've contacted her except you? No one except Finance knows anything about her visit, and they certainly don't give a—"

"*Tessa.*" Luke raised his voice. "It wasn't me."

"Then who was it?" Tessa's tone softened slightly.

"I have no idea," said Luke. "Maybe the first question we should answer is why you did something I explicitly asked you not to do."

"You didn't ask me. You *told* me."

"It's unlike you. We make decisions together."

"Do we, Luke? Because lately it hasn't felt that way." She stepped over to his desk and rested her palms on the edge.

"Tessa, cut it out. If you feel a lack of solidarity, it's because you're too occupied with the Cohort."

"That's my job, Luke." She leaned toward him. "Why don't you tell me how Vivian's trip got canceled?"

Luke paused, considering. In a way, this felt like a stroke of luck, Tessa attacking him for a transgression he knew nothing about. It made him feel certain she knew nothing of the data he'd refrained from sharing with her.

It was almost fun, having her mad at him like this.

Though what she'd done with Vivian Bourne irked him.

"Maybe she chickened out," he said. "Maybe she got cold feet."

"And made up some absurd lie about it? A lie that I could disprove in two seconds? Why would she do that, Luke?"

He pushed his chair back from his desk with his heels, widening the gap between them, and shrugged. "I wouldn't know, Callahan. I'm not the one who's famous for understanding the complexities of young women, now am I?"

He watched the rage take over her face, contracting the corners of her mouth, hardening her gaze. He wished he could take back his words. He'd spoken childishly. Gone too far. But he wasn't used to this—being separate from her, out of sync. Tessa had long been his most important ally, his "co-brain," his friend. She was one of the few women he'd ever truly cared for.

"Look, Tessa, I'm sorry," he began. "I shouldn't have—"

"Oh, that's quite all right," she interrupted, too brightly. "I suggest you save your apologies for later. You'll need them." She grabbed the green fidget off Luke's desk and tossed it over his head toward the window.

"What the hell?" said Luke. In disbelief, he turned to watch the spinner bounce off the smoked glass with a hard ping and fall onto the floor. Instinctively, he rose from his chair and went to retrieve it.

When he stood up, Tessa was gone.

32.

W e're disappointed, Theroux," Borlav said.

Harsh light accosted the seams of his eyelids. Tracy jerked up his head from where he'd laid it on the table in the Blue Room.

Borlav's bulk filled the doorframe.

"Turn off that light," Tracy groaned.

"No can do. This isn't a romantic dinner."

Tracy had been unable to stay awake while he waited for the results of Viv's first screening, in which an Inner Panelist and a Revision Specialist sat her down and laid the facts bare: she needed to shut up about accelerated gestation or pay the price. If she spoke about it again, she would tell their story. Not hers. Not anyone else's. She would stick to the script, or she'd become a permanent resident.

Now that they'd been separated for three days, Tracy found himself unable to stay awake. Viv's absence felt like withdrawal. As soon as he'd gotten back to sleeping in the staff residence zone, he'd begun dreaming of Viv strapped to the bed in quarantine, a cluster of faceless white coats hovering over her, syringes in hand. Nightmares, really. He'd never dreamt of Viv before, not once; he'd read somewhere once that people tended not to dream of things that made sense. He hadn't needed to dream of her because she'd been right there beside him.

Now, she was gone.

Borlav eased into a chair across from him, setting down the single mug of coffee he'd brought for himself.

"Hey, thanks," said Tracy, nodding at the mug.

"I'm in no mood to be nice," said Borlav. "Vivian Bourne's screening was a disaster. What exactly have you been doing for the past four months?"

"My job, Gary."

"Have you? Then why does Bourne seem to have zero qualms about standing her ground? If I remember correctly, you're supposed to be an expert in the art of subtle persuasion. You were supposed to be *prepping* her, Theroux. Filling her impressionable little college brain with respect for the administration. And maybe a whiff of, I don't know, *fear*? A small helping of deference?"

"I didn't have enough time. She's a strong person. I had to work gradually. I couldn't just shoehorn some ideologies that were way out of her zone."

"You had four months. That's enough time to make headway."

"Timeliness with a PIT isn't linear." Tracy willed himself to stay calm, but he felt his anger rearing. "I was holding back for a reason."

"Well, your reason isn't good enough. Bourne's going to require a shit-ton of work. More than we have the resources for. Do you know how many Imports we have happening right now?"

Tracy didn't answer. In truth, Borlav was partially right: he'd ignored the part of his assignment that encouraged him to work on a PIT's powers of resistance. To casually but strategically work in statistics of the current administration's achievements, while subtly reinforcing its power. To remind a PIT that crime in all major U.S. metro areas was at an all-time low, that there hadn't been an act of terrorism on American soil since the assassination attempt on Dewey Falk twenty years ago. That the economy was booming. That the administration's "low-tolerance" policy on the "Disruption of Americanness" was, at least in part, to thank.

The ISA's philosophy was that if a field-op planted and replanted these seeds in the mind of a PIT, they eventually took some kind of hold. Even if only as a faint murmur deep in the subconscious. The ideas were there, irreversibly ingested, making the work of the Revision Specialist a little bit easier.

It was bullshit, Tracy thought. It never would have worked with Viv. He hadn't wanted to humiliate himself by trying.

"Your record isn't spotless, Theroux." Borlav took a gulp of coffee. "You've got some dings. Let's not forget your buddy Irene Brenner. Who's surely gonna come up again before you get that retirement approval you're drooling for."

At the mention of Irene, Tracy's chest clutched. He'd been so occupied with importing Viv that he'd hardly thought about Irene and his long-standing duty to her. He'd brought what she'd asked for. Getting it to her would be the challenge. He would figure it out.

"Is that supposed to be a threat, Gary? Because you'll have to try harder. I've got twenty-six successful Imports on my record. That's more than any other field-op in the ISA. Brenner's one of just a few exceptions."

"You should have *zero* permanent residents, Theroux. My gut tells me that in a week, when Vivian Bourne refuses to get off her fist-waving high horse about an AG conspiracy, her pathetic little attempt to rile up a bunch of kids with dents in their heads, your number will bump up by one. Ending your career on a permanent leaves a bad taste in everyone's mouth. The retirement committee most of all."

Borlav tugged at his collar, the flesh of his neck flushed and sweaty despite the subterranean cool of the Blue Room. Tracy stayed perfectly still.

"What's worse," said Borlav, "is that she's way too goddamn *attached* to you. *Wayne Wayne Wayne.*" He pitched his voice to a falsetto. "Once we break it to her that part of her revision is to never lay eyes on you again, she'll become even more of a mule."

"Shut up." The words flew from Tracy's mouth.

"Cute, how you jump to defend her." Borlav drained his coffee and clanged the mug down on the table. "It goes on my record, too, you know. I'm your boss. Your failure is my failure."

"You're welcome," said Tracy, meeting Borlav's eyes, which were small and deep set. They reminded Tracy of beetles.

"As far as I can tell," said Borlav, "you've been doing nothing but screwing your PIT this whole time. On payroll."

Tracy bolted to his feet, seized with the urge to put Borlav in a headlock. He stood up and balled his fists, summoning every iota of self-control to hold back.

"Watch what you say, Gary."

Borlav blinked but didn't flinch.

"You're supposed to be above this, Theroux. A senior field-op like yourself. When we have no other AG problems out in the field. We're this close"—Borlav pinched his forefinger to his thumb—"to putting the entire Juva situation behind us. Can you imagine that, Theroux? A day when we can stop thinking about this idiotic problem? Don't you know I hate this AG assignment as much as you do? Why would you delay putting it to bed once and for all? Can you help me understand that? Help me understand why you fucked up so royally with Vivian Bourne?"

Tracy paused. Desperation was creeping inside him, dislodging his rationality. It had been Borlav's line about Viv never laying eyes on him that did it.

Goddammit.

He spoke slowly. "Let's take a step back, Gary. Keep Viv in quarantine for a while. Let me work with her. I can turn her around."

Borlav barked a laugh.

"Oh, that won't be necessary, Theroux. You're off her case."

"Excuse me?"

"I put you on probation for . . . let me see. One, failure to execute the psychological component of your mission. Two, becoming intimate with your PIT." He held up his fat fingers to count. "Three—"

Tracy cut him off. "Viv's *my* contact. I'm not sitting around with my thumb in my ass while the rest of you scramble her brain. You'll fail."

"Thumb won't get so lucky, Theroux. You're done with Bourne. But don't worry, I have a new assignment for you. Call it a temp job. Night Survey. Chief. Which means you're not only working graveyard, but you're accountable for everyone else who does, too. Any glitches between the hours of 11:00 p.m. and 7:00 a.m. are on you. Fuckups will just stretch out your timeline to retirement even further."

Tracy had the sensation of falling, as if in a dream. He groped for reason.

"You can't punish me with Night Survey. That's for rookies still popping their zits. I'm not playing Rambo with a bunch of pubescent little fucks. There are more than enough of them guarding this place."

"Rambo?" Borlav brayed a laugh. "Love truly has made you delusional, Theroux. Look, you're on Night Survey, and that's that. It's where we need you to pitch in."

"No. Let me keep working with Viv. Please." He was on the verge of begging Borlav now. But the prospect of being removed from Vivian's case—of possibly never seeing her again—was more than he could bear.

"Sorry," said Borlav, clearly enjoying himself now. "No can do."

"Just give me one week. Seven days and I'll turn Bourne around. If not, I'll report to night watch. I swear to God."

"God's not listening, Theroux. This discussion is over. You're going to strap on your gear and do your fucking Night Survey until we decide to clear you. *If* we decide."

In Tracy's mind, freedom receded from him, a single hurtling car on a vacant highway. A car with Viv inside it.

He ached all over.

"Gary." He spoke slowly to control his tremors. "It's been twenty years. Twenty-six Imports. That's twenty-six human lives I've reconfigured with my bare hands. I've dedicated my life to cleaning up the fallout from other people's mistakes. So they could get rich and win elections and keep *America American*." He let his voice slip into a sneer. What did it matter now?

"My life, Borlav. Some of my Imports took two years to bring in. I had four months with Viv, Gary. Use some common sense. You can't punish me for a tight timeline. Or for being human."

Borlav groaned and held up a hand. "Spare me the pity party. Take a deep breath. Night Survey's not a big deal. Don't jeopardize your retirement more than you already have. Trust me, we all want you out of here, too." He heaved himself upright and stepped toward the door. "In the meantime, why don't we both get some sleep? You'll need it. Your Night Survey duty starts tomorrow."

Tracy pictured the ten-by-twelve structure that served as his "home" when he was at the Colony: *headstones*, the field-ops sometimes called their residences. Inside his, nothing but a sink, a desk with a few ancient photos of Bethany's kids tacked over it, curled up at their edges. The bed was a thin-mattressed twin, "extra long," which was what field-ops considered a perk. He imagined climbing into it alone, the nights ahead of him an indefinite number, nights without Vivian, retirement returned to a vague notion.

He felt he might weep. "You go on," he said to Borlav. "I'll see myself out."

"Good night, Theroux."

~

When he was sure Borlav was gone, he closed the door and paged the nurses' station in quarantine.

He'd brought Irene's gift. The thing she'd asked him for a few weeks ago, when he'd visited her on the tranquil porch of her house in the Colony. He'd promised her.

The voice he'd been hoping for leapt into his ear, melodic and throaty: *Quarantine, Johanna speaking.*

"Johanna, it's Theroux. I need a favor."

"Tracy?" Her voice was like a bright beam piercing darkness. "Hello, baby. What can I do for you?"

"A couple of favors, actually."

33.

*P*eter Grandwein's robot here. Please leave a message for my master.
Tessa tapped "End" and lowered her phone from her ear as she walked down the hallway toward the Cohort's residence. Normally his corny outgoing message made her smile, but she'd heard it so many times lately that it had ceased to amuse her. Peter was often out of signal range and Tessa was often unavailable when he did have a connection. Since he'd begun hiking the Pacific Crest Trail eight weeks ago, they'd managed to speak once a week, and Peter, who avoided texting and social media, messaged Tessa the occasional photo of some stunning vista. Now he was swinging into the last days of the hike, scheduled to exit in southern Oregon sometime in the next day or two and catch a flight back to San Jose. Then he'd spend a night at home in Atherton before heading to Tessa at Seahorse.

Tessa could hardly wait. She'd predicted that as the Cohort neared their collective due date, now just a week away, she'd be so consumed by the culmination of the Trial that Peter would be far from her mind. In truth, the impending births had made her miss him more than ever.

Right now, hearing his voice would help, too. Since yesterday's tension with Luke over Vivian Bourne's canceled trip, a chill had taken hold between them. She regretted accusing him so spontaneously, especially after Viv followed up later, explaining that her parents had pushed up their arrival date at Weldon for graduation, cutting into Viv's trip to Seahorse.

So typical of my parents to barge across the country uninvited, she wrote to Tessa. *Super bummed to postpone but maybe I can come after the births???*

Of course, Tessa replied, though something in Viv's tone annoyed her. It was too offhanded, too light, after her intensity when they'd met on campus, and throughout discussion of her trip. The Cohort would be disappointed. They were heavily pregnant now, deep in the equivalent of their third trimester and eager for any distraction, especially in the form of meeting a child of AG. They'd been almost giddy with anticipation.

Tessa had not yet broken the news of the canceled trip to the Cohort. She also hadn't yet shown them the INR-View. Residual guilt, the g-word, over having wrongly accused Luke of meddling with Vivian Bourne had kept her from debuting the device with the Cohort.

Soon, she thought. For now, she'd hidden it in her room—much more carefully than Luke had hidden it.

Outside the residence door, Tessa knocked to be polite, then lifted her hand to the sensor for Zeus to admit her. She waited for the familiar voice, but it didn't come.

She lifted her palm to the sensor again, more slowly.

Still nothing.

"Tessa?" Kate's voice sounded through the door. It sounded odd. Tentative.

"It's me," said Tessa. "Is Zeus down?"

"Hang on," said Kate. Again, Tessa waited for the door to unlock, but it didn't.

"Hello?" she called through the door. "Can you let me in, Kate?"

Finally, the door swung open. Kate stood on the other side, her stomach bulging beneath a flowy sky-blue dress. She wore no makeup and Tessa noticed her eyes were rimmed with red. "Is everything okay?" said Tessa.

Kate sniffed.

"Tessa," she said, "we need to talk to you."

Tessa followed her into the living area, where LaTonya and Gwen sat on the couch. They both looked somber.

"What is it?" said Tessa.

"Can you come sit down with us?" said LaTonya.

Kate settled beside Gwen, and Tessa sat opposite the three women. A thick, tense silence lodged between them.

"Okay," said Tessa, breaking. "It's *fraught* in this room. What's going on, you guys?"

LaTonya exhaled. "A fuck of a lot."

"Go ahead and show her, Gwen," said Kate.

Slowly, Gwen stood up from the couch, one hand cradling the bottom of her belly. It was massive, Tessa noticed, jutting out from under Gwen's black maternity T-shirt.

"Show me what?" said Tessa.

"Tessa, look," said Gwen. She took a deep breath and lifted her shirt.

"Oh my God," said Tessa. No other words were available. Gwen's pale belly was lumpen with not one bump but two twin mounds: one under her right breast, a half soccer ball, and another over her left hip bone, slightly smaller. Two separate hills, the valley between them shallow but distinct. Tessa fought not to look away.

"Go ahead," said Gwen. "Feel them." She stepped forward and grabbed Tessa's hand and pressed it to the bump above her hip. Tessa wanted to pull away. Instead, she let her palm rest against Gwen's lower bump. It was very firm, the skin stretched tightly across it.

"Feel that?" said Gwen.

"Yes."

Gwen moved Tessa's hand up to the second protrusion.

"And that?"

"Yes."

"Have you ever seen a pregnant woman's stomach look like this?"

"No. I haven't."

"Neither have I," said Gwen, shaky.

LaTonya spoke. "She just woke up from a nap and suddenly looked this way."

"It's true," said Gwen. "I fell asleep with one bump, and woke up with two."

"Why haven't you called a nurse?" asked Tessa.

"I don't know. I'm afraid of what they'll tell me."

"Don't panic," said Tessa, feeling panicked. "Let's get you down to Clinical right away."

"I just had an ultrasound this morning," said Gwen. "Like the rest of you. Everything was normal. Baby boy in head-down position. Measuring seventeen inches. What could have changed in four hours to make me look like this?"

"The baby could just be in a strange position," said Tessa, having no idea if it was true. She removed her hands from Gwen's belly and was grateful when Gwen's shirt dropped down to conceal it.

"No," Gwen whispered. "That's not it."

"I'm fucking scared," said LaTonya, her voice cracking. "What *is* it?"

"Keep hold of yourself, LaTonya," said Tessa. She turned to Gwen. "How do you know it's not just the baby's position?"

"It's the movements," whispered Gwen. "They're separate from each other. Like they're coming from different sources."

"I felt them myself," said Kate. "It's true. Ripples down by her hip bone and up near her chest, at the same time."

"Hands and feet," said Tessa.

"No," said Gwen. "Something's not right." She sat heavily onto the couch and covered her face with her hands. Then she spoke in a muffled voice. "It can't be just one baby. Unless . . ."

"Unless what?" said Tessa.

"There's something seriously wrong with it."

"If that were true, you'd have known long ago," said Tessa. "You're in the care of some of the most brilliant doctors in the world. I brought them here to Seahorse myself."

"Which is exactly why I don't trust anything you say," said Gwen, looking up at Tessa, eyes blazing with accusation. "You're part of the business machine here, Tessa. I read your book, your op-eds, every article about you, before I came here. You're not a scientist. You know nothing more than any of us. You're a PR stunt for Seahorse. You're a way for Luke Zimmerman to validate TEAT faster. And you have no idea what's going on."

"I understand why you'd feel that way," said Tessa calmly.

"Don't pull that empathetic-manager shit on me," said Gwen, her voice breaking. "Something isn't right with my baby." A tear streaked down her cheek. "I never should have signed up for this in the first place. It's fucked up, this thing we're doing."

"Don't say that," said LaTonya.

"But it *is*, isn't it?" said Gwen. "We're meddling with nature. We're putting *human babies* at risk. It's insane. Of course I'm being punished, of course some terrib—" She choked on a sob.

"Oh, Gwen," said Tessa, pulling her into a hug, as much as she could manage.

Gwen pushed her away. "Of course something terrible is going to happen. You can't engineer life this way." She pressed her hands over her face, her body quaking. "I deserve this."

"Stop this," said Tessa. "You're panicking, Gwen. Your mind is spiraling. It's reacting to fear and speaking to it. You are stronger than this. You have the power to calm down right now."

"You're a friggin' goddess, Gwen," said LaTonya. "Listen to Tessa."

"Breathe, honey," said Kate, tentatively putting her hand on Gwen's back. "Just breathe for a minute." When Gwen didn't move away, Kate began to rub her palm in circles.

Slowly, Gwen's sobs dissipated. When she seemed to have calmed, Tessa said, "Let's go down to Clinical and find out what's happening. I'll walk down with you right now."

"*No,*" said Gwen. "I won't. I don't trust them. I want a second opinion."

"From whom?" asked Tessa.

"Another doctor. Unaffiliated with Seahorse. I want to see someone today. Off campus."

"Impossible," said Tessa. "That would violate your NDA."

"So I'll go to jail," said Gwen, shrugging. Her usual archness had returned. "I don't care. That sounds better than living with this feeling I've been having."

"If you leave," said LaTonya, "I'm leaving too."

Kate paused. "Me, too."

For the first time since she'd stepped through the door of the residence wing, Tessa didn't know what to say.

34.

Irene sat on her porch at sunrise, watching bands of color warm the sky over the dry brown mountains in the distance. Dawn had always been her favorite time of day, when her sense of optimism was restored. When the possibility of transformation, yet again, felt just within reach. She remembered stepping off the boathouse dock at Gales Ferry after predawn crew practice, her throat hoarse from coxswaining, the morning coming to life around her. How her heart seemed to rise in her chest, the day telling her *yes yes yes*: anything was surmountable. The new sun on her face was an infusion of power. She let it in, and it carried her.

Even on *that* morning, when she'd steered her car away from the Cades Cove parking lot in Great Smoky Mountains National Park, leaving her baby girl behind, she'd stared into the rosy light filtering through the red spruce trees and thought *maybe*. Maybe it would be okay.

Even on the morning when Henry Duarte had said to her, *You are now in custody of the United States government*, the light had been saffron-bright in her kitchen window, and at first, she'd actually laughed. Surely nothing terrible could be happening against the background of a clean, fresh day.

Even now, when there was nothing left ahead of her, the morning fooled Irene. Even now, sitting alone in her government-issued rocker, in the middle of some nameless desert, she felt it: change, beckoning to her. Offering itself. For a moment, if she did nothing but breathe, she could almost believe it.

Almost.

From the purple-flowered shrubs lining her house, a rabbit hopped onto the lawn. It stopped and sniffed the air, unaware of Irene. She watched it sample several different possibilities, springing toward the road at the end of the lawn and then darting in another direction. It was a lean bunny, she noticed, its body a single tensile arc, tail like a snowball. Her body had once been like that—taut and nimble, ready for commands.

Finally, the rabbit bounced back toward the house and disappeared into the same spot of ruellia from which it had emerged. Irene understood its decision. Here, there was nowhere to go. She rocked and sipped her tea and felt the day's oncoming heat start to press into her.

Soon, a golf cart approached the bend in the road leading to her house, the long, empty loop that circled the Colony's permanent residence zone. She sat up straighter and squinted; she'd left her eyeglasses on her bedside table. It was unusual to see any traffic on the loop at this hour, just after 6:00 a.m. Johanna wouldn't be arriving to make breakfast until after seven.

Swinging onto the straightaway, fifty yards from Irene's house, the golf cart accelerated. The things didn't go very fast, Irene knew, no more than fifteen miles per hour or so, but clearly the driver was flooring the pedal. Her curiosity piqued, she stood from her chair, wobbling as she gained her footing, and went inside to get her glasses. Whoever it was, she wanted to see their face when they passed her house. Even a drive-by would feel like company.

Going inside took longer than she'd expected. The two steps up from the porch were dicey. Bending over to pick up her glasses from where she'd apparently knocked them onto the floor felt like a feat of acrobatics. This was her reality now: simple physical tasks were complicated and arduous. Somehow, she kept forgetting.

When she returned to the porch, Henry Duarte was sitting in her rocker, in head-to-toe camouflage, including a baseball-style cap.

Her hand flew to her mouth. "Henry!"

He jumped up and came to her, pulling her into his arms. Her cheek pressed against the stiff cotton and nylon blend of his uniform, she felt small and safe.

"I'm not supposed to be here," he said. "I can only stay for a minute."

"Don't say that. You always say that." As instantly as the sight of him brought her relief, the prospect of his departure brought sadness. She closed her eyes, letting his presence wash over her. For now, he was here.

"This time, it's more serious," he said. "I don't have clearance to be here."

She stepped from his embrace and he helped lower her back into the rocker. He sat on the ground beside her, legs drawn in a V, elbows resting on his knees. His face looked creased and weary, though he was clean-shaven, with a fresh haircut, a short buzz with clean lines over his ears and at the back of his neck.

"What do you mean, you don't have clearance?" Irene asked him. "And why are you wearing fatigues? I've never seen you . . . isn't that for . . . the others?" She trailed off, having never learned the structure of the Colony's personnel, who did exactly what, or why. She hadn't wanted to. She knew Henry and Johanna, plus a handful of other Permanents, and the doctors she saw weekly, but that was it.

"Long story," Henry sighed. "I got demoted. I'm on night watch now. Basically a security guard, over at Base. Not allowed to travel between zones."

"Then how are you here?"

"Johanna helped."

"She's a good egg."

"She is." Henry shifted to face her head-on and adjusted his hat. His expression was very serious. "Irene, I brought you something."

She didn't have to ask what it was. Inside her body she felt a chemical shift, like tuning forks rubbing together. Instantly, she felt more alive. As if the morning had finally made good on its promise. Possibility. Transformation.

"You did?" she asked softly.

"I did." Henry reached into the breast pocket of his shirt and pulled out a miniature manila envelope, three inches long. "Are you sure you still want it?"

"Absolutely," she said. She'd never been surer of anything.

Beside her, she could hear him breathing. When he spoke, she could tell he was fighting to control his voice.

"Okay," he said. "I'm going to give it to you. But you can't use it until tomorrow night. I'm going to tell you what to do, and I need you to follow my instructions *exactly*."

"Okay. But why tomorrow night?" She didn't want to wait through another dawn. Today's had been enough. Now, in fact, it seemed perfect.

"Tomorrow, Johanna will take you to the Quarry for an appointment."

"I just saw the docs yesterday. There's nothing scheduled for tomorrow."

"Now there is. Trust me."

"I trust you, Henry."

Slowly, he extended the slip of manila toward her. She lifted her hand, wondering if he noticed how crabbed and knotty it had grown. Probably not, she thought. Henry never seemed to notice her deteriorating exterior. Instead, he seemed to see straight inside her.

For this, she'd always loved him. Even though he'd lied to her. Even though he'd brought her here. One of the reasons she refused to revise and leave the Colony—and she had many reasons—was that revision required her to never see Henry again. That, and never speak the truth. To deny that Juva had ever done her harm, to perpetuate an absurd story of rare cancer, to live lie upon lie, while never seeing Henry's face again. It wasn't a life. She'd rather be dead.

She closed her fingers around the envelope.

Tears glazed the surface of Henry's eyes. He rose to his feet.

"Don't cry," said Irene. "You've made me so happy."

He held up his palm. "Please don't say that. I've made no one happy."

She smiled. "That's not for you to decide, Henry."

"It's Tracy. Tracy Theroux. You know that, don't you?"

"I do. I just prefer Henry."

"Speaking of names. One more thing."

"Yes?" said Irene.

"They named her Vivian."

"What?"

"The people who found her. They named her Vivian, and they gave her a good life."

Irene gazed up at him, backlit by the sun, a haggard angel.

"Thank you, Tracy Theroux," she said, and he was gone.

The dawn fooled her every time.

"Vivian?" Johanna's voice eased through the cracked door. "Sweetness?"

"What?" said Viv, foggy with sleep. She fumbled for the light on her nightstand. Pinched at the little chain. Dim light seeped from the bulb. She blinked, roving her eyes around the blank walls, disoriented.

"Is it already time to wake up?" It did not feel like morning, but then again, without cues of sunlight, in this windowless room, how could she be sure?

"No, baby doll, you just fell asleep an hour ago," said Johanna, still outside the door. "You've got a visitor. It'll be quick. Then you can go back to sleep."

Viv bolted up in bed. "Wayne?" she said.

"No, no," said Johanna, stepping backward through the door, pushing it open with her body. "But it's someone Tracy wanted you to meet."

She was maneuvering a wheelchair. Viv watched her back it fully into the room, then close the door. Slowly, Johanna swiveled the wheelchair around to face Viv.

Seated in the chair was an elderly, shriveled woman, her face a fissured desert surface. She wore her bone-white hair long, in scraggly spirals, past the hunch in her back, which rose up from between her shoulders like a turtle shell. She was ancient, ravaged, yet her face was inexplicably beautiful to Viv, a sacred and familiar ruin.

Johanna pushed the woman closer to Viv until her knees met the edge of Viv's mattress. The woman extended her arms. Instead of recoiling, Viv instinctively leaned forward. The woman put one palm on either side of Viv's face and held it between the soft, withered branches of her hands.

Viv closed her eyes. Felt the bird bones of the woman's thin-skinned hands pressing against the flesh of her cheeks. A gauzy memory returned to Viv, from somewhere deep in her muscles. She could not say what it was, but it was there, distinct as an old wound throbbing with the onset of rain.

"Hello, my baby," said the woman. "Hello, and goodbye."

"What?" said Viv.

"I'm sorry," said the woman, her voice chalky, eyes shining with tears. "I just wanted to tell you. That's all."

As if on cue, Johanna spun the wheelchair back toward the door, and pushed. In seconds they were back in the hallway, as if they'd never come at all.

"Who are you?" whispered Viv to the empty room, though somehow, she knew.

35.

Tessa stood before the women of Cohort One, considering the potential disaster of their collectively abandoning the Trial. Their contract with Seahorse could make it difficult, but ultimately, they could leave if they wanted to badly enough. Even if they'd signed away all of Seahorse's liability, even if they conceded to the medical ethics requirements, even if they'd promised not to speak of the Trial outside the gates of the Seahorse campus. If they were willing to live with the consequences, they could devastate the entire organization in one swift coup.

"No," said Tessa. "That is absolutely . . ."

Suddenly, she knew what she needed to do: empower them to want to stay.

"Are you okay, Tessa?" said LaTonya.

"Wait here for just a minute," she said. "I need to get something from my room."

Ten minutes later, she returned to the living area, holding a maroon toiletry case and her phone, and set both on the table between the couches. The Cohort stared at her without speaking, their curiosity palpable. Tessa rolled the case's lock into proper alignment, clicked it open, and removed the wand inside.

"Whoa," said LaTonya. "Is that an INR-View?"

Tessa flicked it and connected it to her phone.

"Gwen, lift your shirt," she commanded. Gwen obeyed.

Tessa skimmed the wand slowly over Gwen's belly, as she'd seen Gupta do dozens of times. The blue light flicked and flicked, and then held steady, indicating it had gathered a full image. Tessa held up her phone so they could all see the corresponding image.

"Jesus Christ," said Kate.

"I knew it," said Gwen, her voice dead flat. "I knew it."

On the screen were two babies, suspended in fluid, facing each other, attached at the sternum.

Conjoined twins.

In the warm track lighting of the living space, the sun bright gold outside, Tessa was suddenly freezing. The INR-View slipped out of her hand and bounced off the rug. Her phone went dark. Gwen pulled her shirt back over her belly and dropped onto the couch.

Kate began to cry. "Now I have to check mine, too. But I'm afraid."

"Me, too," said LaTonya.

Tessa summoned her calm. "Of course," she said. "We're going to look at the other babies together. But first." She turned to Gwen, desperate to provide some comfort—but what? Gwen stared at Tessa, terror immobilizing her gaze, eyes dark and cold.

Tessa reached for Gwen's chin and cupped it in her hand. Gently, she stroked the woman's face.

"Listen to me, Gwen. Everything is going to be okay. I know that sounds impossible, under the circumstances, but I'm promising you."

"Impossible," said Gwen, toneless. "It's over. They've been lying to me for all these weeks, and now my babies are going to die."

"They will not die," said Tessa.

Gwen gave a rueful laugh and removed Tessa's hand. "You can stop right there, Tessa. Spare us the motivational speech. You've lost me. It's over. You've probably known about this all along. You're part of the *team*, after all."

"No," said Tessa, more sharply than she'd intended. "You're welcome to every negative opinion of me except that one. I promise you, Gwen, that I knew nothing of this."

"If she did, why would she bring us an INR-View?" said Kate, swiping at her tears.

"I don't think she knew," said LaTonya.

"Think about it," said Gwen. "Think about who she is. A woman so obsessed with practicality and efficiency"—she spat the words—"that she's trying to reconfigure the way people *get made*."

"Wait," said Tessa. "That's not why—"

"Actions speak louder," said Gwen. "You can spin it any way you like, but in the end, you are a woman who encourages other women to entrust their bodies and their babies to artificial manipulations. To take a pill so they don't feel their pregnancies. To hand over their breast milk so it can be replicated. Did you ever consider that nature might be sort of wise? That maybe we're *supposed* to feel sick during pregnancy? Maybe we're *supposed* to suck it up and nurse our own babies, inconvenient as it may be? You say don't blame the women, blame the system, but aren't you expecting *us* to take all the risk?"

"We applied to be here," said Kate. "No one pressured us into the Trial."

"You're wrong," said Gwen. She pointed to Tessa. "She did."

"What?" said Tessa.

"We all read your book," said Gwen. "We know how eloquent it is. How persuasive, how exciting, how inspiring, how much of a . . ." Her voice cracked. "A complete and total mind-fuck it is for desperate women like me."

Tessa waited for Kate or LaTonya to jump to her defense, but both remained silent. She felt them abruptly receding from her, crossing into solidarity with Gwen.

"You've misunderstood me," said Tessa. "I have deep respect for the wisdom of nature. It's expectations of women that've become unnatural. In a better world, we'd be allowed to stay home sick with nausea and nurse on demand around the clock. In a better world, women would get a stipend every year until their youngest child went to kindergarten. In a bet—"

"In a better world, you'd have enrolled in the Trial yourself," said Gwen. "If you really believed in Seahorse one hundred percent, if you believed in everything you're peddling in *Pushing Through*, then you would've put your money where your mouth is. We all know you're married. We all know you're rich. What was stopping you?"

"I . . ." Tessa fought to compose herself. "I couldn't get pregnant. I mean *we*. My husband and I. Peter and me." Her words sounded sloppy; she could not seem to compose them.

"Weak excuse," said Gwen. "A woman like you wouldn't let a detail like that stop you. A little show of uncooperativeness from nature. You're a pioneer of reproductive technology, Tessa. Don't tell me infertility really got in your way."

Tessa stumbled back to the couch opposite the Cohort and let it catch her. She felt woozy, as if Gwen had spun her around and around, dislodging something at her center in the process. She leaned back against the couch and shut her eyes. Bile rose to the back of her throat. She felt violently queasy and pulled in air hard through her nostrils, willing herself not to throw up.

When she'd steadied herself, she opened her eyes. From the opposite couch, the three women watched her, waiting for answers.

"You're right," Tessa said slowly, meeting Gwen's eyes. "I didn't want a baby badly enough. I *don't* want one badly enough. Peter wanted it, and I pretended to want it, but I didn't. That's why I'm not pregnant. That's why I'm not in the Trial."

"Okay," said Gwen, with a hint of kindness. "Then it's okay."

"Oh, Tessa," said Kate.

"I never gave a fuck that you weren't in it," said LaTonya.

Tessa's hands were shaking and her nausea was still intense, but with great effort she summoned her focus. There was a situation to deal with.

"I didn't know about your babies," she said to Gwen.

"I believe you," said Gwen.

"But I'm going to help you," said Tessa. "I'm going to help you, and I'm going to punish whoever knew this and hid it from you."

"Can retribution wait until Kate and I see our babies?" said LaTonya.

"Yes," said Tessa, picking up the INR-View from where she'd dropped it on the floor.

"Technology is a feminist weapon, right?" said Kate weakly.

"Prepare for battle," said Tessa grimly. She waved the wand through the air like a sword.

36.

To make the call, Tracy went to the Blue Room, one of the few spots at the Colony where he might operate unnoticed, at least for a short time. The room was designed for secrecy, for the secure transfer of ultrasensitive information, and thus digital communication that happened inside was protected by extra layers of encryption. Sure, there were plenty of folks at the ISA who could crack it, who'd probably only need a few minutes to trace who Tracy was calling and what he was telling them, but it might take hours before anyone looked at the data stream.

If he was lucky.

All he needed to do was delay their noticing. After that, they could discover him. They could penalize him any way they liked. As long as he executed his promises to Irene and Vivian, he no longer cared what happened to him afterward. His life was not worth the sum of theirs. Not by a long shot.

The underground room was dark and cool. He secured the door's multiple locks and stood with his back against it. Just in case.

On his phone, he pulled up a photo of Viv, one that he'd taken on the plane he'd forced her to board in New Hampshire. It was the most troubling one he could find: her mouth slack, eyes half closed, head tipped back.

He tapped out a message: *This is Wayne Bridger. I sat next to you on a flight from San Jose to Boston. I'm contacting you because Vivian Bourne is in grave danger and needs your help. I need to speak with you immediately in order to ensure her safety. Please place a blocked video call to me at this number ASAP. The situation is urgent.*

He took a deep breath and texted the photo and the message to Tessa Callahan.

A few minutes later, his phone lit up with a blocked call.

37.

Tessa was on the footbridge, en route to Luke's office from the Cohort residence, trying to piece together a strategy in her mind. In the past, she would have tried to appeal to Luke's integrity. To what she'd once believed to be his inherent goodness, lodged deep beneath his ambition and his insecurity and his little-boy desperation to please the looming ghost of his father.

Except now she wasn't sure the goodness was there. She was no longer sure who Luke was.

Or for that matter, who *she* was.

But now was not the time for introspection. She had to do whatever it took, no matter how calculated, to find out the exact status of Gwen's babies, and how they could save them. She knew that conjoined twins, if connected in certain parts of the body, could survive. She'd read a few accounts of their successful separation, even watched an interview with twins who were leading healthy, normal lives.

More commonly, though, she knew the outcomes were different.

Her anger at Luke was a curious thing, so large and solid that it had calcified inside her. It was like carrying a load of bricks. She had to step carefully, with great concentration, or she might fall into such a dark place, she might not know how to climb out.

If she wasn't careful, she might lose all control.

But she was famous for self-control. Peter had reminded her of this more than once, when he was trying to get through to her.

I need the real Tessa right now, he would say.

Too often, she had not granted him this, claiming she was unable. That it was not in her nature to soften on demand.

But nature was malleable.

Wasn't it?

Somehow, she would get through to Luke.

Below her, midday at the Seahorse Center, the floors teemed with life and industry. Young engineers in T-shirts and jeans, a couple of dogs, lab techs in white coats. The sun filtered down through the dome, gilded and generous. Briefly, she thought of flight. Of gliding in the elevator to the ground floor, stepping onto the Thought Floor and walking straight through security, out into the open afternoon. Of driving somewhere—a hospital in San Francisco, or the Stanford med school, where she knew the dean—and simply asking for help.

She knew many people, beyond Seahorse, who would help her.

She'd just stepped off the footbridge and into the hallway of West Lobe when the text from Wayne Bridger arrived.

She remembered him instantly: the charming, handsome man with faded acne scars who'd sat beside her on the flight to Boston. She glanced at the text midstride, but when she saw the photo he'd sent, she stopped in her tracks.

On her screen was a photo of Vivian Bourne, appearing pale and unconscious. She scanned the accompanying text, then veered down the hallway to her own office instead of Luke's. She locked the door behind her and stared at the ocean beyond the window, a dazzling cobalt blue beneath the afternoon sun.

Then she sat down at her desk and did as Wayne Bridger had asked.

In seconds, his face filled her screen, backdropped by a blue wall.

"I wanted you to be able to see me," he said, forgoing a greeting. "In case you had any doubts about authenticity."

"Explain the situation," said Tessa.

Wayne explained.

Tessa gripped her phone tighter.

"I need you to come and get her," Wayne said. "You'll need a helicopter."

"Where?" said Tessa. "How?"

"I'm sending you the coordinates," said Wayne. "Any good pilot will be able to find us."

"Then what?" said Tessa.

"Then you take Viv with you," he said. "We'll meet you there. Twelve thirty a.m. Mountain time tomorrow night."

Tessa's heart sped.

"I want to help," she said. "But why me? Why not her parents? Why not—"

"Too risky," snapped Wayne. "And plus, Tessa, you owe her."

"Owe her? Why?"

"Not just Viv. You owe any number of them."

"Any number of who?"

"The mothers and children who suffered from AG. Your methods are sloppy, Tessa. Egregious disregard for scientific procedure. We're well aware that Seahorse obtained the source material for your glitzy *product* illicitly."

"Illicitly? What?"

"Don't play dumb." Wayne's voice was hard. "Nothing gets past the ISA. We've known for years that your buddy Luke Zimmerman helped himself to tissue samples from Configuration Labs. You've been riding a loophole all these years. The ride is over now. You might as well comply and show up exactly where I tell you to show up, or I can send you and your skateboarder boyfriend to jail tomorrow."

Tessa felt she was hurtling through space, as if she'd fallen from the footbridge and was plummeting down, down.

Wayne kept talking.

"If you want to cooperate, maybe you can save yourself and your precious company and maybe even your billions. Maybe that loophole you've been clinging to won't disappear."

"I . . . I don't understand." Tessa heard her voice shaking. "What loophole?"

"Let me put it this way. Until now, the ISA and Seahorse have had an unspoken agreement. You do your demented little experiments, tool around with human bodies, and we'll look the other way. But it couldn't last forever, now could it? Unless you help Vivian Bourne, forever ends tomorrow. I can have the Feds at your fucking techie Xanadu *tomorrow*."

Tessa could do nothing but stare into her phone at Wayne. His face was so clear she could see his scars. They regarded each other through the screens. She recalled something she'd written in *Pushing Through*, in the section devoted to tips on running a successful meeting as a woman.

Do not hesitate to employ intimacy, albeit strategically and appropriately, in professional conversations.

"I'm waiting for a yes," said Wayne.

"What happened to you?" she asked.

"Come again?"

"I'm curious," she said, "how you landed in a career as a spy." He'd never used the word *spy*, but she'd deduced, based on what he'd told her, that he was.

"This is not a goddamn therapy session," said Wayne. It was striking, Tessa thought, how different he was now from the relaxed cowboy–grad student persona he'd presented to her on the plane.

"Just tell me. Was secrecy necessary in your earlier life? Did it sustain you?"

He squinted at her, incredulous.

"Of *course* it was fucking necessary," he said. "I'm sending you the coordinates now. Be there at 12:30 a.m. on the nose tomorrow. As in, after midnight."

His screen went dark.

Suddenly, Tessa knew her strategy.

~

Luke was exiting his office just as Tessa arrived.

"Hey." He greeted her with a single flat word. His expression—impatient, startled—suggested she'd caught him in the middle of something. He appeared packed up and ready to go somewhere: office lights off, monitor dark, bag slung over his shoulder.

"I need to talk to you." She'd coached herself on appearing perfectly composed. As if she were paying Luke a social visit, as if she'd simply missed him.

"Now's not a good time," he said.

"This is important, Luke."

"Can we walk and talk? I have a meeting."

"What meeting?"

She could see in his hesitation that he would not be telling her the truth.

"San Francisco," he said.

"Luke. Please. I need you. Ten minutes."

He craned his neck down the hallway, as if to verify its emptiness.

"In here," he said, summoning her back into his office.

She followed and shut the door. Despite the room's airiness, it felt claustrophobic.

"Do you want to sit down?" He gestured toward the Lucite.

"I don't," she said.

"What's up?" He was impatient. "I have to be somewhere in an hour." She heard an uncertainty in his voice. She reminded herself of the basics of communicating with Luke. With all men. Joining them emotionally, wherever they were. Not letting the vicissitudes of your own wild, unhinged, female feelings take charge. Corroborating those feelings, that state of being, and then soothing it.

"What is it? You seem . . ." She searched for the word. It was *squirrelly* or *skittish*, but that would only make him retreat from her. "Preoccupied. Worried. I can tell you're upset about something." She could. It was in the way he was holding his lips, contracted around his teeth. Pursed. The membrane holding his vulnerability was porous. Even now, with Gwen's situation teeming in her mind, making her whole body feel on edge, she could see that to accuse Luke of anything would be foolish.

"What's going on, Luke? You can tell me. As friends having a conversation. It's not work unless you say it is. We're partners, remember?"

"So what's up?"

In *Pushing Through*, she'd instructed her readers to begin confrontational conversations with statements of feeling.

"I'm feeling worried, Luke."

"About?"

"About information recently shared with me. Unexpected information."

"No games, Tessa, remember? Tell me what you mean."

She looked him in the eye. "I'm feeling concerned about Gwen's pregnancy. I know you think it's a psych issue, but I'm certain it's also phys—"

He cut her off. "Okay, so you know."

"I know what?"

"That she's carrying twins. I've been wanting to tell you. But it posed a conflict."

"What?" Tessa's body electrified, as if she'd been plugged into a socket. "A conflict with *me*? What about the conflict of not telling *her*?"

"It was risk mitigation. To keep her from doing something dangerous before we knew we could stabilize the situation. We have every intention of telling her."

"When? The Cohort's due in a week!"

"When she goes into labor," said Luke calmly. "When she's officially no longer a flight risk. As you know, she's demonstrated instability since she arrived here. It's only progressed. Plus, there are some complications with the twins."

She already knows, you bastard, she wanted to say.

"Complications?" she said, playing dumb.

"That's where we're fortunate, actually. The situation is extremely rare. The embryo Gupta implanted spontaneously divided. But it didn't cleave entirely. The babies are conjoined, yes. But they're attached at the sternum. Nothing but cartilage and tissue connecting them. No organs involved. They'll be easy to separate."

Relief flooded her, but she reminded herself not to trust him.

"Easy?" she said.

"Milford has it under control."

"Really? And did Milford endorse this decision not to tell her? To willfully deceive a mother about the ultrasound images of her own baby?"

Luke sighed. "*Endorse* is too strong a word. Let's say he consented. It was a matter of unleashing Gwen's hysteria over the span of many weeks, or containing it to the brief window of her labor. It wasn't an easy decision, but it was the right one. The future of Seahorse was at stake."

"You've lost your mind," she said. "You're not saving Seahorse. You're just postponing its implosion. You think Gwen's going to meekly slip back into the world with newborn twins and keep this story to herself?"

Luke steadied his gaze on her, contemplative.

"She's not going back into the world. Not for some time, anyway."

Tessa almost laughed. "What are you going to do? Hold us hostage?"

"Of course not. We're putting together a protocol that will be in the best interest of all parties involved. Mothers, babies, and the Center. When everyone goes their separate ways, it will be in the spirit of calm and goodwill."

When. Tessa felt a cold seep of dread in her shoulders. Over the years of working with Luke, she'd experienced a broad range of feelings toward him, but fear had never been one of them.

Until now.

Luke took a step toward the door of his office, apparently done with the conversation. "I know I can count on you to keep this conversation in total confidence, Tessa. I know nothing is more important to you than our work here, and the well-being of your Cohort. I know you'd never do anything to compromise either of those."

His voice sounded deeper than usual. Ominous.

"I have a favor to ask of you, Luke."

"Anything," he said, with sarcasm.

"I need you to run an errand for me."

"In what direction? Because I'm headed up to the city."

"I'll show you," she said, and presented her phone.

Degrees Lat Long	37.5775000°, -105.4856000°
Degrees Minutes	37°34.65000', -105°29.13600'
Degrees Minutes Seconds	37°34'39.0000", -105°29'08.1600"
UTM	13S 457122mE 4159050mN
MGRS	13SDB5712259050
Grid North	-0.3°
GARS	150LR37
Maidenhead	DM77GN18RO44
GEOREF	EJQH30863465

"What the fuck is that?" said Luke.

"It's in New Mexico," said Tessa casually. She'd entered the coordinates Tracy had sent into a mapping application. "The middle of nowhere, actually."

"This is getting weird, Tessa. Why the hell would I go to New Mexico for you?"

"Because for once, it's the right thing to do."

"For once?"

"I know about the Config samples, Luke. Have you heard of informed consent? Do you know there are serious penalties for using stolen genetic material for profit? The Feds don't like it, Luke. It's an ethical snake pit. Not to mention a PR nightmare. Have you heard of Henrietta Lacks?"

Luke stared at her, blinking. His unwashed brown curls splayed over his brows; Tessa resisted the impulse to brush them away from his face.

He was so young.

It was no excuse.

"You'll need your plane," she said matter-of-factly. "Plus a helicopter. So please check to see if your pilot's available. You'll be picking up a friend of mine tomorrow after midnight."

"Tessa, hang on. Wait. I think you've gotten some bad information."

"Just follow instructions," said Tessa. "Don't be late." She made her way to the door.

"Wait," Luke repeated. "Don't be insane. Is this your hormones talking? Did you catch something from Gwen?"

"If you need me, I'll be with the Cohort," said Tessa, delivering a smile. "Have a safe trip."

38.

Tracy lay in his residence and waited for his 11:00 p.m. shift to start, watching an opal half-moon take its post in the sky. Sleep had begun to evade him again. His body refused to sign off during the afternoon, so that he might be alert for his guard shift. Instead, he lay awake in his hut while the day burned on beyond his blackout shades, staring at the photos of his sister's kids, his nieces and nephews, that he'd tacked to the wall above his bed ten years ago. He knew that even inmates, in time, usually had the desire to personalize their cells, but he'd never been able to bring himself to do it. Bethany had sent him more photos over the years, updated ones, routed to him at a snail's pace via the post office addresses the Agency required him to use. But those kids, the ones in the new photos, were different people than the ones who'd climbed up his leg and bounced on his lap. They were teenagers now, full of restless desire, foreign to Tracy in a way that made him unable to put up their pictures. You couldn't know someone unless you understood, precisely, what they wanted. What they feared. So he'd left the pictures of toddlers and kindergartners up for so long that they'd faded and curled at the edges, and beyond that paltry decor, nothing else. His "home" was nothing but an efficiency studio in the desert, blanker than his fake apartment in Cambridge.

Evidence that the life he was hiding was emptier than the one he'd presented to Viv.

Viv. He tried not to picture her, cloistered in the Quarry, getting dinner delivered on a cart by Johanna or some other nurse. Instead, he tried to think of her as he'd known her until just days ago, in her life as a college student in Boston. He tried to think of them together in their ordinary places: breakfast at the Piehole, walking by the river, lying in his bed until fifteen minutes before he had to "teach his class at MIT." All the phrases that had come so effortlessly, all the little inventions, not because Viv was easy to lie to but because he'd let himself believe that they wouldn't matter. That together they would somehow transcend the phony history he'd spun to her, that the inner truth of him was bigger than the surface of his lies.

What an idiot he'd been, he thought now, lying on the thin mattress of his bunk. Inner truth. As if he could do one thing and hope for another, expecting the hoped-for thing to prevail, powered by the Force. He and Bethany had loved Star Wars when they were little, had used brooms and rakes as lightsabers and battled each other in the dirt yard of the trailer. Neither ever wanted to be from the dark side, so they settled for Good versus Good: Luke versus Leia, Obi-Wan versus Hans, R2 versus C3PO.

That's how his work with Viv had felt. He was technically in opposition to her, technically baiting her so that he could make her disappear, but he always felt they were on the same side. Good versus Good.

If he complied, he'd be free in three months. Pending paperwork, passage of his final polygraph, et cetera. He'd always thought he'd go back to Montana, build a cabin deep in the northern Rockies— somewhere up near Whitefish—and live out his days beside a frigid river in the mountains. Since he'd been with Viv, though, a wintry climate no longer appealed to him. Too much of his life had been spent in the cold. He was picturing a beach now, palm trees and cake-flour sand, no seasons. He didn't want to wear layers. He wished to hide beneath nothing.

Tracy's phone bleated an alert. He sat up to silence it, but when he looked at the screen, it read 10:52. Time to go to work. It was going to be a long night.

39.

Luke sipped a club soda and stared out the window as his plane angled toward the clouds. Outside, night was claiming the sky, but the dregs of the sunset were still ferocious, bleeding wild colors. Luke could see the burning eye of the sun, fading, and he stared right at it. His whole life he'd done that, and his eyes had never suffered for it. His father had chastised him for it, which, of course, only encouraged him. He thought of Reed now, of how deep his disappointment would be if he knew Luke had failed him. That he'd lost Seahorse before it had managed to transcend a single imperfection in humanity. All because of Luke's slovenly, idiotic mistakes.

Over the loudspeaker came his pilot's voice. "Flight time: two hours, forty-seven minutes."

Luke sipped his water.

They were headed to Tremble City, the closest airstrip his pilot, Trey, could find, twenty miles from the coordinates Luke had gotten from Tessa's phone. From there, they'd have to take a chopper. It was going to be a long night.

But he had no choice. Tessa knew too much.

Some time later, a message pinged in, waking Luke from a light sleep. He yawned and pulled out his device.

The message was from Rita Gupta.

Gwendolyn Harris was in early labor. Contractions four to five minutes apart. They would move forward with a C-section as planned. Gupta and Milford were already preparing for surgery. The anesthesiologist had arrived.

No one seems to know where you are, Gupta had written. *But everything is under control. We'll keep you updated.*

Luke pulled on his headset to communicate with the cabin.

"Trey," he said, "how long have we been up?"

"One hour, forty-eight minutes."

Almost two hours.

It would take him at least three, including traffic, to get back to Seahorse. It was best if he stayed away. There was nothing he could contribute to Gwen's situation; for that, he'd hired the best doctors in the world, spent millions. His presence might only make his staff feel pressure they did not need.

He replied to Gupta: *I'm OOO until tomorrow. Unexpected necessity. Gwen is in the greatest of hands.*

Then he turned off his device.

Perhaps everything would be okay.

He believed in Milford and Gupta and the rest of the team, in all the work they had done. Perhaps they'd pushed TEAT to trial a bit prematurely, perhaps they'd sourced material too aggressively, tweaked the data a bit; but then, as Tessa had written in her book, *waiting for a clear green light is the cowardice of a wasting life.*

Luke believed this with all his heart. Even if they'd waited to launch the Trial, risks would still have been involved. The Cohort knew this. They embraced it. People had been taking voluntary risks with their bodies for generations: gender reassignment surgeries, transplants of every kind, breast implants. Face-lifts and vaginal tightening, Botox. They'd undergone lobotomies, they'd had bacteria purposely introduced into their brains to eat away cancer.

Some had taken a little-known drug called Juva, in hopes of stretching their fertility into their forties, their fifties, even beyond.

Human pioneers would always be necessary for progress. Without them, the world would not continue to flourish. It would stagnate and wither and die.

It was all one unified system, Luke thought, one organic pattern: risk and consequence, setback and progress. They were all working together, generations of humans, pushing through the darkness toward the light, sacrificing now so that others could have a better future.

There was no shortcut around sacrifice.

Still, Luke hoped very much that things would turn out well for Gwen and her babies. As it was, he had enough troubled women to worry about.

Outside the window of his plane, the night sky turned to black velvet, pocked with hard white stars.

40.

Tracy knocked lightly on Viv's door in the Quarry. She opened it with the tap of a button, still lying in bed, assuming he was Johanna. Her breath staggered inward when she saw him. He held a finger to his lips. Moved across the room to her. She sat straight up in bed and then cowered, shielding her face with her forearms. As if fending him off.

"Please," he whispered at her bedside. There was little time before they would find him. Perhaps just minutes before the rest of Third Shift Surveillance noticed that their squad captain was MIA. Before the alerts beamed to screens and alarms shrieked.

Viv lowered her arms from her face. In the dim light, he could see she'd advanced maybe to forty. Still fully herself. Maybe even more so. Her face was her own, just deeper settled, her cheekbones more prominent. She wore a nightgown, something loose and white. Her hair spilled over her shoulders. It had salted and peppered in places, ash-colored. He'd never seen her more beautiful.

"No," she said to him. A single syllable, stark and cruel. "And why are you dressed like a soldier?"

His heart boggled in his chest. He lifted his hand to her cheek, on instinct, needing to feel her skin. She batted him away.

"It's too late," she said. "It's over. Go away."

"It's not. I found a way."

"A way?"

"I can get you home. To your parents, or to Weldon, or wherever you want to go. But you'll have to promise me you'll never tell anyone what you've seen and heard here. Not ever, to anyone. Do you understand?"

"No, I don't. I've already been over and over this with what's-his-face. I'm not going to stop talking about AG. I'm not going to stop talking about it or writing about it. I'm not going to pretend that something didn't happen to us. *Look* at me, Wayne," she said, jumping out of bed and grabbing a fistful of her hair. "It's turning *gray*. Which wouldn't be so bad except that I've also got"—she jerked her index finger toward her eyes—"crow's feet. Not to mention wrinkles I shouldn't have for another twenty years. Not to mention a gimpy leg because I broke my leg falling onto *grass*. You know who breaks their bones falling on soft surfaces, Wayne? *Old people.* That's who. I'm not going to shut up about this until I find out why it happened."

He swallowed with effort. "You're not sick," he said. "You're healthy."

"So what? I'm starting to *look* shitty. It's got to be only a matter of time before I start feeling that way too."

"Not necessarily." Irene, despite looking ninety when she was forty-two, hadn't ever been truly "sick" for a single day. No illnesses, no deterioration of her mind. There were the physical changes, of course—gradual at first, then rapid—but she'd never really been ill. "And you don't look shitty at all. You look . . . perfect."

"Give me a break."

"Sorry, it's true."

"I need to know why this is happening to me."

Tracy paused. "Okay. I'll tell you why."

She tipped her head to the right, something she did when her interest was piqued, a gesture that he found inexplicably endearing.

"What?"

"I'll tell you."

"You know something about AG?"

"Yes. I know a lot that I haven't told you. I wanted to, but I couldn't."

Viv stood silently, her eyes on the floor. He moved one hand back to her cheek, then another. This time, she did not push him away. Let him cradle her face in his palms.

"I'll tell you everything I know about AG. But I don't have time right now. If I'm going to get you out of here, you have to follow my directions."

"You *abducted* me. Why would I ever trust you again?"

"Viv, please. I'm begging you, okay? Come with me now. And then I'll tell you what I know about AG, and I'll get you out of this place. Don't you want to get out?"

"Yes. Just not on their . . . terms."

"I'm offering that to you. Just do what I tell you, and I'll get you out of here. To your parents, to Weldon, wherever. No one will be that suspicious—we've dealt with them."

"Dealt with them?"

"We've been in touch. We've kept them from worrying."

Viv tilted her head at him, quizzical. "I don't see how that's possible," she said. "I can't disappear for a week and not cause people to worry."

He fought the urge to take her in his arms.

"You can, actually," he said. "But if anyone's skeptical, if you have to explain these last few days, blame it all on me. Play the unstable boyfriend card."

"It wouldn't be a *play*."

"Say I dragged you on some spiritual quest to the desert. Say I'm loony tunes, that I'm in a cult, whatever you come up with. Say we shroomed and did yoga or something. You freaked out and wanted to go home. So you called for help. Leave it at that. Blame me all you want, feel free to get creative, but don't use a single detail of the truth. Do you understand me?"

"And if I don't?"

"If you don't, they'll hurt you. And the others. And me."

She did not ask him to identify the pronoun.

"Please come with me now. It's going to be uncomfortable, but then you'll be safe. You'll be free." He extended his arm to her. "Let's go."

Time was moving fast, bearing down on them.

"So you're not leaving with me? You're going to stay in this place?"

He breathed out, long and slow, snagged with trembling. "Yes. For now."

Her deliberation felt eternal.

"Okay," she whispered.

She lifted her eyes.

He held out his hand and she reached for it.

41.

"Help me understand," said Tessa to Rita Gupta.

Gupta pushed the red lever of a hot water dispenser and filled her mug. She chose a bag of tea from the colorful array of boxes on the counter and dropped it into her cup. Then she took a seat across the table from Tessa. They were alone in a small break room of East Lobe, with a window that looked out over the topiary garden. At eight in the evening, it was almost dark, and the path lamps had turned on below, lighting the geometric shapes of the artfully pared trees.

"I've already explained," said Gupta, blowing at the steam rising from her tea.

"You're a renowned obstetrician, Rita. At the top of your field. Affiliated with one of the best med schools in the country. How could you agree to deceiving a patient?"

"I agreed to nothing of the sort," said Gupta. "I was misled by Luke. Egregiously so. He substituted ultrasound images without my knowledge. They were highly convincing. If he weren't so repulsive, I'd be impressed with his technical acumen."

"Are you telling me you didn't know you were looking at bogus ultrasounds?"

"I am." Gupta met Tessa's eyes and blinked slowly: a request for trust. Tessa nodded back. She had a great deal of respect for Gupta. Before arriving in the States to work on the artificial womb, she'd delivered babies in the slums of Mumbai. She'd seen every natal emergency imaginable.

Perhaps she really hadn't known.

"You have two children, Rita, right? In college?"

"Princeton and Caltech," Gupta said, brightening. "Twins, actually."

Tessa had not known they were twins. "Can I ask you a question, from a motherly standpoint?"

"Of course."

"Because I'm not a mother myself."

"I'm aware."

"Would you have used the Seahorse Solution, if you'd had the chance? Back when you were pregnant?"

Gupta looked thoughtful. She took a small sip of tea. "I'm completely committed to the work we do here. But I would never use Seahorse myself."

"Why not?"

"I loved being pregnant. I remember feeling all-powerful and extremely vulnerable at the same time. On one hand, I was growing an entire life inside me. On the other, I could hardly walk a block without having to rest. My lower back hurt all the time. I gained sixty-five pounds. And yet . . ." She trailed off.

"And yet?" Tessa prodded.

"Pregnancy was an important time. The bridge from one life to another. I needed the gradualness of the nine months. If it had happened in nine weeks, I would have been a different sort of mother."

"A lesser sort?"

Gupta considered.

"Yes, lesser," she said.

"Why?"

"I'm sorry. I know this isn't what you wanted to hear. But having a child is a relinquishing of self. For a woman, it's the beginning of her death. A sort of torch passing, from one generation to the next. Nine weeks isn't enough to prepare for that. I would have resented my children, I think."

"And what about men?" asked Tessa. "Is it the beginning of death for them, too?"

"Quite the opposite. It's the beginning of their freedom."

"Freedom from what?"

"Their partners, of course. The tedium of married life. Of course, children are a new sort of tedium, but mothers absorb the lion's share of that. Fathers do the fun part of parenting."

"You're making a lot of generalizations," said Tessa.

Gupta shrugged. "General, and true."

"If you don't believe in Seahorse, Rita, then why are you here? You already had an amazing job."

Gupta smiled. "Milford may have brought me here, Tessa, but I stayed because of you. I don't agree with most of what you say, but I admire how you say it."

Before Tessa could answer, Gupta's phone emitted a high-pitched beeping sound from the table.

"Dr. Gupta here."

She listened for a moment, then nodded her head vigorously.

"On my way." She put the phone down and spoke to Tessa. "Gwen Harris's labor has progressed to the point where she is expected to deliver soon."

"Oh my God," said Tessa, the weight of their conversation instantly evaporating.

"Shall we go?"

Tessa stood up.

"Oh, and Tessa. One more thing." The doctor seemed wildly calm at the prospect of delivering conjoined twins. Tessa followed her to the door.

"Luke is a very confused young man," said Gupta, "possibly lacking a moral center. But inadvertently, what he did for Gwen was an act of kindness."

"What?" said Tessa. The falling sensation was returning, faint nausea rising, her sense of order spinning into chaos. She reached for the wall to steady herself.

"It's best that she didn't know," said Gupta. "Now let's go and help her."

42.

Tessa sat on one of the couches of Room 801 of East Lobe, where Cohort One had gathered for orientation almost nine weeks ago. LaTonya and Kate sat on either side of her, staring at the paintings on the opposite walls. The spare tranquility of the room during orientation had turned to something coldly inhospitable—the polished concrete floor like tundra, the blue-green hues of the abstract paintings like hypothermic skin.

Gwen's babies had been in surgery to separate them for the past three hours, and the Cohort was waiting for news.

"Why aren't they communicating with us?" asked Kate. "Tessa, can you do something?"

"They'll communicate when they have something to tell us," said Tessa. "Dr. Gupta won't keep us in the dark."

"Glad one of us is so confident," said LaTonya. "Because I sure as shit am not."

If any doctor could handle Gwen's situation, Rita Gupta could.

Not that Tessa wasn't scared. Not that alarm wasn't a reasonable state.

LaTonya made a choking sound. Tessa moved closer and put her arm around her. On cue, LaTonya's baby gave a hard kick.

"I felt that one!" said Tessa.

"Tough little dude," said LaTonya.

Subtly, minutely, Tessa felt the mood among the three of them lift.
Spin your vision toward optimism, Tessa had written in her book.
Young women had turned the edict into a chant at Tessa's speeches as
she took the stage: *SPIN your vision / toward OP-ti-miiiiiism!*

Now more than ever, she thought, it was crucial that she take her
own advice.

"Kate, LaTonya," Tessa said. "We can't lose our courage now."

"Mine's gone," groaned LaTonya.

"Don't be ridiculous," said Tessa. "Of course it isn't."

"And how're we supposed to be courageous, exactly?" said LaTonya.
"What's the point? What can we do except wait here for news from the
docs on Gwen's fucked-up situation, and then wait longer to go into
labor ourselves?"

"That's it," said Tessa. "You'll go into labor, and you'll deliver your
babies and be absolutely fine."

"And what if we're not fine?" said Kate. "Why don't you explain,
Tessa, what we can expect if Gwen and her babies are already not fine?"

"You can expect me to make everything fine," said Tessa, willing
herself to believe it. "That's my job. I will not fail you."

Neither woman challenged her assertion.

"Gupta, Rita. Authorized to proceed." The metallic voice of Zeus
admitted Dr. Gupta into the room. Kate bolted upright.

"Good afternoon, Cohort One," said the doctor, eyes smiling as she
approached the couches. "I have good news. Gwen and her babies—
both of them—are in the clear. You can come see them now."

43.

Irene's bed became a plush ship, rocking gently on a calm sea. She floated in the center of it, sinking down into a deeper, warmer place. Into a tepid liquid. A welcoming syrup. Peace. Finally. Henry had done what he'd promised, and now she could rest.

She'd met her daughter, Vivian. Now Irene was ready.

The syrup around her thickened, became too viscous to move inside. To keep her eyes open. She let them close, expecting darkness. Never had she heard any descriptions that hadn't involved the darkness. Descending, enshrouding, swallowing.

But behind her eyes, only light. Tame and golden, like sunshine at the end of an autumn afternoon. Everywhere was the gilded, honey illumination, surrounding her, filling her, claiming her, becoming her.

Very slowly, Irene moved her hand through the heavy liquid to her mouth. Put her thumb inside it. An ancient reflex. Often practiced in the womb.

The ensuing peace deeper than bone. Further down than the center of the earth.

Somehow, inside the liquid, it was still easy to breathe. In fact, Irene didn't have to breathe at all. Something else was fortifying her, taking hold, nourishing her from both inside and out, like an umbilical cord.

44.

"Time of death, 11:42 p.m.," said Johanna briskly into the phone. She'd placed a call to a supervisor at Base to report Irene's death and request authorization to transport the body, for examination by the medical team in the morning.

Tracy was amazed by the nurse's composure. She'd assisted a suicide and was now proceeding to aid the escape of a PIT from the Colony. And yet she appeared completely unaffected, as if this were simply another night at work.

He knew it was an act. He knew how hard Johanna must be fighting to keep it together, because he was fighting himself. He'd always felt a deep kinship with her, a sense of being cut from the same cloth.

To watch Irene's life extinguish, even though she'd wanted it so badly, had cut through Tracy like a blade. He wanted to sit and let himself weep, to talk to Viv about it. Surely she was upset, but right now she stood beside him, straight-backed and stoic, ready to spring into action.

"Shall I bring her to the morgue, or do you want her in cold storage until morning?" Johanna was saying into the phone. "Got it. Yes, very sad. But she was so frail and frankly unhappy. So yes, I'll complete the Pronouncement of Death and then transport her to cold storage."

She lowered her phone.

"All clear," she said. "I'm authorized to move her from the Quarry to Admin B."

On the gurney, Irene's body appeared even smaller than it had in life, just minutes before. She probably weighed ninety pounds. A perfect coxswain, Tracy thought.

He wished he'd known her then.

Tracy touched Viv's shoulder and gestured to the gurney.

Beneath his touch, Viv stiffened. "I can't do this."

"You can," said Tracy. "It's the only way."

"He's right," echoed Johanna softly. "It'll only be a few minutes. Get on."

Viv stepped to the gurney and lay down on it, next to her mother. Johanna billowed a sheet down over them and wheeled the bed out of the room, managing to plant a kiss on Tracy's cheek without breaking stride.

"Good luck to us, honeycakes," she said to him. "See you outside Admin B."

~

At 11:58, the Colony's alarm screamed through the night. Tracy had been waiting for it. He'd resumed his rounds on foot after parting ways with Johanna and Viv, moving slowly from building to building, cutting the darkness with his flashlight. It had been under fifteen minutes since he'd left them but already felt like a lifetime ago.

The Colony had endured two decades with no intrusions into its airspace. Hikers had stumbled upon the Base, weird loners doing time in the desert for spiritual reasons, but Base was not of particular interest, the squat cluster of ugly tan buildings. Easily explained away as a research facility. Strategically positioned for detection so that outsiders could be intercepted and escorted away.

The intruders had always been on foot. Easily removed.

But now there it was, a satellite map on Tracy's surveillance screen, a jumble of numbers at the bottom indicating flight position. Roving across the screen was a pulsing red dot. Something flying low in the desert sky.

Seconds later, a message arrived on his phone. *LANDED. Lat 37.5775000°, Long -105.4856000°*

He tapped a fast response and distributed it to the surveillance team: *THEROUX DISPATCHING.* Summoned Jensen, the carrot-haired rookie, for backup. The type who'd follow directions, without asking too many questions.

A moment later, Jensen pulled up in a Humvee. Tracy could practically see the kid drooling, he was so eager to bust the intruder.

"Evening, Theroux. Where we headed?"

"Admin B."

"What? Why to an admin building? I thought we were headed for an interception." He waved toward the open desert. "Out there."

"Just drive."

Jensen swung the Humvee around the central circular drive of Base and toward Admin B, one of a half dozen squat stucco buildings.

"Pull up by the door," said Tracy. "And close your eyes."

"Excuse me?"

"You heard me."

He didn't really care what Jensen saw. Tracy's own chances of salvation were over. But he didn't mind discombobulating the kid a little.

Jensen screeched the Humvee to a halt right in front of the building. He closed his eyes.

"Now cover them with your hands," said Tracy, beckoning toward the door, hoping Johanna was behind it with the gurney to hand off Viv and then transport Irene's body to cold storage. Jensen raised his hands to his face, and as if on cue, Viv stepped out of the door. Tracy helped her lie flat in the back of the Humvee.

He reached over and chucked Jensen on the shoulder.

"Open your eyes and drive. Straight to the exit. Then follow this." He pointed to his phone affixed to the dash, its GPS glowing.

Jensen accelerated sharply, the redneck in him rising as he pointed the Humvee into the open desert. Tracy gripped the frame of the Humvee with one damp hand. He was sweating despite the low temperature. The desert night whipped his face.

With his free hand, Tracy reached down and switched on the stereo. Noise did not matter here, miles away from anything. He figured the music might rattle whoever was waiting for them out there, death metal blasting in the middle of nowhere. The music was all discord and violence, a vocalist making an incoherent growl. All the Humvees played the same songs. Tracy could never discern the lyrics. He didn't want to.

They rolled past cactus and rock and thorn trees. The moon burned brighter. Beside him, Jensen wore a manic grin. Rookie courage, all muddled up in the animal fear Tracy could practically smell on the kid. He glanced at the GPS; the target was getting closer. He palmed the slick metal of his submachine gun, an MP5. His pulse was faster than he wanted it to be; he could feel it moving in his neck.

Point-four miles, point-three, point-two.

When they were two hundred feet from the target, Tracy hit the floodlight. The beam smashed into a little chopper, a special-ops ultralight that no one from the ISA had probably ever flown. Tracy recognized the machine: a Baby Wasp. Designed for rescues in combat zones, covert reconnaissance flights.

Not for dicking around in the middle of the New Mexico desert late at night.

Tessa Callahan had done well.

45.

When the lights of the Humvee hit Luke, he'd already been shaking from the cold. The temperature had plummeted wildly since they'd left Tremble City for Tessa's spot in the desert. It hadn't occurred to him to bring a winter jacket. As the oversized vehicle hurtled straight toward him, headlights blinding, he began to shake harder.

The Humvee parked a dozen feet from the chopper, and a man hopped out of the passenger side. Then he opened the back door and extended his hand to help someone out. A woman, Luke could tell from her shape, wearing a hooded sweatshirt.

The man wore fatigues and carried a gun. He held the woman's hand as they made their way from the Humvee to the chopper. Luke strained to see her face, but it was obscured by her hood. When the couple reached the base of the Wasp's ramp, the man lifted his gun to Luke's head.

Luke could almost feel the hard carbon fiber against his temple. His heart thudded.

"Please put that down," he said. "Tessa Callahan sent me here."

"I know that," said the man. "And now that you're here, you're leaving. You're going to fly the fuck away from here and never come back.

My friend is going with you. You'll deliver her safely to Tessa Callahan. If you don't, you'll be dead in twenty-four hours. All clear?"

"All clear," said Luke.

The man released his grip on the woman.

Finally, she removed her hood.

Luke recognized her instantly.

She was Vivian Bourne.

The CleftKid. She looked just as she had on LikeMe, only older. Quite a bit older.

"It's time," said the man with the gun. He lowered it and flicked his wrist toward Luke. "Time for all of you to go." He dropped Viv's hand and she stepped onto the ramp of the Wasp followed by Luke.

Luke detected the hint of a tremor in the man's voice.

"Trey," Luke called toward the cockpit. "Rev up."

The rotor blades began to whirl, and the chopper lifted, pitched, and rose into the deep night sky.

PART FOUR

Personal risk is a barometer of true passion.

—*Tessa Callahan,* Pushing Through: A Handbook for
Young Women in the New World

46.

On Friday evening, in the room that served as the Seahorse Center's miniature intensive care unit, Tessa sat in a nursing rocker holding Gwen's baby girl, who was swaddled in a lavender muslin blanket, nursing from the Mammarina Tessa wore. Two lamps lit the room in a soft glow; the windows were covered with blackout shades to help Gwen and the babies sleep. Beside Tessa, Viv sat in a matching chair with the boy in the crook of her arm. He'd fallen asleep nursing, still latched onto Viv's Mammarina. Ten days after surgery, the twins were healing rapidly, but Gwen was recovering slowly from her C-section, and breastfeeding, now her most critical duty, was challenging and painful. The babies' mouths, she told Tessa, felt like hot pins to her nipples each time they latched. Gwen bit down on her lip and kept trying, but each feeding brought tears to her eyes.

And there were so many feedings. The babies seemed perpetually ravenous, mawing the air with their tiny mouths less than an hour after they'd nursed, demanding more.

"Let us help," Tessa had said to Gwen, after watching her wince through another feeding session. "The lab will fast-track your supplies."

Gwen rubbed a viscous organic salve over her nipples and sighed. "Fine." An hour later, she allowed the techs to collect colostrum samples and take nipple moldings.

Two days later, her kit arrived: an ample supply of powdered FormuLove, which, when mixed with purified water, produced a liquid with a very strong molecular resemblance to Gwen's breast milk. There were also two identical harnesses—Mammarinas—outfitted with pumps that adjusted the flow of FormuLove through silicone nipples, shaped exactly like Gwen's, according to the strength of the infant's suckle.

The improvement was striking. Now, for example, Gwen had been asleep for almost two hours, getting the rest she desperately needed, while Tessa and Viv held and fed her babies.

The boy in Viv's arms, whose name was Daniel, made a small mewling noise and opened his eyes.

"Hello, Danny boy," said Viv, smiling down at him. The baby began a sputtering cry.

"Hungry again, already?" she said, and expertly maneuvered the Mammarina back into his mouth. Tessa watched him stretch his jaw and squirm before clamping onto the prosthetic nipple. After a few seconds, he relaxed and his body quieted again as he settled into nursing.

Viv turned her head to Tessa. "Amazes me, every time," she said.

"Me, too," said Tessa. From her lap, Gwen's daughter, Alexis, gazed up at her. The baby's bright brown eyes fastened on Tessa's, roved away, and returned again. In the moments of eye contact, Tessa felt she alone was anchoring the tiny girl to the world. It gave her an expansive, giddy feeling in her chest, as if something were flowering inside her.

Then she caught sight of Gwen sleeping across the room and remembered: the baby was *hers*, not Tessa's. And the flowering vanished.

Alexis wore matching socks and a hat striped with yellow and blue. Tessa gently lifted the hat off her head.

Viv caught her. "Are you checking *again*?"

"Yes," said Tessa, abashed.

"I don't think it works that way," said Viv. "I was born with mine. It didn't suddenly appear."

"I know that," said Tessa. "It's just heartening to see." She appraised the baby's head, ran her fingers lightly over the downy tufts of dark hair, then replaced the hat. Viv was right, of course: there was nothing beneath Alexis's hair but smooth scalp and a standard fontanel, which Tessa had seen pulsing a few times, like a heartbeat, and she had irrationally worried the spot was going to cave inward. But it did not.

Daniel's head was the same as his sister's.

Rationally, Tessa understood the absence of clefts in the babies did not guarantee the normalcy of their development in the future. But it also wasn't meaningless.

"I don't want to go home," said Viv softly.

"You don't have to," said Tessa. "You can stay here."

"Without you? Really? That just seems strange."

"Bonding Camp doesn't end for another month. The Cohort will be there. They'd love to have you. You'd be so helpful."

"I don't know. The other two seem so . . . capable."

Kate and LaTonya had each given birth to healthy babies five days ago, a girl and a boy, just hours apart. Both weighed nearly eight pounds; neither had a cleft.

"Trust me," said Tessa, turning the baby around to the other side of her Mammarina. She was surprised at how easily she'd caught on to the delicate mechanics of handling a baby. The fragility of their bird-necks, their soft heads, the tiny, slippery bullets of their bodies, had always secretly repelled her. But now that she'd spent hours holding Alexis and Daniel, the little creatures seemed much sturdier than she'd imagined. Adjusting them in her arms felt less precarious every time. "There'll be plenty for you to do. Think about it."

Viv sighed. "Well, my parents already hate me for skipping my college graduation. Might as well let them keep on hating me."

"They don't hate you," said Tessa. After Luke returned from the desert with Viv, she hadn't wanted to return either to Weldon for graduation or to her parents' house in Orange County. She wouldn't tell Tessa where she'd been, only that she wished to remain within the secure confines of the Seahorse Center for a time. *Please don't ask me to talk about it,* she'd said to Tessa of her time in the desert. Tessa agreed. She also agreed to let Weldon and Viv's parents know that Viv had been hired by Seahorse to assist with an intensive new project.

In the meantime, Viv moved into a spare residential room in East Lobe. She allowed Dr. Gupta to conduct lengthy examinations. She allowed every sort of testing and analysis of her body: her vitals, bone density, muscle tone, reflexes . . . the list went on. During the day, she was Tessa's shadow. Tessa introduced her to the staff as her summer intern. Viv went to meetings and helped with the Cohort and their babies: holding, rocking, feeding, swaddling. Despite her wrinkles and her limp, her energy was boundless. Gently, Tessa asked her if she'd like to dye her hair. Viv said yes, and Tessa invited her personal colorist to the Center.

At night, Dino or Michael, the Seahorse guards whom Tessa trusted most, stood watch outside Viv's bedroom door. Viv hadn't needed to ask. Tessa simply offered.

The Cohort loved Viv.

She was a natural with the babies. Tessa was impressed. Now, for example, Daniel had finished another Mammarina feeding and Viv had maneuvered him from her lap to upright on her shoulder and was patting his back.

Across the room, Gwen shifted in her bed, sighed, and then slowly sat up. She no longer winced when she moved, Tessa noticed. Her C-section incision was healing.

"Morning," said Gwen, yawning as she pushed her long, loose hair behind her shoulders. It was the same salt-and-pepper shade Viv's had been until her appointment with the colorist yesterday. "Or I guess it's afternoon? I've lost all sense of time."

"Early evening, actually," said Tessa. "Almost dinnertime."

"How can it possibly be so tranquil in here?" said Gwen. "Last I checked, I had *twins*. Are you two baby whisperers?"

On cue, Alexis began to cry. Tessa stood and brought her over to Gwen, transferring her carefully into her mother's arms.

"Viv's the baby whisperer," said Tessa.

"Nah," said Viv, "the Mammarina gets all the credit."

"I still think it's a creepy contraption," said Gwen. "But I'll take a little creepiness for the sake of sleep."

"Daniel's gained almost a pound now," said Tessa. "He weighed five-fourteen today. It's amazing."

"Did he really? Or did the docs just swap in a substitute baby?" Gwen deadpanned, her tone cutting. She still had not fully absorbed the shock of delivering conjoined twins. Luke had formed an entire damage control team to manage the situation: an attorney, a psychologist, a neonatologist with specialization in rare births. In various professional language, they'd explained to Gwen that her twins had not been expected to survive. That, among other factors, maternal stress levels during pregnancy weighed significantly in determining whether the babies lived or died.

We knew you would survive, said the neonatologist. *But the unique nature of your gestational term, in combination with the delicate status of the fetus, left us with a grueling decision . . .*

You are entitled to deep anger, said the psychologist. *It is a natural and healthy response to a highly unusual situation. At the same time, the twins themselves did not do anything wrong . . .*

Page 28, Section A, Clause VI, said the lawyer. *The Cohort Member relinquishes all rights to medical decisions made in support of the safety of herself and her child to the Seahorse Natal Staff.*

At first, Gwen had wanted to speak only to Tessa. She'd been virtually incoherent with shock and confusion. Then the twins emerged from surgery, almost five pounds each and howling with need, and Gwen shifted. She was still angry, but her anger deferred to the urgent, wild demands of her babies.

At the moment, sipping guava juice as she cradled Alexis, Gwen did not look angry, Tessa thought.

Tessa's own outrage at Luke's decision had crossed over into something quieter. More contemplative. She was struck by the fact that he considered the Trial a win, that he was already meeting with his PR people to formulate a campaign. This campaign would launch after the Cohort and their babies completed their bonding period at the Center, announcing the triumph of TEAT and the impending availability of the Seahorse Solution to women everywhere.

Tessa would handle Luke. Of this she was completely sure. Exactly *how*, she had not figured out yet.

Tessa saw that baby Daniel had fallen back to sleep in Viv's arms, his fist balled into a tiny lump. Viv eased Daniel down into his plexiglass-sided bassinet with great care and wheeled him over to Gwen's bedside.

"You're a godsend, Vivian," said Gwen. "You're so good with them."

"They're good babies," said Viv.

"Dinner is here!" trilled a bright voice from the doorway, and Tessa turned to see Mindy, a chipper young staff nurse, standing behind a rolling cart with several covered dishes atop it.

"Thank God," said Gwen. "I'm starving."

"We'll leave you to it," said Tessa, rising from her rocker.

"Bye, my sweets," Viv said to the babies. "See you later, Gwen."

Exiting Gwen's room, Tessa and Viv walked in step toward the footbridge. Viv's limp seemed to be diminishing, Tessa thought, but it was hard to tell.

"Would it really be okay if I stayed here and helped during Bonding?" said Viv. "I'll do anything the Cohort needs. Diapers, baths, laundry . . ."

Tessa laughed. "We have staff for that."

"Then wherever I'm needed. Surely another set of hands can't hurt with four newborns around."

Tessa paused, thinking. "We'd need to discuss the terms. I'd want you to keep seeing the doctors here, to monitor your own situation."

"Fine," said Viv. "Although I feel *good*. My leg hurts less every day. The new wrinkles aren't showing up as much."

"Still. You'd need to consent to daily checkups with Dr. Gupta."

"I like Dr. Gupta."

"And still no internet connectivity," Tessa continued. "It's not personal, just general security policy for guests. Not until you've left the Center permanently."

"How would I? I don't have a device."

"It's not so much a matter of capability. It's whether you're okay with being cut off from the world like that."

"The internet isn't the world," said Viv. Tessa thought she detected an ironic note in her voice. "It can wait."

"It's a deal, then," said Tessa. "You can stay here for a few more weeks. Until Bonding ends."

Viv exhaled a sigh of relief. "Tessa. Thank you."

They exited a long hallway and followed the inner periphery of East Lobe, which offered a view of the Thought Floor below. Friday evening was the quietest time of the week at the Center; most employees were gone by seven. Tessa counted just five lingering staffers.

Overhead, the mossy hue of evening dimmed the massive skylights; the sun had set and the fog blown in. Soon the domes' Kevlar caps would close for the night. As they walked, their elbows inches apart, Tessa stole a look at Viv. Her profile revealed details Tessa hadn't noticed earlier in the day: liverish spots above her jawline. Loose, crinkled flesh where the underside of Viv's chin met her neck. Were those new developments, or had Tessa just missed them? She'd been distracted in the past few days, after all, by the presence of Gwen's babies.

She was fairly certain they were new. She looked straight ahead again as they approached Tessa's office in West Lobe.

"You can have my room," said Tessa. "It's much bigger and nicer than the one you're in now. I'm leaving the Center the day after tomorrow, as soon as my husband, Peter, arrives. Then it's all yours."

"Why aren't *you* staying? You've been here for the Cohort's pregnancies. Don't you want to stay and see how Bonding unfolds?"

"I . . . do," said Tessa. "But Peter and I have been apart for ten weeks. We need some time."

"How romantic," said Viv, as they reached the door to Tessa's office.

Tessa presented her palm to Zeus. The door swung open, but the automated lighting system did not activate. Her office stayed dark.

"The lights are glitchy after-hours sometimes," said Tessa. "Let me turn them on."

She stepped into the dim, silent office to find Peter sitting at her desk.

47.

Night had settled over the Center. Above the ocean, moonlight struggled through the fog. Tessa took Peter's hand and led him on the footpath toward a bench on the western edge of the Center's grounds, a favorite spot of hers. They walked in silence, a damp, saline breeze on their faces. Peter was leaner than he'd been ten weeks ago, and harder-looking, his jawline sharper, as if his hike through the wilderness had stripped him to his essence. Even his hand felt different around her own: cooler, less assertive. She'd always loved the way he held her hand, with a certain confidence, underpinned by pride. It felt more tentative now, as if he were doing her a favor.

Tessa tried to keep her nerves in check, though she was disoriented from the surprise of seeing him forty-eight hours early. After the shock of his presence in her office abated, she'd been infused with happiness, until she'd stepped into his arms, and he'd whispered into her ear, *Sorry to show up unannounced like this. But I needed to talk to you. It couldn't wait.* Viv had taken the cue and quickly excused herself. Alone in her overlarge office with Peter, Tessa felt abruptly unsteady, as if she were seasick, in desperate need of air, and suggested a walk.

They arrived at the bench, just off the footpath hugging the bluffs, a half dozen feet from where the land dropped off to the sea thirty feet below. The waves roiled and crashed, invisible in the darkness.

"Talk to me, Peter," said Tessa. "I'm ready to listen." She could feel her pulse rabbiting in her neck.

Peter inhaled, as if preparing. "Remember Python?"

Oh. Relief coursed through Tessa. This was just about the dog.

"Remember him? What do you mean, honey? How would I forget our dog?"

Peter turned to her on the bench and crossed an ankle at his knee. "You didn't ask about him once."

"About Python?"

"Right. We talked a half dozen times, and you never mentioned him."

"I . . . I." She suppressed the urge to laugh. "I'm sorry. I've been totally occupied with the Trial. You know that."

"Of course," he said. "The Trial." Was she imagining bitterness in his voice?

She swallowed and tried again. "But that's no excuse. You're absolutely right. I should have—"

"He's dead, Tessa."

"What?"

"He's gone. Bitten by a rattlesnake on the trail. We did everything we could, but we just didn't have access to antivenom quickly enough. It was . . . it was . . ." His voice wobbled and Tessa put her hand on his leg. "Pretty awful."

"Jesus, Peter. When did this happen?"

"Two weeks ago."

"Two weeks? And you're just telling me now?" She was incredulous.

Peter was quiet for a moment.

"I thought it would be disruptive. We were hardly able to find any time to talk anyway."

"You don't withhold this sort of news." Tessa's disorientation took hold again, this time blended with fresh sadness, though it sprang more from Peter's delay than from losing Python. Which made her feel even worse.

"I don't want to hurt you by saying this, but I honestly didn't think you'd care that much."

"Python was mine first," she reminded him.

"I know," said Peter. "But after a time, he was really only mine, wasn't he?"

"Yes," she said quietly. She moved her arm from his leg to over his shoulder. He did not move. "I'm so sorry, Peter. I know this must be so painful for you. We'll get another dog."

"Python isn't really what I wanted to talk to you about."

"He isn't?"

Peter gave a weak, sad laugh. "No. Though he fits into the bigger picture of what I wanted to say."

"Just say it. I'm listening."

"Okay." He took a deep breath. She heard the faint wheeze and her heart trembled. On some gut level, she knew what was coming.

"I met someone on the trail."

Around her, the mild June night turned wintry. She wrapped her arms around herself and shivered.

"*Met* someone?"

"I told you that Eric and Dalton left the trail before I did. And that I kept going with other hikers I'd met at one of the supply points. You never asked for any details, because you weren't interested—"

"That's not fair. I was occupied. At any other time in my life, I would have asked. But Seahorse was consuming me." Now Tessa couldn't stop shivering.

Peter pulled off his sweatshirt. "Here. Put this on."

She waved it away.

"So you had an affair on the Pacific Crest Trail? With someone you met while restocking your granola bars?"

"I didn't have an affair," he said evenly. "I wouldn't do that to you. But the problem is . . ." He paused, his voice unsteady. "I *wanted* to."

"Why?"

"I love you, Tessa, but love isn't enough anymore. I need . . . dailiness. I don't just want to admire and respect each other and have these parallel lives. I want to *do* stuff together. I want you to hike a long wilderness trail with me. I want to adore our dog together. I want you to take pleasure in food instead of thinking how *inefficient* mealtimes are. Because isn't that what it comes down to? The hours of the day? I'm lonely in this marriage. Aren't you?"

She seriously considered the question.

"No," she said finally. "I'm not."

"That's because you have your work. And your work people. The people you spend exponentially more time with than me. I used to tell myself, *quality over quantity*, but now I think actions are what count."

He gazed at the blacked-out horizon.

"It's temporary," said Tessa. "Now that the Trial is wrapping, I won't be so immersed in—"

"That's not true," said Peter. "You'll write your next book, you'll be lauded for your courage and activism, you'll stir up controversy, and then you'll be on to your next thing. Back to working nine hundred hours a week with"—he paused, as if steeling himself for the words that would follow—"Luke Zimmerman."

"Luke is my colleague."

"He's your other husband."

Tessa felt genuinely queasy. "That is not true." Her teeth chattered.

"It's not Luke, per se," he said. "It's your priorities."

The night felt like it was pressing down on her. Closing in. "I thought you loved our life together," she said. "I've never been anything but up-front about my priorities. About who I am."

"I know that. It's not your fault. But I'm just not okay with it anymore. It hit me on the trail. The purpose of Seahorse is to prevent a pregnancy and baby from disrupting your life and your work. To keep it all seamless somehow. But having children is supposed to be disruptive. All the clichés formed for a reason, didn't they? There's nothing like it and you'll never be the same and all that? I know you spin Seahorse as this feminist breakthrough, but now I'm seeing it as a way to keep women far from their maternal instincts. I'm sorry if that offends you." His voice was tight, tamping down emotion.

"Don't blame this on Seahorse. Don't make it loftier than it is. You *met someone.* That's what this is about, isn't it?"

Peter sighed. "Chicken or the egg."

Anger cut through her incredulousness. "Does the baby have anything to do with this? Did my lack of fertility let you down, Peter?"

"Tessa, God! How could you say that? No. Not at all."

"How old is she, Peter? The hiker?"

"Your fertility had nothing to do with it."

"Thirty-two? Thirty-four?"

"Your lack of enthusiasm for a baby might have had something to do with it. But it's just one factor."

Tessa felt herself begin to deflate, steadily, like a punctured tire. She wanted to punch him and to collapse into him. Then a line from *Pushing Through* flashed to mind:

In the throes of opposition, validating one's opponent is critical to success.

She gathered herself.

"Peter. Okay. I hear you. And you're absolutely right. I've been absent. I've taken you for granted. I've put my work first when you should be first. You have every right to consider another person."

"I'm not *considering another person*," he said. "I'm in love with her."

The words slashed through Tessa. *In love with her.* But she pushed on, keeping her voice low and calm.

"I understand your impulse, Peter. But I'm asking you, as your wife of four years, not to give up so quickly. We can work through this. I think if you let yourself find meaningful work, it would—"

"See?" he snapped. "There you go."

"There I go what?"

"Pushing your value system onto me. I don't want to find meaningful work. I just want my life to feel meaningful. I want to do whatever it takes to get by and then spend as much time as I possibly can—wait for it, Tessa—*enjoying myself.*"

"When have I ever judged you for enjoying yourself?" She felt genuinely wounded.

"Since about day one, when you foisted ZSY on me. You knew I wasn't the entrepreneurial type. You knew the store would fail. But you just couldn't accept that I might be happy and unambitious at the same time."

"That's outrageous. I only wanted to help. You were dissatisfied."

"Correction. You made me *think* I should be dissatisfied. And I went along with it. Which was a failure on my part."

Impulsively, Tessa pressed her head to his chest, so that she could feel his heart thumping beneath his shirt, and stayed there until he finally lifted his arm from his side onto her back, lightly, not reciprocating her embrace, but responding to her at least. She closed her eyes and heard him sigh. Rational conversation was out of the question.

Tessa straightened to face him, putting her arms around his neck. "Peter," she said. "Please give me another chance to show you."

In the darkness, he met her eyes. Overhead, a gust of wind rustled the cypress branches, making their conversation suddenly feel less private.

"I'm sorry," he whispered, turning back to the invisible sea. "But I can't."

Tessa's stomach lurched and she bolted up from the bench, back toward the footpath. She began to run back toward the Center, its domes arched like the backs of angry cats in the weak moonlight.

48.

2021

When she woke the next day, marigold morning light was already illuminating her bedroom. She'd fallen asleep without closing the shades, curled at the far edge of the queen mattress, still wearing her jeans and beige linen top from yesterday. The room was too sunny; she covered her eyes with her forearm and lay still, breathing, her mind bleary, her body wobbly with a low-grade, unlocated nausea. Not just in her gut, but everywhere.

With effort, she shifted to face the other side of the bed, hoping for an illogical second that Peter might have followed her back to the Center and stayed. But the white comforter was smooth and blank, folded once at the top beneath two plump pillows.

No one had been there.

She groped for her phone on the nightstand and was startled at the time: 9:06 a.m.

Impossible. She couldn't remember when she'd last slept so late.

Slowly, she began to sit, but bile rose in her throat and she lay down again.

"Tessa? Hello?" A familiar, bell-bright voiced lilted through the door. "It's Rita Gupta."

"And Vivian."

"Can we come in?" said Gupta.

"Yes," said Tessa, wincing at the croaky sound of her voice.

"Oh," said Gupta, stepping through the door. "I had no idea you were still in bed. I'm so sorry."

"We were worried," said Viv. "You never sleep late."

"No, no, it's fine," said Tessa.

"Are you feeling okay?" said Gupta carefully.

"Not at all," said Tessa. "I'm not feeling okay at all."

"In what way?" said Gupta, concerned. "You look worn out."

"Did you sleep in your clothes?" asked Viv.

Tessa nodded.

"May I have a look?" said Gupta, stepping closer to Tessa's bedside. "When did you start feeling sick?"

Tessa made an effort to sit up, and this time made it upright without feeling like she was going to vomit. Still, it was arduous. She closed her eyes and sat with her back against the headboard.

"Do you mind if I touch your forehead?" asked Gupta.

Her hand on Tessa's face was dry and cool, somehow comforting.

"No fever." She pulled an ocular scope from the pocket of her white coat. "Can I look at your eyes? Can you open them?"

Tessa opened them and blinked, willing the room around her into focus.

"You can look," she said. "But I'm definitely not sick."

"You're not?" said Gupta, curious. "Because you don't look entirely well."

"No offense," said Viv. "But you don't."

Tessa breathed deeply to steady herself. She pictured the queasiness exiting her body. It did not budge.

She looked into Dr. Gupta's doe-brown eyes.

"I'm not sick, Rita," she said. "I'm pregnant."

49.

Thirty weeks and four days later

I ce chips?" Kate proffered a plastic cup.

Tessa waved it away. Her contractions were three minutes apart.

"You're doing amazing, Tessa," said LaTonya.

"Breathing like a champ," said Kate, nodding.

Gupta lifted Tessa's gown to check her. "Close to nine centimeters," she said, pleased.

The next contraction hit her like hot, deep rods to her center, from all directions. A cramp dialed way beyond its natural limits. All the analogies she'd heard: *Take your worst menstrual cramp and multiply it by a thousand. Like running the twenty-sixth mile of a marathon over and over and over.* They were apt but also completely wrong. Childbirth was its own, specific pain. It was shaped from fear. The fear of cleaving one life from another. She understood: A separation this profound must be momentous. Pain was the form of expression. It was how the body mourned.

The baby was leaving her in order to join her.

She unleashed a ragged scream.

When the pain receded, she heard Gwen's voice: "I'm glad I got to skip this part."

"Gwen!" said Kate. "That's not nice."

But Tessa tried to smile. "It's okay, Gwen."

Tessa was no longer afraid. Her friends had all done this and survived, without partners. Not simply survived, but flourished. They were out in the world with their babies. Working and mothering, working and mothering. They were using Mammarinas and the Intimizer and they were happy. Exhausted, yes, and still stretched thin, but with a minimum of the g-word and a strong sense of fulfillment.

If they could do it, Tessa told herself, she certainly could. Without Peter. Their divorce had finalized last month, and he'd moved to Oregon with the hiker. Lindsey was her name. A cute, sporty name. She was thirty-three. An avid hiker and climber. This was as much as Tessa had learned; she wanted to know nothing else.

Almost as soon as her last contraction ended, another began.

"More breathing," said Gupta.

"You're okay, Tessa," said Kate. "It's almost over, over, over."

"Push through," said Gwen. "Get it?"

"Shut up," said LaTonya. "Tessa, honey, breathe."

"Stop telling me that," said Tessa, inhaling as deeply as she could, but it was harder than ever. She heard herself making guttural, goatish sounds.

"Stay present," said Gupta. "Stay right inside this moment."

"Fuck this moment," said Tessa, as Gupta peered between her legs again.

"Ten centimeters," said Gupta. "Congratulations. It's time."

Tessa had the wild, intense urge to push.

"I need to push," she said.

She pushed.

"Crowning," said Gupta.

"Beautiful!" said Kate.

She pushed again.

The ring of fire felt more like a crown of thorns. Burning.

"Aaaaahhhhh!" she yelled. Her voice filled the room.

"One more," said the doctor.

Tessa squeezed herself and felt the baby moving through her, felt the smooth tangle of limbs passing through her.

"Reach down and grab her," said Gupta.

Blindly, Tessa reached between her legs to the slippery thing emerging.

"Now bring her onto your chest," the doctor said.

"Oh my God," said Gwen. "Oh my God."

Tessa obeyed, and suddenly the baby was there, damp and bleating, her weight tiny but essential on Tessa's chest.

At her bedside, the three women of Cohort One stood weeping. Tessa lowered her face to the top of her daughter's perfect head, covered in a scrim of dark hair, like Peter's, and kissed it.

Epilogue

Tessa and Viv sat in side-by-side chaises on the empty beach near Big Sur, baby Petra parked on her swim-diapered bottom between them. She was busy poking holes in the sand with a plastic shovel, grabbing at shells and rocks, flashing a gap-toothed grin at her mother each time the gentle surf lapped at her toes. When the rising tide splashed over her chubby thighs, she squealed in surprise.

Viv reached to lift the baby to dry sand.

"No, let me," said Tessa. "I don't want you to strain yourself. She's twenty-two pounds now." At ten months, Petra was in the ninetieth percentile for both height and weight, a healthy and exuberant child. Already Tessa could not imagine life without her. This was what had surprised her most; she'd always imagined a baby would make her feel displaced, that it would muscle into her life, helpless and teeming with insatiable needs, and fracture the person she'd once been into disparate pieces. She'd assumed a baby would cleave her into mommy Tessa and grown-up Tessa. That her life would require the permanent juggling of these roles.

In reality, Petra had quite the opposite effect. She was demanding, yes, but she felt like a natural extension of Tessa. Her effect was expansive, unifying. It was as if Tessa had brought a part of herself out into the world that had formerly lain dormant inside her.

Peter, she realized, had been the one who'd made her feel divided. In a perpetual struggle to tamp down certain parts of herself, to cultivate others. It was not his fault. He'd done the best he could. He'd loved her. But deep down, she understood now, he'd wanted her to be a different kind of woman. The kind who equated his needs with her own. Perhaps all men sought that, Tessa thought. Perhaps she was inherently undesirable in that regard. Destined to be alone.

Except that she had Petra now. She was not alone. But it felt right: having Petra and not having Peter. It was simply a feeling, not an idea. She was not suddenly pro-baby; she did not feel her life was "complete." She still felt hungry for her work, an itch to keep moving, to build and test and accomplish.

"It's okay, I've got her," said Viv, maneuvering the baby onto her lap. She made a happy, gulping sound. Tessa's daughter adored Viv.

Viv was getting stronger by the day. Yesterday she'd insisted they rent bikes, one with a child seat on the handlebars for Petra, and pedal the full length of an eight-mile path along the coast, the sea spangling beside them, moist salt air on their faces. It had been a glorious day, and Petra was endlessly delighted, pointing and giggling the whole of the ride. But the best part about it, for Tessa, had been watching Viv ride her bike with relish, hardly winded, the muscles of her thighs and calves visible as she pedaled.

REVERSA, Tessa's new project, was still in the early phases of development, still classified as experimental. The treatment involved stepping into an insulated stainless steel chamber and being misted for twenty minutes with a proprietary liquid formula developed at Seahorse Labs. The objective of the mist was to restore youth and vitality. It would be targeted to the general public, but Tessa's private mission was to make sure every child of accelerated gestation gained free access to it.

So far, REVERSA was working on the nine subjects who'd agreed to try it: Viv and a handful of other natural AG young adults who'd responded to the call for volunteers. The group had been receiving the treatment twice daily over several months. Six were presenting evidence of positive effects: more energy and stamina, increased muscle tone, even higher bone density. Their wrinkles and sun spots weren't disappearing, but they weren't proliferating, either.

Amazing, Tessa thought, what Luke Zimmerman could accomplish when he was truly motivated. When he was enlightened with just a few items of information: for example, that Tessa happened to know what he'd taken from Config, because an acquaintance of hers—an agent in the ISA, in fact—had confided in her. But not to worry, Tessa told Luke. The Feds would leave him alone, as long as he agreed to the cease-and-desist order her lawyers were sending him. A notice prohibiting future applications of Targeted Embryonic Acceleration Technology. Per the order, she'd told Luke calmly, the TEAT component of the Seahorse Solution would be eliminated immediately. This would free Luke up to work on other projects. New and exciting innovations.

As she'd spoken, Luke sat at his desk and spun his fidget, flicking it to a faster and faster spin. He'd dropped his feet from the desktop to the floor and tapped them on the polished concrete. He'd swiped his hair out of his face with his pinky and index finger, several times.

Tessa informed him that Seahorse Solutions would be fast-tracking a new project immediately: REVERSA. For this, she'd need Luke to provide capital. Angel funding, unlimited amounts. The project would be expensive; Tessa could not be fettered by cost.

Luke nodded slowly, his eyes latched to the spinning green plastic on his desk. He refused to look at Tessa. But he was listening.

Within weeks, he'd gotten the REVERSA team up and running.

～

The sun was high in the sky; it was almost noon. Soon, Tessa thought, they'd need to get back to the house so she could give Viv her midday REVERSA treatment, then put both the baby and her friend down for their naps. Viv was getting stronger by the day, but still needed her rest.

"Shall we head inside?" she said to Viv, who was bouncing Petra on her lap.

"Not quite yet," said Viv. "Petra's so happy."

"Okay. Tell me when you get tired."

"I'm sitting down in the sunshine," said Viv. "I'm not going to get tired."

"I'm going for a quick swim, then."

The ocean was cold, but Tessa didn't mind. She headed straight out into the surf, and when it reached her thighs, she dove under a wave and swam. She stroked and breathed, stroked and breathed, her skin numbing against the water, which felt both plush and bracing. Her swimming had improved a great deal; it had been her favorite activity when she was pregnant. Peter would be proud; she'd come a long way in the water since she'd flailed in a half panic against the frigid shallows of San Francisco Bay, unable to banish her childish thoughts of monsters lurking below.

She no longer feared swimming in the ocean.

Back on shore, she found Petra and Viv dozing together on a chaise. Tessa spread a blanket in the sand and lay down on it, closing her eyes and listening to the waves. The beach had been empty all morning, not a soul but for the three of them. As she reclined with her eyes shut, though, she began to sense a presence. As if she could hear footsteps in the sand.

She opened her eyes and looked behind her, steered by a feeling.

From the line of palm trees at the periphery of the sand, a man was descending onto the beach. Medium height, muscular, his gate quick and sure. Face largely concealed by a thick brown-red beard and mustache, plus sunglasses. Headed straight toward them. Hurrying, really.

Tessa swung her legs off her chaise and planted her feet in the sand, sitting up straight. Motherhood had equipped her with an instinctive vigilance, a readiness to spring at any moment in defense of her baby. Or of Vivian, who was still weak, despite steady improvements from the REVERSA. The man looked ordinary, but his gait was oddly deliberate.

Who would be beelining toward them on this pristine beach?

She stood up.

Viv opened her eyes. "Where are you going?"

"Nowhere," said Tessa.

The man drew closer: twenty yards or so.

Tessa reached for Petra. "Let me take her."

In Tessa's arms, the baby woke with a wobbly cry.

"Shhh, sweetie," said Tessa. "Shhhh." She bounced Petra on one hip, clutching her tightly as the approaching stranger broke into a jog, closing the remaining gap between them.

"Hello there," Tessa called out.

The man arrived at their chaises and stopped right in front of Viv's, as if she'd been the finish line. He placed his hands on his knees to catch his breath, and Tessa stepped toward him, her protective reflexes now extending to Viv. When he straightened and faced Tessa, she could see the scar lines etched just above his beard.

No one spoke. Even Petra fell silent.

"Howdy," said the man, finally.

"You came," Viv said.

"I'm here," he said.

Tessa watched as her baby extended her plump arms up toward the man, the stranger, reaching for him on instinct, full of trust and wonder.

ACKNOWLEDGMENTS

Wild thanks to:

Susan Golomb, for making this happen when I'd almost accepted it wouldn't.

Carmen Johnson, for never wavering from this project and seeing exactly what it needed to be.

Kelli Martin, for her wise eagle eye.

Lucy Silag, for bringing this book to the world.

Kris Widger—my husband, my ally, my defender, my love. Without your boundless patience I could not have seen this through.

My children, Townes, Kirby, and Cassidy—lights of my life, sparkers of joy, crafters of so many motivational notes, chanters of *Mama, write like the wind* when I needed it most.

My mother, Cathy Schwarzkopf Wolfson, a.k.a. Moopy—for taking care of my children while I wrote this book, and adoring me no matter what.

My friends, who saw me through this madness, end to end. My bestie and literary kindred spirit, Julia Fierro. My great commiserater, Justin Feinstein; my favorite brunchers, Katherine Satorius and Amy

Bourne; my fellow ninja, Claire Bidwell Smith. My earliest editor, Linda Larson. I love you all to the moon.

Rebecca and Jonathan Benefiel Bijur, for my title.

The Wolfson men—Gary, Gregory, Jonathan, and Justin—for always being ready to listen, read another draft, take my side, and crack me up.

ABOUT THE AUTHOR

Caeli Wolfson Widger is the author of the novel *Real Happy Family*. Her work has appeared in numerous literary journals, the *New York Times Magazine*, and Amazon's *Day One* and on NPR. Caeli lives with her husband and three children in Santa Monica, California, where she runs a recruiting firm focused on tech startups.

More about Caeli can be found on her website, www.caeliwidger.com; on Facebook at www.facebook.com/caeliwidgerauthor; or on Twitter at @wolfwidge.